The Columbus Option

'Have you heard of the Cartagena Group? It's a standing conference of South American debtor nations, named after the place it first met in Colombia. There've been rumours of other debtors joining the group to form a cartel – like OPEC, in a way – so they can negotiate jointly with the West.'

'I know about OPEC. But that's a cartel controlling the selling price of oil.'

'Sure. And for some years it earned billions of dollars profit which its members deposited with Western banks and the banks then lent to other developing countries, who now can't pay it back.'

'So why are my pictures going to make me rich?'

'Because if my hunch is correct, what's going on at Columbus Cay right now is a meeting of all the big debtors discussing how best to put the Western banks' $580 billion down the tube.'

'And?' She couldn't visualize $580 billion.

'The entire US deficit is only $160 billion. This would make the 1929 crash look like a picnic.'

RICHARD COX

The Columbus Option

A Methuen Paperback

A Methuen Paperback

THE COLUMBUS OPTION

British Library Cataloguing in Publication Data

Cox, Richard, 1931–
  The Columbus option—(A Methuen
  paperback).
  I. Title
  823′.914[F]   PR6053.D969

  ISBN 0-413-17050-0

First published in Great Britain 1986
by Martin Secker & Warburg Ltd
This edition published 1988
by Methuen London Ltd
11 New Fetter Lane, London EC4P 4EE

Copyright (c) 1986 by Richard Cox

Printed and bound in Great Britain
by Richard Clay Ltd, Bungay, Suffolk

ACKNOWLEDGEMENTS

I owe a debt of gratitude to many people who helped me with this book. In particular to Miss Noel Acheson for her research; to Anatole Kaletsky's Twentieth Century Fund paper, 'The Costs of Default'; to Martin Mayer's *The Money Bazaars* (Dutton, 1984); to the publisher of the *International Herald Tribune*; to Mr and Mrs Werner Walbrol for their hospitality; to Mr and Mrs Roger Daniell; to Mrs Sara Fisher, who typed the manuscript meticulously; and finally to my wife for putting up with the strain.

Richard Cox
July 1986

CHAPTER ONE

Marsh Harbour, Great Abaco. Friday June 7th

For a few seconds the tropical water calmed and the diffused images beneath the surface achieved recognizable forms. The rock was a broken head of coral. The straw-coloured sea anemone became what it had paralleled: the frayed end of a rope, which wormed into the sand as if rooted near the curious shape. The shape itself resolved into the bleached rib cage of a skeleton, half embedded in the sand, the skull and legs only to be guessed at. Then the swell returned, the rope wavered into motion and the skeleton again began to tremble and shift, as if trying feebly to escape.

'A stupid man,' Garrard commented reflectively, 'axein' questions what were never his business. Should've stayed nights in de hotel, stayed wid de right guys, like wid me. Few tings more dead in dis world dan dead reporters. Ain't dat so, Mr Pendler?'

The Bahamian's accent was the sing-song of the deep South though local idiosyncracies studded his language. He was a big, tall man and a thick fringe of beard outlined his broad, black face. His manner was self-confident and convivially menacing – like a friendly preacher warning a guest about hell-fire round the corner. He surveyed the sweep of the bay, which began at the low promontory of coral rock on which they were standing.

'Jesus Lord, man, we been drinkin' dis view long enough. I oughta be takin' you places. Go see de boat-buildin' at Man O'War Bay. What else you wantin' for writin'?'

'Local colour. A few hotels. Markets. Eating places, maybe.' Stuart Pendler kept a grip on himself. He had seen more intimidating sights than a skeleton in the water before, even one with a rock attached to it. If those bones were the earthly remains of a reporter, imperceptibly being ground to nothing by the tides, then he must have been a freelance or a local. No American news editor would fail to ask questions if a staff man went missing. Pendler himself was a specialist writer, an expert whose name carried authority at the head of a column of newsprint. More, he had warned the *Herald Tribune* that he was on to a story in the Bahamas vastly more significant than his original assignment to report on the islands as a tax haven cum leisure paradise. In fact he'd been on to it before he came and he didn't propose to be intimidated out of asking questions.

'You have conferences here on Abaco?' he demanded.

'Conferences?' Garrard gripped his arm and began steering him forcibly back along the overgrown path through the palm trees towards the road. 'No conferences goin' on here. Who axein' about conferences? Dey kin go to Nassau for dat, or Paradise Island.'

'I guess so,' Pendler agreed. If you can't get it by confrontation, his motto ran, get it by guile.

'Know sometin'?' Garrard relaxed his hold a trifle, apparently pleased. 'Dat place ain't Paradise Island for real. Used to be called Hog Island, 'til dat guy Hartford bought it, and dey put up all de hotels. Plain Hog Island. You say dat if you want, just treat Abaco right. People havin' a different lifestyle here, all right? Sailin', fishin', scuba-divin', going on de flats after bone-fish. Dis a friendly island, man, all one hundred tirty miles. Beautiful beaches and relaxin' friendliness. You write dat, we'll be glad.'

Goddam it, Pendler thought as his shoes scuffed through spiky grass and kicked up dust, why am I being hustled like a convict while this goon parrots the junk out of the brochures? Yesterday, when they had called him at his hotel in Nassau and said the government would be delighted to offer him hospitality on his trip to Great Abaco, his regrettably *brief* trip because accommodations were so overbooked, he had recognized the hand of whatever security service there was in the enforced invitation. Sure enough, when he and Maggie alighted at the Marsh Harbour airport and they were greeted by this creep Garrard, he had known his instinct was right. Garrard was no more an official guide than he himself was a travel-writer.

'All right, man,' Garrard announced as they emerged at the road where he had parked the 'hospitality' car, 'let's go find your lady. Reckon she be done by now.' He evidently felt his message had sunk in.

As they drove back to Marsh Harbour Pendler wondered if Maggie had taken the pictures. Probably not. As a professional photographer she had a mind all of her own. She only knew the official background to the assignment and he anticipated problems guiding her lens in the right directions. He needed the evidence of camera shots to back his story, to confirm without question who was attending the secret meeting on Great Abaco this out-ofseason June weekend.

All the scraps of evidence Pendler had gathered from around the world over the past two weeks had pointed to a major news scoop. Individually they might be just scraps: ministers cancelling appointments; a Central Bank director's speech in Mexico City; a sharp comment in a broadcast; an expected currency devaluation postponed. But if his hunch was correct, the decisions of the next few days here in Great Abaco could bankrupt millions of ordinary people in the United States and Europe, could ruin great business corporations and topple governments. This catastrophic outcome, however, moved him less than the importance of getting his story. To him, like any true, ink-in-the-veins newspaper man, the story was everything. He cared about it as passionately as a detective cares about arresting a criminal or a doctor about identifying a disease. He was a totally committed professional and he didn't intend letting a small-time spook like Garrard stand in his way.

Maggie Fitzgerald waited at the seafood restaurant on Marsh Harbour's main street, her cameras on the table: two Nikons, one fitted with a 70 mm semi-telephoto lens, the other with a wide-angle. If you saw a good shot coming up there was no time for fiddling around. Not that she did here. She was unimpressed by the town, even if it possessed the only set of traffic-lights in the out islands. She wanted to be around the white coral sand beaches and long palm-fringed bays, getting the kind of pictures she could sell long after this assignment was over. She was Irish, thirty, her hair near blonde, slimly attractive and suffused with a demonic determination to make a name for herself as a photographer. The more she thought about this trip, the more she suspected the real reason Stuart had persuaded the *Trib* to pay her fare was quite unconnected with journalism.

So she sat with a half-consumed fruit juice in front of her, watched the lunchtime human traffic on the street outside, and gradually raised a head of steam at being kept waiting. She didn't care a toss that the restaurant was supposedly renowned. She resented wasting time, even Bahamian time, which Garrard had been at pains to tell her meant arriving minutes, hours or even days late.

When Stuart and his mentor were half an hour overdue and Maggie had begun tapping on the table-top impatiently with the vulgar green-plastic swizzle-stick which had decorated her drink, her eye was caught by a group of men entering the restaurant. There were five of them, three pale-faced Europeans and two

3

swarthy Latin Americans. They entered and stood briefly waiting to be allotted a table. It was the way they related to each other during those few moments that excited her curiosity.

The senior European was a man of perhaps sixty, out of character in a flowered shirt and lemon-yellow slacks, yet as imperiously self-assured as if he owned the place. He clearly expected the manager to hasten and greet him. Meanwhile, his younger companions adopted the positions which intrigued her. The first, thin and intellectual-looking, hovered a step back as if ready to interpret or assist. The second, more burly and wearing a wide-shouldered cotton jacket with a distinct bulge beneath the left armpit, planted himself alongside the door and swept the restaurant's patrons with his eyes. She had never seen a trio who looked less like tourists.

She was just turning her attention to the two Latin Americans, equally clearly master and adviser, though more at ease in their tropical vacation clothes, when Garrard's car came to a halt outside.

'About time,' she muttered to herself, determined to extract an apology and not waving. They could look for her. She watched the manager materialize and start welcoming the five strangers, obsequiously showing them to a reserved table. Then Pendler entered ahead of Garrard, saw the group, stopped dead, hastily recovered himself and looked around for her. His moment of astonishment had been so brief and so quickly concealed that the Bahamian, following behind, had noticed nothing odd.

'And where have you been, I should like to know.' She tended to overplay her Irishness when she was annoyed.

'Sorry,' Stuart darted a glance over his shoulder, as if fearful the curious group of men would vanish. 'We saw a remarkable bay.'

'Sure did,' Garrard confirmed, though making no move to sit down. He had no wish to be manoeuvred into paying for a meal in the town's most expensive establishment.

'We'll see you later,' Pendler said, reading the hesitancy aright.

'Be back terreckly,' Garrard agreed. 'Tings I should be attendin' to.' With that he ambled across to the manager, spoke a few words and left.

'And what did he show you?' Maggie asked. 'The local sex shop? What wasn't fit for my lovely Irish eyes?'

'Nothing much. Wanted to give me some friendly advice.'

She scented the sarcasm in his voice and let the question ride. A waiter came up with a menu describing every dish in over-succulent detail. They chose conch chowder followed by red snapper Creole with white wine to drink. Across the room a pair of waiters were attending to the group.

4

'Say,' Pendler exclaimed, with transparent insincerity, 'wouldn't it be something to have a picture of a restaurant? Like here?'

'Are you joking?' Her professional judgement surfaced instantly. 'This place? Overweight tourists, bad light. They don't even have a big display of food, like a buffet. Why waste film?'

'Shouldn't we have a crack, though?' he tried to cajole her, realizing how anglicized his language had become. 'For the record. Hell, Maggie, we're leaving again tomorrow on the afternoon plane.' He nearly added, 'thanks to that damn spook', but thought better of it. He had no wish to alarm her. 'Restaurants have to be part of the story.'

'Listen, Stu. You decide the words, I decide the pix, right?'

'If you find it embarrassing, forget it.'

She flushed in spite of herself. He'd touched a nerve, damn him. Deliberately. On their last assignment – their only previous assignment together, the one where he had made a clumsy pass at her – she'd been shy of taking the Nikons to a diplomatic party to which he had been invited and she had not. In consequence she'd missed a semi-historic handshake between the Secretary of State and a Russian arms-control negotiator. The *Trib* had had to buy from an agency. She'd cried herself to sleep that night out of simple frustration at her failure to compete.

'All right,' she said, angered by the memory, 'I'll take your wretched picture. I suppose you want those men in it?'

'Yes,' Pendler said calmly, 'that is exactly what I want. Why not ask the manager first and use a wide angle with them to the side so they assume they're not in the picture at all.'

She almost exploded. But she went and smiled nicely at the manager, indicating a view of the restaurant which appeared to omit the group. By the time she was through, she had captured all their faces, and because she wasn't using flash either, their initial apprehensions had faded.

'And now,' she said, as she sat down again to find the conch chowder already served, 'perhaps you'll explain what this is all about.'

Columbus Cay, Great Abaco

The Club at Columbus Cay, an island half an hour by launch from Marsh Harbour, was one of the most private conference centres anywhere. It had hosted the General Motors board for a long weekend hammering out a secret new corporate strategy and catered for the most confidential meetings. On one occasion its founder, the white-bearded but not so old Pat McLellan, had realized too late that the executives renting his facilities were the top management of the New York mafia. He had made no fuss. Columbus Cay's watchword was discretion matched by luxury – the precise opposite of the huge hotels in Nassau or Paradise Island which widely publicized their off-season sales conventions. By contrast McLellan knew that word of mouth among the kind of clientele he sought was enough, given the smallness of his club. So although you would find Columbus Cay on a nautical chart, one of the 600 islands in the Stream, it never featured on a tourist map.

When the Bahamas government requested Columbus Cay's entire facilities at short notice, McLellan had jibbed. He had existing room reservations. Then the Minister telephoned him personally with some open threats about hotel- and bar-licence renewals. McLellan, listening angrily, stared at the pencilled-in bookings on his daily accommodation sheets and realized that if the government could shift the meeting by a day he would only have to make three cancellation calls. The Minister had agreed but refused to donate free holidays for the disappointed guests. McLellan responded by quoting a high-season room rate, which was easy since he had no printed brochure prices anyway. And that had been that.

'There will be no requirement for passport or guest-card formalities,' the Minister had said. 'My office will send a list of names.'

When the list had arrived, a day before the first guests, McLellan realized that all the patronymics were as phoney as the proverbial plastic dollar.

José-Maria Garcia Lopez-Santini slouched contentedly in the stern of the launch, a straw hat bought from a street vendor in Marsh Harbour tilted over his eyes. The brim appeared fuzzily out of focus in his vision, the strong sun creating a kind of circular halo at the edge. He pretended to be half asleep while watching the crystal water churned into spray by the twin outboards, then shifted his eyes to the men standing in the bow, the elder stiff and curiously correct as he held on to a chrome rail and stared ahead.

It's fine for him, Lopez-Santini thought, he may be sixty but in Communist countries politicians last for ever, they're all gerontocracies. All he has to do is follow the party line and keep his nose clean. In the Argentine it is very different. Holy Mother, he himself had only been Minister for the Economy since January, the task the President had set him was impossible, and even if there wasn't a military coup he doubted if he'd still be holding office in a year. A man had to grasp the fruits of office while they were available.

Take this trip: it was so secret that even his wife Mercedes had to be kept in ignorance of his destination. She would be expecting presents on his return, lavish ones. Every international conference he had attended, whether as a minister or before that as an adviser, had carried a domestic price-tag attached. If Mercedes could not accompany him, that price rose. If she could not telephone and check what he was up to, it hit the roof. He prayed this private club would possess a boutique. If not, he would be in trouble. He belched, automatically raising his hand to his mouth. That baked crawfish had been excellent, though he was beginning to regret the cheese sauce. What a crazy fuss the Pole had made about going to the restaurant, complaining about lack of security and actually quivering when an American tourist started photographing her companion. That was the problem with Communists: they could never relax.

The Communist in question, Henryk Kaminski, Finance Minister of the Polish People's Republic, was troubled by very different thoughts. As he watched the green blur of the island they were approaching gradually resolve itself into the shapes and colours of beaches, trees and a small settlement, his instinct struggled against his orders. That instinct, honed by thirty years' experience of balancing Poland's interest against Russian demands, of trying to render the doctrinaire workable, made him suspicious of Lopez-Santini. His feelings were encapsulated by the remark the Argentine had made after their chartered plane from Nassau touched down at Marsh Harbour's small airport:

'My friend, if we are going to travel from an airport to a harbour at lunchtime, and the best seafood restaurant in the Bahamas lies between the two, then the setting for our discussion is pre-ordained. Let us make the most of it.'

The attitude summed up the man, Kaminski decided: pleasure-loving and therefore unreliable. Lopez-Santini had even remarked casually that he had his shirts made in London and his wife shopped in Rome. The Pole believed that when one's country was enduring a period of extreme austerity its leaders had a duty to share the people's discomfort, not frequent foreign fleshpots. As for Lopez-Santini's disregard of that woman who took photographs, it was inexplicable. Only the assurances of his own aide, young Jozef Kryst, that her camera lens was definitely not pointed in their direction had allayed his fears. Even so he had demanded that she should be traced and her film confiscated.

Kaminski wondered if the official who had fetched them from

the restaurant would take his request seriously. West Indians were notoriously unpredictable and he presumed these people were the same. Besides, the Bahamas government was not involved in this meeting in any plenipotentiary capacity. Its government had merely agreed to a request for facilities. All the ministers concerned preferred to meet on neutral ground, and from that point of view the islands were perfect: an international playground, served by airlines from all over the world, where strange faces would arouse no comment, and yet complete privacy could be guaranteed. Except that this damned Argentine had broken the rules the moment they arrived. Kaminski contented himself, not very adequately, with the knowledge that his orders had been to establish a *rapprochement* with the Argentine delegate before the conference began and that he had done so.

The launch slowed, the bow slumping into the water causing Lopez-Santini to lift his hat and look around openly. They were passing the end of a jetty supported on wooden poles. A line of gleaming white boats lay moored inside a tiny marina, each sporting a high and frail superstructure above its cabin, each with the delicate antennae of fishing outriggers rising alongside. On shore, a number of thatched villas were just visible among the palm trees near a large rotunda-shaped building with a two-tiered roof.

'Columbus Cay, folks,' the boatman announced, rolling the words like an impresario, 'de out-islands' private paradise.'

As each group was shown to its private villa, to be greeted by the Club's attentive room servants, McLellan realized he had something more than the conventionally unusual on his hands. In total there were due to be twenty-four groups. The nearest any came to checking in was when their security men appeared at the front office and insisted on being shown the entire establishment, from the air-conditioned conference rotunda to the perimeter fence. He had founded the Club to give himself a retirement occupation after a career as a hotelier, and he could guess most of the nationalities – guesses reinforced when peculiar meal orders started coming in. He was hosting representatives from South America, Africa and Asia, among whom the Poles seemed curiously out of place. The pressure they put on the staff became so acute that he wound up abandoning his sundowner and taking the swing shift at the reception himself. He was there when an unscheduled visitor arrived, long after dark.

'How you doin'?' the visitor asked rhetorically and gave his name as Garrard. He was not a local, McLellan recognized that.

8

Garrard leant his elbows on the teak counter, not attempting to stay out of earshot of the desk clerk, and made it plain that if any attempt was made to identify the guests the Club would be closed down.

'No one else comes here, all right? No one at all. No tourists, no fishin' guys, no scuba-divers. Nobody going to be givin' trouble, right?'

'Except you, I presume,' McLellan remarked caustically. He was no respecter of spooks.

'If God spare life.' Somehow Garrard's accent gave the colloquial phrase a threatening twist. 'Be seein' you, man.'

Marsh Harbour, Great Abaco

Stuart Pendler ordered a pina colada for himself and a sea-grape soda for Maggie then settled himself on one of the balcony chairs and watched the evening light fade over the ocean. A faint click from his room made him look hastily over his shoulder. For a few seconds he was puzzled, wondering if it was her unlocking the communicating door. No hope. Locking it more likely. She'd laid down the law about sex and work during the afternoon. He flicked through the pages of the hotel brochure.

'Your jumping-off point to Abaco adventure,' it enthused ... 'we can arrange sailing sojourns ... motor-boat outings to deserted cays ...'

A buzzer announced the waiter with the drinks. He let the man in and found Maggie behind him in the passage, wearing some kind of sarong. When the Irish go overboard, he thought, they sure do.

'Like it?' she asked, out on the balcony again, twirling round for his inspection. 'I bought it in Java.'

'Here's looking at you!' he raised his glass. 'How about a boat trip tomorrow? Escape from that Garrard fellow, find some of those locations you want.'

'Remember we have a plane to catch.'

'There's always another.' He waved aside her doubts. 'And this hotel isn't full. No way. All that about accommodations being overbooked was a load of crap. We could stay on. The *Trib* won't mind.'

She agreed, reluctantly. The harbour where Stu had insisted on spending half the afternoon chatting to fishermen had been photographically limited – frustratingly so.

'Any place you wanted to go in particular?' she asked, still suspicious of his motives.

'I heard of an island called Columbus Cay.' He fell back on an expression he'd picked up in London: 'Let's play it by ear.'

Columbus Cay, Great Abaco. Saturday June 8th

The conference suite was planned around a hexagonal hall in the rotunda, which from the exterior resembled a low pagoda with outbuildings. Inside, a horseshoe shape of teak desks confronted a small podium. Each desk had microphones and headsets, linked to interpreters who could watch the proceedings through a wide glass panel in one wall, while doors in others led to a bar and to offices for secretaries and telex machines. At most the hall could accommodate only fifty-two delegates, but it did so superbly. Today it hosted ten less: twenty-one ministers, with twenty-one advisers seated alongside them. Three groups had failed to arrive.

Lopez-Santini had been among the first to take his place this morning. His bon-viveur image concealed a sharp and serious mind and he didn't want to miss a single nuance of this meeting, which aggravatingly started late because the two Nigerians kept them waiting: a bad augury, he thought. How could you propose threatening the whole Western banking system if you couldn't get your own act together?

In fact he had very limited sympathy with the aims of this conference. Its purpose was for the finance ministers of the world's twenty-four main debtor nations to present a united front in negotiating with the Western banks. Between them those nations owed close on $1,000 billion. Standing united was one thing. What Lopez-Santini disliked, both intellectually and emotionally, was what he was sure the Mexican convener of this conference intended proposing; namely, some form of co-ordinated blackmail of the banks.

'Your Excellencies.' The Mexican delegate had mounted the podium with the Brazilian flanking him and was acknowledging a murmur of spontaneous applause. He was a paunchy man in his early fifties with a misleadingly expansive smile under a pencil-line moustache. His name was Alvarez. 'Your Excellencies,' he repeated, 'we all know why we are here today. We are here because we are crippled by our debts to avaricious Western institutions. If we ask the International Monetary Fund for help we are subjected to humiliating conditions. When American, British or

German bankers do agree to reschedule the repayment of loans they impose huge fees and impossible interest rates. We have to defend ourselves and our peoples . . .'

Otherwise, Lopez-Santini reflected sardonically, we shall not be re-elected. Except that the Africans and Asians here mostly represented dictatorships. He didn't agree with the kind of chip-on-the-shoulder Third World arguments that always distorted United Nations debates. Ten years ago Brazil had demanded respect as a regional industrial leader. She had the world's largest power-generating project at Itaipu and 10,000 trainees in a Volkswagen automotive-engineering school. San Bernardo do Campo had been the Detroit of Latin America. Investment and loans had poured in. And now that a chill wind of recession was blowing even her leaders wanted sympathy, as if their country was some exploited banana republic.

'I am sorry to note,' Alvarez continued acidly, 'that some of our neighbours prefer not to stand shoulder to shoulder with their comrades.' His glance swept the delegates, resting long enough on Lopez-Santini for the implications to be read by others.

Lopez-Santini sat impassive. The Argentine might technically be a developing country, but materially she was self-sufficient. It had only been the unbridled spending of the military, culminating in the tragedy of the Malvinas War, that had turned one of the finest farming areas in the world into an economic chaos where a one million-peso banknote had become worth less than a cup of coffee, merely the tip you gave the waiter for serving it. But that was over. The new democratic government had accepted the IMF's tough conditions for new loans, and inflation had dropped from its crazy 1,000 per cent to fifty per cent and lower. Why threaten the achievement?

'For my country, I can tell you,' the Mexican was into his stride now, his eloquence fired by his subject, 'our President has warned that we will not pay our foreign debts with recession, nor unemployment, nor hunger. We refuse to sacrifice our people for New York bankers who spend more on an evening out with their wives than our labourers earn in a month.'

That was true of all their nations. Lopez-Santini himself knew of a family of seven in Buenos Aires living off a single $190-a-month wage packet. The dilemma that haunted almost all the ministers present was how to tell the poorest of the poor that the price of grain or rice must go up because a team of slick-suited foreigners insisted price rises were a condition of more development aid. Ironically, it was easier for the dictatorships than the recently restored democracies. Glancing at the faces around the horseshoe table – some friends, others men he mistrusted intensely – Lopez-Santini reminded himself of their predicaments.

The Mexican was worst off, still struggling to bring his country through the aftermath of natural calamity. Following on the $4 billion cost of the 1985 earthquake had come the collapse of oil prices. Mexico's exports had been hit when she needed them most. He had every sympathy for the Mexicans.

The Bolivian Finance Minister, doodling on a pad as he listened, had to devise an economic policy for a chaotic democracy, racked by an annual inflation rate of 14,000 per cent and heavily dependent for foreign exchange on illicit drug-trafficking into the United States. But the aide seated beside him was no normal aide, and everyone knew it. The youngish, macho-looking gentleman who held the titular position of Bolivia's Deputy Finance Minister constituted the government's unofficial and necessary link with the drug-traffickers. His name was Rodrigo Suarez and he would favour breaking with the Western bankers for less than altruistic reasons: the drug barons wanted the American government off their backs, and the way the US government kept after them was by linking drug-enforcement measures with aid. Suarez must be hoping a debt default would put an end to both.

By contrast, the Sudanese, a coal-black Nubian of impressive stature and respected ability, was trying to pick up the pieces of life for a population much of which was still starving years after the last Sahel drought. In his country IMF policies had directly contributed to riots and the overthrow of the former president.

While Lopez-Santini continued trying to judge which way the others would vote, watching the disparate faces of Indonesians and Zaireois, of Filipinos and Chileans, the Mexican on the podium worked up his oration.

'What weapon have we against this terrible burden, this thousand-billion dollars which the West encouraged our governments to borrow and which now threatens to destroy us?'

The irony was that from the oil boom of the early 1970s onwards, the Western banks had been desperate to lend. They had huge deposits coming in from the Arab oil states and had to lend them out again to make a profit. They told themselves it was safe to lend to governments and did so in huge amounts, both to the deserving and to some of the most corrupt regimes the world has ever seen. One London bank even lent $10 million to the notorious Mobutu of Zaire to stage a world-title fight between Carl Foreman and Muhammad Ali. When the debt crisis showed its head at the end of the decade they lent more so that their debtors could continue to pay the interest on the original loans. If the treasurers and boards of the giants had it coming to them, it was largely their own fault.

'I can tell you what our weapon must be.' The Mexican was suddenly calm, standing back confidently from the lectern with his arms outstretched, hands resting on it. 'We must threaten to bankrupt the banks.'

A ripple of appreciative laughter greeted this. The idea was not new. President Castro of Cuba had long been urging Latin America to form a debtors' cartel. His pleas invariably fell on deaf ears for good reason. Cuba was a satellite of the Soviet Union and the proposal was transparently a Soviet-inspired manoeuvre against the West. But when Brazil, an industrially advanced nation, supported the Mexican initiative it acquired greater respectability.

'Do I need to remind you,' Alvarez went on, 'that at least 580 billion dollars of the developing countries' current debt is owed to commercial banks, and that many have lent far more than their capital and reserves?'

Lopez-Santini consulted the notes his aides had prepared. To be exact, twenty-four major United States banks had lent more than their total issued share capital. Another 185 were seriously exposed. At the head of the list came the prestigious Manufacturers Hanover whose loans to only six of the nations represented here today – Argentina, Brazil, Chile, Mexico, the Philippines and Venezuela – totalled 269 per cent of its shareholders' equity. In other words, it had lent over two and a half times its capital. If those six ceased paying interest, then after three months under American law the loans would have to be classified as bad debts and the banks concerned would go bust. A crude term, but correct. Furthermore, a domino effect would run right through the US banking system because many small banks had participated with the giants to form lending consortiums. The major European and Japanese banks would be savagely hit too.

'If we can agree to tell the bankers of the West, with one voice, that we decline to either pay more interest or to repay loans, then the United States, Britain, Germany, Japan and Switzerland will be forced to negotiate a new deal. Their governments cannot allow them to collapse. They cannot risk a financial crash. They will be forced to mount a rescue operation so that the banks' half of this 1,000 billion dollars can be written off.' The Mexican Minister paused. 'This is the proposal we should transmit to them.'

At this point he began to lose control. He might have convened this meeting but he could not keep effective order among twenty-one delegates, all of whom wished to express their views at once.

Lopez-Santini listened with increasing concern. The possibility of this outcome was, of course, why South Korea and Israel, both major debtors, had declined to be represented at the meeting. They were not about to sabotage their allies. The Yugoslavs had presumably not come because they thought of themselves as being European. Of the Eastern bloc debtors, only Poland had sent its Minister and Lopez-Santini knew that Kaminski's mission was not to give assistance. Kaminski, sitting aloof on the far side of the half circle of tables, had his own fish to fry.

For many minutes Lopez-Santini kept silent, except to whisper to his aide, Felipe, who agreed it would not be in the Argentine's interest to join this cartel. Their inflation was coming under control, their international reputation was improving. Far better to let others be intransigent while they themselves bargained.

'Everything is relative,' Lopez-Santini chuckled. 'For a change we shall be the good boys.'

'Excellencies, gentlemen.' The Mexican had to shout into the microphone, 'Order, señores. Many have asked how we can achieve this. Let me tell you. We give an ultimatum.'

'And if they refuse it?' Kaminski's interruption had to be through an interpreter, though no one could miss the harshness of his tone.

'If they refuse, señor? If they refuse to negotiate, we give them one week. If after one week they have not agreed, we release the news. The media will do the rest. Within hours Wall Street will be in turmoil, stock prices will collapse in London and Tokyo. Small depositors will fight to withdraw their savings from banks. It did not only happen in 1929. It happened on a small scale in the United States with the Penn Square Bank's collapse in 1982 and the fall of many thrift institutions in 1984 and 1985. There will be panic.'

A great roar of laughter from the Nigerian echoed across the hall. 'I like that,' he shouted. 'I like that. Now they can be the victim of their own damn press.'

'But the West will refuse to trade with us again, except for cash,' the Philippines' Minister insisted. His country was striving to re-establish itself after two decades of the Marcos family's corrupt misrule. Both trade and aid were desperately needed. It was one thing for Mexico to seek escape from an impossible $97 billion of debt. By contrast his own country's $27 billion might eventually be paid off, and if American military aid ceased, the generals would rapidly become restive.

'In Latin America,' Alvarez replied, 'there were defaults in the 1820s, the 1870s and the 1930s. Within a few years of each, our governments obtained credit again. History will repeat itself. We can afford to keep our nerve even though we do not advocate a total default. We must threaten the banks with disaster because they understand that, but our aim must be to negotiate a deal that stops a millimetre short of it.' He raised his hand for silence. This altercation had aroused argument among the other delegates. 'Our aim is to lift the burden from our backs, not destroy the system. Only if the banks refuse will we default. This afternoon, we must elect a representative negotiator. Meanwhile, I repeat the need for secrecy. Even the fact that we are meeting at all could fuel speculation. Secrecy is the one benefit we can offer our creditors, while the bankers plan how to keep themselves solvent. Secrecy and a small amount of time.'

As he left to lunch at his villa, Lopez-Santini conceded to his aide that this approach might be international blackmail, but it had a degree of sophistication. However, he did not believe it could be kept quiet.

Maggie was still inwardly raging when the speedboat nosed into the white coral sand of a deserted beach, fringed by a crescent of casuarina trees, and the lean young Bahamian who had ferried them out announced that this was Columbus Cay.

'Dis side no one goes,' he explained. 'Dey have de Club round de udder side where dere is no wind.'

She stood up, the fibreglass hull rocking slightly as her weight shifted, and began working out shots. If the boatman posed unaffectedly this would be an idyllic scene.

'Pretty good, huh?' Pendler suggested. 'Isn't this what the islands are all about?'

'They'd be better still if you kept your thieving hands out of other people's camera-cases,' she snapped. How dare he rifle through her belongings and then, when she discovered her exposed films were missing from the aluminium case, calmly admit that he'd posted them to London. 'Just a precaution,' he'd said. Disdaining his assistance, she scrambled over the gunwale and dropped into two feet of water, splashing her jeans up to her thighs. She straightened, moved a step or two and began photographing the beach, with the boat in the foreground.

She first saw movement among the trees through the camera lens, took no notice because it seemed insignificant in the wide-angle view, then stopped because the men walking down the sand were spoiling the shot. She lowered the Nikon. The men were closer than she had realized. Out of the corner of her eye, with that peripheral vision which professional photographers learn to cultivate because a lot of things happen to one side, she saw Stuart stiffen into immobility. Then she saw why. Both men had guns.

The policewoman was fresh and neat in a sparkling white tunic with gilt buttons. Her hat, black-brimmed with a white crown and gilt badge, sat squarely over a cheerful native face. She had never had an assignment quite like this before, but she smiled at the manager of the hotel, as did her male colleague, and the manager agreed it was far better to be discreet about a search. If the Irish tourist was not carrying drugs then this could all be quietly forgotten. If she was, then the law had to take its course. He handed out a duplicate room key and let them get on with their job. Personally, he preferred not to know more.

The cocaine was supposed to be concealed in a roll of film – that was what she had been told. A used one, one with the film wound back so no length of celluloid protruded. But although there were packs of unexposed film, not one answered the description. What should she do with the replacement they had given her? She asked her colleague.

He frowned. This should have been simple. 'No dice,' he said, 'We leave.'

The inspector of police hadn't told them the cocaine was in the cassette they'd brought, for the reason that the inspector didn't know himself. Only Garrard knew and Garrard was out at Columbus Cay.

McLellan looked over at the two tourists the guards had rounded up and felt sorry for them.

'This is a private island, I'm afraid,' he said, firmly none the less. 'We'll have to send you back to Marsh Harbour.'

'Can't we even buy lunch?' Pendler pleaded. It was clear that some kind of meeting was breaking up. In the distance he could see people leaving a curiously shaped building. They moved in small groups, talking animatedly. He was one hundred per cent sure this was the place. 'Couldn't you stretch the rules?'

McLellan shook his head. 'I'll find you someone to escort you back.' He left them in the care of the guards and returned a few minutes later with Garrard.

'Jeez,' Pendler muttered, 'it's our old friend again.'

'How you doin'?' Garrard declared with unexpected *bonhomie*. 'I was jest axein' after you. No time at all you be missing de plane. Lucky I bin speakin' to de airport now, tellin' dem hold everyting, two passengers is missin'. Lucky I phone de hotel too, tellin' pack your bags.'

'Our boat's on the other side.'

'Jesus Lord, dat boat have some unlucky owner. We're leavin'.' He hustled them down to the jetty and into a launch.

When they were on the way across, with the helmsman making a tidy eighteen knots, the wake creaming behind, Garrard broke a long silence.

'All right, now, give me de film,' he ordered Maggie. 'No givin' trouble. Out de case and out de cameras.'

'No.'

'Give.' A gun appeared in his hand.

'Do as the man says,' Pendler said wearily.

Garrard took the cassettes one by one and threw them into the sea.

'Next time,' he said, 'it be de cameras. Except dere ain't goin' to be no next time. You don't take warnin', you're a stupid man.' He left it at that because he wanted them out quietly. The arrest could be made when the baggage was searched at Nassau.

CHAPTER TWO

Buenos Aires. Morning, Saturday June 8th

Ruiz the chauffeur had orders to vary the route each day, but there were limits to his ingenuity. Every morning the two young girls had to be driven from the Lopez-Santinis' large apartment overlooking Palermo Park to San Andres School in the Olivos district of Buenos Aires. In the afternoon they had to be brought back. The apartment block and the school were inescapably fixed points in the itinerary. The school hours were fixed times. A few miles of broad highway linked the two fashionable areas and were safer than the backstreets. Ruiz always held the white Ford Falcon sedan at a good speed on the dual carriageway and kept a close eye on the rear-view mirror, especially near the spaghetti-junction interchange with the other main road. He used to tell his girlfriend Ana, 'Sometimes I get worried.'

'If anything happens,' she would reply, 'worry for yourself, Ruiz. Don't be a hero. They're not your kids, for God's sake.' Ana was working class and practical. The Lopez-Santini family could afford to pay ransoms. Her boyfriend only had one life.

On Saturdays Ruiz worried less. So, for that matter, did Mercedes Lopez-Santini herself. There were no classes on Saturdays, only sport in the mornings, so the timetable varied. In the first term of the year the school played hockey – at private schools hockey was *the* game – and Mercedes was delighted that both her daughters loved it. Teresa, twelve years old, chubby and dark-haired, was also a promising player. On Saturday June 15th she would be in the junior team for a match against Michael Ham School. This Saturday, the 8th, San Andres was having a practice and her younger sister, Gloria, aged ten, was in a less important game. They were excited and chattering as they ran past the hall porters to the car waiting in the driveway.

As Ruiz swung the Ford out into the road he noticed that the joggers were there again, despite its being a cold and windy morning – June was mid-winter in Argentina. The joggers were a young couple who wore distinctive maroon track suits and arrived on a motor scooter. Driving past, he glimpsed the man parking the Vespa under a tree, while the girl ran on the spot to keep warm. Rather her than me, he thought, as he accelerated away, then forgot them as he concentrated on a deviation he had planned for this morning, turning into one of the broad avenues which intersect the park, just to check he was not being followed. Palermo Park is to Buenos Aires what the Bois de Boulogne is to Paris, a huge lung through which city-dwellers can breathe. It is best known for the Hipodromo Argentino racecourse, for the rose gardens, for the polo, golf and tennis clubs which adjoin it and for the finest livestock show-ground in the world, that of the Argentine Rural Society. All kinds of people go to Palermo for all kinds of activity. After the white Ford had turned left, the man and the girl began their run, as they had done for the last four Saturdays, always coinciding with the departure of the Lopez-Santini children.

The workers' demonstration at the Plaza de Mayo in downtown Buenos Aires was less spontaneous than the union organizers would have admitted. It was deliberately being staged the Saturday before Lopez-Santini was due to sign yet another stop-gap loan agreement with the International Monetary Fund on behalf of the Argentine government. But if the banners and slogans had been prepared in advance, the anger felt by the participants was real. They might not know the technical pre-conditions for IMF assistance, usually referred to as 'economic adjustment', but they did know what keeping the Western bankers happy cost in practice: austerity and frozen wage-packets which would no longer buy the necessities of life for their families.

By eleven the police estimated the crowd was 100,000 strong, its members waving a forest of patriotic blue-and-white flags, while huge banners flapped in the breeze above their heads.

'PEACE, BREAD, WORK AND TO HELL WITH THE IMF,' read one. Others advertised unions and movements, like the 'CGT' and 'JUVENTUD PERONISTAS', harking back to memories of the glorious days of President Peron. The speeches were aggressive too.

Soon after midday the vast crowd began surging up the Avenida de Mayo towards the Congress building. The police knew better than to try to stop the procession, though they sealed off many streets leading into the city centre.

With no other job on hand, Ruiz lounged in the Ford and listened to the radio. He heard news about the workers' demonstration and decided it was unlikely to affect him. About the same time that the downtown crowd marched on the Congress the school games finished. Teresa and Gloria emerged from the buildings, flushed and happy, clutching their hockey-sticks. A teacher escorted them to the car: no one was taking chances with a minister's children.

It was not until Ruiz reached the neighbourhood of Palermo Park that he encountered any problem, and because of the broadcasts he was unfazed to find his intended route blocked by a uniformed policeman, who firmly waved him down a different avenue. He was less than five minutes from the apartment, anyway. A short distance into the park he realized with momentary shock that there had been an accident ahead. A girl in a maroon track suit was standing by the side of the road, shouting and gesticulating. Beyond her, toppled on its side, lay a motor scooter with the body of a man inert beside it. Ruiz slowed, recognizing the familiar joggers, instinctively horrified at what a hit-and-run driver had done to them. The girl stepped out on to the road, waving him down with despairing gestures. He stopped, pressing the button that actuated the electric window.

'*Señor, señor,*' she screamed. '*Por favor*, help us.'

For a few seconds Ruiz hesitated. Then the feeling that he already knew her overcame his mistrust. He told the children to stay in the car, got out and ran across to see how badly the man was hurt. The girl stood wailing that her boyfriend was dead. As Ruiz bent down she drew a gun out of the track suit's pocket and shot him in the back of the head.

Thirty seconds later she was in the Ford's driving seat. To her relief the chauffeur had left the keys in the ignition. She ordered the children to keep quiet, executed a tyre-screeching U-turn and drove away, waving to the policeman at the crossroads. The male jogger scrambled to his feet, glanced dispassionately at the dying chauffeur whose blood was spurting into the grass, righted the scooter and set off in the opposite direction.

Southampton, Long Island. Midday

Sheldon Harrison was regretting this lunch at the Meadow Club in Dune Road on the most exclusive part of Southampton's seashore, where one of his two guests, the president of the bank he worked for, was not a member. The social cadences of Southampton were complex, muted, physically near-invisible to outsiders, and carved in stone so far as the residents were concerned. The President of the Bartrum Bank, Ray Roth, was a reasonably average small-town businessman. But the town he had settled in, and which Sheldon Harrison's ancestors had helped to found 300 years earlier, was about as far removed from middle America as any place on the same continent could be. By the unwritten rules of the Meadow Club, Ray Roth would never be elected to membership. It had been stupid, Harrison now admitted to himself as they ordered pre-lunch drinks from a steward, to entertain Ray here.

The reason he had risked it was that Harrison's house guest liked the atmosphere of the Meadow Club: it was his kind of place. He was a recently retired British banker named James Warburton, a distant relative and a regular visitor to Southampton ever since Harrison could remember. Though thirty years apart in age, they understood each other. More important, Warburton understood the social structure of Southampton, which was half the reason Harrison wanted him to meet Roth. Harrison was a shareholder in the Bartrum Bank and was far from happy at the direction Roth had been taking it. You had to know something about the town to appreciate why Roth had made the kind of loans he had.

In winter, when Mecox Bay froze solid, Southampton's population was around 8,000 souls. In the height of summer that number swelled to nearer 60,000, and the white clapboard-clad mansions along Dune Road and South Main Street rented out for $10,000 a week – if you could get one – as the rich flew in like swallows from as far afield as Australia and Germany. Together with Sag Harbor, and the other Hamptons, it was to New York what Deauville and Le Touquet are to Paris, even rivalling Newport, Rhode Island.

All this wealth – the snobbery and the disparity between the winter and summer populations – created opportunities for backbiting, envy and graft which would have astonished old Thomas Halsey, the many times great grandfather of Sheldon Harrison and the remote ancestral cousin of his house guest. It went some

21

way to explaining why Ray Roth was being so aggressively loud-mouthed now, lecturing Warburton about the importance of Long Island and, by implication, of the Bartrum Bank. He was forty-four, but looked older, his face tinged grey from heavy smoking, and he emphasized his points by pounding the air with his fist.

'Let me tell you something, sir. Long Island is one whole lot more than just resorts like this. In terms of wealth, Nassau and Suffolk Counties amount to being the fifth largest city in the United States. You talk about per capita income, we're number one.'

'Is that so, Mr Roth? You intrigue me.' Warburton's reaction was characteristically understated. He was sixty-one, with silver-grey hair and a pink complexion which made his face look freshly scrubbed. He wore a conservatively coloured sports coat, while a silk cravat formalized his open-neck shirt. He would have passed as an elder statesman anywhere; and the benign innocence was totally misleading. Beneath it lay one of the shrewdest banking brains in Europe, which was why he had been called to New York for consultations on Third World debt. He sipped his gin and tonic and diplomatically challenged Roth's assertion.

'I had always understood Marin County to be the United States' most prosperous small community.'

'Marin County? Forget it. Not in the same league.' Roth hammered the air some more, his paunch threatening the waistband of his purple tartan trousers. 'Have you seen the service industries around JFK?' he demanded. 'You heard about the computer companies at Hauppage? Okay,' he leant forward as if forced to concede a point, 'I agree. Farmers around the Hamptons here, small-holders out at Montauk: those guys are down. But if they own land, they are not. No, sir. Along with all that goddam history, they're sitting on millions. And back in Nassau County, they're making more. Long Island's a high-tech area, Mr Warburton. Those guys bank with us. We know.'

Oh Christ, Harrison thought again, why didn't I guess Ray would start boasting instead of encouraging Warburton to unload some of the unofficial advice he was almost uniquely well qualified to offer. The Bartrum Bank, of which Harrison himself was a junior vice-president, was a minnow compared to the giants like Bank America, Chase Manhattan and Citibank. So why pretend?

However, Roth went right on beating his own drum.

'I tell you, sir, we know Long Island because it's our business to know.'

In fairness, as Harrison had explained to Warburton over breakfast this morning, the Bartrum Bank did have a certain amount going for it. Founded over a century ago, it had a reputation for friendliness, prudent management of funds and absolute probity, which had enabled it to expand to a capitalization of some $71 million and assets of $840 million, despite competition from the Bank of Long Island and the Bank of the Hamptons.

None the less, the real reason for Long Island businesses maintaining accounts with the Bartrum Bank was the McFadden Act. Back in 1926 a long-standing Congressional mistrust of monopolies had solidified into a law which made it illegal for banks to open offices outside their home states. Sixty years later, despite computerized cheque-clearing systems operated by the Federal Reserve and such competitors as Bank Wire, it was still easier for companies to pay their employees through one of the nation's 15,000 local banks than through a Manhattan giant. Eventually the revolution in financial services might change this. For the moment a bank president like Roth could justify his self-importance.

The self-importance was Roth's Achilles' heel. Sheldon Harrison had explained that too, while his housekeeper served them bacon and eggs and hash browns – he was a bachelor maintaining a large, inherited house a couple of miles out at Water Mill.

Sheldon suspected that it was because he wanted to belong to the international set – or at least talk as if he did – that Roth had committed the bank to foreign loans which would have sent his predecessors into shock.

'Were the loans as bad as that?' Warburton had asked.

'Mostly syndicated by Plaza in New York: one of their vice-presidents has a house out here. They sounded profitable at the time.'

Warburton had understood instantly. Banks were in the business of accepting deposits and lending them out again at a higher rate, making a profit on 'the turn'. During the boom years before the 1982 recession it had been easy to attract local deposits at high interest rates, but less easy to lend out again at higher. So the large-scale financing needs of Third World governments, offering those higher rates, had seemed a godsend. Hundreds of banks were persuaded to take part in syndicated loans arranged by the big money centres which acted as leaders. By the early 1980s Plaza, like some others, was no longer committing its own funds: just taking a fee for organizing syndicates.

'Ray used to argue that if Plaza said the deals were okay, well they must be.'

'So you would like me to advise him whether those loans will go bad?'

'If Ray can be persuaded to ask,' Harrison had said. 'I hope he can. The longer he holds off, the harder we'll be hit. Our loans are all years past maturity and not repaid.'

As they transferred themselves to the dining-room of the Meadow Club Warburton was reminded of this breakfast-time briefing by the way Roth continued trumpeting the Bartrum Bank's virtues: almost as if he were afraid to stop.

'Let me tell you,' he exclaimed, surveying the throng in the wide room, 'a community like Southampton needs a bank like ours. Maybe that's hard for an outsider to appreciate. I guess you don't have local banks the way we do.'

'They were mostly amalgamated into large groups years ago.' Warburton allowed the point to lapse while a steward took their orders, then explained briefly how, for example, a number of small family banks in the eastern counties of England had evolved into the worldwide organizations which still traded under the name of one of those families: Barclays. 'I was with Lloyds myself. They, the Midland and the National Westminster have branches in virtually every town in Britain, even in many villages. And the Royal Bank of Scotland, of course, up north. Ours is a somewhat different scene.'

When, he wondered, would this conversation get to the point? Suddenly Roth brought it there, and took his breath away with the naivety of the question.

'Your people do much foreign lending?' he asked casually.

'It's why I'm over here.' Warburton managed to retain his sang-froid, choking back a retort about the 6,000 branch offices of British banks overseas. Few Americans knew that British capital had originally financed development in many Latin American states nor imagined it still did, which was the snag. Ordinary high-street customers of British banks at home were equally ignorant of how exposed certain of them were out there.

Although Barclays, with extensive commitments in Africa, had been steadily building reserves against the possibility of default, and likewise NatWest was in no danger, the Midland reportedly had three times the value of its capital and reserves in Latin America. Lloyds, which had absorbed the Bank of London and South America, was exposed to around £4 billion overall. It was not a lot of consolation that jointly the British banks were only owed some seven per cent of Third World debt as against American exposure to fifty per cent. A default could still be deeply embarrassing to them.

'James was Deputy Chairman of the Latin American Re-scheduling Committee,' Harrison cut in, anxious not to let his boss back off. 'They asked him to come across again.'

'So what's the problem?' The edge of alarm, of fear even, was audible in Roth's voice.

'We are hoping it's only short-term.'

Harrison glanced across the table anxiously. His guest had not explained the precise reasons for being in America, only that his advice had been asked.

'Yeah?' Roth's hand, clutching a square-cut tumbler of whisky, began to tremble. He hastily put the glass down, as if betrayed.

'Strictly between ourselves, the Banco do Brasil has temporarily suspended foreign-exchange payments. Began on Friday. That's why the committee is reassembling.' Warburton smiled gently, 'Not that it's often been out of session, these days. It was I who retired and am now being recalled to the colours.'

'But they can't do that!' The blood was seeping from Roth's normally florid cheeks. 'You mean those bastards are defaulting?'

'They're very carefully not saying so.' Warburton noted the greyish pallor spread across the American's face and guessed he must have outstanding loans on which the interest was seriously overdue. Under US law a debt became 'non-performing' when the interest was more than twelve weeks late. If all South American debt went bad some of the most famous names in banking would be insolvent: Bankers Trust, Chase Manhattan, Citicorp, First Chicago and Wells Fargo among them.

'Are you heavily exposed in Brazil?' he asked.

'We participated in a couple of syndicated loans, for a whole stack of government projects. Hell, how could anyone . . .' Roth left the rest unsaid, but Warburton could guess it. Legally, Bartrum could not loan more than twenty per cent of its undivided surplus to any one customer. However, by nominally splitting the amount among a number of enterprises, this restriction could be evaded. The snag was that most Third World countries only possessed one channel through which foreign-exchange payments could be made. That channel was the central bank.

'How much is involved?' Warburton asked.

'At the rate we were offered, I couldn't refuse.' Roth slid away from answering.

Greed, Warburton reminded himself. It was always the same, and the banks to whom he was acting as consultant in his retirement had been no differently motivated. Making a huge loan on a single transaction was infinitely simpler than lending out in half-million- or million-dollar packets, especially if you had to investigate the credit-worthiness of each borrower. In the late 1970s and early 1980s nobody had questioned the credit-worthiness of governments. So there was no administrative bother over that, either. And the lead bank received a fat fee up-front for arranging the loan. It had all been too easy.

'No!' Roth suddenly came to life, hammering the table. 'They can't do this to us. They can't do it. We have to act. Call the White House, tell our Senator, do something.'

Other people began to stare. Harrison caught at his boss's sleeve. 'Ray, please. Keep your voice down.'

'We have to do something.' Roth rose to his feet, knocking over his whisky, staining the white cloth. 'I'm sorry, Mr Warburton, we have to leave. Sheldon, we have to work on this.' He began to stride towards the door, while the waiter hurried across to ask what was the matter.

At the front door, looking out towards the driveway where their cars were parked, Roth suddenly appreciated that their British guest had no means of getting home unless Harrison took him.

'Okay, okay,' he half shouted. 'Go to Water Mill first but come right back to the office. This is an emergency, and I mean that.'

'Could the loan be written off?' Warburton demanded quietly, as they drove along Dune Road, past the high hedges and service driveways that shielded the resort houses of the rich, past a lake and the site where old Thomas Halsey had planted his original homestead in 1640, and out through flat farmland to the village where Harrison lived. 'How much is involved?'

'Twenty million in Brazil. Almost half of the bank's capital.'

'Did Mr Roth take part in other developing-country syndications?'

'The Argentine and Mexico,' Harrison said grimly. 'If they default, we'll be insolvent. A lot of people round here would lose their life savings and have the mortgages on their homes foreclosed. Fifteen years ago the Bartrum Bank wouldn't lend outside the State, let alone the country. Then Ray let himself be sweet-talked into thinking he could be part of the big time. The size of the syndicates just mesmerized him. And the rates. As I told you, he used to boast at parties here about our international activity. Crazy.' He eased the car to a halt at the Route 27 intersection until a gap in the steady flow of traffic allowed him to pull out and cross the main road to go down a lane signed Old Mill Road. 'Nearly there. What do you suggest?'

'Keeping your nerve,' Warburton answered, as they stopped by a white-painted picket fence. 'Four or five hundred other banks must be in the same hole: British, German, Swedish, Swiss, Japanese, as well as American. They'll have to get organized. When was your last interest payment from Brazil due?'

'Ninety days ago yesterday. Officially it can no longer be counted a performing asset.'

'You do have a problem.' Warburton drew in his breath. 'Well if I were you I'd look for some technical way to postpone the due date and persuade your Mr Roth to calm down. Nothing gets around faster than news of a bank in trouble. And then, if you will forgive a colloquialism, the shit really will hit the fan.'

Nassau. Afternoon

'Excuse me, sir. If you and de lady wouldn't mind steppin' dis way.'

The Bahamian customs officer who singled out Stuart Pendler and Maggie from the passengers off the Marsh Harbour flight felt he could afford to be polite. This pair were dead meat, oh man they were. They'd collected their baggage, and he knew just exactly where the coke was concealed, the tip-off had been that accurate. He had them cold.

'We don't have to go through customs, do we?' Maggie said it for them both, though glancing at Stuart for support.

'If you don't mind, ma'am, I jest likes to see your bags.' A fraction more insistent this time, the Bahamian guided them away to the customs examination rooms. 'Jest likes to see what you may be carryin'.'

They hadn't much option. Pendler consented, scenting a frame-up. This must be why that spook Garrard had arranged for their cases to be taken to the airport. He could kick himself for not having thought of it before, and there was nothing he could do about it now.

Twenty minutes later, their belongings lay strewn along the customs bench and the official was less relaxed. In order not to make the tip-off obvious, he had gone through all the usual hiding-places and found nothing: the make-up in Maggie's vanity-case smelt and felt like what it was supposed to be. No packets of white powder had emerged from among Stuart's correspondence or his clothing. That didn't worry him. What did was that far from the pair becoming frightened, their antagonism was increasing.

'What's the idea?' Pendler demanded. 'What are you trying to find?'

'Dose.' The Bahamian disregarded the protests and pointed at Maggie's box of film. He'd followed his orders. Now he could go for the kill. 'Open dose.'

'You can't.' Maggie interrupted. 'They're sealed.'

'Can't? No such word as "can't". Open dem.'

'But you'll spoil the film! Don't you understand?' She felt like screaming at this bully.

27

'You can't. I will.' He pulled out a pocket knife and one by one ripped through the side of the rolls, pulling out the celluloid inside and shaking the little round containers over a sheet of paper. When all twelve were ruined and not a sniff of cocain had fallen from them he lost his cool completely.

'Okay. You play fool wid me, I know what I'm doing.' He shouted for a woman assistant and they hustled Maggie and Stuart into separate cubicles for a body search.

Having stripped naked, Stuart was forced to stand with his legs wide apart, hands high above his head, palms against the wall. The customs man thrust plastic-gloved fingers into his backside, causing him to twist and jerk with pain. Instinctively he lashed backwards with one foot, his heel catching the Bahamian in the groin. Then he managed to stumble away from the wall and turn defensively with his back to it. The Bahamian, clutching his crotch, glared at him.

'Listen,' Pendler grated out the words, acutely conscious of his own vulnerability, 'the US Consul knows we're arriving. He'll be waiting for me to call. You want a diplomatic incident? Give me my pants.' He felt both furiously angry and absurd.

For a moment he was afraid he was going to be beaten up. Instead, the customs man straightened himself and tossed the trousers across contemptuously.

'You git deported for dat. Assaultin' an officer. You trash.' He moved suddenly to shake his fist in Pendler's face. 'Where you hidin' it, huh?'

'What?'

'De snow. De coke. Don't play fool wid me.'

'We don't take drugs.' Pendler managed to pull up his trousers and stand straight. The whole scenario was abruptly clear. 'Your friend Garrard got it wrong. I phoned the Consul because he threatened us.'

The name Garrard produced an instant effect. The Bahamian hesitated, stared, then said, 'Jest wait,' and left, locking the cubicle door. Through the thin walls Pendler could hear Maggie's voice, pitched close to a scream.

'How dare you! How dare you call me a junkie!'

In the other cubicle the woman officer reluctantly let her dress again, leaving her in tears.

Through the wall Pendler heard a low-voiced confabulation outside. Then the door was unlocked.

'You pack dose bags. You're leavin',' the man ordered.

As he obeyed, reckoning that the bluff about the Consul had worked, Maggie was also let out, wiping her eyes, taking control of herself.

'Why are they doing this, Stu?' she asked. 'What's the point?'

'Have to ask Garrard that.' He turned on the man. 'I want to make a call.'

'You kin do that after. I told you, you're leavin', man. We got orders about you.'

He refused to elucidate. As soon as they had repacked their cases, before Maggie could even fix her make-up, they were escorted to a police office, handed tickets to New York, and then taken to the US Immigration and Customs control. Technically they had left the Bahamas. Two hours later they were airborne.

'Well,' Maggie demanded, accepting a whisky with a nervous laugh of relief, 'perhaps now we're out of that hell-hole you can tell me what it was all about. And it had better be good. Do you realize I've come out of that trip with absolutely nothing? Not a single picture!'

'I posted a roll to Paris, remember?'

'Those stupid pictures in the restaurant!' She was not mollified. 'Who can I sell those to?'

'Those stupid pictures,' Pendler just stopped himself from adding 'if they come out', 'are of the Polish Finance Minister lunching with the Argentine Economy Minister, when both were officially someplace else.'

'For the sake of which you just got us roughed up and deported?' She twisted in her seat so as to look at him. 'Why didn't you tell me who I was photographing. Don't you trust me that much?' Her anger was beginning to flare. He'd simply been using her to confirm some other story he was working on. The whisky did nothing to dampen her temper either. 'What do I get out of this, apart from never being allowed back in the Bahamas? You're a real four-letter man, Stuart Pendler.'

'I'm sorry. That creep Garrard made a fairly explicit threat when he took me for a drive. He warned me off looking for conferences, which told me we were in the right place.'

'So?' The very quietness of her question would have heralded an explosion to anyone who knew Maggie well.

'I thought it safer to keep you in the dark.'

'Which you have done since the start of the trip! Holy Mother of Jesus, the conceit of the man. Who do you think you are: the Financial Correspondent of the *Herald Tribune* or the Lord God of Hosts? And are you writing a travel piece at all, may I ask?'

'Sure. As a blind. The real story is the people the Argentine and the Pole are meeting with. How could I prove the whole thing wasn't an invention unless I had your picture?'

'Oh, I see.' When she wanted to be withering she could be. 'So now every time you're on a story I have to go too, just to show it happened.'

Pendler took this lightly. He was accustomed to abuse. 'This thing is the biggest financial story in years and the photos are going to be worth a sack of dollars. "Photos", plural, because I'm going to need more.'

'What is "this thing"?' In spite of her indignation she was becoming intrigued.

'Have you heard of the Cartagena Group? It's a standing conference of South American debtor nations, named after the place it first met in Colombia. There've been rumours of other debtors joining the group to form a cartel – like OPEC, in a way – so they can negotiate jointly with the West.'

'I know about OPEC. But that's a cartel controlling the selling price of oil.'

'Sure. And for some years it earned billions of dollars profit which its members deposited with Western banks and the banks then lent to other developing countries, who now can't pay it back.'

'So why are my pictures going to make me rich?'

'Because if my hunch is correct, what's going on at Columbus Cay right now is a meeting of all the big debtors discussing how best to put the Western banks $580 billion down the tube.'

'And?' She couldn't visualize $580 billion.

'The entire US deficit is only $160 billion. This would make the 1929 crash look like a picnic.'

'I wasn't around in 1929.'

'A great many people could be ruined. The debtor countries could hold the banks to ransom: announce some impossible write-off option and say, "If you don't accept, we'll default. Our people are starving: yours can have a taste of the same medicine."'

'You think that's what we stumbled on?' She could see that if Stu's hunch was correct, he had a front-page story that wouldn't just run for a day.

'Hardly stumbled. I've been watching for signs. A few weeks ago the Mexican Finance Minister made an unpublicized swing around the world. Every city he stopped at was the capital of a debtor nation. Except for Nassau. That suggested the Bahamas for a conference. The rest was legwork and enquiries.' He smiled happily. 'A lot of enquiries. I had one lucky break. A travel-agent friend was furious because he'd made firm reservations for clients at Columbus Cay and they'd been cancelled. That gave me a probable place and the date.'

Maggie glanced sideways at him with something akin to admiration. 'You know, Stu, as well as being the biggest male chauvinist this side of Hollywood, you are actually quite a pro. But what if by reporting this you start a panic?'

'You mean the media should have kept quiet about the Chernobyl disaster?' he poured a slug of whisky from the tiny bottle the stewardess had brought, suddenly dead serious. 'You mean the *Post* should never have investigated Watergate? My job is to find out the truth, not cover up for the authorities. Okay, one shouldn't publish military secrets and we don't. This is different. This is of legitimate public concern. You don't save people from a time bomb by pretending it isn't there.'

Water Mill, Long Island. Afternoon

'How did you get on?' Warburton looked round from the lounger in which he was reclining by the pool. It had been a perfect afternoon and the sun was still warm. Martha, the housekeeper, had brought him tea. He felt deeply content and had to force himself to show interest in conversation about a man whom he had decided was basically an overblown non-entity. 'Has Roth calmed down?'

'Not a lot.' Harrison mixed himself an early drink at the bar in the pool-house. 'What can you do on a Saturday afternoon except go through figures. Can I offer you a martini?'

'Later perhaps.' He listened to the clink of ice and watched a boy paddling past in a yellow canoe. The lawn of the Harrisons' family house, where Sheldon had lived alone since his mother died, ran down to a large pond, fringed with reeds. Through the reeds he caught glimpses of the boy manoeuvring himself across the water. The sight reminded him of his own childhood paddling a boat on the carp pond at Gaddesden, where the Halseys originated.

Harrison followed his gaze. 'There's a kind of tunnel under the road through to Mecox Bay. People row through sometimes.' He settled heavily into an adjoining chair. 'What's scaring Ray is if the Argentine does the same as Brazil. He put ten million out there a couple of months before the Falklands War.'

'And Galtieri promptly spent it on military toys, eh?' After the Argentine military junta fell, following the Falklands defeat, it had proved impossible for the incoming democratic government to disentangle the military's web of unaccounted-for spending, not even its totals. Warburton sat up, accepting that he was going to have to concentrate. 'Personally I don't think the Argentine will default, though it's one of the few Latin American countries that can afford to thumb its nose at us. It's economically all but self-sufficient. The only others that would gain despite the trading penalties are Brazil and Venezuela. Mexico's so hopeless it's been on the verge of default for months. Those three might go bad, but I don't think the Argentine will.'

'Why should the Argentines want to honour debts?'

'They'll get national growth of around 3.8 per cent without default. That's better than many European countries. So, what with wishing to prove they can function as a democracy, I think the Argentines will stay with us. Lopez-Santini will certainly want to.'

'You know him?' Harrison stopped dead, almost spilling the glass he was bringing. 'Christ, I wish *we* did!'

Warburton grunted non-committally, accepted the drink, then said suddenly, 'There are things one can do on a Saturday. I can telephone Buenos Aires, for example. José won't discuss Argentine policy, but he might express a view on Brazil's.'

The pool-house had a telephone extension. While Warburton went indoors to find his address book, Harrison checked the codes. Five minutes later the number of the apartment overlooking Palermo Park was ringing.

'What person are you calling?' a voice demanded in Spanish. 'Who are you?'

Warburton explained.

'It is not possible to speak with this number.' The phone clicked.

'Curious,' Warburton commented, reluctantly replacing the receiver, 'they're ex-directory, of course, but . . . I wonder what's wrong.'

Columbus Cay, Great Abaco. Afternoon

The afternoon session had been sluggish so far, despite a siesta break. Or perhaps because of it. An indulgent lunch, Lopez-Santini reflected mordantly, seldom encouraged either common sense or fine oratory. He and Kaminski had been basically in agreement: for diametrically opposite reasons both their countries would be reluctant to participate in a debtors' cartel. The Polish government had to prove that a Communist economic system could work without total dependence on Russia: Lopez-Santini had to show that the Argentine's recently restored Western democracy could also survive alone. To his credit, Kaminski had appreciated the humour in their being bedfellows.

The conference itself, however, had been humourless and histrionic. Lopez-Santini was being subjected to heavy lobbying. Success for the Mexican organizers would depend above all on persuading the heavyweight debtors to collaborate. The heavyweights were snidely nicknamed the MBA nations – Mexico, Brazil and the Argentine. The pressure put on Lopez-Santini was unlikely to be intellectual.

The Bolivian Deputy Finance Minister, Suarez, set a tone which Lopez-Santini particularly deplored. It had consisted largely of a virulent attack on a US lady senator who was campaigning for cutting off aid to Bolivia if its production of narcotics was not reduced. Bolivia produced half the entire world supply of cocaine and no amount of statistics on child mortality, malnutrition, nor even an exponential rate of currency inflation could make poisoning the youth of North America by drug addiction desirable. The thought of Teresa and Gloria becoming junkies made Lopez-Santini tremble. He was proud and protective of his daughters as only a Latin can be.

My problem, Lopez-Santini told himself as the Sudanese began a more reasoned speech, is that I'm an economist, not a gut politician. I wasn't educated on election platforms. I'm trying to consolidate unpopular reforms which reason tells me are essential.

To his horror, as the session neared its end the Mexican Chairman offered him a role he could not conceivably accept.

'Señor Lopez-Santini,' Alvarez announced sententiously from the podium, 'I propose that this conference should offer you the greatest honour within its gift. Your acumen as an economist is well known, your negotiating skills as a diplomat have gained you prestige and a wide circle of friends. We should like you to negotiate on behalf of what we propose to term, informally, the Columbus Group. Are you willing?'

Flabbergasted, Lopez-Santini had no alternative but to rise to his feet and reply. He saw through the manoeuvre instantly. Mexico and Brazil were co-sponsors of the default-threat plan. By far the most effective way to neutralize his own opposition and maintain solidarity was to appoint him as spokesman. Applause greeted his standing up. None the less, he would have to refuse. He was steeling himself against the inevitable jeers and insults when there was a minor disturbance at the entrance to the hall. He looked round and saw the white-bearded manager in the doorway, whispering to the security man who must have allowed him in. The security man, young, with thick black hair and a moustache, cast around like a bird-dog, then headed behind the horseshoe of desks.

'Señor Lopez-Santini?' He wasn't one hundred per cent sure he had approached the right minister. 'Señor, we have Buenos Aires on the line. They say it is urgent.'

Both perplexed and relieved, Lopez-Santini excused himself and was taken by the apologetic manager across the compound to a private office behind the reception. McLellan's apologies were for interrupting the meeting. He was too experienced to express regret at the breach of security involved in identifying the Argentine's real name. If the Bahamas government wanted to play Mickey Mouse games, that was their affair.

Lopez-Santini, hurrying through the palm trees to the office, had a presentiment of disaster which was rapidly confirmed. The caller was the Buenos Aires Chief of Police, whom he had met a couple of times at receptions, but otherwise barely knew. His memory was of a small, portly and extremely pompous man, in an immaculate and heavily decorated uniform.

'What is it, Jefe?' He was apprehensive rather than angry. For the Chief himself to have called, the matter must be truly urgent.

'Bad news, I am afraid, Excellency. Your daughters have been abducted.'

'How? Not both of them?' A vision of Ruiz in his uniform flashed through his mind and he knew it must have been the school run; protecting children was impossibly difficult.

'Both, I regret. Your chauffeur's body was found in the Park shortly after one today. The car is missing. Your wife has received a ransom demand. I myself am with her now at your apartment. I am advising her personally.'

Lopez-Santini checked his watch. Four thirty-five here was two hours later in Buenos Aires. Probably six hours since the kidnap. The girls could be anywhere by now. Mercedes must be crazy with worry. Before talking to her he must have the facts.

'What is the ransom?'

'Half politics, half money, Excellency. Unique in my experience. Your daughters will be killed unless the Government refuses any new agreement with the International Monetary Fund and renegotiates the terms of the current loans. That is the first condition. The second is a payment of $1 million. When they have the money and are satisfied negotiations with the IMF have been broken off, your daughters will be released.'

'Bastards,' Lopez-Santini swore. 'But that's open-ended. They might never be satisfied. Who are they?'

The answer reinforced the shock.

'They claim to be the ERP. We have no proof.'

Lopez-Santini felt his grip on the telephone tighten, as though by instinctive physical pressure on the instrument he could somehow influence events, and his hand began to shake. The initials stood, in Spanish, for the People's Revolutionary Army. It was the ERP whose guerilla activity had led to the overthrow of Isabelita Peron all those years ago and to the 'dirty war' in which tens of thousands of civilians had died at the hands of Argentine's military. President Alfonsin had tried to cauterize those terrible wounds on society by bringing the officers responsible for suppressing the ERP to justice. Talking on a long-distance telephone, Lopez-Santini could not discuss, let alone analyse, the devastating political implications if the ERP had genuinely surfaced again. The only certainty was that his daughters were in extreme danger.

Although when his wife Mercedes came on to the line she was controlled at first, she rapidly turned hysterical, insisting on his immediate return. He promised to charter a plane to Miami first thing in the morning. His aide Felipe would have to observe the rest of the meeting on his behalf. For him to represent the Group was impossible. But when he returned to the pagoda-shaped building a strange hush greeted his discreet reappearance, followed by vigorous clapping.

'When you were gone,' Felipe told him with embarrassment as he sat down, 'they took a vote. They elected you. There was nothing I could do.'

'But I cannot . . .' He broke off, torn by the realization that his loyalties were now impossibly divided. Accepting would compromise his government's freedom of action. However, if the kidnappers could somehow be informed of this, then his unwelcome role might ensure his daughters' safety. It would prove he was meeting the first condition. Suppressing his anger, he rose coldly to his feet, bowed and joined Alvarez on the podium.

CHAPTER THREE

Buenos Aires. Sunday June 9th

The Jefe had personally received the Minister and his wife, not failing to underscore that it was solely on account of the importance of this distressing matter that he had come to Police Headquarters on a Sunday afternoon.

The Jefe's office overlooked the central courtyard of the handsome old building in the city centre – a courtyard planted with palm trees and surrounded with balconies. On every other day of the week there were scores of people around: girls in overalls typing; fat sergeants lolling at their desks while queues of ordinary citizens waited. Today there were only a few young policemen, armed with sub-machine guns, guarding the ground-floor entrance. Lopez-Santini had noticed this lack of activity as he and Mercedes were escorted up, but he did not bother to ask if crime ceased on Sundays. The police were, all too literally, a law unto themselves.

'Naturally it would be my wish to take charge of your case myself.' The Jefe's navy-blue uniform, liberally adorned with silver buttons and braid, looked band-box fresh. He smoothed the tunic over his paunch. 'However, it is better to be advised by an expert in this unhappy field.' He pressed an intercom button. 'Comisario Alfaro, kindly come to my office.'

When Comisario Alfaro appeared, a slightly younger, slightly less corpulent replica of the Jefe himself, the ceremonious explanations continued.

'The Comisario will have my full authority and backing. Although he will, of course, use his own discretion in interpreting the evidence we have already obtained.'

Lopez-Santini had understood the purposes of this charade perfectly. The Jefe was distancing himself from possible failure.

In such a corrupt police force this was always wise: who could tell what junior officer might not betray an operation?

Next they had been shown to Alfaro's own office, where a tape-recorder stood ready on the desk, and real tension made itself felt.

'This may be upsetting, Excellency,' he apologized in advance. 'I regret it is essential to identify the voices. You may even, by a miracle, recognize the kidnappers.' He watched Lopez-Santini sitting on the leather sofa, his wife beside him, her hand clasped in his. Mercedes had long black hair which framed a well-shaped face, but her olive-tinted skin was pale and her eyes puffy from weeping. She trembled. An unusual couple, he reflected, the university economist lured into the despised world of politics with his well-heeled socialite wife. An attraction of opposites? She *was* attractive, too: had kept her figure in spite of child-bearing. In less distressing circumstances . . .

'We can both face facts, Comisario,' Lopez-Santini said, feeling far from certain that Mercedes would be able or anxious to proceed. He never trusted policemen. They always had ulterior motives. How had this recording been obtained, for example? All Alfaro would say was that it had been received while His Excellency the Minister was on his way back from the Bahamas. Did he know how to deal with kidnappers? How much useful experience lay beneath the silver badges of rank and the decorations?

Alfaro switched on the tape and a sound like paper rustling came from the loudspeaker. Then a voice succeeded it: Teresa's voice subdued and frightened.

'When can I talk to Papa? I want to talk to Papa, please.'

'Oh God, it's her, it's my baby.' Mercedes tightened her grip on her husband's hand, hardly able to restrain herself.

'Shush, my love. We must listen.' Every word could carry a message, but he missed the next few.

'. . . your sister.' A man's voice, gruff and with a provincial inflexion.

'Papa?'

Lopez-Santini could visualize his daughter screwing up her courage. She knew all about tape-recorders, of course. Yet perhaps in her fear she was expecting him to reply.

'Papa. Gloria is with me. We're all right. In a room. I don't know where exactly. They gave us supper. We're going to sleep in bunks.' He felt Mercedes shivering. 'Please fetch us soon.' There was a muffled interruption. 'Here's Gloria.'

It was like a travesty of the conversations when the girls were staying with their aunt and phoned in the evening to relate the day's excitements.

'I'm frightened. I don't want to be here.' Gloria, whose awkwardness had always been more pronounced on the telephone, began stumbling over the phrases. 'Please come, Papa, I don't like the lady . . .'

'Shut up.' The man's voice cut in, there was a sound like a slap followed by a scream.

'Oh, I can't bear it. They're hitting her. Oh my babies.' Mercedes began to sob, trying to start up from the sofa, then burying her head on her husband's shoulder.

'You heard them.' The man had evidently returned to the microphone alone. 'They're okay. They're lucky. Millions of ordinary workers aren't. Now listen, Lopez-Santini. Listen well. This time you're going to do something for the democracy you keep shouting about. You're going to do something for the workers. No more pay cuts. No more devaluation. No more bleeding our country to death for foreign vultures. They can sing for their money, okay? There won't be any IMF agreement next week. No IMF deal, no more debt repayments. You're going to make a public statement, okay. Official. That's the first thing. The second's easier. Private. A million dollars. You can afford that, Lopez-Santini. You fat cats in the Congress have plenty salted away in Switzerland. You buy your shirts in London, don't you? Our people can't afford shirts, from anywhere. Think about that for a minute.'

The pause in this almost telegraphic speech was dramatic. Lopez-Santini's thoughts raced. Today was Sunday. The IMF talks were due Monday week. He had eight days. More if they could somehow stall.

'What else does he want?' Mercedes was despairing and the answer came on cue.

'You got that, Lopez-Santini! Two things. From you, one million dollars. Private, no publicity. From the government, a public statement. No more debt repayment, no more licking the IMF's boots for loans. Then you can have the girls back. If not, you never see them again. We might kill them. We might sell them. They're old enough. Think of that, Lopez-Santini. Tell your wife. Some people would pay good money.'

'I can't bear it.' Mercedes almost screamed. 'Beasts! Devils! How can they?' She burst into a flood of tears.

Even though the man had paused again – his sense of timing was uncanny – his words became lost in Mercedes' sobbing. The Comisario had to replay the end of the tape.

'We're not fools. We know you have to be seen to negotiate. We'll give you a week. We'll be in touch.'

Alfaro leant across his desk and turned off the machine.

'Oh my babies, my poor darling babies. Why does it have to be them?' Mercedes, though intelligent, had always been more concerned with her friends and family than her husband's day-to-day work. He had been a professor. She understood that. Now he was a minister: and she enjoyed the status. But the IMF? 'What does he mean?' she moaned. 'What have we done?'

'We have talks due with the IMF. Its officials are certain to want more austerity as the price of a new loan. What that criminal doesn't understand is that our own policies are already more stringent than theirs. Perhaps it's good that people blame the Fund, instead of us.'

As a 'free market' economist Lopez-Santini found it ironic that the International Monetary Fund should have become a hated bogeyman in so many developing countries. The way this had come about proved that the surest way to lose a friend is to lend him money.

The IMF belonged to its 148 member countries. Although they all contributed it was basically the rich who put in and the poor who took out. The idea of the Fund, back in 1945, had been to help iron out international balance of payments problems by short-term lending. After the 1973 oil price shock its activity had hugely increased. Financed mainly by the industrial members, it went into long-term loans, giving poorer members a quota each. The quotas had to be increased rapidly. Some countries like Jamaica, the Ivory Coast and Sudan went four and a half times beyond their limit. Inevitably, because its rules forbade rescheduling, the IMF had to get tough, insisting debtors adopt orthodox financial policies to put their economies in order.

Orthodoxy meant aiming for solvency by reducing inflation and stimulating productivity. The orthodox measures included controlling prices and wages, cutting government spending, devaluing currencies. This was understandably unpopular. In the Argentine, struggling to pay off the profligate borrowing of the previous military government, the austerity measures had initially been welcomed. But then the adjustment began causing recession, unemployment, bankruptcies and union unrest.

'The man's right in a way,' Lopez-Santini said wearily. 'The poorest will suffer most from another IMF deal. They always do.' Comforting his wife with his arm still round her shoulder, he stared enquiringly at Alfaro. 'Have you handled a kidnap before?'

'I have indeed.' Alfaro gave his reply heavy emphasis, deliberately omitting to call the Minister 'Excellency' as an implied reprimand. 'I cut my teeth on the Born case. You will remember the Monteneros kidnapped the Born brothers in broad daylight on their way to work.'

Lopez-Santini shuddered. The family company of Bunge Born had paid a $60 million ransom back in 1975. A year later the activity of the Monteneros and the People's Revolutionary Army had sparked an army coup and the long, searing years of the 'dirty war'.

'You think the ERP is holding our children? Surely they were eliminated?'

'You asked, Excellency, if I had experience. I merely observe that before the Born brothers were released the Monteneros also made political demands. Until these kidnappers identify themselves we can only guess. Your daughters were snatched during a left-wing demonstration in the city. There could be a connection.'

'How did you get the tape?'

'An anonymous caller told us to look underneath a certain bench in a suburban park. There is every likelihood that your children are being held in one of the suburbs. The voice on the tape is middle class. It told us there is also a woman involved. Historically most of our revolutionaries have been recruited from among discontented students and graduates. We shall hear from them again. Then we can negotiate.'

'But we must pay!' Mercedes interrupted. 'Even if we have to sell everything, we must pay.'

'No, señora, we must negotiate. They have not forbidden you to inform us. The contrary. They have positively thrown their threat in our faces. We shall get your children back, but to do so we must talk. In secrecy, always in secret. At all costs the kidnap must be kept out of the papers. At the same time, we might use the press to our advantage. Can you release a statement suggesting the IMF faces tough negotiations?'

'If His Excellency the President agrees.' Lopez-Santini smiled mirthlessly. National pride would have demanded that he be seen to put up a fight against the IMF, anyway.

'It would be helpful, Excellency. Meanwhile I shall intensify the search for witnesses.'

'You can't do anything now?' Disbelief and horror mingled in Mercedes' expression.

'Unhappily, señora, we have to wait until they contact us. Then we shall act.' Helping Mercedes to her feet, the Comisario escorted the couple downstairs to where an official car was waiting at a side entrance. He wished he could feel as confident as he tried to sound. The very word 'kidnap' meant to seize a child and all too often kidnappings of children had ended in catastrophe. It might be half a century since the Lindbergh baby was murdered in the United States, but the danger remained as acute today.

Long Island. Evening

'Better than getting snarled up in Sunday evening traffic, I suppose,' Warburton observed, as the pilot began taxiing the twin-engined commuter plane out to Easthampton airport's runway. He felt less relaxed than he tried to sound. The seat was narrow and his knees were jammed against the back of the one in front. On the other hand, he had a dinner date in New York of pressing importance: though not, unfortunately, with a pretty woman.

'I guess it's faster,' Harrison conceded. In fact by the time one had checked in, flown, found a taxi at the Marine Air Terminal at La Guardia and reached Manhattan, the air service wasn't so much quicker than the Hampton Jitney. Or more comfortable. But Warburton had insisted. 'Listen, Jim,' he asked, not for the first time today, 'are you sure you want me involved?'

The engines roared as the pilot revved up for take-off, and Warburton didn't answer until they were airborne and the Long Island shore was slipping past beneath.

'If the Western banks face a crisis, and I think they do, the international committee is going to be busy. Bill Osborn of First National has never left off working on the debt problem. He'll be Chairman. He wants me as Deputy again to represent the Europeans. I ought to have an American assistant. You know how I work. I'd like you with us.'

'If Ray Roth agrees.'

The plane rocked and Warburton wondered whether this local Long Island airline was among the businesses in hock to the Bartrum Bank. If so, the turbulence they were suffering now would be nothing compared to what the management was heading for.

'Your Mr Roth,' he said, in as measured tones as the noise allowed, 'would be wise to release you. We've been anticipating either a Mexican or a Brazilian default. If other debtor nations follow suit it may not be a question of whether any banks go under, it'll be which ones do.'

Paris. Monday June 10th

'Are you sure your imagination isn't running away with you, Stu?'

The editor of the *International Herald Tribune* leant back in his chair, fingertips pressed together as if making a Hindu greeting, and gazed at Pendler over them as sceptically as only a man who has been in journalism all his life can gaze. The editor was a medium-built, rather portly man with thick though greying hair. He'd been a football player at Harvard thirty years ago, but his muscles had run to fat in a way occasional games of squash at a sporting club in the Paris suburb of Neuilly couldn't combat. These days he waddled slightly as he walked. However, that didn't make him any less shrewd. His name was Harry Grant and when people misheard it as 'Cary' he always laughed indulgently. He also had to put up with a certain amount of ribbing about connections with the famous Harry's Bar, which wasn't far from the old *Trib* office off the Champs-Elysées.

'I tell you, Harry,' Pendler insisted, 'what's going on at Columbus Cay is a secret meeting of the debtor nations. It has to be. It's a big story.'

'What did you actually see? A skeleton in the water, two fellows who might be a Pole and an Argentine eating lobster, and some highly objectionable local officials.' Grant let his chair come down four square on the carpet and slapped his palms on the desk. 'I'm sorry, Stu. We have a million words a day of genuine news coming into the computers from AP, the *Post* and the *Times*. We're not in the business of sensationalism. The *Trib* is a paper of world coverage and informed comment. Why don't you stay with the project we sent you out for. That Bahamas tax-haven piece should be the one the *Times* will take from us.'

'So would the western banking system being held to ransom.'

'Stu,' impatience became visible in Grant's expression, 'a while back we sponsored a conference in Oxford on Latin American debt. Maybe you recall its conclusions? A debtor nations' cartel is not considered probable. Okay?'

The *Trib*, Pendler reflected, was both a privilege and an inhibition to serve. Established here in Paris jointly by the *Washington Post* and the *New York Times* after the old *New York Herald Tribune* folded, most of its stories came from them and from the big agencies like Reuter. Editorial comment was reprinted from distinguished papers around the world. Only a handful of specialist writers and reporters like himself provided original material. 'Special to the *Tribune*' as the byline always said, though the arts and financial pages had particularly high reputations.

'What would we want with an exclusive anyway?' Pendler remarked provocatively. 'Except for the *Post* or the *Times* to follow up.'

'Put your cartel theory on the back burner. I'd like the tax-haven copy by the end of the week.'

'Did it ever occur to you, sir,' Pendler tried mock-formality to get his point across, 'that when we have a world story we're uniquely positioned to put it across?'

This was no exaggeration. Every night except Saturday the *Herald Tribune* was transmitted via satellite to printing centres in London, Zurich, The Hague, Rome, Singapore, Hong Kong, Miami and other cities. It took only four minutes to send the entire paper – layouts, pictures and all – ready for printing. The local process was actually slower, because the motorbike courier needed twenty minutes to reach the plant, in a Paris suburb. Over-all, the *Trib* had a world readership of influential citizens that no other journal could match within a comparable timescale.

'Go away, Stu.' Grant waved at him as if flicking ash off the desk.

Reluctantly Pendler obeyed and went down to the feature-writers' area on the second floor, where he grabbed a free desk. For the next forty-five minutes he rang numbers in Britain where he might locate a man who had been intimately concerned with debt rescheduling on behalf of British banks and who, being retired, might be willing to offer a lead. He failed. The nearest person to his quarry with whom he managed to speak was a house-keeper and she affected ignorance.

'I'm very sorry, sir,' she said with the restrained dignity of the English family retainer, 'Mr Warburton is abroad and we do not know when he will be back.'

London. Morning

For a man who controlled £5 million of investments, Leonard Slater lived unusually simply. The only accountable perquisites of office which he and his wife Gladys enjoyed were a four-bed-room brick-and-tile house in the London suburb of Hendon, a modest-sized Ford saloon car and a free subscription to various newspapers, ranging from the *Financial Times* to the Militant Tendency's weekly. As a committed Socialist he read the latter rather more closely than the former.

However, this breakfast-time on Monday June 10th, it was the distinctive pink newsprint of the financial paper which he turned to first, while Gladys bustled round bringing him bacon and eggs, toast and tea. He had an important meeting today and she didn't like him to want for anything she could provide. In his job he was responsible for the wellbeing of quite a few people. At home she looked after him. That was right and proper and how things should be. She didn't read the papers much, just heard the radio's brief daily output of news about murders, terrorism and disasters and put them out of her mind as soon as the music came on again. The outside world was Len's affair. She would have been horrified if she had known that he was almost as ignorant of it as she was.

The cherished 'perks' of a house and car which Len and Gladys Slater enjoyed were his reward for his lifetime's service as an official of the Amalgamated Union of Clerical and Accounting Staffs, known throughout the Labour movement as AUCAS. His shrewder, more militant and distinctly less honourable colleagues hadn't wanted him in the leadership, because Len would never lead anyone to victory in the class struggle. He was a hard-working non-entity. At the same time he was renowned in the Union for being straight and they didn't want to be seen ditching him before his time. He was already a Trustee of the pension fund. So by way of a compromise they gave him the running of it as a final job. Politically, the solution was ideal – except, perhaps, that he knew nothing about investment management. But then the other Trustees didn't either. Nor, legally, were they required to. It was common in the trade-union movement for pension funds to be controlled by unqualified leaders.

'I suppose Keith will be there?' Gladys asked, refilling his teacup. Keith Norris was the General Secretary, a bit of a rat, she thought, always out for himself. You needed your wits about you with Keith.

'Can't hold the meeting without him,' Len replied, his eyes on the paper, his right leg stuck at an awkward angle beneath the kitchen table. He was an angular man altogether – thin and stiff-legged from a long-ago accident – the very opposite of his plumply rotund wife. 'Thanks, love,' he murmured as she poured the tea, then exclaimed, 'Jesus! Those bloody blacks.'

'Len! You're not supposed to talk about them like that.' She wasn't shocked, merely practical. 'What if you said that in public? There'd be no end of a to-do.'

'Look!' He held the page up and found his finger shaking as he pointed.

TALKS ON $20 BILLION NIGERIAN DEBT POSTPONED
Creditors of the Nigerian military government, currently owed $20 billion, may be forced to accept further rescheduling. An announcement over the weekend that talks with IMF repre-

sentatives have been postponed suggests terms may be made even tougher. Altogether the Finance Ministry is understood to have received some 200,000 requests for repayment.

The story continued across another column, with an explanation that Nigeria had already limited interest payments on its debt to a maximum of thirty per cent of the country's foreign-exchange earnings, which meant many loans would not be fully serviced. However, Gladys made no attempt to follow her husband's finger as he tremblingly pointed to the sentences that mattered.

'What's Nigeria to do with us?' she asked impatiently.

'We lent their government £2 million.'

'What on earth for?'

Unwittingly she had posed a question that was being put to themselves by bankers in many Western cities. Usually the answer was that with its tremendous oil wealth Nigeria had seemed secure. Certainly, very few would have made a loan there for such solidly non-commercial reasons as AUCAS.

'After Keith closed our account with Barclays because they were involved in South Africa he insisted we make a positive contribution to the fight against apartheid.' Len remembered bitterly how Keith had told him to shut up or get out when he objected. 'He wanted to invest in black Africa on principle. Told me to find somewhere suitable.'

'Doesn't sound very suitable to me, dear.'

'Well, love,' Len found himself being defensive, 'we always do keep a lot of our money in what they call "fixed-interest stocks". That way we can be sure of the income.'

Although the AUCAS fund was tiny compared to major industrial or commercial pension funds, because it served only those eligible among 500 employees of the Union – like Slater himself, not the 51,000 Union members – it still had to maintain acceptable ratios of income to capital. So the investments were divided between property, shares in British companies, and fixed-interest government bonds. The property and shares gave capital appreciation, the bonds gave guaranteed income.

'The new bankers we went to said Nigeria was the one country in Africa that couldn't go wrong, and the interest they offered was higher than we could get here. But now the buggers aren't paying.' He got to his feet as decisively as his stiff leg permitted. 'I'd best be going, love. I have to talk to those bloody bankers before we start the meeting.'

The abruptness was deliberate. He wanted to escape any more awkward questions. Gladys wasn't only mistrustful of Keith. She had been scathing at the time about the lunches at the Ritz to which he and the third Trustee had been entertained by the new bankers' London manager, a persuasive young man named Richard Stephens. At the time Len had felt flattered. Now the Union was paying the price.

Normally he walked the short distance from their house to Hendon Central station on the Northern Line, getting exercise with the aid of his favourite stick. This morning Gladys insisted on driving him.

'I doubt that that Stephens man'll be offering you any fancy lunch today,' she observed tartly before saying goodbye, then relented. 'Don't let them do you down, love. Keep your pecker up.'

None the less, Slater spent the train ride into London morosely kicking himself for his folly and stroking the dark wood of the stick as if it were a talisman, which in a way it was. The stick was encircled by a chromium band just below the curved handle. Words in unfamiliar Cyrillic characters engraved on the band expressed fraternal greetings from his Soviet hosts at the Russian Black Sea spa where he had taken a cure five years ago. The treatment had not improved his leg much, but the gift had been meant to symbolize comradely friendship, and it still did. As the train swayed and rumbled into London he wondered if the Russians had any clout with Nigeria these days. Someone must have, for God's sake. Britain hadn't.

He was still mentally chewing at the problem when he reached the AUCAS headquarters, a drably converted pair of houses in the major thoroughfare of Camden Road. He went straight to his first-floor office, its Georgian windows double-glazed against the roar of the traffic, and used the time he had gained to phone Stephens.

In left-wing political terms it had been correct for Keith to insist on shifting to a bank that had no undesirable connections – either with South Africa, Israel, or the United States. But as Slater waited to be put through he pictured the man they relied on now with misgiving: podgy-faced, lips moist like the inside of an oyster, only the eyes sharp and darting. If the eyes were the windows of the soul, then what lay within Richard Stephens might best be left uninvestigated. Keith had not been at those Ritz lunches. There was no need. His militant friends had recommended the Bank of Commercial Credit and no one in AUCAS could gainsay Keith.

'Yes, indeed, Len, I have seen the report.' At his monumental mahogany partner's desk in the City, Richard Stephens doodled as he answered, trying to remember how many military coups had taken place in Nigeria since he arranged the loan. Two was it? Or

46

three? 'The new President is determined to put the national house in order, but the oil-price fall hit them when they were already down.' He consulted the VDU on its special mounting and had to suppress a whistled intake of breath. The shortfall on the interest payments had become appalling. 'Of course, Len,' he tried to sound consoling, 'your two million is at a full percentage point over the London Interbank. We were lucky to get such a high rate.'

'That two million's close to half our assets,' Slater's voice rasped as much from fear as anger. 'We have more pensioners depending on us every year.'

'Believe me, I understand your concern.'

Stephens played with a calculator while he spoke, evaluating the analysis of his client's assets and liabilities which he had called up on the VDU.

Contributions from the AUCAS pension scheme's 423 members yielded £576,000 a year. Not all the employees had worked long enough for the Union to join. But of those 423 many were over fifty and he knew Keith Norris was determined to kick out the old guard of moderate officials and replace them with young activists. He'd do it too. As employers the unions were liable to ride roughshod over their staff. So the twin factors of early retirement and a membership that was ageing anyway would sharply increase the Fund's dependence on its investments. The figures shone on the calculator's liquid-crystal display. Jesus, no wonder the old fool was uptight! Overall, AUCAS was earning less than five per cent on its £5.2 million of investments, which meant that the £2 million in Nigeria loaned at one per cent over LIBOR – the current London Interbank Offered Rate – of $9\frac{7}{8}$ per cent accounted for £223,000 out of the total £260,000 on investment income. Jesus wept! Slater was in deep trouble. If the Nigerians defaulted he'd either have to raise members' contributions hugely, make savage cuts in benefits to the retired, or wind up the Fund.

'Is there no way of obtaining repayment? The other Trustees will demand to know. We must get that money back.'

Stephens pursed his lips, suppressing the desire to say, 'Len, you must be joking.' Dear old Len was for the chop. As Fund Manager he might not need to be qualified, but he did have some obligation to act prudently. When the crunch came there was a chance of rescuing a normal commercial pension fund, as when the UK Provident Institution was refinanced after it lost a bomb in unlisted gas and oil securities. But who'd want to rescue a fund headed by a militant Trot like Keith Norris? Colonel Gadhafi, perhaps. No one else.

'Well, Len,' he suggested the only way out he knew, 'it is sometimes possible to trade foreign debt on the New York market. One brokerage firm specializes in helping banks reduce or realign their exposure. Sometimes they swap debts – exchanging debt in South America for debt in Poland, for instance – sometimes they sell it for cash. At a discount, of course.'

The discounts were huge. Tactfully, he omitted that fact.

'Find out for us then.'

'It's still the middle of the night in New York. I'll telephone as soon as they open for business.'

'Please do so. Urgently.'

After Slater had rung off, Stephens made further calculations. The idea of extracting more commission from this particular deal amused him. It had already been very profitable for its size. Not only had the Bank of Commercial Credit taken a conventional one-quarter of one per cent plus expenses for arranging the loan, but the Nigerian Finance Minister of the time had also been personally generous: only £1,800,000 had gone anywhere near Africa. The Minister's cut had been £200,000, transferred direct to Switzerland. Obligingly, he had allowed Stephens personally a quarter of that, firstly for obtaining the loan and secondly for turning a blind eye to where it had been sent. Quite a joke really, given the Union's explicit orders to lend to Africa. And now he could take a further profit by getting AUCAS out of the hole Keith Norris' doctrinaire policies had dug for it. If, that was, anyone in New York was fool enough to buy the debt.

While Stephens occupied himself with the more instantly profitable matter of acting for yet another Arab wishing to buy a stake in the Harrods department store, the meeting at AUCAS was reaching a stormy conclusion in a committee room hung with photographs of former Union leaders.

'When all's said and done,' Keith Norris was half shouting, 'you're the Fund Manager, Len. It's your bloody job to get the two million back. You lent it out.'

'On your orders, Keith, on your orders.' Len Slater, sickened with worry, knew he was bleating like a goat before its throat was cut. ' "Governments can't go bust," you said.'

'But we can't sue them, can we? We can't sequestrate their assets, like the bloody Tories can ours. You should have known that, Len. You're the responsible official of the Union.'

'Keith's right, brother Len,' the third Trustee added. 'If we're going to invest in the capitalist system, and we haven't much alternative, it's your job to do it right.'

'The bank might find someone to take over the loan – there's what they call "a secondary market" in international debt.'

'For the full amount?' Norris could be bitterly sarcastic when he wished. 'Just because they like your pretty face? Come off it!' He became serious again. 'Maybe you should go out to Africa yourself. Tell them our pensioners need the money. Remind them we took our investments out of South Africa.'

'I could try.'

Len's doubt about tackling a government run by tinpot generals must have shown in his expression, because Norris' concluding remark was typically menacing and snide. It hadn't been through merit that Keith Norris had reached the pinnacle job of General Secretary for life of AUCAS. It had been through intrigue and in-fighting.

'You'd better try, Len, because we can't have a free house and a free car wasted on a comrade who doesn't try, can we? Our members wouldn't approve of that, would they? Not if we can't pay their pensions any more.'

Len Slater was no match for such threats. When the meeting was over, he rang Stephens and sought further advice. He would go home in the evening a deeply worried man.

Buenos Aires. Morning

For a few hours on the Sunday evening His Excellency Señor José Lopez-Santini had considered the kidnap of his children might provide a defensible reason for not returning to the Columbus Cay conference. His wife was pleading with him to stay; he had to raise at least some of the ransom; he had to obtain the Argentine President's agreement to delaying the IMF talks.

Then on Monday the second message came.

Ana, the girlfriend of the murdered chauffeur, telephoned from a call-box before breakfast. She had opened the door of her family's tenement apartment to let the cat out and found an envelope addressed to His Excellency. What should she do?

Lopez-Santini told her to hurry round. Fortunately, she lived relatively close. He instinctively shied away from fetching her in case it was a trap baited for himself. Then he rang the airport and postponed his departure for the second time. The President had authorized a government jet. The crew could wait.

When Ana arrived, she stood wringing her hands fearfully in the hall, as though personally responsible, while Lopez-Santini felt the letter cautiously. He decided it was too flimsy to conceal explosives and was right. With Mercedes looking over his shoulder, still in a flimsy lace dressing-gown, he drew out a single sheet of cheap notepaper, ruled with feint lines.

'So you returned from a conference. If it helps the peoples' cause, you must go back. We will make allowances for co-operative behaviour. The girls miss you. We told them you are too busy to phone.'

'Too busy . . . the devils,' Mercedes swayed, then controlled herself in front of their lower-class visitor.

Ana began to cry, providentially giving Mercedes something to do. She took her through to the kitchen, leaving her husband gazing at the strange message. He turned it over and saw what amounted to a postscript.

'Show this to your friend the Comisario if you want. He doesn't worry us.'

The implications were discomfortingly clear. He was glad the kidnappers knew about the conference, yet how could they unless a police officer had leaked it to them? The police always had been notoriously prone to collaboration with criminals. Not that these were ordinary crooks. Everything about their style identified them as being from the educated middle class, confident of their intellectual superiority. Yet why had they chosen Ana as an unwilling courier? The corollary must be that they had studied poor Ruiz's habits and routine carefully.

For an entire agonizing hour after Ana had left, the Minister debated with his wife as to whether they should inform the Comisario or not. Suppose Ana was then murdered? In the end they concluded they had no alternative. They would take him the letter, and Lopez-Santini would depart for the Bahamas immediately afterwards.

'I must be seen to do what the kidnappers want, my love,' he argued, 'and I believe they have as much interest in keeping this secret as we have.'

New York. Midday

To James Warburton, the Carlyle Hotel on East 76th Street and Madison Avenue was a civilized and sophisticated home from home in New York. Some of the richest men in the world stayed there and the staff were discreetly adept at screening their guests from the attentions of the media, or any other unwelcome visitors.

If the Carlyle was half an hour from Wall Street in a cab, well, that was a minor inconvenience he could cheerfully put up with. On Sunday he had checked in for only two nights. But the reception clerks were unsurprised when he rang down from First National's offices at midday this Monday morning and enquired, with self-deprecating British politeness, about the possibility of extending his reservation.

'Sure, Mr Warburton. That will be no problem. How long do you plan to be with us? A month maybe? Our pleasure, sir.'

He turned to Sheldon Harrison, with whom he had been working all morning in an office thoughtfully provided by the First National Bank.

'I fear we have to assume the worse. The Brazilians are neither releasing foreign exchange nor talking. My old friend Lopez-Santini is still having his calls intercepted, the Mexican and Venezuelan Finance Ministers are "out of town". The whole situation stinks, and before we know where we are the market will sense the same. Can our friend Roth release you?'

'He won't like it. But he can.'

'Then that is today's good news,' Warburton smiled. 'We had better arrange a meeting of the full creditors' committee as soon as possible. Germans, Japanese, Swiss. Everyone. Make it the day after tomorrow, if they'll agree.' He smiled again. 'And if they don't, make it Wednesday just the same.'

A scant quarter mile away, the president of a loan-brokerage firm named Aurelius Incorporated was speaking across the Atlantic to Richard Stephens in London. Not speaking too politely, either, since like many people whose activity bordered the public domain he hated having his own words quoted back at him.

'Maybe I said that. Bankers don't always have to live with their mistakes. Most particularly the big money-center banks don't have to. With respect, Mr Stephens, your Bank of Commercial Credit is not in that league. Your activity isn't so widespread. You're going to find it harder to adjust your portfolio.'

'We *are* offering you business, Mr Aurelius.' The waspishness was latent in Stephens' words, though he kept it subdued. 'As we understand it, you handle over $500 million of debt sales a year. Is $3 million a problem?'

'It's not the amount, it's the place. South America we can handle. We could find some corporation wants to start a $10 million project in Argentina tomorrow. They buy some American bank's ten million of Argentine debt for eight and trade it to the

51

Central Bank for the full amount in local currency. Everyone's happy. The big bank gets shot of a poorly performing debt, the corporation saves two million, the Argentine loses a foreign-exchange repayment problem, we take a commission. But where is Nigeria for Chrissake?'

'It's the largest country in Africa. It has oil. I'd appreciate a quote for around $3 million of eight-year Nigerian government bonds at one point over LIBOR.'

'If you insist, Mr Stephens, but it won't make your day. Last week we could get only ten cents in the dollar on Nicaraguan debt. And Nicaragua's in our own backyard.'

And they probably wish it wasn't, Stephens thought vengefully as he replaced the phone, given the fighting there.

An hour and a half later, Aurelius Inc. was back on the line.

'Like I warned you, Mr Stephens, the markets are uneasy this morning. Everyone's jumpy. We can get you twenty-seven cents in the dollar.'

If it had not been for the earlier Nicaraguan example, Stephens would have thought he had misheard. Twenty-seven per cent was an insult. There was no way the Trustees of AUCAS would accept losing seventy-three per cent of their investment.

'I don't think my clients would agree to such a low figure,' he said. 'What's going on at your end?'

Aurelius' attitude became more friendly. He enjoyed unloading bad news on foreigners.

'Mainly rumour, I guess. Brazil's temporarily suspended foreign-exchange payments. Doesn't take much to cause a panic these days.'

After this second conversation, Stephens devoted a few minutes to considering his position. He would have to give some kind of an answer to Len Slater. Furthermore, there was the future: the more often AUCAS could be persuaded to shift its investments, the more commission his bank would make. Eventually he decided to put the proposition the other way around and manoeuvre the Union into dictating the unacceptable conditions.

'Mr Slater,' he announced in the reverentially unctuous tone of someone who has just located the Holy Grail, 'our New York correspondents believe it may be possible to find a buyer for your Nigerian loan. The question is: how much discount can you permit us to give?'

'Discount?' Slater was still so traumatized by the morning's meeting that he momentarily failed to understand. 'Discount?' he repeated, with the puzzlement one of his own pensioners might have displayed at not being able to withdraw the full amount of his savings from the Post Office. 'Oh yes. I suppose there has to be some kind of incentive. Can we say ten per cent? The other Trustees would probably accept that.'

'Excellent, sir.' Stephens tried to project the feel of a beaming smile down the line. 'I will instruct them to start work on it straightaway. Of course it may take a few days.'

Trading, he joked to himself, was the art of the possible. The possible was unlikely to include selling on a Nigerian loan except at a catastrophic loss. Tomorrow he would tell that old fool Slater that he had been unsuccessful. At least he would then have shown willing, even if it had earned him no immediate commission.

Paris. Evening

The candle-lit restaurant was on a boat moored to the Seine embankment near the rearing landmark structure of the Eiffel Tower. Every few minutes a huge *bâteau mouche* laden with tourists would pass by, its floodlights illuminating the buildings on each side of the river. Then the floating restaurant rocked gently and the garish light flickered over the diners' faces. It didn't faze either Stuart or Maggie. In every other respect this warm June evening was a dream.

'You deserve the nicest place I know,' he touched her fingertips across the linen cloth, earning a secretive smile. 'I'm sorry about the weekend. I can promise no repeat performances are planned.'

'But you're not giving up the story.' She sat up straight, clowning outrage. 'Let me tell you, Mr Pendler, after putting me through the hoop like that you are *not* abandoning the story.'

He shook his head. 'Calm down. I've spent all afternoon . . .'

'*Excusez-moi, m'sieur, 'dame. Vous avez choisi?*' The head waiter had materialized by their table, order-pad in hand. He was elegant in a white dinner-jacket, positively capitalizing on his advancing age with a neat white beard and an air of unchallengeable experience.

Maggie looked up, aware that she had not yet consulted the distinguished menu, saw the man's face and almost seemed to choke.

'Is your name McLellan?' she demanded, in English.

'Pardon, madame?' He stepped back, mystified, quickly smoothing the movement into an inclination of the head. 'When you are ready, m'sieur, 'dame, when you are ready.'

'What gives?' Stuart was equally taken aback.

'If he isn't the Columbus Cay manager's brother, then he's his double. Don't you see the likeness?'

Pendler glanced after the retreating waiter. 'Sure, he has a beard. Hey, now you are stretching probabilities!'

She dropped the subject until they had ordered and been served the entrée, then reactivated it.

'What did your travel-agent acquaintance say about the Club?'

'Had a European manager and French cuisine. So do a thousand restaurants in the States.'

'Are you being deliberately dim? McLellan was either Scots or Irish. He worked in Europe. People in the hotel trade here must know him.'

'So?'

'They could ask questions about him that we can't. Maybe your travel agent could. They could find out when the meeting ends and who was there.'

'He'd smell a rat at once.'

'No, he would not.' She grinned happily. 'Not with the scenario I've just thought of.'

Ten minutes later, Stuart Pendler was beckoning the McLellan look-alike who had triggered Maggie's imagination to order champagne.

Columbus Cay, Great Abaco

Despite having a helicopter waiting at Nassau to whirl him direct to the out islands, Lopez-Santini only reached Columbus Cay as the closing session was about to begin. McLellan was standing waiting by the palm trees, white hair blowing in the rotor's downwash, together with the Minister's aide, Felipe. The aide's expression was enough to warn Lopez-Santini of trouble as he clambered ungracefully out of the aircraft, McLellan assisting him.

'Excellency,' Felipe had to shout to be heard above the engine's roar as the chopper clattered away again, silhouetted against the evening sky like a giant dragonfly, 'we must have ten minutes in private.'

'The assembly is waiting for you, sir,' McLellan said, none too happily. The way he had been ordered to give the message stank of intrigue, and he disliked being given orders on his own territory.

'Thank you.' Lopez-Santini sensed the manager's unease. 'Tell them I shall be there in ten minutes. Come, Felipe.' He led the way to their villa. 'What's the trouble now?'

Those ten minutes, extending inescapably to twenty, were among the worst of the Minister's life: something he would have thought impossible after the kidnapping.

'They have voted for abrogation of all loan agreements,' Felipe told him once they were alone. 'The mood is vindictive. Many would welcome the collapse of the Western banking system. They don't want to negotiate. They would like to start withholding payments immediately.'

'Can they be so stupid?' His reaction was instinctive. OPEC had faltered. This cartel would also fail if it gave unqualified ultimatums. There had to be some give and take, some margin for negotiation. Then he remembered the kidnap terms and actually groaned out loud. Was it coincidence that the kidnappers had also given him a week?

'There is worse, Excellency.'

'Go on.' Lopez-Santini had now begun gearing himself for a struggle of wills. Although inclined to laziness if events did not demand much effort, when a crisis arose he could display great intellectual resilience. Physically he might not be strong, mentally he was. 'What exactly is worse?' he asked.

'Señor Rodrigo Suarez has been named as your co-negotiator, if what they propose can be called a negotiation.'

'Holy Mother, but that *is* unacceptable!' For a few moments the Minister sat completely still, recovering his composure. Then he began pacing the room, as if the activity would help him ponder the implications.

Rodrigo Suarez, thirty-six years old, a millionaire, insolent, boastful of his prowess with women, was notorious for his connections with the drug mafiosi of Bolivia – indeed, effectively he was one of them. He had come to public prominence after the so-called 'Cocaine Coup' in 1980, when General Luis Garcia Meza seized power and released the majority of drug-traffickers from jail. Meza was long gone – the tenure of Bolivian presidents averaged less than a year – but Suarez had proved indispensable. Most government is based on compromise of some kind. The compromise in Bolivia revolved around the technically illicit export of cocaine, earning in excess of $2 billion a year in foreign exchange. If those earnings could have been legitimized they would have solved the nation's foreign-debt problem overnight. An unofficial arrangement between the administration and the drug mafiosi was a running necessity and Suarez was the intermediary, which was why he held the otherwise empty title of Deputy Finance Minister.

'It was Señor Suarez who suggested a one-week deadline for the ultimatum,' Felipe offered.

'That does not surprise me.' Suarez would naturally insist on hitting the American banks a knock-out blow if he could, because American government aid was normally linked to agreements on prosecuting drug-traffickers. However half-heartedly those prosecutions might be pursued, they did inhibit the drug trade. A break with the banks might also end the aid and the mafiosi's power would be hugely enhanced.

'The only alternative, Excellency,' Felipe correctly read his master's mind, 'is to stand down.'

'Impossible.' Such a decision would leak back to Buenos Aires within hours, especially with Suarez involved. Again the co-incidence of the week's deadline given by the kidnappers being identical to that proposed by Suarez to the conference hit him. But the word 'alternative' sparked thought. If they could offer the Western banks some kind of option ... 'I have not yet addressed the meeting,' he said abruptly. 'Let us go across.'

When he entered the hall Lopez-Santini was greeted by pro-longed applause. Seizing advantage of the welcome, he strode straight to the podium, held his hands high for silence and launched impromptu into the most important speech of his entire career.

'Excellencies, comrades in adversity,' he began histrionically, you have done me an inexpressible honour ... By skilled dip-lomacy we can achieve total abrogation of our foreign debt ...' Gradually he weaned them to his theme. 'Unqualified ultimatums too often fail. Intransigence is its own worst enemy. Yes, we must threaten the public announcement of default which would destroy the confidence of the capitalist countries in their banks. Yes, we must give a deadline.' Here he gave the briefest possible nod of acknowledgement to Rodrigo Suarez, sitting with his elbows self-confidently resting on the desk in front of him, a thin smile on his moustachioed face. 'However, Excellencies, I suggest we must allow the Western banking system some form of option.' He paused to judge how the theatricality he so despised was being received, and was accorded a distinct hum of approval. 'The option I propose will cost us almost nothing in the long term. What it will do is enable the Western banks to save face. Not save the capital of their loans, Excellencies. That they will have lost. But retain a face-saving fraction of the interest due. May I explain the technicalities?' A less enthusiastic murmur greeted this. 'They are as follows ...'

Five minutes later he reckoned he was still holding his audience, but only just. The more aggressive of those present, Suarez leading, shouted demands for total humiliation of the system that had so humiliated their nations in the past.

'Excellencies, you have invited me to negotiate. To negotiate I must have some discretion.'

'Agreed.' Alvarez, the Mexican, who had remained on the podium throughout, stood up authoritatively. 'Is anyone opposed?'

Only three hands were raised, the Nigerian's and Suarez's being two of them. Lopez-Santini breathed a silent sigh of relief. Some degree of sanity had prevailed. The threat of catastrophe was stark enough without a refusal to talk.

'I say there should be no option for the banks,' Suarez's coarse voice cut into the momentary silence following the vote. 'Except a financial crash.'

'Then take that message to New York yourself.'

Throwing down such a personal challenge was dangerous in the extreme, given Suarez's vengeful nature. But it had to be now or never, and in front of the others, if Lopez-Santini was to exercise any control over events. He was gambling on Suarez not daring to take up the challenge for reasons of which the Latin Americans were well aware, though the Indonesian, Nigerian and Pole looked mystified. If the Bolivian once set foot on United States soil he faced certain arrest by the Drug Enforcement Agency.

Suarez flushed, scowled, and stayed silent.

'In that case, Excellencies,' Lopez-Santini spoke with a smooth self-confidence he did not feel, 'I shall draft a message for despatch tomorrow to the leading creditor banks of the United States, Britain, Germany, Japan, Sweden and Switzerland. It will give them one week in which to come to terms. I suggest we reassemble here seven days from today and that to preserve confidentiality, we refer to my proposal as the Columbus Option.'

CHAPTER FOUR

New York. Tuesday June 11th

The telex message was alarmingly brief, Warburton considered. He and Harrison were handed copies within moments of being welcomed into William Osborn's office on the fourteenth floor of First National Bank's headquarters on Water Street, down near Wall Street in the financial area of Manhattan, and a short walk from the austere building of the New York Federal Reserve. Although it was only nine thirty-five in the morning, Warburton already knew that no Brazilian payments of any kind had been received overnight, and as he had ascended in the elevator he had wondered if Ray Roth or one of his executive officers would be calling on the Fed for emergency money today. But the telex drove Roth's problems straight out of his thoughts:

> DEMAND IMMEDIATE CONSULTATIONS.
> LOPEZ-SANTINI.

The formality of the date and time, 10.03 on June 11th, only emphasized the abruptness of the text.

'More significant for what it doesn't say than what it does,' he observed, while Sheldon Harrison listened, intrigued because it had not told him much at all. 'For a start it can only refer to rescheduling.'

'Agreed,' Osborn occupied himself with the ritual of lighting his first cigar of the day, cutting off the tip and roasting the end gently, though his gaze never really left his colleagues. Part of Osborn's success as a negotiator lay in always 'letting the other guy put his ten cents' worth in', a quality he shared with Warburton. Both men listened a lot, and when they did speak they spoke politely. It was this natural affinity of approach which had prompted Osborn to call on Warburton again, even though the Briton was ten years his senior and officially retired.

'It can only refer to the debt business, but our friend Lopez-Santini doesn't want the world to know that.'

'Also agreed.' Osborn pressed his desk-buzzer and spoke into an intercom. 'Sally, just check there are no other copies of that telex around the building, please.' He drew on the cigar. 'Speaking for ourselves, we have a $20 million loan to the Argentine falling due for repayment in a month and we were pretty much expecting Lopez-Santini would come to an agreement with the IMF next week. Then we'd have been prepared to reschedule. The telex could simply refer to that.'

'Those words "demand" and "immediate" are out of character, Bill. Lopez-Santini may get emotional occasionally, but ultimatums are not his style.'

'You think we should speak with him?'

'I've been trying his home all weekend.'

'Let's call his Ministry.' Osborn pressed the buzzer again and asked his secretary to obtain the number. Then he killed time by addressing Harrison. 'It'll be a pleasure to have you on board, Sheldon. Not that this may be anything except a rough ride. We could probably live with the threat of an Argentine default – if that's what this telex is in fact about – US banks are only exposed there to the extent of around $9 billion. Brazil or Mexico would be far worse. If the whole of Latin America went bad . . . well, I prefer not to think about that too often. Quite apart from making a load of banks insolvent, the US economy as a whole would lose over a million jobs within a year. We've had a number of simulations done and . . .'

The Buenos Aires call coming through interrupted him. He spoke fluently in Spanish, waited, spoke again, waited again, finally abandoned the attempt.

'His Excellency the Minister is already on his way,' he repeated for Warburton's benefit. 'His plane will be landing at Teterboro in three and a half hours. The Argentine Consul will be meeting him.'

'But,' Harrison checked himself, though the corollary of this news had been immediately apparent.

'Go ahead.'

'Surely, sir, that's impossible. Even allowing a two-hour time difference, he would have to have left before the telex was sent. Several hours before.'

'Or else he is not coming from the Argentine at all,' Warburton suggested. 'He's been somewhere a great deal closer, rallying support.'

'That,' Osborn said, blowing out smoke reflectively, 'is a point which bears thinking about. Maybe we should alert the Fed.'

*

Contrary to many people's belief, the largest known accumulation of gold in the world is not locked away at Fort Knox. Nor is it in South Africa, though mining engineers on the Rand might argue on behalf of their underground mineral reserves. The largest known stock of gold in the shape of bars that can be physically counted lies – or did lie at the moment Bill Osborn 'alerted' the Fed – in the vaults of the Federal Reserve Bank of New York. That stock constituted one quarter of the world's accountable gold reserves: $14 billions' worth. The bars themselves lay stacked eighty feet down beneath the Fed's stone-faced skyscraper, lying 'on the bedrock of Manhattan', as officials liked to remark. By a coincidence, each foot below street-level represented a foreign nation, foreign bank or international organization which had assets stored there, usually US government securities. The vaults held $115 billions' worth of these, in addition to the gold.

The bank officer to whom Osborn spoke, one of a large staff working atop this latter-day Aladdin's cave, was a senior vice-president of the Fed named Edward D. Channon. He was forty-six years old, clean-featured, happily married. As befitted his status, he dressed conservatively. He had recently been elected commodore of a small yacht club in Westchester, where he lived. Occasionally his picture appeared in financial magazines and what you saw in the photo was the regulation trustworthy pillar of the Wall Street financial fraternity – in so far, that was, as anyone trusted Wall Street. Although plenty of people hated the Fed, they usually found it hard to hate Ed Channon, which was just as well when he had to enforce unpleasant decisions.

'People at parties sometimes ask what I do,' he was fond of saying, with an impishness which did not fit the regular appearance. 'I tell them I help exercise the Fed's statutory primary supervisory responsibility toward State Chartered banks that are members of the Federal Reserve System. After that they usually change the subject.'

Within the maze of relationships between the twelve Federal Reserve Banks and their controlling Washington Board which collectively made up the Federal Reserve System – the central bank of the United States – the New York Fed served New York State, New Jersey and Fairfield County, Connecticut, domestically. It was also the international arm of the System, providing banking services for some 150 foreign central banks and for the IMF. Hence all that gold and securities in the vaults.

With the dollar the world's pre-eminent reserve currency, in the way sterling used to be, the Fed's overall mission of maintaining a safe and flexible monetary system for the United States had inescapable global repercussions. If the dollar fell, so for example did the revenues of other oil-producing states around the world, because oil was priced in dollars.

Therefore although Channon himself did not work on foreign-exchange questions, he was instantly aware that Bill Osborn's guarded reference to a problem in that area had implications both for his colleagues and for the well-being of the New York money-centre banks which were so heavily exposed abroad.

'Could you come over?' he asked. 'There are times when I don't trust the confidentiality of Mr Bell's invention.'

So Osborn left Water Street and hurried across the Chase Plaza to the Fed's building on the corner of Liberty and Nassau Streets.

'I'd heard Brazilian interest payments have been delayed,' Channon remarked as soon as Osborn had sat down. 'You think the Argentine's following suit?'

'It's a pretty peremptory telex.' Osborn handed a copy across.

Channon read it, remembering with chilling clarity the December day of 1982 when Brazil had followed Mexico into effective default, unable to repay the $5 billion-a-night borrowings on the New York market which had been keeping the Banco do Brasil afloat. The Treasury and the Fed had been forced to borrow hurriedly around the world – extremely hurriedly – in order to keep the financial system out of crisis until long-term re-negotiation of those nations' mammoth debts could be arranged. The arrangement had been politely called 'rescheduling', meaning the duration of the loans was to be extended, often by many years. If they hadn't been, many of the most prestigious New York banks would have become legally insolvent in a major financial crisis both for them and for the dollar. That was when Channon and Osborn had first met, and now the Banco do Brasil was suspending payments again.

'I'll warn my colleagues on the foreign-exchange side,' Channon said. 'I assume you're calling your committee together again?'

'Tomorrow. Hopefully this will only concern loans to Brazil and the Argentine.'

Channon knew that was tougher than it sounded. At least 1,500 American banks had become involved in loans to Latin American countries. So had major British, German, Swiss, Swedish and Japanese banks. At this point all this commercial debt was Osborn's problem, however. His committee would be representing the Western banks in direct dealings with the debtor governments. The Federal Reserve would only become involved if American banks faced actual collapse. By Congressional order, the Fed was 'the lender of last resort'. When a bank couldn't get backing anywhere else, it turned to the Fed. But this was nowhere approaching a last-resort situation.

'Provided we're prepared,' Osborn observed, mirroring Channon's own thinking, 'there need be no crisis. We'll keep the whole thing under wraps until whatever the Argentine wants is fixed up.'

'I'll inform Washington, though.' Channon extended his hand in farewell. 'And we'll be in touch with the Bank of England and the others as routine. Keep me posted, Bill. We must have lunch sometime.'

The suggestion was deliberately indefinite. Even though he knew they were all sitting on a powder-keg of debt, he reckoned this time round they could keep the fuse well damped. There wasn't going to be another 1982, let alone a 1929.

Southampton, Long Island

For Ray Roth, ensconced with the Bartrum Bank's Treasurer, Dale Schuster, at his unnecessarily plush offices in Southampton, this was a week when, despite glorious summer weather, Black Monday had been succeeded by Black Tuesday, with every prospect of Black Wednesday being next in line.

In fact Roth was learning very quickly and very painfully what any lending officer dealing with foreigners would have learnt in his twenties working for an international bank. But Roth had never been a junior bank officer, with Bartrum or anyone else. He had quit running a real-estate business to come in at board level when he inherited a shareholding.

'What precisely did Plaza say this morning, Dale?' he asked, for the second time, one eyelid twitching briefly.

'There's a "delay" in the Brazilian interest coming through,' Schuster repeated, a trace of impatience showing. 'They're "working on it". Same as they said Friday and yesterday.'

Plaza Central was the New York money-centre bank which had lured them into this Brazilian loan late in 1981. The bait had been an interest rate two points higher than could be obtained locally in Long Island, where demand for money had been slack due to the recession. Plaza Central was a rival to Chase Manhattan, Citicorp, First National and the other giants. Roth had been impressed by its famous name and international connections. So had Schuster. They had trusted its judgement. Roth still remembered the moment of decision.

'Listen, Ray,' Schuster had said with his characteristic free-wheeling enthusiasm, 'why do we futz around lending in penny packets to stores and dealers, taking up references, monitoring credit-worthiness, getting all the hassle and overheads, when we can make a single, safe, twenty-million loan at a rate that should make the stockholders' eyes pop. Twelve and three-eighths per cent! Jeez! And like the guy at Plaza says, "governments don't go bust".'

In fact, Schuster's training had been with Savings and Loan institutions, where his racy self-confidence appealed to depositors. It went down well with the minor businessmen of Long Island too. But he had none of the personal contacts in South America which a major bank would have considered essential for a treasurer instituting business there. He and Roth had left all that to Plaza, which later bear-led them into Argentine and Mexican loan syndicates as well. 'Mexico's an oil-producer. Petro-currencies can't go wrong.' Those were the Plaza vice-president's words, and Schuster had sagely agreed.

Besides, Roth found the ease of the transactions breathtaking. Bartrum just made the transfer and there the bank was, featured along with fifty-one others in the 'tombstone' advertisement in the *Wall Street Journal* which announced the $100 million loan 'For purposes of record only'. Translated, this phrase meant it was too late for anyone else to get in on the act. The ad was a roll-call of the victors. Roth had a copy framed to hang on his office wall and paid Plaza's up-front fees with happiness.

He felt less happy about the loan today.

'Dale,' he asked, squaring up to the worst immediate problem. 'We already credited our accounts with the interest, didn't we?'

'Sure.' Schuster tried to brush the worry aside, his mind obstinately mesmerized with memories of small-borrowers' collateral, of houses, Treasury bonds, factory plant and stock which could all be sold if the worst happened. 'Up to three months overdue it's normal practice to treat the interest as paid. All the big boys do that. They know it's on the way.'

'The debt should be classified as a non-performing asset after three months, though. What if some wise guy from the State Banking Authority starts asking if Brazil *has* paid?'

Thus Ray Roth raised the spectre that was haunting far larger outfits than Bartrum. Bankers would never dream of crediting a private individual's account with money that had not been received. Yet they did exactly that for themselves with interest due from governments, and they did it routinely.

'I never have liked this game of treating interest as if it has

63

been received when we know it hasn't,' Roth complained. Psychologically what he needed was for someone to tell him this was okay, even though it made no sense.

'I tell you, there's no cause for worrying.' Dale slid naturally into the role of country-style counsellor. His friends used to joke that he could have sold a savings account to a fruit-machine. 'Everyone from the Chairman of the Federal Reserve downward wants to avoid these loans being non-performing. They're only non-performing if the interest don't get paid within three months of the date.'

'I know that, for Christ's sake.'

'Right. So the big boys like Citicorp and Chase give more loans so our friends south of the border can pay the interest on the old ones. They don't call it capitalizing that interest. No sir! If they did they couldn't write it in the profit column. But it's gotten to be all book-keeping, Ray. It doesn't put any cash in the vaults.'

Schuster had no qualms about explaining in homespun terms which would have insulted a professional. For one thing it was his style, and for another he knew his president only followed financial news of direct relevance to Long Island. Ray was the original small-town businessman, with both the wiles and the innocence of the breed. If a stranger asked him what a bank did, he'd give a cagey kind of smile.

'A bank makes float,' he would answer, enjoying the obscurity of the phrase.

If the stranger wasn't going to burst a blood-vessel on discovering that banks had been legitimately chiselling their customers ever since cheques were invented, he would go further and explain what 'float' was.

'Float' was the time between when the cheques which customers had paid in were credited to the bank by the federal clearance system and when those same amounts were credited by the bank itself to the customer. Legally, banks did not have to credit an out-of-State cheque for ten days. The average period they held on to customers' funds was five working days. It might not sound much, but specialists like the banker author Martin Mayer reckoned it gave American banks the free use of around $60 billion a day. In Europe 'float' could be even longer. Funds telexed from Lloyds Bank in Geneva to Lloyds Bank in central London averaged fourteen days in transit, so for two full weeks Lloyds would be lending out those funds on the markets at a good percentage.

Ray Roth fully appreciated these advantages of the system, and why large companies would pay their bills, or even their employees, with out-of-State cheques, if they could get away with it, in order to delay being debited. Every prudent housewife paying for her marketing with a cheque exploited a personal float at the store's expense.

What had never occurred to him before was that the big-time international bankers could have gotten themselves into a situation where the balance of advantage was against them, where the loan books showed profits and the vaults were bare.

'Jesus,' he exclaimed, thoroughly alarmed by what Dale had told him. 'We not only can't participate in another Brazilian re-structuring if those bastards at Plaza ask us, we've got to have that interest.'

'We can get by for a while without the cash. We're not strapped.'

'Sure. But if the goddam Brazilian loan goes non-performing and we have to declare a twenty-million bad debt, we're going to be in all kinds of trouble. What happens when stockholders wake up and read in the paper that their capital's gone?'

'Well,' Dale's mind ranged over the standard practices for evading reality, 'I guess we can massage the date the loan became operative by a couple of weeks. Make it like the interest isn't due yet.'

'The giants can do that, maybe,' Roth said doubtfully. 'You reckon the State authority will play ball with us?'

'Sure. They won't make waves even if the examiners do come around. Who wants insolvencies after Continental Illinois? Not that we would be insolvent,' he added hastily, realizing he had accidentally expressed Roth's worst fear. 'Let's be sensible, Ray. We've done everything the law demands. We've declared the per-centage of our loans that are foreign. The stockholders can find that out anytime.'

'If they know,' Roth observed moodily. 'I'm getting worried someone could tell them.'

'Don't be so goddam depressed. Who can blame you? All we did was make the same loans everyone was making a few years back. We've obeyed all the rules.' Dale began rattling off the practices they had observed correctly, as if drawing curtains round a corpse, then added, 'Might be wise to begin putting aside special reserves against the Brazilian loan going bad, though. That way we keep sweet with the International Lending Supervision Act . . .'

The buzzer on Roth's desk interrupted them, just as he was about to ask what else the Act required.

'Mr Gianni to see you, sir.'

'Gianni? Am I expecting him?' Roth was thrown off balance in a way he would not normally have been. Gianni was one of those clients he had boasted about at lunch on Sunday. 'Long Island's a high-tech area, Mr Warburton. Those guys bank with us.' A long moment passed. 'Oh, you mean Paul Gianni of ACE Techtronics?'

'Yes, sir. He would be grateful for a few minutes with you.'

By the time Gianni entered – a small, black-haired man in his late thirties, wearing thick-rimmed glasses – Roth had recovered his usual Christian-name affability.

'Good to see you, Paul,' he shook hands warmly. 'You're welcome anytime. Meet our Treasurer, Dale Schuster. Dale, this is Paul Gianni, the chief executive of the fastest growing electronics company this side of Silicon Valley. Dale and I were just through.'

Taking his cue, Schuster began moving towards the door when the visitor stopped him.

'As Treasurer I guess you should hear about this.'

The harshness in Gianni's voice caused Roth to react instantly. With local businessmen he was on familiar territory, not like goddam Brazil.

'Take a chair, Paul. Sit down.' He indicated the cream-leather chairs around the small conference table, 'What's your problem?'

'You remember we've been supplying the Brazilian airplane industry?' Gianni settled himself at the table, leaning forward earnestly on the polished yew surface, though not missing the way Roth stiffened at the word 'Brazilian'. 'On your advice we consigned goods against a bill of exchange.'

'Yes,' Schuster said cautiously, thinking ahead of the obvious bad news.

'The bill covered the first part of a $1.7 million order for transceivers and radars. It was due for payment after ninety days. We shipped ninety-five days ago. Your people downstairs say nothing's come through.'

'We'll speak to the officer concerned right away.' Roth lifted his phone and gave rapid orders. 'Be responsive' was his number-one rule with customers he valued, 'Be seen to act'.

Meanwhile Schuster jotted down details. 'This bank bill was for $700,000? Drawn on the Banco do Brasil? Our correspondents in New York sent it for collection?'

'Whad'ya mean, "correspondents"?'

'Conducting foreign business isn't within our charter, Mr Gianni. We have to do that through a correspondent bank.'

'You guys told me this bill of exchange was no different to a post-dated check. Since when have a bank's checks bounced?' Gianni's Italian ancestry was rapidly surfacing in aggression.

At this point the officer who had done the paperwork came in, handing over a file to Schuster. Bartrum's systems were computerized, but not for international dealings. A bill of exchange was a formal document and they had kept a copy. Schuster scrutinized it, while the young man waited.

'This was due Thursday June 6th?' he queried. 'What's gone wrong?'

'I've spoken several times to New York, sir. They confirm the bill was presented in Rio for collection Thursday and accepted. The funds just haven't been telexed through yet.'

'Listen here,' Gianni cut in angrily. 'We have more than 400 men and women working in our plant. They have families and kids. We have to pay them, we have mortgage payments, we have to buy raw materials. We need that money.'

'Call New York and ask again what's causing the delay,' Roth said quickly. He didn't want juniors witnessing the kind of scene that was boiling up. Even as he spoke, he realized that by using the word 'delay' he was slipping into the very same jargon of deceit that Plaza was employing to string him along. If Brazil was failing to honour bills, then sure as hell that country was in trouble.

'We need those dollars,' Gianni repeated. 'And I hold you responsible.'

'I'm sorry, sir,' Schuster could no longer escape a formal disclaimer. 'Your bill was guaranteed by the Bank of Brazil. We acted only as agents. Did you have credit insurance?'

'Insurance? Your guys said if it was with a bank it was safe.' Gianni's temper was rapidly mounting. 'Listen, we never had a goddam foreign order before. We asked you to fix the payment.' He rose to his feet. 'You better get that seven hundred thousand.'

'Could we provide a bridging loan?' Roth looked at his Treasurer, his basic cowardice revealed by attempting to pass the buck. He had to live in social proximity to Gianni and his workforce. Many of the employees banked with Bartrum. He couldn't afford to antagonize them.

However, Schuster wasn't about to shoulder the blame for a refusal, and a twelve-year-old could have seen this was a potential bad debt walking through the door. ACE Techtronics couldn't survive a $1.7 million default. No way.

'When do you need cash in your account, sir?' he asked.

'Friday.' For a few seconds Gianni thought he was going to be saved. 'The weekly pay-checks go out Fridays.'

'Give us forty-eight hours. We'll get working on this right now.' Schuster stood up too, smiled, held out his hand, did his best. 'Believe me, sir, we appreciate your concern.'

The soft soap failed.

'If you pair of schmucks let my company go down, you'll pay for it.' Gianni spat the words at them. 'Your names'll stink from here to the Triboro Bridge.' He stormed out.

'Jesus Christ,' Roth looked despairingly at his Treasurer. 'If Brazil goes bad on us for $20 million, how can we lend out more?' He was up against a crisis so far beyond the dimensions of his own experience that he was unable to comprehend it.

'I'll tell you one thing for free.' Schuster spoke as if he had unexpectedly stumbled on a hidden truth, which in a way he had. 'If a bank like ours got into a fix it used to be the small depositors who stood in line for their savings and lost out. This time it won't be. They're covered by Federal Insurance up to $100,000. Nor's it gonna be the borrowers like Gianni who have long-term loans.' He stayed silent while he thought about this. 'It'll be us who'll have to go and discount those loans at the Fed for cash.'

London. Late afternoon

'Mr Slater?' A short enquiring pause. 'Richard Stephens here. I have been finding out about those Nigerian bonds for you.'

'Ah.' Len Slater tried to sound as if he had not been steeling himself for this call all day, taking refuge from his anxiety by dealing with the least demanding routine letters while he waited. Yesterday he had deluded himself into believing the other Trustees might agree a ten per cent discount to be rid of the bonds. This morning Keith Norris had shot that tiny hope from under him. A normal broker's commission was the maximum the Union could afford.

'Good news, I hope?' he said weakly.

'Not tremendously good, I'm sorry to say.' Stephens accented the 'tremendously'. He habitually employed hopeful words to convey the reverse of hope. 'The New York market is jittery again, prices slipping badly. The Dow Jones Index is down eleven points.'

Slater knew that meant share prices had fallen and presumably Nigerian loans too, except that they were not quoted on any stock exchange.

'Might as well know the worst, then,' he said, sub-consciously squaring his bony shoulders as if facing an intruder.

'I'm afraid we have so far been unable to find a buyer.'

This was untrue. However, Stephens preferred a greyish lie to quoting the price he had been offered, which was even lower than yesterday's. Keep one's image good, was his motto.

'You mean to tell me . . .' Slater was sitting bolt upright now, his thin face suffused with indignation. 'Listen to me, lad. It's no time ago you were recommending us Nigeria. Soundest country in Africa, you said.'

At his end of the line Stephens paled. He did not appreciate being called 'lad', even by a trade unionist with £5 million at his beck and call. He licked his drying lips, choked back a remark about Africa being a disaster area however you looked at it, then suddenly decided to let fly.

'With respect,' he said, acidly, again implying the opposite, 'you specifically ordered us to participate in that bond issue. It is hardly our responsibility if the only offer obtainable wasn't worth passing on.'

'So there was a buyer!' In his relief Slater let his guard down completely.

'At twenty-seven cents in the dollar, yes.'

The disbelieving silence with which this was greeted caused Stephens to smile. If old Len wasn't on the skids already, he deserved to be.

'Do you wish me to accept?'

'Twenty-seven cents? Twenty-seven per cent?' The eventual reply was a husky whisper, £540,000 in exchange for our £2 million investment?'

'Its better than nothing.'

'No! We can't rob our members like that. Never!'

'Whatever you wish, sir.' Stephens rang off, wondering if he ought not to have a quick private word with the General Secretary, if he was to keep AUCAS as a client. Keith Norris would be on his side. They had a kind of freemasonry in common, he and Keith.

A few minutes later, Len walked slowly to Camden Town station, leaning on his stick and so distraught that he only narrowly escaped being run over at the traffic lights. Two thoughts were revolving in his mind with the compulsive dementia of whirling dervishes. He must somehow keep this disaster from the other Trustees and he must fly to Nigeria as soon as possible – those bloody blacks were supposed to be Socialists, they ought to be sympathetic.

London's Fleet Street, long a synonym for the press, was changing as more newspapers followed *The Times* out of the area. In a curious way, Stuart Pendler was sad. He had never enjoyed swilling beer in the Fleet Street pubs so beloved of reporters or propping up the crowded bar of El Vino's. However, he had liked the International Press Club situated on the first floor of the glass-fronted mini-skyscraper known as the International Press Centre, where the *New York Times* and the *Wall Street Journal* had their London bureaux. The Club had been within walking distance of his own office, but it too had fallen prey to change and gone into liquidation. There was no place Pendler could rely on bumping into American colleagues for a drink and gossip, except perhaps Scribes. He went there.

This evening of Tuesday June 11th there were barely half a dozen people in the bar. Fortunately, the man he had hoped to find was one of them. He bought a scotch and joined him.

'How's tricks, Tom? Mind if I join you?'

Tom Mahon was a veteran correspondent of the *Wall Street Journal*, and he had excellent City contacts.

'Haven't seen you around.' Mahon lifted the olive out of his dry martini, ate it carefully and deposited the stone in an ashtray. 'Been away?'

'Paris.' Pendler killed the query and settled himself into an armchair. 'All the French talk about is their budget deficit.'

'And the British about take-overs. Hell of a shake-out going on, as I guess there was bound to be once the Big Bang was over.'

The Big Bang had been the opening of the British Stock Exchange to outsiders, but it was less than fascinating to Pendler at this moment. He tried to steer the conversation on to foreign-exchange problems. If Tom didn't have his ear to the ground, no journalist did.

'The French should never have nationalized Rothschilds,' he said. 'The Swiss haven't trusted them since. Won't even help them with balance-of-payments lending.'

'One thing about the Swiss, they run a bank like a bank, not a goddam lottery. That reminds me. You know what my big event is this week?' Mahon let loose a spluttering laugh. 'Lunch with the Swiss–American Chamber of Commerce in Zurich.'

'The fun party of the century. Why did they pick on you?'

'Shush.' Mahon put an finger to his lips. 'It's the gnomes' idea of a rare honour – for a pressman, that is. Besides, they have an American speaker. I guess they'd like it covered in the *Journal*. In fairness, they have had some distinguished guests in the past: NATO commanders-in-chief, former presidents. This time it's William Osborn of First National.'

Pendler had to take a quick gulp of whisky to conceal his surprise. If there was one man who must know about Columbus Cay, that man was Bill Osborn.

'His usual subject?' he asked casually.

'I have the title on me someplace.' Mahon fumbled for his diary.

'Yep, "Political Risk in Sovereign Lending". Might be worth half a column. It's not often Osborn makes a public appearance. You interested?'

'If I could get away.' Pendler tried to make that sound unlikely. 'Which day is it?'

'Thursday.' Mahon consulted his diary again. 'Twelve for twelve-thirty at the Dolder Grand Hotel. I'm going the night before. Why don't you come along?'

A couple of whiskies later Pendler had allowed himself to be talked into requesting an invitation which, he reflected, didn't say much for Mahon's opinion of the *Trib* as a competitor. Well, basically it wasn't one. Anyway, he wasn't going to lose out on buttonholing Osborn either at the pre-lunch drink session or afterwards. When he left Scribes he returned to his office, rang Paris to obtain the editor's okay, then called Maggie to find what she had achieved. He had a hunch his luck was on the turn.

'How much you pay me?'

'For what?'

'Very best quality top-class information.'

'Come on, honey, I've had a busy day.' The moment he let his irritation sound through on the phone, Stuart regretted it. 'I didn't mean that. What gives?'

'For you, sir, very best special price I am offering. Nowhere else are you finding such excellent facts.' Maggie relented and dropped the teasing mock-Asian accent. 'About the manager of Columbus Cay, love. About McLellan. Who else?'

'That was quick.'

His surprise made her feel like purring. She was lying comfortably, propped up with cushions on the sofa of her high-ceilinged attic studio in Paris, basically one vast room with great exposed beams supporting the roof, and windows facing south and west over the Marais district. The evening sun gilded her flowers and plants in their window-ledge pots and cast an elongated pool of warm light on the carpet. A few minutes ago she had kicked her shoes off, curled her legs up under her and taken the first few sips of a glass of kir – white wine made tangy with cassis. She was as content as a cat. Quite apart from the delight of being in a place totally her own, with her own photos and drawings pinned around the walls, she had made a discovery today. The secret of successful research was simpler than she had imagined: it lay in knowing where to look.

'Finding Mr McLellan was easy,' she told Pendler lazily. In

fact she had consulted a French catering-trades' directory. 'He's had a curious career. Born in Marseilles, just before World War Two. Educated in England. Banqueting Manager at the Ritz when he was only thirty-one, House Manager after that. Then a spell advising a group in Switzerland – must have had something going for him to be teaching the Swiss about hotels. Finally back to Paris as Deputy General Manager at the Crillon.'

Pendler was intrigued, visualizing the Crillon's stately classical façade overlooking the Place de la Concorde. A lot of hotels claimed to be among the greatest in the world. The Crillon didn't bother. Everyone knew it was. McLellan had been close to the top of his profession.

'You said "finally". When did he leave Paris?'

'The barman remembers him.' Maggie went on, thinking that if she wasn't clocking up instant Brownie points for initiative, she ought to be. 'Wouldn't say exactly what the scandal was, just that Monsieur Patrick walked out a couple of years ago. No one has seen him since.'

'I guess I owe you a drink.'

'Not to worry.' She uncoiled herself and stretched her legs out luxuriously, savouring the moment. 'You can pay for one in the Bahamas.'

'I can what?'

'Your friendly travel agent booked us into Columbus Cay for tomorrow week. The scenario we cooked up in that boat restaurant has come to life'

'Are you kidding? That's fantastic.' But how could they get away with returning to the place they'd been deported from? 'Just one thing. Both the immigration people and McLellan might remember my face.'

'I thought of that.' She wiggled her toes happily. 'Which is why I've included you out. "Us" means a girlfriend and me. I shall also dye my hair back to its proper colour. How d'you think I'll look as a brunette with glasses, Stu?'

'Hey. Wait a minute. This is my story.'

'Don't worry, you won't lose it. The *Trib*'s paying.' She allowed a few seconds for this shaft to sink in, then added the barb: 'Harry Grant felt the least they could do was compensate for the pictures I lost. Now I can take them all over again. He feels the place itself is visually more interesting than Finance Ministers at airports.'

'Listen, Maggie, it's a great idea, sure. But those goons stamped your passport.' He tried to sound reasonable, though he was boiling inside.

She reached out for the kir and took a cool, delicious sip. She hadn't enjoyed a phone conversation so much in years.

'I didn't tell you, Stu. A ghastly thing happened after I left the Crillon. As I was going down the Concorde Métro entrance, one of those wretched Arabs knocked into me and stole my bag. He was gone before I knew it. Luckily the only important thing inside was the passport. I shall have to get a replacement from the Irish Embassy tomorrow.' She paused for another sip. 'This time I shall fly in direct from Miami. I agree that Nassau was most unpleasant.'

Silently cursing the whole monstrous conspiracy of women in journalism, Pendler was about to ring off when he remembered Zurich.

'Before you leave on this exotic trip, can you make Zurich on Thursday.' He explained. 'Osborn is very seldom photographed. May not be too easy, of course.'

'Challenge accepted, dear.' She clinked her glass delicately against the receiver. 'I'm drinking to success. Where do we meet?'

New York. Midday

Early evening in Europe was lunchtime in New York. While Stuart Pendler conversed with Maggie and Len Slater clutched his stick in the Underground train home – convinced that the other passengers were staring at him – Lopez-Santini was arriving in Manhattan. Or, to be more exact, he was sitting impotently in a limousine edging its way through solid traffic towards Wall Street, while the young Argentine Consul attempted appropriate conversation, which wasn't easy because he had no inkling of the Minister's mission. Eventually Lopez-Santini tired of the charade.

'Can I phone home on this?' he picked up the car telephone.

'Of course, Excellency. What is the number?' The Consul was relieved. He could pretend not to be listening.

Lopez-Santini himself hoped he would be able to find out, obliquely, if there had been news of his children.

'Praise God that you have thought of us at last.' Mercedes did not wait for explanations before launching a storm of emotional abuse. 'It's fine for you, jetting around the world. You ask has anything happened? If you cared about us you would know. Nothing has happened, José. Nothing, nothing, nothing! I am going crazy with worry.'

'My darling,' he tried to temporize, 'at this moment I am with our Consul in New York. I have seized the first opportunity . . .,' cupping his hand over the mouthpiece he explained to the young

73

man, knowing he must be hearing every syllable, 'We have family problems; my wife is a little overwrought.' He allowed her to continue, until he could interject, 'I wish there was someone you could talk to.' He meant this as a reminder of the need for secrecy. Her reply horrified him.

'If there wasn't I should go mad. Mercifully, Gabriella Menendez has come round. She is saving my sanity.'

Gabriella was a cousin of his wife's and a legendary gossip.

'We must be discreet, my love,' he glanced sideways at the Consul, who was tactfully staring at the traffic. 'You do understand? We must keep these matters to ourselves.'

'Only a man would say that!' Her half-scream made him jump. 'I suppose you don't trust me, is that it? When you're enjoying the fleshpots, leaving me to cope all alone.' She continued in this vein for a further ten minutes, during which time the limo progressed two blocks. When the conversation ended he had been unable to tell her that his next stop would be Switzerland. Not that he could have mentioned the ransom in front of the Consul.

Buenos Aires. 3 pm

'You see!' Mercedes turned theatrically to her contemporary and cousin, perched on the edge of an armchair, tea and cakes beside her on a small table. 'My poor darling babies are in peril of their lives, in mortal danger, and where is José-Maria? In New York!'

'A Braun-Menendez would be where he is needed. With his loved ones.' Gabriella bit into an eclair, savouring the cream. She had dropped in unannounced for a social call, only to discover the drama afflicting her unfortunate relative. 'As I said when you married him, my dear, the Lopez-Santinis are not a family of distinction. Brains perhaps, but not blood. He should be with you now, whatever his job.'

'You forget he is a Cabinet Minister, Gabriella. A key member of the government.' Mercedes instantly became defensive. She wasn't having others attack her husband. 'He has important meetings abroad. But even so,' she shook her head sadly, not unwilling to let the tears flow again, 'if only we could talk to the kidnappers.' A sudden fear struck her heart. 'You won't tell anyone, will you? The Comisario warned us, secrecy is crucial. If it once got out that our girls were being held to ransom . . .'

'My dearest, of course not.' Gabriella abandoned the cakes to dart across and embrace her unhappy cousin. 'You poor darling . . .' As Mercedes began to sob, she comforted her tenderly. It was all too awful for words, like a television soap opera come to life. Her friends would never believe. . . .

New York. *1 pm*

The lunch organized for the Minister in one of First National's private reception rooms was strictly private, strictly a working one. Osborn liked to cut the frills and get on with the business.

'The fewer of us around, the less posturing there'll be,' he agreed with Warburton. 'If Lopez-Santini arrives alone, then we should ditch Sheldon Harrison. I don't want to make him feel uncomfortable.'

When the limousine finally did reach Water Street the Minister dismissed his Consul. Thus it was simply the three men who foregathered on the twenty-ninth floor: three mature, conservatively dressed men who from their appearance might as easily have been senior diplomats as bankers or industrialists. The proverbial fly on the wall – in this case oak-panelled and hung with expensive Audubon wildlife prints – could equally have supposed it was a reunion of old friends. In a way it was. They had met many times before in the context of rescheduling, when Lopez-Santini himself had been an economic adviser to the eleven-nation Cartagena Group of Latin American debtor countries.

'Well, José-Maria,' Osborn said pleasantly when the immediate civilities were over and they were standing, drinks in hand, admiring the view of the East River, 'your country has some kind of emergency on its hands?'

'Not only mine. The developing nations are all under the most extreme pressure, social and political as well as financial.'

'The price of democracy,' Warburton commented. 'Any sensible man would want to pay it.' One of the ironies of so many South American dictators having been overthrown was that the elected governments succeeding them were a lot less responsive to outside creditors. 'Are you representing the Cartagena Group again?'

'Those and others.' Lopez-Santini turned away from the view to face his hosts. 'You could say that I am here as an ambassador for twenty-one nations.' He allowed them a quick half-smile. 'Naturally I have brought my credentials.'

'We'll believe you,' Osborn showed more cheerfulness than he felt. 'More whisky?' He fetched the decanter himself. He hadn't wanted staff cluttering the room, at least until the meal had to be served.

'So,' Warburton said amiably. 'Are you here to deliver a diplomatic note, or to make an informal *démarche*?'

Lopez-Santini waited until his glass had been refilled. The first essential for this mission, as in all diplomacy, would be a combination of good manners and personal detachment from the message being handed over.

'The governments which have asked me to represent them are those of the principal debtor nations in South America, Africa and Asia. The grouping was formed only at the weekend. Poland has joined it, South Korea has not. This is a list.' He opened his briefcase and extracted a typed paper, which he gave to the two bankers. 'They wish, collectively, to present a proposal.'

'Naturally we will consider it,' Osborn said.

'Personally – not in my capacity as a Minister of the government of the Republic of the Argentine – I regret that this proposal is thought necessary.' Lopez-Santini was aware that he was becoming pompous, but saw no escape. 'Do you wish me to read it?' Finalizing the draft had taken him and Felipe most of the night, attempting to soften what edges they could. He was still far from happy with the result.

'You can give us the gist.'

'The proposal is that repayment of all loans should be suspended for thirty years.'

'Pretty hard to sell that to the banks.' Osborn's only observable reaction was to adjust his thick-rimmed glasses and peer at the list again. 'I suppose certain of these governments wouldn't be too sad if the major US banks did go into liquidation.'

'There were some emotional speeches at our conference.' Lopez-Santini made his distaste clear, whilst not disguising the threat.

'And the interest payments over those thirty years?' Warburton enquired.

'Only nominal.'

'I guess that will need thinking about,' Osborn remarked, 'Might be easier on a full stomach.'

An hour and three courses later, neither Osborn nor Warburton had succeeded in finding a chink in the Argentine Minister's armour. He had clearly been allowed extremely little, if any, scope for compromise.

'So what's the alternative, José-Maria?' Warburton demanded.

'The alternative,' Lopez-Santini paused, 'is, I regret, a default – a public renunciation of all our countries' debts next week.' He spread his hands with Latin eloquence. 'I do appreciate, perhaps better than some of my colleagues, the scale of the financial crisis that would cause. They reply that the only measures left to them are desperate ones.'

'That's no option, José-Maria,' Osborn said, asperity tingeing his voice for the first time, 'that's blackmail.'

'I am sorry.' He genuinely was. This pseudo-option lowered him to the same moral level as his children's kidnappers. 'I must demand a "Yes" or "No" answer by six o'clock on the evening of Monday June 17th.'

After that there wasn't much to be said, and the Argentine left.

'Deep down,' Warburton observed when they were alone again. 'Lopez-Santini's no more sympathetic to this than we are.'

'You think someone has a hold over him?'

'I wouldn't be surprised.'

Osborn considered the possibility and dismissed it.

'We have to deal with facts, Jim. Our committee meets tomorrow. We have to construct a strategy and a timetable.'

'Aren't you due to give a speech in Zurich on Thursday?'

'You're damn right, I am.' Osborn swore gently. 'Clean slipped my mind. Would you stand in for me?'

'Bad tactics. If we want to keep this quiet we should all behave as normally as possible. Publicity is a major part of the threat: we don't want to stimulate speculation.'

'I guess so.' Osborn grunted in uncharacteristic annoyance. 'All we need is a leak. Then the panic will start and it won't be a question of whether the banks survive, at the best it'll be which.'

CHAPTER FIVE

Buenos Aires. Tuesday June 11th

The messenger came to the suburban apartment block after dark on the Tuesday evening, checked that he was not being followed before he entered, then walked up the uncarpeted service stairs instead of taking the lift. He was lanky, tousle-haired and dressed in jeans and a windcheater that was grubby at the neck and wrists – a typical student, looking younger than his nineteen years, more like a boy. At the door of the apartment itself he waited a full minute, listening for footsteps or the whirr of the lift machinery. Then he tapped the recognition signal and slipped inside as soon as the catch was released.

'Your name?' The slim, dark-haired man who confronted him rapped out the question.

'Jorge.'

'Turn around. Face the wall.'

The body search which followed was swift, efficient and revealed no weapon. The man's tone relaxed a trifle.

'Come through.' He guided the student down a passage past closed doors to a bedroom, in which a young woman was sitting on the side of the bed. Her eyes followed the boy's movements, though she did not speak.

'Well?' asked the man.

'Tomas wants them moved. Tomorrow. He says they are to be sedated. A small van will be in the basement garage at midday.'

'Do we go with them?'

'I don't know.' The boy began to be frightened. He had been warned that the couple might object. 'I heard the police have a description of you.'

'Is that so?' The woman broke her silence. 'Do you know any more?'

'I was only asked to give the message.'

'Which you have done,' the man agreed, though with no great amiability.

'Then I'll be going.' He shifted his weight awkwardly from one foot to the other, anxious to be released. But the man made no move.

'Who exactly gave you this message?'

'It is from Tomas.'

'Tomas himself?'

The boy wilted under this interrogation. He had been told about Tomas by the student friend who had asked yesterday, out of the blue, if he seriously wanted to help the Party. A broad hint conveyed that the Party was the Ejertico Revolucionario de Pueblo, the ERP, and the boy was proud to be chosen. As instructed, he had gone to a cheap bar and met an alert and mean-looking thug whom he knew instinctively was no revolutionary. The thug had given him the verbal message, made him repeat it back, ordered him to report again after delivering it, then offered a few snorts of cocaine in a twist of paper as advance payment, which the boy declined. He wasn't after drugs or money. He would have refused to take the message at all if he had not already become scared.

'Tomas spoke to you?' the man repeated.

'Not himself.'

The man and woman exchanged swift glances, as if agreeing what to do next.

'Well,' the man said, 'you found us. Now forget us, right. Forget our faces. Forget the address.' He escorted the boy to the door.

'You think we're in danger, Miguel?' The woman asked when he returned, though in a tone of assessment rather than anxiety.

'Not from the cops.'

'We should have handled the negotiation as well as the snatch.'

'Too risky. Tomas was correct about that.' Each cell had its function and only one link to the group. The newer Junta de Coordinacion Revolucionaria, to which they actually belonged, was so secretive that next-door neighbours could belong without being aware of each other's allegiance. Basically it was a student and middle-class movement. 'But why didn't Tomas come himself?'

'We could phone him.'

'No, Maria.' For good reason telephone contact was forbidden except in the most extreme emergency.

'Miguel.' She had made up her mind. 'Things are going well. Lopez-Santini's announced that the IMF are in for a rough ride –

we heard that on the radio. The political aim is the main one. We weren't going to make any move on the ransom until after the weekend. The more we look like an ordinary couple whose nieces are visiting the better. Besides, those kids trust me now. We even bought them new clothes. We were never meant to hand them to anyone else.'

'Tomas could have changed his mind.' Miguel was still uncertain.

'I don't believe he sent that boy.' She felt under the bedding, pulled out the Beretta with which she had killed the chauffeur Ruiz, and began checking it. She was a professional with small arms. 'We must think carefully about tomorrow,' she said.

New York. Wednesday June 12th

If guessing the future correctly kept you awake at night – and that was what burnt out foreign-exchange dealers faster than anything – then New York was a bad place to be. This was the conclusion Sheldon Harrison had reached by the morning of Wednesday June 12th, his third full day as Warburton's aide. The resources of First National's analysts and economists had been opened to him, with some plausible excuses about his needing to familiarize himself with international debt problems. He had been astonished at the amount of information available, even if less than mind-blown by the twenty-nine-year-old whizz-kid conducting his initiation.

'Man, we have data here you could be shot for possessing in a lot of countries. You know why? They don't have it themselves, that's why.'

'Is that so, Mr Roach?' Harrison failed to keep a hint of mockery out of his appreciation. Willard J. Roach was one of a breed of computer-programmers who had been elevated to executive status as the financial-services revolution speeded up. When a bank was shifting billions of dollars a day, its computer systems had to work, and work well. Roach designed programs that did. In consequence, he earned twice his contemporaries' salaries and had self-consciously bought a couple of Brooks Brothers suits. However, what projected out of the well-cut clothing remained a ginger-haired older relative of the freckled youth who graced the cover of *Mad* magazine. He was no kind of a banker and the other bank officers of his own age had little hesitation in pinning uncomplimentary nicknames on him. About the kindest was 'Roachy'.

'Call me Willard,' he told Harrison, always hopeful of gaining respect from someone new. 'You mean you don't know what these IBMs can do?'

'Not in forecasting.'

Although computers had transformed Bartrum Bank's accountancy and cheque-clearing, the wider applications of technology had passed it by. Ray Roth didn't need computer simulations of how his local customers might behave.

'Gee. Well,' Roach waved a proprietorial hand around the arrays of computer terminals and displays in this open-plan area where the analysts worked, 'we research plenty in-house, and we're taking data from other institutions all the time. Forecast anything you want.'

The snag, Harrison knew, was the range of choice. When an ancient Greek consulted the Oracle at Delphi about the future, he received only a single answer from the mystical voice. It might be cryptic and idiosyncratic, but it was definitive. The modern American banker could obtain as many differing views as he could afford to commission. Which could be confusing. He put the point.

'Oh,' Roach replied confidently, 'the computer fixes all those kinds of problem. One thing we've done for Mr Osborn is make like a model of the economy in countries where the bank's exposed.'

'Figuratively a model?'

'Sure. A simulation.' He was glancing down at the keyboard on his desk as if he had itchy fingers. 'We can feed in changes the analysts come up with – like higher interest rates, lower export growth, a drop or rise in the oil price. We feed those in and the model gives out new predictions.'

'Let's try the Argentine.'

'Have to be more specific. This is a complex model. Like I said before, we have data the Argentine government itself won't have.'

Harrison paused to think. One key factor in a country's ability to service debt was the growth of its economy.

'Let's have Gross National Product.'

'Okay.' Roach began tapping keys.

'SELECT SCENARIO,' the computer demanded, displaying a choice.

'You want "Base", "Pessimistic", "Weak" or "Crisis"?' Roach asked. 'Short-term, medium-term or long-term? Flavour of the month is "Crisis, short term".'

'I'm an optimist. Give me "Base, medium".'

Roach happily continued his dialogue with the machine. Columns of figures appeared on the screen. He underlined a few of them with light.

'ARGENTINE REPUBLIC. GNP GROWTH PERCENT-AGES 1960–1970 4.3: 1970–1980 1.9: 1981–1986 − 1.16: 1986–1990 2.96.'

'They must have had some kind of hiccup down there in the early 1980s, I guess. Went into below-zero growth.'

'The Falklands War.'

Roach stared at the machine, discountenanced. 'Oh, yeah.' He was an expert in computers, not current affairs. 'You want to see non-oil developing countries generally?' He needed to retrieve his loss of face. 'Like for comparison.'

'Good idea.'

'NON-OIL LESS DEVELOPED COUNTRIES,' the display announced, 'TWENTY-FIVE LARGEST BORROWERS GNP GROWTH (IMF) 1981–1985 2.92: 1986–1990 4.6.'

'Are those for real?' Harrison could hardly believe the figures. In the mid-1980s the United States' own growth had been far less than this. The figure of 1.2 per cent for 1985 stuck in his mind. 'You mean countries that owe us $1,000 billion are doing better than we are?'

The opening was too obvious for Roach to miss. 'If you lent me a thousand billion without security,' he asked innocently, 'and I never paid any interest on that loan, which of us two would be better off?'

He began playing with his console again and a whole column of country names appeared with statistics ranged alongside.

'What did I tell you. Korea's heading for 6.5 per cent growth; Thailand for 6.3; Malaysia 6.4; even lousy Colombia should be hitting 3.2.' He swivelled around on his chair for a moment. 'I give you an idea for free, Mr Harrison. Those guys don't need to bug out. Any bank lets them default must be soft in the head.'

Harrison looked at the computer expert with something nearer respect. He had unexpected common sense and common sense was hardly an attribute of the bankers who had landed themselves in the debt crisis, from clowns like Ray Roth right up to the presidents of First National, Chase, Citicorp and the others.

'Growth isn't the whole story,' he reminded Roach. 'I mean, if the interest payments are swallowing up all a country's foreign exchange, there must be a strong temptation to bug out. How do they pay for imports?' He was expressing it simplistically, he knew.

'Our model has those parameters. Funny thing you mentioning temptation. Guy called Kaletsky extrapolated some temptation ratios from the same sources we use.'

'Can you calculate a temptation?' It was a quirky idea.

'Kaletsky did. Took figures from Wharton Econometrics and Data Processing Inc. Pretty interesting. We used the same formula. I wrote the program.' Again he began typing commands into the computer. Fresh columns of figures appeared on the screen. 'See that. Brazil's temptation would be higher than anywhere's except Mexico. Argentina's not so high. Peru is nil. Philippines a minus. So are Malaysia, Korea and Thailand. Like I said, those guys would be crazy to break with the banks. They'd be worse off. Brazil ought to be thinking twice if any long-term restructuring was on offer. Only Mexico spells catastrophe.'

'Has Mr Osborn seen this?'

'We reckoned he had other things on his mind. Until this new crisis blew, that is.'

'What d'you mean "new crisis"?' Harrison froze. He simply stood, gazing at the awkward figure of Roach in his shirt-sleeves, so un-put-together as a person, yet so competent with his machines, until the man noticed and straightened up.

'Isn't there some kind of a default?'

'Who told you?'

'People talk.' Roach was defensive. 'The word gets around.'

'If that word gets around Wall Street, there could be a panic. You understand what that means? Your gossip could cause a crash. You'd be out of a job. We all would. Let me tell you something. Mr Osborn has things under control. Right? You just tell people crisis is not the flavour of the month.'

'If you say so.'

'Bill Osborn does, okay? And I'd like printouts of those ratios sent to his office. I think they'll interest him.'

As he walked out, Harrison hoped he had achieved two things: stamped on a gossip brush-fire just in time, and discovered a cache of the exact ammunition James Warburton was looking for to persuade member nations out of the cartel. If, that was, an intellectual approach would work with leaders whose citizens were starving.

Buenos Aires. Midday

Even at midday the basement garage was a shadowy forest of concrete pillars: the vacant spaces oil-stained and obscure, the parked cars like hulks whose paint and chrome faintly reflected what daylight seeped down the entrance ramp. The van would come down this ramp, once the electrically operated gate had been actuated. Security still mattered to the building's owners, though they seldom replaced neon tubes lights that had burnt out.

Maria was counting on the security gate, the dim light and the apartment block's porter maintaining his routine. This morning he had been outside in his navy-blue dungarees as usual, washing the pavement, swapping anecdotes with the porters of the neighbouring buildings, whistling at pretty girls who passed. Come twelve he would disappear to his own apartment for his midday meal and a siesta. Whoever had sent the messenger must be relying on that, and so was she. Now she waited upstairs, trying not to be distracted from her planning by the Lopez-Santini daughters' questions. She had only given them a mild sedative. They had to be awake enough to obey.

'Are you taking us to Papa?' Teresa asked for perhaps the twentieth time. She was sitting on a sofa beside her sister, who was sucking her thumb as if she was six again.

'Soon.'

'We want to see Mama and Papa very much.'

'I know. But you must do as you are told. Now shut up.'

Maria was on edge, anticipating trouble of some kind and painfully aware that she and her hostages had become emotionally bound to each other. It was one thing to hate a capitalist like Lopez-Santini, another to hurt these little ones, whose reactions tore at her gut. She could never have children herself and was unable to avoid emotional involvement as Gloria retreated into tearful baby behaviour, while her older sister comforted her and seemed stronger-willed by the day. Teresa was going to grow into quite some lady, and Maria – the same Maria who had calmly shot the chauffeur – was determined she should get out of this alive.

The door buzzer sounded. She hurried to peer through the observation hole, saw Miguel's features spread-eagled by the tiny lens and slid the catch.

'Three,' he whispered. 'Two with hoods. The boy is driving. Maybe its better you don't come.'

'We're in this together,' she was angered at his protective instincts. 'Is Ramos there?'

'Ramos is hidden and the porter has gone.'

'Remember. Stay close to one of those pillars.'

'I am not a fool.'

Miguel had become as angry and suspicious as she, though for different reasons. Maria was the political one. She had suggested the kidnap and Tomas had added the financial demand. Miguel agreed with that. They always needed funds. Yet they were about to hand over a million dollars on the hoof, as it were, without Tomas' personal confirmation. He had tried the usual way, walking across the city at breakfast-time to a contact address, but found no one in. The set-up stank, especially with the men in the van hooded. The only trick up their own sleeve was Ramos, lurking in the shadows of the garage with his gun.

Maria had exchanged her habitual indoor moccasins for calf-length leather boots, her jeans tucked into them. You had to behave and look well-off in this kind of apartment block, and anyway, she was. She took a short fur-trimmed jacket from the peg in the hall, checked the Beretta was in its pocket, picked up a canvas grip with a Hechler and Koch sub-machine gun inside, and hustled the girls out to the lift.

'Now,' she said as they descended. 'When I tell you to get inside the car, you must stay in it. You understand? Otherwise you will not see your Papa.'

Teresa trembled and said, 'Yes.' She was prepared to do as she was told because although she did not believe the stories about Ruiz being a bad man, Maria had been kind and played games with her and Gloria and also talked about important things, like the way the poor and the peasants had suffered under the army. Her mother never told her things like that. Nor did the teachers at school.

They emerged from the lift to find a white mini-van standing in the main central space of the garage, facing towards the curving incline of the ramp. Two men in leather jackets and black hoods were standing by it. The boy, Jorge, was in the driver's seat, his face visible. He did not look at them.

'These the girls?' demanded the first of the men, as if assessing merchandise.

'They're called Teresa and Gloria,' Maria said defiantly as the girls themselves huddled against her, terrified.

'Better be the right ones. Get them in.'

She pushed the girls ahead of her towards the vehicle, the grip clasped in her left hand, deliberately pausing before stepping in herself.

'Not you,' the first man said. 'We're taking care of them now.' He indicated the grip. 'That theirs?'

'No.' She moved back. 'Don't you know my name?' She had a cover name, as well as her own.

'Names aren't necessary.' The man slid the door shut and turned to Miguel. 'Open the gate.'

'It's automatic going out.' He stayed obstinately still. These men weren't Party members. Their accents, their build and clothes, the way they walked, everything told him they were mobsters. He wished he knew exactly where Ramos was positioned.

For a few seconds there was silence, all four holding their

ground, while the girls shrunk out of sight inside the van and Jorge pretended not to notice, nervously ready to start the engine.

'Okay. Stay here,' the first man agreed roughly, balancing expediency against his orders, deciding to pick off these jumped-up idiots in a fractionally different way. 'Let's go,' he called to the boy.

Jorge eased into first gear and drove slowly towards the ramp. The men walked on the side away from Maria, giving themselves cover.

As the van rounded the corner of the ramp, Maria dodged behind a pillar and unzipped the bag. The sub-machine gun was in her hands by the time the vehicle stopped, now three feet above the floor-level and headed straight for the gate. A few feet further and the mechanism would function.

'Hey, you,' the first man yelled, 'it's not working. Come here.'

Tricked, Miguel responded. As he began walking towards the ramp the second man leaned around the back of the vehicle, took swift aim with a revolver and fired. Miguel fell. Both the mobsters raced down, exploiting their advantage. It was short-lived.

Ramos rose from his hiding-place behind a Ford sedan and shot one, while Maria stepped out and sprayed the other with bullets, which ricocheted off the concrete, reverberating like a road-drill in the confined space.

The boy revved the engine frantically, drove further up, found the gate was opening only slowly and stalled. Seconds later, Ramos was dragging him out of the driver's seat. The van itself stayed put, held by the gears. Inside it the girls were screaming.

Miguel, wounded in the thigh, had crawled behind a pillar. He was clutching at it, trying to regain his feet, as Maria walked over to the dying men. Rivulets of blood fingered across the concrete from beneath them. She pulled the hood off one's head, finding a swarthy, moustachioed face she had never seen before. Then she yanked at the other, ripping the cloth. He too was a stranger.

She dropped the hood and went to Ramos, who had the boy's left arm twisted high behind his back, the bones close to snapping.

'Who sent you?' she demanded, searching his pockets as she spoke.

'Tomas.'

'You're lying.' She pointed to the bodies. 'How did they come into this?'

The boy shook his head.

'I give you twenty seconds.' She began to count, methodically changing the gun's select lever to single shots. 'Eight, six, four, two. Who are they?'

The boy still shook his head vehemently, terror in his eyes. If anything went wrong, they had warned, he would be killed. He believed it.

'Let him go, Ramos,' she said coolly, and shot him in the back as he stumbled away. The echoing noise reminded her how little time they had before the porter sounded the alarm. 'Get Miguel to the apartment,' she ordered. 'Don't let him drip blood. 'I'll bring the girls.'

This proved less easy than killing. She found them crouching on the floor of the van, Teresa hysterical yet still protecting her sister. Quick attempts at reassurance failed and she had to slap sense into them, before half dragging them to the lift.

The porter had heard the shooting distantly, muffled by the intervening walls. He had decided many years ago to keep out of gunfights and delayed fifteen minutes before telephoning the police. When he did dare to emerge from his retreat and enter the hall of the block, all he saw was the retreating backs of the couple from Apartment 34, going for a walk with their nieces. Much later he would recall that the husband was limping.

New York. Morning

'As I said yesterday, Lopez-Santini is acting completely out of character.' James Warburton was having a final discussion with Osborn before the bankers' committee meeting began, while Harrison listened. 'He may be emotional with his family – what Latin isn't – but professionally his approach has always been cool and intellectual.'

'Logically, sir,' Harrison said, indicating the print-outs which Willard Roach had sent up, 'quite a number of countries ought to be unwilling defaulters. What if you spoke to the ministers individually?'

'We do that all the time,' Warburton said mildly – he didn't believe in put-downs – 'not only when there's a crisis.'

'The political factors are the ones Roach's computer can't quantify.' Osborn was hunched behind his desk and chomping a cigar, something he only resorted to under stress. 'Take the President of Mexico. He may not give a damn about refined calculations. He'll want to know broadly what his voters stand to gain by default and how much they'll suffer if the West retaliates. Could US banks persuade Uncle Sam to impound Mexican ships and airliners, or freeze the country's dollar assets? We froze Iran's, but that was over human hostages. Banks aren't viewed with such sympathy. It's the human factors Roachy can't punch into his temptation ratio.'

'I see that, sir,' Harrison refused to give up, 'but as Mr Warburton just said, the Argentine Minister is an economist.'

'He also represents a government that wants to prove democracy can work,' Warburton added in his slightly drawling accent. 'In his case, logic and politics should be running on the same track.'

'Okay, then. Let's ask him for dinner.'

'He left for Switzerland last night, sir.' Part of Harrison's brief was to keep tabs on VIPs' whereabouts.

'The devil he did!' Warburton exclaimed. 'He won't even get the time of day out of the Swiss.'

'Tell you something, Jim,' Osborn peered through a cloud of smoke. 'maybe you should deliver that speech for me tomorrow rather than have me cancel. Give you a reason for being there.'

'I might brush up a few other acquaintanceships in Europe too. The Poles, for instance. We need to prise as many of these parrots off their perch as we can.'

'There you have a point bears thinking about. We need a new strategy. Up to now we've always persuaded banks to re-structure while attaching strings to the new loans by way of IMF economic-adjustment programs. That way the defaults have always been conciliatory. This time the debtors are telling the IMF to screw off – if you'll forgive the expression. We may have to resort to inducements that don't figure in young Roachy's ratios. Like persuading Congress to stop giving US aid to Bolivia, Colombia, Peru and the other drug barons, instead of just threatening. Suppose we could pressurize a few Latins, could you organize anything with the Africans and East Europeans?'

'That was more or less my idea, though I might express it more diplomatically.'

'Fine,' Osborn said. 'Then we have an attack strategy at last.'

London to Lagos. Evening

Len Slater shifted around, trying to settle his ache-prone body. Economy-class airline seats were not designed for elderly men with gammy legs. Within minutes he knew that the blanket and diminutive pillow handed out by the stewardess would not alleviate an agonizing night. He had never flown further than Odessa before.

Worse, the whisky-flushed businessman next to him started making conversation.

'Going to Lagos, are you?' he asked in a North Country accent. 'Best have a few quick ones while you can afford to.'

'Nigeria's expensive?' Since he was going to be jammed up against him for seven hours, Slater elected to be polite. 'What with the hotel being paid in advance, I'm hoping not to need much cash.'

'Not need cash, eh? You must be joking! Second most expensive capital in t'world, Lagos. You've plenty of five- and ten-dollar notes, I hope.'

'I have some pound coins.'

'Won't go far with those.' The man twisted to look at him. 'You've never heard of "dash"?'

Slater shook his head. 'Is that a tax?'

'Good as!' The man scratched his palm with his fingernails. 'Have to dash every mortal bloody being. Immigration, customs, check-in staff, taxi-touts – digital watches go down a treat. Mind you, except for the baggage part, it's easier going in. Leaving's the nightmare. Need a walletful then. If you don't mind my asking, what kind of business are you in? Missionary?'

Slater was unable to decide if this was a joke.

'I'm trying to obtain repayment of a loan, since you do ask,' he replied stiffly.

'No offence meant. Large amount?'

'It is for us. Two million pounds.'

The man suffered a sudden convulsion. When he had ceased spluttering he pressed the overhead button for the stewardess.

'I'm standing you a drink, friend,' he said, between the coughs. 'Because you're going to need one. We're providing things they can't do without down there. Necessities. Total bloody necessities of life. And we're still having to barter. I'm swapping armoured-cars, machine-guns and grenades for oil! Though with luck we can sell it forward on the spot market.'

The last part was Greek to Slater, but the main point struck home.

'You think I may have difficulty?'

'You'll learn what "dash" means and no mistake. Here.' The man took out a gilt-cornered memo-pad and scribbled a name. 'You might need a lawyer. He'll cost you, but he is in with the new regime.'

After the miniature whisky bottles had been brought, the man raised his plastic tumbler, jingling the ice.

'Here's to the white man's grave,' he said. 'And the best of British luck there.'

New York. Afternoon

For Sheldon Harrison, nurtured on old-fashioned Protestant values, the bankers' rescheduling committee was a revelation. Though not, unfortunately, of probity and wisdom.

Superficially, the thirty-one dark-suited people gathered in First National's conference room after lunch this Wednesday looked like paragons of prudence. Waiting for the proceedings to begin, the men talked in the low tones of high finance, occasionally flashing gold cuff-links as they made a gesture, cracked a subdued joke, or nodded sagely at a point made in conversation. Almost without exception they also served part-time on the boards of other institutions: insurance companies, industrial corporations etc. Their personal credit-ratings were so high they scarcely needed credit cards. They were here today because – without any exception whatever – they had authorized loans that a kid playing Monopoly would instinctively have considered unsound.

The Europeans who had arrived in a gaggle on Concorde from London and Paris this morning represented famous banks – Lloyds, Dresdner, Credit Lyonnais – who were exposed in Africa, Eastern Europe or South America, but not catastrophically. They could draw comfort from the fact that forty per cent of the $970 billion Third World debt had come from governments, the IMF and the World Bank. Of the $580 billion or so owed to commercial banks the British were embarrassed to the tune of only seven per cent; the Germans, Swiss, Japanese, French, Swedes and others to around forty; the Americans to over fifty.

It was his own countrymen, Harrison reflected morbidly, who were about to reap the whirlwind, and they deserved to. Collectively, the top nine US banks had lent Third World governments one and three quarter times their own capital: 173.3 per cent, to be exact. Bank America, Chase, Citicorp, Manufacturers Hanover, First Chicago – even Morgan Guaranty, reckoned shrewdest of them all – were among those which had loaned out far more than the value of their issued capital and reserves and, if this default happened, would be instantly insolvent. For them, this could be the apocalypse.

Sheldon's grandmother used to read from the Bible when he was a boy out at Water Mill, sitting in her chair by a log fire in the living-room of the rambling clapboard house, while the wind sighed in the trees outside and every hour or two the banshee wail of a passing train disturbed the night. Her favoured passages about fire and brimstone destroying the wicked remained as firm in his mind as the names of his earliest schoolfriends. With her Puritan instincts she would have reckoned the thirty men and one woman in this room were about to receive no less than their just deserts. Furthermore, what with Bill Osborn having given no advance details of the agenda, divine retribution would be coming as a total surprise.

'I regret to tell you,' Osborn announced, when they had settled down, 'that the Finance Ministers of twenty-one debtor nations have formed a cartel. They've given us an option which I would call an ultimatum. They've said, in effect, "Either we don't pay for thirty years and remit only a nominal one per cent interest, or we don't pay at all". That's our agenda for today.'

Silence fell: a shocked, unbelieving silence. Then people began exchanging *sotto voce* comments.

'Holy cow!' one ambassadorially distinguished delegate from Chicago remarked to his neighbour. 'We're loaned up to seven hundred million in Brazil and eight hundred million in Mexico. How are you fixed?'

'Half a billion each.' The heavy-featured man next to him represented a famous West Coast banking house. 'Mexico gave us an extra eighth on the interest spread. Guess we'd have been better off shooting craps.'

Harrison listened, fascinated, and at the same time appalled. That eighth had not been eight per cent. It had been one eighth of one per cent. It might return $625,000 more on a $500 million investment than they'd have obtained from investment at home, but only if the Brazilians and Mexicans both paid the interest and repaid the capital. These apparently responsible men had gone out of their minds for relatively tiny fractions of profit on huge quotients of risk.

Traditionally, the banks had always been in the business of borrowing at one rate and lending out again at a higher one – the 'spread' was the difference between these two. In Long Island, the Bartrum Bank borrowed from local savers and lent out again for real-estate purchase or to auto-dealers needing to floor-plan their showrooms with new models. The big money-centres had done the equivalent on an international scale.

'I guess the goddam OPEC gave these guys the cartel idea,' someone else remarked.

'Those Arabs have a lot to answer for.'

Too simplistic by half, Harrison reflected. OPEC's oil cartel had only fouled up the banking system because the men around this table had allowed it to.

Constantly expanding loan portfolios were what bank lending officers had been instructed to aim for. When those tenfold oil-price hikes of the 1970s suddenly gave Saudi Arabia and the Gulf States revenues beyond the dreams of sheikhly avarice – more than they could conceivably spend on airports, yachts or women – the Western banks were delighted to scoop up the vast residue. Furthermore, since oil was priced in dollars, at some point in the chain those petrodollars had to be traded through New York and American banks.

Enter the problem, Harrison reflected. To whom were the banks going to lend these billions of dollars?

Demand for investment in the late 1970s was low in both the States and Europe – because the oil crises had brought about recession. So the next choice was the so-called developing countries, which had been steadily growing since the 1960s. These countries were a real mish-mash. There were ex-colonies in Africa and Asia, dozens of them, all fired by what one economist neatly named 'the revolution of rising expectations'. There were nations with real potential like the Argentine, except that its rulers became more interested in guns than profits. There were natural basket-cases, like Haiti. Some had their own oil, some didn't. They all wanted loans. So the bankers lent the non-oil ones money with which to buy oil and continue their growth, and after that they lent the oil-producers money because with oil they couldn't go wrong. They then compounded the potential for disaster by adding American capital to the petrodollars. By the end of the 1970s half the profits of the big American money-centre banks were derived from international lending.

'When I think we were giving our Treasury Department people bonuses for placing those funds!' the ambassador look-alike muttered. 'A monkey could have sold them.'

'If we'd have stopped in '82 we'd have been okay.'

Harrison recalled 1982 with bitterness. Though a shareholder in Bartrum Bank, he was working in London that year with Warburton, and was not even aware of Ray Roth's decision to participate in Argentine and Mexican loan consortiums. He probably would not have been able to influence him, anyhow. Roth was only one of hundreds being sweet-talked into the fresh lending which the big banks' enforced restructuring entailed.

Roth, whose predecessors wouldn't have considered lending outside Long Island, leapt at the chance. And what could be smarter than taking *three* slices of cherry cake by adding Brazil as well? Before 1983 was over both he and others, like the Bankers

Trust of South Carolina, were having to extend their six-month loans to eight years. Eight years! And now the interest wasn't being paid, either. Altogether there were some 1,500 American banks in the same predicament, great and small. The whole financial edifice had become as stable as a house of cards on a windy day.

'Gentlemen.' Osborn called the meeting to order and the buzz of worried conversation died away. 'We have to face some unpalatable truths. We've all effectively been loaning debtor countries the money to pay their overdue interest and we've been reporting it as profit. But there's been no real profit and no real cashflow for years. If the World Bank had taken over the burden, things might be different. It hasn't. What's more the oil-price fall of '86 is doing what it was bound to in the end. The Arabs are asking for their money back. The restructuring's over, gentlemen. We are into a totally new ball-game.'

'One that we should refuse to play, *hein*?' interrupted a German named Treichler.

'One we have to play, sir, if we don't want another 1929.' He turned to Sheldon. 'Mr Harrison will pass around some strategy notes we have prepared.'

While Harrison did this, Osborn conferred briefly with Warburton about keeping the Federal Reserve informed.

'As you see,' he continued, 'there are two aspects to this strategy: defensive and offensive. We propose regional sub-committees to examine the defensive.'

'By what day do they report?' Treichler demanded.

'Before leaving New York.'

A murmur of dismay greeted this announcement.

'Gentlemen.' Osborn was uncompromising. 'Today is Wednesday. We have to give a collective reply by Monday evening. In between we need agreement from your correspondent banks.'

'But that is impossible!' Treichler himself had marshalled funds from over a hundred different firms, including merchant banks which in turn represented pension funds, insurance companies, corporations and private investors.

'Herr Treichler, I have already explained. What we have received is not an option. It is an ultimatum. However, I will request an extension of time.'

'And this offensive strategy?' The German disliked being cut down in public. 'What such strategy is possible, may I ask?'

'The offensive?' Osborn smiled for the first time. 'Why, I'm going to break up the cartel, if I can. What else? Care to join me?'

*

'Your Excellency.' The benign if heavy-jowled president of the Swiss bank was outwardly sympathetic. He had received Lopez-Santini as a favoured client in his private sanctum, a modern office rendered traditional with hunting trophies and oil portraits of past presidents on the walls. They sat in deep leather armchairs and coffee had been served. 'It would be our wish, *natürlich*, to give you personally all possible assistance.'

He emphasized the 'personally' for several reasons. Numbered, secret accounts for Third World politicians were a valued part of the bank's stock-in-trade. However, he had to differentiate between what the bank could do for Lopez-Santini himself and what it could do for the government the Minister represented. This very morning one of the bank's senior officers was in New York discussing the default threat: yet here was the debtor-countries' principal negotiator flying to Zurich to ask a favour. Something major must be in the wind. If Lopez-Santini was straight with him, then he could be helpful. If he was devious . . . well, business was business.

'How much do you need?' he asked.

'A million dollars, Herr Seiler.'

The Swiss consulted a document. 'The investments we manage on your behalf are valued at less than four hundred thousand. You have fifty-two thousand on deposit.' The implication was obvious in the way the banker smiled. As one professional to another, that faintly twisted smile said, you must surely appreciate. . .

'I can assure you of repayment. My wife has substantial assets.' Lopez-Santini passed across the letter from Mercedes giving him power to pledge her credit.

'There was really no need, Excellency.' Seiler none the less kept the letter. 'Those assets are in the Argentine, I presume.'

'Principally.' This was the sting, and Lopez-Santini flushed, knowing that Seiler might now suggest a trade-off.

'Of course, Your Excellency, if anyone can give assurances, you can. However, these new negotiations are causing all Swiss banks grave concern. We ask ourselves if all foreign-exchange transactions from Latin American countries may not be suspended, we wonder if debt to Swiss banks will continue to be serviced.'

Decoded, this oblique enquiry meant: if we accommodate you, will you guarantee the Argentine will not default on Swiss loans generally? Seiler knew it was a long shot, since it would undermine

94

the new cartel's united stand. But how could Lopez-Santini ask for a million dollars in this week of all weeks without expecting to give a *quid pro quo*?

'Personally, Herr Seiler, I am not in sympathy with current moves.' He wished he could have been explicit, could have revealed that his children's lives were at stake.

'You will forgive my asking the purpose of this loan?'

'It is for an investment.'

Seiler nodded sagely and tapped his solid-gold pen gently on the back of his hand in a deliberate pantomime of decision-making. Then, as if the whole business pained him inexpressibly, he slid a telex out of the folder.

'We received this half an hour ago from our Buenos Aires representative.'

As Lopez-Santini read the short message, the slip of paper seemed to swell into a monstrous fog in front of his eyes, blotting out all coherent thought:

NEWSPAPERS REPORT LOPEZ-SANTINI CHILDREN MISSING SINCE WEEKEND. FAMILY DENY KIDNAP RUMOURS.

'You have my deepest sympathy,' Seiler said, interpreting his guest's expression, and instantly abandoning all thought of trade-offs. From this moment the Minister was no different to any other client in trouble.

All the latent despair of the past few days surfaced in the Argentine's voice. 'They want the money by Monday.'

'I would advise most strongly against paying. Can the police do nothing?'

Lopez-Santini thought of the Comisario's medals and silver braid, of his arrogant self-confidence – and his failure to turn up a single clue so far.

'The police are probably involved themselves,' he said flatly. 'They usually are.' How much information was suppressed before it could reach Alfaro?

Seiler sighed. He had recently assisted an Italian industrialist in a similar heart-breaking predicament. The ransom had been paid and the child found dead a week later. By contrast this Argentine was not a rich man. No responsible adviser could encourage a client to ruin himself.

'Excellency,' Seiler said at last, 'on average, ransoms are settled for one-fifth of the original demand. You must negotiate, preferably through a third party. If it is of any assistance, I will provide a letter stating that the maximum obtainable on your assets at short notice is $250,000.'

'My wife wants to pay, not argue.'

'A mother is especially vulnerable. I would not offer you the million even if you were a Swiss. But a quarter million is at your immediate disposal.'

'Thank you,' Lopez-Santini said wearily. 'I wish I felt that this will avert the catastrophe.'

Herr Seiler was still pondering the meaning of that remark when he stepped out of his Mercedes under the broad entrance canopy of the Dolder Grand Hotel to attend the Chamber of Commerce lunch.

The Dolder Grand Hotel surveyed the city of Zurich and the mountains beyond from a forested hill. The less well-heeled local citizens could reach its exclusive neighbourhood via the top station of a short funicular railway. The hotel arranged private transport for its distinguished visitors.

On this Thursday morning, James Warburton was ferried up from the airport in one of the Dolder's luxurious limousines and ushered to a suite. An excellent breakfast, his second of the day, was wheeled in on a trolley by a white-coated waiter. Then he attempted to finalize his speech. What worried him was that when he left New York, the four sub-committees had all been dead-locked. Ought he to utilize this semi-public occasion to make a plea for flexibility to European bankers? A number would be present. How much dare he suggest?

He was still polishing phrases upstairs when Stuart Pendler debouched from a taxi below. Pendler did not expect to be treated as a distinguished guest. However, he was acutely fazed to learn that he was not a guest at all – the more so because the person who told him was Maggie. She had been waiting disconsolately on a gilt chair in the lobby, her camera-cases at her feet, while the receptionists eyed her with a mixture of disdain and suspicion.

'You're not on the list,' she hissed in an undertone, 'your famous Mr Osborn isn't coming, and the staff are just longing for an excuse to throw me out.' She glared at him. 'Not that they'll need one in a minute. If there's no picture, I'm leaving.'

The truth was, she'd had a struggle of conscience over dressing for this assignment. Should she wear a neat little suit as a re-spectable Swiss businesswoman might? Or should she be herself? Her individualism had won. She had chosen the alternative uni-form of jeans and now looked completely out of place. Her request to photograph the people arriving had been icily refused.

'There has to be a mistake.' Pendler refrained from saying her outfit was certainly one. 'Let me find Tom Mahon. He should be here.'

A reception was visibly in progress in a room off the lobby, where two chic women at a table by the door were checking invitations and handing out name-tags. He strolled across and began his explanations. Within minutes it was all smoothed out. But Maggie? In those goddam jeans?

'They squeezed me in.' He tried to make his apology convincing: 'I'm sorry. They just won't . . .'

'I imagine this place has a restaurant,' she snapped, 'where they will not require me to look like some crappy Swiss gnome. You'll find me there.' She hefted up her camera-case and walked away, tossing her head.

The lunch did little to make up for this. Pendler was allotted a place with Mahon at a table for eight, next to a Swiss public-relations executive of alpine girth who kept saying 'Aach, so!', alternated with 'I am not speaking Engleesh so gut'. It was a relief when, punctually at one-thirty, the chairman called on James Warburton to speak.

Herr Seiler, at the top table, clapped warmly, wondering if there would be an opportunity to mention Lopez-Santini afterwards. Not to betray confidentiality, of course. Merely to probe.

'Mr Chairman, Distinguished Members of the Swiss–American Chamber of Commerce, Ladies and Gentlemen. Those who play second fiddle seldom have the chance to call the tune. Today it is both my pleasure and regret . . .'

Warburton had to limit himself to half an hour exactly. The Swiss liked their money's worth; equally they believed in getting back to work after lunch. He followed his notes carefully, inserting the occasional mild joke, until reaching the passage he hoped the bankers present would interpret correctly.

'A default today would pose unquantifiable risks for both sides. Could the banks rely on multinational trading companies to support them? I doubt it. When Cuba, Libya and Peru expropriated Western assets – to name only three of many countries – did the banks boycott them? They did not. So why should the multinationals help the banks? Why should the many other kinds of organization which nowadays provide credit? Why should governments be expected to impose sanctions on those regimes they support politically?

'If, which God forbid, a new debt crisis arose, bankers would have to be flexible enough to face unprecedentedly tough negotiations. There comes a time when the kissing has to stop.'

'Kissing?' the PR man beside Pendler asked. 'Who is making kisses please?'

But Pendler was busy scribbling a question in his notebook, and when Warburton had finished he rose to his feet.

'Sir, you mentioned corporate reactions to default. Surely all those companies' employees bank someplace. What if they panicked?'

'No government could permit a major commercial bank to actually fail.' It was the stock answer.

'Like the Bank of England saving the Johnson Matthey Bank?'

Warburton winced. The fraud scandals attending that narrowly averted collapse had been deplorable. He believed the Bank of England should have let JMB go under, '*pour encourager les autres*'.

'Some casualties might be unavoidable.'

'So there could be failures?'

'No more questions, I think.' The chairman hastily closed the proceedings and initiated the applause.

Out in the lobby afterwards, Pendler succeeded in button-holing his quarry.

'Surprised to see you here, Mr Pendler.' Warburton neatly cloaked his unease with affability. 'Between ourselves, you had a point over JMB. Some banks would hardly deserve rescuing.'

'Would, sir? Or will?'

'My dear fellow, I was speaking entirely hypothetically.'

'You don't know about the debtors' conference?'

'Conference?' He pretended to misunderstand, wondering how much the *Herald Tribune* knew. Too much, probably.

The flash from a camera startled them both. Maggie had evaded the hotel staff and got her picture.

'Really, Pendler,' Warburton remonstrated in his most British manner. 'I must protest. This was a private meeting, completely off the record.' He backed away.

Two uniformed flunkeys pushed through the guests to seize Maggie's arm. Five minutes later she and Stuart were tramping up the road to the funicular railway, the porter having declined to call a taxi.

'I'll say one thing for you, Stu,' – she began to see the funny side as they waited on the tiny platform for the train – 'you do have a genius for getting thrown out of places.'

Buenos Aires. Morning

The photograph of the Lopez-Santini girls was blurred and a year out of date: cut out and enlarged from a school sports group.

But even reproduced on newsprint, the faces were recognizable.

MINISTER'S DAUGHTERS MISSING

Fears for the safety of Teresa and Gloria Lopez-Santini were being voiced yesterday. Teachers at San Andres School in the fashionable Olivos district said the girls, aged 12 and 10, had not attended classes this week. They were last seen at a hockey match on Saturday.

Their father, the Minister for the Economy, is at present abroad. Calls to the family apartment near Palermo Park are being intercepted by the exchange. The Minister is married to the former Miss Mercedes Braun-Menendez.

This front-page story of Thursday June 13th continued for several more paragraphs. Miguel spread the newspaper out on the kitchen-table of the new hide-out apartment in Quilmes, near the Boca railway. His leg hurt like hell. The bullet had passed right through his thigh, missing bone but tearing muscle. He leant on the table for support and stared both at the story about the girls and the report in the adjoining column, while Maria read over his shoulder.

WAS GANGLAND KILLING KIDNAP ATTEMPT?

Police called to an apartment block in the Flores district found three men shot to death in a basement garage. Two have been identified as minor drug-traffickers. The third carried a Student Association card. His name is being withheld until relatives are traced. Mystery surrounds the affair, but sources suggest a kidnap plot aimed at acquaintances of the student in the building.

'Tomas sold us out,' Maria said. 'And the police do know.'

'Or the boy.'

'You want to ask Tomas?' she laughed harshly. 'So he can tell the *traficantes*? We should release the girls and quit. Go to Europe.'

'Fine for you.' He twisted round to argue. 'You have money.' Suddenly he felt dizzy and was forced to sit down on the simple wooden chair. 'What did we do this for?'

'The Party.' She was a lot tougher-minded than him. 'But the Party's betrayed us. We should let the girls go.'

'And say goodbye to a million dollars?'

'Your friends will be back on Monday. What then?' This was Miguel's private bolt-hole they had come to, an apartment to which he had a key for emergencies. But the owners would recognize the girls from the newspapers. 'If the story's correct, we can't phone the Lopez-Santinis.'

Miguel thought. Something in the paper had given him an idea.

'We can phone the school from a call-box,' he said. 'Pass a message. Tell the Lopez-Santinis to unbug their line.'

'And then?'

'We'll settle for half a million by Sunday.' He shifted painfully on the chair. 'We'd better work out a plan.'

CHAPTER SIX

Hauppage, Long Island. 8.30 am, Thursday June 13th

'There must be some guy can give a straight answer!' Paul Gianni, talking to himself, slammed down the phone after yet another fruitless conversation. He wasn't only exasperated. He was becoming worried with the insidious, gut-creeping fear which eats into a man who finds himself grappling with forces he cannot understand, let alone control.

He had begun self-confidently enough on Wednesday morning, addressing Schuster of the Bartrum Bank with contemptuous forcefulness: 'Tell me who the man is at Plaza and I'll speak with him.' After demanding to know from several officers there why the company's $700,000 Brazilian letter of credit was not being honoured, he had reluctantly been given the name of Plaza's correspondent in Rio de Janeiro. The correspondent made excuses. By mid-afternoon, which was the close of work in Rio due to the time difference, he had progressed as far as the name of an official in the External Debt Department of the Banco do Brasil. The official was in a meeting and would not be available until tomorrow.

To make it worse, in the evening he and his energetic, personable, blonde wife Trudy had been hosting a dinner at the country club for the company's principal backers. It was to celebrate completion on time of the largest order ACE Techtronics had ever won: the Brazilian order.

'Another success like this,' he had told her savagely, as she smoothed down his tuxedo before they left their colonial-style home in Westhampton, 'and we'll be on the breadline.'

'No we won't, darling,' she joked, trying to cheer him up, 'we have three hundred thousand tucked away in Treasury bonds. Remember?'

The celebration had gone smoothly enough. No one doubted that in financing Gianni they had backed a winner. For a few hours he had forgotten about Brazil.

However, he had been up earlier than usual on Thursday morning, acutely aware that if he achieved nothing today he could be laying off staff tomorrow. This was no kind of a week for celebrations.

Cruising out along the Old Riverhead Road to join Route 27, he had felt momentarily embarrassed by his new, bright red, Mercedes roadster. It was fine for him to indulge himself in fancy foreign cars. Aside from their shareholding in ACE, he and Trudy owned their house outright and had sizeable savings. Men like Mike Donovan, his senior supervisor, had savings, sure, but they were normally up to their necks in hire-purchase agreements as well. The feeling had still been with him half an hour later when he eased off the Long Island Expressway towards Marcus Boulevard on the outskirts of Hauppage, where the company was located.

Gianni deliberately had his office looking inward on the assembly lines. He liked to see what was going on and he liked the operatives to know he was there, not practising golf-shots on the carpet while they laboured. The first of them were trickling in as he settled to his desk. Many were women, whose nimble fingers were suited to such of the intricate work as was not automated. They worked seated, each adding his or her components to the transceivers and other electronic equipment slowly proceeding past them. The conditions of light and cleanliness were a model for workplaces anywhere.

As he dialled the first of the damn Brazilian calls – his secretary wasn't in yet – he noticed Donovan, clad in a white coat like the other supervisors, answering questions below. That man, in his late forties now and with a lifetime's engineering experience, was the kind who had enabled ACE Techtronics to establish a reputation for technology that didn't fail and to land important defence contracts. It was one thing producing home computers for discount sales to kids; it was something else supplying airforces and airlines, where if the systems blew, people got killed. Shit, he muttered to himself, as he listened for the connection, we didn't build this outfit to see it abandoned through some other jerk's incompetence.

A woman operator answered at the other end. The official he asked for was not available.

That was when he slammed down the phone, feeling he might as well be chasing a will-o'-the-wisp on Halloween. No one would admit responsibility. Every official had a buck-passing let-out. Except for himself. He was going to get some straight answers if it was the last thing he did.

Five calls to Rio de Janeiro, and several hours later, Gianni had answers: and they were unnerving ones. The Brazilian bank official was more honest than anyone else had been.

'Señor, I regret that while certain bank negotiations are in progress all foreign-exchange payment is temporary suspended.'

'How long is "temporary"?'

'Next week we hope these problems can be settled.'

'Problems!' Gianni exploded. 'You think you have problems? We need paychecks for four hundred staff tomorrow. We delivered the goods three months ago, goddam it.'

'Sir. I like to tell you something person to person. Not as an official. Do you wish to hear?'

'Yeah, okay.' There was nothing to lose.

'Last night we have riots. The store my wife shops at is looted and burned. This morning she does not dare to go out. The army is in the streets. I myself walk seven kilometres to work. I show my identity card twenty-three times. Do you have this kinds of problems?'

'I guess not.' Gianni was taken aback at the man's frankness. 'Is that what's going on? I never knew.' Or had he seen it in the paper and taken no serious notice?

'For three days, señor. The President is telling the people to be calm. How can they when the prices go up every day?'

'I'm sorry.'

'Until this situation stabilizes we can do nothing.'

'When might you release our $700,000?'

'There are many others, many millions of dollars. We ask short-term creditors to be patient. We do not wish to lose friends. You will all be paid. May I suggest, señor, you keep in touch with the bank who make this exchange bill for you.'

This time Gianni did not crash the receiver on to its rest. He replaced it slowly and thoughtfully. In a few minutes of long-distance conversation he'd received his first meaningful lesson in foreign affairs. The people down there in Brazil were no different to anyone else. Except their difficulties sounded worse. If you talked to them, they'd tell you. His mistake had been to assume that the smooth-suited representatives who'd placed the electronics order came from a normal, stable industrial country. Furthermore, all that unending stuff in the financial pages about Latin American debt wasn't only for bankers, it was for real. If Bartrum Bank's officers had been any damn good at all, they would have warned him. He picked up the phone again to make a formal appointment with Ray Roth in Southampton. Roth had it coming to him: and then some.

Buenos Aires. 11 am

'I'll murder the stupid bitch! How could she do this to us!' Mercedes was determined to divert her husband's wrath on to someone else. 'Gabriella! Whom I trusted!'

'Either she's gossiped or the police have planted the story.'

Lopez-Santini himself sat by the window drinking fresh coffee, for which he was grateful, and enduring his wife's self-justifications, for which he was not. The flight via Madrid had been delayed, he was exhausted, and he had been greeted by the devastating newspaper headlines.

'I told you secrecy was essential,' he said.

'And where were you? Abroad as usual! What do you think I am? An automaton? A woman of stone?' She paused just long enough for him to reflect that he should never have married an heiress. Never. No matter how great the attraction for an underpaid academic. 'I'll kill that bitch. How dare she speak about the bad blood of the Lopez-Santinis. What has her husband ever achieved?'

'Mediocrity has its compensations.' He could imagine Gabriella's comments on his ancestry. 'At least no one will kidnap *their* children.'

'For once you are right. *She* isn't suffering!' Mercedes seized the obvious way out of this impasse. 'Oh my babies! Where are they?'

Lopez-Santini choked back a retort. Enough was enough. He wanted his daughters back as desperately as she did and he must forgive her for being overwrought. Thank God she had not appreciated the significance of the story in the adjoining column of the newspaper. It was an old journalistic trick to print two reports next to each other, if the editor did not dare link them directly. But why should the kidnappers be fighting off the *traficantes*? It was inexplicable and frightening.

He was enjoying a much-needed bath, washing away the clinging sweaty grime of two successive nights' travelling, when he heard the phone ringing. Seconds later, Mercedes dashed in.

'Quick. It's the school.'

He lifted the intrument off the tiled wall, the warmth of the water still soaking into his bones, his whole body still relaxing. Until the headmistress explained in her precise and carefully modulated voice.

'Señor Santini? A woman has just spoken to me from a call-box. She claimed that your daughters were with her. Naturally, I demanded proof. She put Teresa on the line. Yes, Your Excellency. It was Teresa, quite unmistakably. She said they are both well and are sorry to be missing school.'

'Is that all?' He could scarcely believe it.

'The little girl sounded, you must forgive the absurdity, as if she had confidence, as if she were being protected.'

'And the woman?'

'Educated.' The headmistress had tried to achieve a mental picture as soon as she appreciated what the call was about. 'In her late twenties or early thirties, I should say. Very articulate. Very determined. Refused to give a name, of course. She said that if you remove the 'interference' she will telephone your apartment. But you are not to inform the police. About this she made a most curious remark: "I've saved the girls once already. Tell Lopez-Santini nobody can be trusted."'

'Thank you, señora. I am most grateful.' How ridiculous she would think it if she could see him in the bath, the water lapping his toes. He hoisted himself more upright. 'One point, señora. You must keep this completely to yourself.'

'I shall, and believe me, Excellency, I shall also be interviewing every member of the staff to trace this morning's disgraceful newspaper report.'

'I hope you will emphasize that you have spoken to me and that there is no truth in it. The girls have merely caught an infection.'

Which was true, in a sense, he reflected as he towelled himself dry. They were victims of an infected society and one thing was evident: whoever held them now was also protecting them against a potentially worse enemy. Therefore they might be in a hurry, might settle quickly. There were grounds for hope. He called Comisario Alfaro and ordered the phone intercept removed. Now all he could do was stay in and wait.

It was not for a further half hour that he realized he had done precisely what the kidnappers had forbidden. He had effectively 'informed the police'.

*

In Zurich, Stuart Pendler had gone to a local newspaper office before transmitting his story to Paris. As routine, before leaving, he read through the incoming agency telexes again. A new item had appeared, datelined Buenos Aires: 'FEARS EXPRESSED FOR MINISTER'S CHILDREN'.

What followed was an extremely brief resumé of that morning's local newspaper report. The agency man had omitted the adjoining account of the shooting, although he had appreciated its positioning. He had no wish to foul his relations with the authorities by making the connection before they announced it.

Even so, Pendler felt justified in telephoning the *Herald Tribune*'s editor.

'That copy you just filed,' Harry Grant remarked candidly, 'is unlikely to set the world on fire. Osborn is somebody. Who ever heard of Warburton?'

'He's just about admitted there's a debt crisis blowing up and I know Lopez-Santini's involved. So the disappearance of those kids must be relevant.'

'The rumoured disappearance. Our readers need facts, Stu, not rumours.' He tipped his chair back, running his fingers through his hair and thinking. 'I agree there have been riots in Brazil. We also have word from New York that Brazil is delaying some foreign-exchange payments.'

'What have I been saying? It's all part of the same thing.'

'Maybe.'

Sitting there in his grey-walled office in Neuilly, constantly passing judgement on what was significant in world affairs and what was not, Grant sometimes felt cut off. He would like to consult on this one before committing himself. His financial correspondent could be right.

'Okay, Stuart,' he relented, 'if you think it's all the same big story, you prove it. We're short of copy for Saturday/Sunday. I'll hold over what you just sent in and you can wrap it all up for tomorrow night. But I'm telling you, if there are no demonstrable connections between these events, I'll be holding it over again until there are.'

Pendler was too wise to argue. As it used to say at the foot of old-fashioned letter columns, 'The Editor's decision is final.' He couldn't hang around here, either. With only twenty-six hours in hand, he needed to be back in London. He wished the hell he was going with Maggie to Columbus Cay.

'Let's get this straight Sheldon. You still work for us, right? How about being available when I need you?'

Ray Roth was blustering because he was worried. In less than an hour, Gianni would be arriving from Hauppage, spitting fire, and he had no idea what to say to him. The only person who might help was Harrison. Because Harrison was an employee, Roth shouted at him down the phone as though he'd been playing hookey.

'We've been a little busy here, Ray.' Harrison was not cowed. 'Jim Warburton's in Switzerland and Mr Osborn's had me act as rapporteur to one of the committees.' To be exact he had been with the rescheduling group and was astonished to realize that the lead bankers were willing to go some way towards a compromise. Almost anything was preferable to their loans becoming non-performing. However, he had no authority to discuss that with Roth. 'How can I help?' he asked.

'I want to know if those Brazilians are going to pay, Sheldon.' Sweat dampened his shirt-collar at the mere thought that they might not. 'I have to know.' He explained Gianni's problem with the bill of exchange.

'I'm not the expert, Ray, I'm the dogsbody.'

'Even the fly on the wall at those meetings must get to learn something. You think Brazil will release this foreign exchange?'

The question was both embarrassing and dangerous. Osborn and Warburton were successful partly because they avoided giving outright opinions. Instead, they guided their colleagues towards a consensus, always listening a great deal more than they spoke.

'Well,' Harrison said diplomatically, 'there's a school of thought that whatever else these countries do they'll honour short-term trade debts. They have to, if they want to go on importing and exporting. They can't afford to antagonize the big multinationals.' This was a weak point in the banks' position which Warburton had intended mentioning publicly in Zurich, so he didn't feel he was shooting his mouth off.

'You mean Brazil will release Gianni's money?'

'Most likely. They can hardly sell airplanes without radios or electronics.'

'You reckon we could advance Gianni funds against that bill of exchange?'

Harrison all but exploded. 'Listen, Ray, I'm a shareholder in Bartrum Bank just as you are and I wouldn't like to think we were making any more large loans without security.'

'There's no way we would,' Roth retreated hastily, feeling the droplets of sweat inch slimily down his back.

'I'm glad,' Harrison said shortly. He felt sorry for Gianni, but here they were back at the central idiocy of the whole problem. No one in their right mind would loan money against a Brazilian bill at this moment, yet Roth would clearly have liked to. It wasn't hard to guess that three months back he had told Gianni how safe Brazil was, the same way Plaza had earlier reassured him, even though the circumstances were totally different.

'Thanks, Sheldon,' Roth said weakly. 'Thanks for your advice. Keep in touch, huh?'

For some minutes after replacing the phone, he sat in lonely thought. Sheldon was right. No matter how many fancy titles were attached to lending, there were only two kinds of loan: secured and unsecured. Security involved the bank having a legal lien over some asset which it could sell, if the worst happened. What could he demand that Gianni pledge? His house? Stocks or bonds? How would Bartrum's other board members react? One was in real estate, another a car-dealer, a third's full-time occupation was insurance. They were all local businessmen with far-reaching local contacts. Even though the bank was legally under no obligation with that damned bill, the others might by instinct side with Gianni. So what the hell was he to say when the man arrived?

Buenos Aires. 1.30 pm

By the early afternoon, Mercedes Lopez-Santini was literally prostrate with anxiety, propped up with cushions on a French Empire-style *chaise-longue*, while the maid brought cups of a mildly sedative drink. They had been waiting all morning for a call which never came. Even the Minister himself was finding it impossible to concentrate.

On the desk in his study lay the notes of his meetings with Osborn and Seiler. He needed to decide what mix of eventual debt repayment and of 'nominal' interest might in practice satisfy the Columbus Group without ruining the Western banks involved. From the banks' point of view, the key would be having time to build up reserves against the debt . . . but, but, but.

The photographs of his daughters, in polished-brass frames, stared at him from a side-table. Every time he looked round, they seemed to catch his eye, reproaching him. He thrust his paperwork aside.

When the door-buzzer sounded, he jumped up as agitatedly as if a bomb had gone off.

The visitor was Ana, through whom one message had already been passed. She entered nervously, pulling at her shawl, as Mercedes appeared from the living-room, anxious to know what was going on.

'I found this when I got home, Excellency.' She handed over a small envelope. 'It had been pushed under our door.'

'What does it say?' Mercedes half-screamed. 'Holy Mother of God, open it!'

Lopez-Santini, however, wanted to avoid destroying finger-prints and was holding the envelope in his handkerchief whilst looking around for a knife. When he finally slit the flap, what he found inside was a crude sketch-map of the Rose Garden in Palermo Park with one place ringed in red crayon. Written at the side were the words: 'Go there when the line is cut off after you answer the telephone.'

'Ana,' he turned on the girl, 'have you spoken to anyone about our daughters?'

'No, señor. I swear not.'

'To the police?' She had, of course, been questioned immediately after Ruiz was murdered. 'Have they come to you again?'

'I told them nothing, I swear.'

So Alfaro's men were still nosing about. He warned Ana to speak to no one about this new message and sent her home.

'What is that?' Mercedes tried to take the map from him. 'I don't understand.'

'It shows where we leave the ransom or else where they place something for us. We have to wait, my dearest. We can only wait.'

Twenty minutes later the phone rang at last and he almost ran to pick it up. He could tell from the noises that the caller was in a public booth.

'You have received the message?' a woman's voice demanded, and Lopez-Santini knew that this must be the kidnapper who had spoken to the school.

'A few minutes ago.'

'You have the money?'

He steeled himself for an argument that would be one thousand times more difficult with his wife listening.

'I can give a draft drawn on a Swiss bank to pay the bearer a quarter of a million dollars. It was impossible to obtain used American notes in such quantity.'

There was a momentary pause while this was digested.

'Half a million.'

'A quarter is all the bank will provide.'

'You're a rich man, you bastard.' She spoke very quietly. 'Already we have reduced the amount.'

He wondered why she did not make a more explicit threat, then realized that if she was in a call-box there could be other people standing near. In Buenos Aires the booths were not fully enclosed. Furthermore, they worked with a metal token called a *costel* which had to be purchased at the nearest newspaper *kiosko*. With inflation changing the value of money almost daily, coin-operated phones were impractical. This phone must be very close to the *kiosko*.

'Say we will give more later,' Mercedes hissed in his ear. 'Keep her talking.'

He shook his head against this dangerously open-ended approach, while continuing to speak.

'You gave us too little time,' he insisted with all the finality he could muster. 'However, I can give a guarantee from the bank in addition to the draft.'

'We'll think about it,' the woman announced curtly. 'If we agree, then we'll give the signal. Come straight there. Make sure you are not followed.'

'Today?' he asked.

'When we decide.' A pause. 'I think your phone is still tapped. If you don't get the goods safely it will be your own fault. Come completely alone.'

The *kiosko* where Maria had bought the *costel* was hardly more than a hole in the wall with a counter and racks around the inside holding cigarettes, chocolate and newspapers. As she walked past, the woman's gaze followed her. They saw too much, those *kiosko*-owners. Maria quickened her pace towards the apartment, reinforced in her instinct to settle with Lopez-Santini as soon as possible. The obstacle was going to be Miguel.

While she had looked after the girls, heating up *empanadas* from a local grocery for a midday meal – and having to admit the meat in the pies was tasteless – Miguel had been out laying the ransom trail. A note taped to the underside of a bench in the Rose Garden was only the start. Lopez-Santini would then have to follow a whole series of instructions before finding his daughters, giving Miguel and her time to escape. But the bank draft was a lousy idea. With a proper organization they'd have kept the girls until Lopez-Santini had obtained cash. That could not be done without other collaborators. They were under pressure and the only alternative was for her or Miguel to take the enormous risk of staying on with the children until the draft had been cashed.

'A call-box in Quilmes? *Gracias*.' The fat police sergeant monitoring the phone-tap wrote the street location on a slip of paper, printing it carefully in capitals, then took it upstairs to his superior.

The lieutenant added this address to the transcript he had received seconds earlier and prepared to present himself to the Comisario.

'The problem, sir,' he explained after saluting briskly, 'is that we do not know the rendezvous or the recognition signal.'

Alfaro lounged in his wide chair, his silver-braided tunic unbuttoned, and read the transcript. He was not as inexperienced at this game as his detractors claimed. He could sense unusual urgency in the woman's words. Why was she willing to lower the price so dramatically?

'They're on the run,' he observed. 'Something's gone wrong. It must have been they who massacred those *traficantes*. What do you suggest?'

'All we can do is keep surveillance on the Minister.'

'And scare the kidnappers away from the drop? They'd go straight back and kill those girls. Any shadowing must be exceptionally discreet. I shall direct it myself. If we cannot trace the woman in Quilmes in the next few hours we may not be able to make any arrest until after the ransom is paid. Report to me the instant anyone speaks on the Minister's phone.'

Alfaro dismissed the lieutenant, telephoned his wife to say he would be home late, if at all, and then fell to considering whether to approach Lopez-Santini direct. One thing was clear: if his department contributed to the Minister's children dying, they would all be in trouble.

Downstairs, the lieutenant told his colleagues he was going out for cigarettes. He went to a bar two streets away and as he paid spoke to the barman in an undertone.

'Tell Tomas they're in Quilmes and it's soon.'

*

Journalistic scoops are often dictated by luck. Had Stuart Pendler been around the Dolder Grand Hotel in the early evening of June 13th, instead of at lunchtime, he would have made a quantum leap towards confirming his theory. Even the *Trib*'s editor would have accepted that. But today luck was against him.

The event Pendler missed was the arrival of a thin, beaky-nosed man, wearing an indifferently tailored dark suit, who asked at the reception for Herr Warburton. The man was Jozef Kryst. Six days ago he had been consuming crawfish at a restaurant in Marsh Harbour; today he had flown in from Warsaw for 'an informal discussion'. He was enjoying more foreign travel in a week than he normally secured in a year, if one excluded trips to other Soviet Bloc countries. Despite his bleak appearance, he was in good humour.

'Minister Kaminski regrets that he could not come in person,' he explained after being welcomed into the elegant suite. 'He hopes you will shortly visit our country.'

'The Minister has a great deal on his mind, I know.' Warburton inclined his head gracefully. That burden included $30 billion of still-growing debt. Fortunately, over half of it was to other Western governments, though British banks had claim to a tenth, which was troubling enough. 'I am sure you will convey our proposals to him as clearly as if he had heard them himself.'

Over drinks in Warburton's suite – he was not risking their being seen publicly together – the probing evolved slowly into a measure of agreement. The key factor was Poland's economic subservience to the Soviet Union, coupled awkwardly to a Catholic and Western cultural heritage. Few Poles wished to tighten the bonds with Russia.

'Trade between your country and the rest of Europe ought not to be prejudiced,' Warburton observed, tactfully acknowledging Poland's affinity with the West. 'If anything, we must make it easier for you to earn foreign exchange.'

'Our debt-service ratio has been 125 per cent. That cannot be maintained.'

'I understand.' To pay out all one's foreign-exchange earnings plus 25 per cent on interest charges would be an impossible equation. It meant borrowing to import at all – other than from the Soviet Union – at a penal exchange rate. The austerity imposed on ordinary citizens had been severe. Anything worse might spark riots and even revolution, which the Soviet Army would instantly put down. No one, except perhaps the Politburo in Moscow, desired such an outcome. Certainly the Poles did not.

'You should not judge us by our action against Solidarity,' Kryst said. 'We are on a tight-rope all the time. That is the price for giving our citizens some future economic hope.'

'So what do you need?'

'At least $800 million of new lending. Austria and the German Federal Republic will make contributions. Unhappily not enough.'

'They would help even less if there were a default,' Warburton reminded him.

'Also in two or three years substantial repayments are due.'

'Suppose we could reschedule to the end of the century?'

'You will give this to all countries?' Kryst was incredulous.

'Only in special cases. We might accept lower rates of interest so that your trade can be maintained.'

At this point the Pole began making notes instead of attempting to memorize points, and Warburton guessed he was hooked. 'You are authorized to make this offer?' Kryst asked suspiciously.

'Our committee is in session in New York at this moment. Agreement could be formalized at the weekend.' Warburton decided to risk an indiscretion. 'Would this relieve the political pressures on your government?'

Kryst's eyes flickered. He sipped a little mineral water. Warburton was asking, in effect, if the Russians wanted Poland to default. He knew they did. Though whether to promote a Western banking crisis, or for the less far-reaching purpose of strengthening economic control over his country, he could not be sure.

'It would relieve certain pressures,' he agreed cautiously. He hoped Warburton would not quote the remark and found himself fearing he had said too much. 'In my personal estimation it might relieve those pressures.'

When the Pole had left, Warburton rang Osborn in New York.

'I think they'll take the bait, if we can come up with a significant long-term restructuring.'

'Not interest-forgiveness?'

'Not unless the committee suggests that.' Forgiveness – that is to say, letting debtors pay an artificially low interest rate – might be something bankers regularly offered their own staffs for house purchases. But the idea of doing it on an international scale, whilst still paying their depositors' market rates, made their blood freeze.

'Either way,' Warburton concluded briskly, 'we should put pressure on our central banks to offer immediate talks. My guess is that the Russians are leaning heavily in Kaminski and he'd be happy to get off the perch. This is the time to rescue him.'

'You have a point there, Jim,' Osborn said. 'This sounds like the best news we've had all week.'

Lagos. Early evening

Walking out of air-conditioning into Lagos' humid heat felt at first as if someone had lit a fire under his backside. Len Slater had made the transition more often during the past twelve hours than he could recall. Following advice, he had hired a car and driver for the entire day – there was no certainty of finding taxis – and had called on the appropriate government departments without appointment. He had sat for hours on a bench in the Finance Ministry, along with some remarkably good-humoured Africans and one remarkably unamused German, until it emerged that the official through whom they were all required to channel their requests was absent.

'Back tomorrow. Come again.' A beaming, broad-hipped African secretary in a vivid print dress had told them. 'Today I think he may be stuck in traffic.' She roared with laughter. 'Tomorrow he is coming.'

Now Slater stood shirtless at the window of his hotel room, gazing at the ships in the harbour, and pondering if he could afford a beer from the mini-bar.

Unbelievably, he had already spent over £100. He decided to disregard the price-list. He sat down, glass in hand, feeling suddenly chilled by the air-conditioning and wondering what to do if the official was still not there tomorrow. Should he remain over the weekend? Then he remembered the name given him by the man on the plane.

'He'll cost you,' the man had remarked vulgarly, 'but he is in with the new regime.'

Half an hour later, after a prolonged battle with the telephone-dialling system, Slater was speaking to an Oxford-accented lawyer named Ayokolo who expressed delight at being able to assist.

'A friend of his is a friend of mine. With goodwill all things are possible.'

When Slater finally fell asleep on the bouncy foam mattress, he was still wondering how much goodwill he would be able to afford.

Few people visited the Rose Garden of Palermo Park in winter, and this afternoon it was deserted. Lopez-Santini set off there immediately after the phone-call signal. This had come very soon after the previous call and he interpreted it as meaning the kidnappers were under pressure. He left his car on a side-road near the Garden and walked at a quick pace, looking over his shoulder occasionally to see if he was being trailed. He did not appear to be.

He continued until he found the spot marked on the diagram, then paused in confusion. He was standing at the intersection of two paths between the rose-beds. The plants had been pruned back, The earth around was bare. Nothing lay on the paths. He seated himself on a bench, and puzzled until he realized that the bench itself must conceal the message. Sitting upright, trying not to make his search obvious, he felt underneath the slats. His fingers found paper. Abandoning caution, he bent over and detached an envelope taped to the wood. Inside it were orders.

'Go to the Bar Parador, in Quilmes. In the men's lavatory there is a letter behind the cistern. Leave your packet in its place. Go there immediately.'

Lopez-Santini folded the piece of paper carefully and put it in his wallet. Then he walked to his car, reprimanding himself for ever supposing that this kind of exchange would be simple.

No one watched him drive away, because there was no one there to watch. This had been designed to prepare him for a complicated and time-wasting treasure hunt. Besides, Miguel could not be in two places at once, and Miguel was at the Bar Parador, establishing his surveillance for the drop.

'You're a fool, an idiot.' Comisario Alfaro glared across his wide desk at the lieutenant, suspicions forming in his mind as he castigated the man for belated reporting. 'You think Lopez-Santini has received no recognition signal when his phone goes dead the moment he answers it? Can you not imagine? He has been waiting all day, his wife is probably in tears if she's indulging herself as usual. He is worried, frightened, completely on edge and you tell me that when a call is cut off he doesn't try to re-establish contact?'

The lieutenant muttered apologies, hoping he had given Tomas enough time.

Alfaro was already dialling the Lopez-Santinis' number. He spoke for some minutes to Mercedes, then shouted angrily at his subordinate.

'We've missed him, damn you.' No matter that a few hours ago he had been talking about extreme discretion. He had to act. 'I'm going to talk to that *kiosko*-owner myself.' He began stripping off his coat. He wasn't doing this in uniform.

Miguel had chosen a small table in one corner of the Bar Parador and was on his third beer. He had been there ahead of time because they had none to spare. From where he sat he could watch both the main entrance and the door at the back leading to the toilets. He sheltered behind a copy of *La Nacion*, which someone had left, reading desultorily with one eye open for his victim's arrival.

The newspaper reported the police as having new clues in the bizarre Flores shoot-out case. The dead student was believed to have been tricked into acting as a courier. Examination of the mini-van had revealed traces of coca paste – unrefined cocaine – and the vehicle itself had originally been registered in Tucuman, up on the far side of the Pampa, near the borders of Chile and Bolivia.

It occurred to Miguel that he and Maria might have been set up by Tomas from the start. He was speculating on reasons for Tomas double-crossing other members of the Party when Lopez-Santini entered. Miguel knew him both from studying photographs and from his behaviour. The Minister's impatience was like an uneasy presence about him, made visible in the way he perched on his chair. Within moments of being served he disappeared to the toilets.

If Lopez-Santini did as instructed, he would now drive to another bar, in another district, where another envelope had been concealed. And so on. Eventually this convoluted trail would lead to a letter from one of his daughters. By then Maria would be out of the country with the bank draft. The letter would include an unpleasant surprise. Miguel had no sympathy for the Minister. If he couldn't lay his hands on dollar bills who could?

When Lopez-Santini reappeared, he clattered loose change on to the table by his almost untouched drink and hurried out. He did not even look around. Perhaps he was afraid to.

So far so good. Miguel waited a few minutes, then went to the toilet and stood on the seat. A long brown envelope had been thrust behind the old-fashioned cistern mounted high on a graffiti-decorated wall. He drew it out, climbed down, dusted it off and hastily slit it open. Inside were three documents: a letter of authority; a letter of guarantee from the Swiss bank; and the bank draft itself. He slipped them into his pocket, flushed the lavatory, and left.

Outside the bar he glanced briefly around, then began an indirect walk back to the apartment, occasionally crossing the street and glancing sideways at reflections in shop windows to check that no one was tailing him. He felt cautiously exultant as he limped along. All they had to do now was lock up the girls and get Maria to the airport. He would fly out tomorrow. It did not improve his temper that this delay was due to his own lack of foresight in failing to obtain an American visa.

Southampton, Long Island. *12.30 pm*

'I'm real sorry about this, Paul.' To Roth's relief, his customer's arrival had been delayed, enabling him to call together enough members of the bank's six-man lending committee to establish a quorum. 'I called an emergency meeting and we don't feel we should advance this much without security. To anyone.'

'Never?' During the drive from Hauppage, Gianni had got one thing clear in his mind: his was a special case.

'We have to observe banking principles. Commercial lending officers are allowed a line of credit up to a certain limit. In our case its $500,000. Any loan above that must be approved by the lending committee, all full-time bank officers, all experienced men.' This was Roth's let-out and he was hanging on to it like a shipwrecked sailor to a raft. 'You must know its normal practice to ask for collateral.'

'What's gotten into you, Roth?' Gianni became acid. 'You lent to Brazil and Mexico. What's different?'

'They're governments.'

'Sure. And our contract's with a Brazilian government company. Are you telling me you won't lend against a bill of exchange they've accepted?'

Roth did his utmost to appear pained, regretful and adamant, all at once.

'I'm sorry,' he said, adding as a sweetener. 'Our latest information is this hang-up will only be temporary.'

But Gianni wasn't letting go. 'How come your guys didn't tell me a letter of credit was safer? You told me a bill of exchange would be fine. Aren't you the experts?'

Evidently Gianni had been boning up on the subject. He was correct, of course. The truth was, no senior Bartrum officer would have dared counsel openly against trusting a country to which the bank had committed such a high proportion of its capital. That would be to invite awkward questions from stockholders. So when Gianni had enquired about a bill of exchange, the desk officer who referred it to Schuster had been told to go ahead. Equally, if Gianni had asked for the safer method of a letter of credit, they would have fixed one. Schuster's aim had been to avoid making waves, especially public ones. Well, Roth thought, it was tough luck for the desk officer, but he was young.

'In confidence,' Roth splayed his fingers on his desk before making the portentous announcement, 'although the bank accepts no liability, the officer concerned is being assigned to other duties.'

'While I lay off my workforce, huh?'

'How much do you need for next week?' he asked nervously. Gianni certainly was in a fighting mood.

'One hundred and eighty thousand. If I delay a few payments.' Gianni had prepared his figures. 'And don't ask me to mortgage the plant because we haven't paid for it yet.'

'As a concession,' Roth still wanted to head off confrontation if he could, and he already realized it had been a mistake to offer up the desk officer as a sacrifice, 'I'll advance one hundred and eighty if you provide security for one hundred. Only because we've been with you from the start.'

Gianni thought about it, about the three hundred thousand in US Treasury bonds he and his wife held, about taking out a second mortgage on his house.

'I'll have to talk to Trudy,' he said. 'I'll call you in the morning.'

'Believe me,' Roth assured him as he left, 'we are confident this problem is only very short-term.'

Like all those bastards, Gianni reflected furiously as he drove home to Westhampton, they only offer you an umbrella when it isn't raining. Suppose no money came through next week, and the week after? Whether Roth was confident or not, Gianni was going to have to start laying men off tomorrow.

CHAPTER SEVEN

Beni region, Bolivia. 1 pm, Thursday June 13th

Six of the seven men seated round the table in the rambling old Spanish-style ranchhouse, a traditional hacienda, were worth a billion dollars each. At least. Mostly in young middle age, they were far and away the largest foreign-exchange earners in South America. They had flown in for what their host, Amado Canelas, called 'informal deliberations' and lounged around the long dining-table in slacks and open-neck shirts, pulling on Canelas' fine cigars and appreciatively rolling generous measures of his twelve-year-old single-malt whisky around their tongues as they noisily debated the future.

Canelas himself was the elder statesman of their $100 billion business, a hard-eyed and energetic fifty-one-year-old, handsome in the crease-featured, worldly-wise way that gunslingers are portrayed in films. It matched his image for a gold-plated handgun to be holstered on his embossed leather belt. He had convened this meeting and after listening to an hour of argument and table-thumping he abruptly decided enough was enough.

'Quiet!' he roared, and when that had no effect, drew the golden gun and fired a single shot into the ceiling. As wood splintered and a trickle of dust fell, the others at last stopped talking. The Colombian, distinctive in a roll-neck cashmere sweater, began to reach for his own weapon, then saw the smile spread across Canelas' leathery face and relaxed.

'Señores,' Canelas said very quietly, exploiting the silence, 'what we need to know is if Rodrigo here can hold his group together.' He turned to the seventh man, the politician who was a mere millionaire. 'Can you, my friend? Because if you cannot we are wasting our breath.'

The menace implicit in Canelas' soft speech was far more telling than the others' obscenities. Rodrigo Suarez, his paid henchman and acknowledged puppet in the job of Deputy Finance Minister, found himself suddenly nervous.

'I cannot hold the entire Columbus Group, no.'

'We'll have your guts if you don't, you son of a bitch,' the Mexican interrupted. 'What in hell are you paid for?'

'Let him finish,' Canelas said.

Smarting at the insult, Suarez glared at the Mexican, then continued.

'What matters is that our own countries stay firm. We can never control Asians or Africans. We don't need to. South America's crisis is acute enough for us to earn the pay-off we want. All that is necessary is to provide the foreign currency for a few months' international trade. Then our governments will have the courage to default.'

'And screw the filthy Yanquis,' commented the Peruvian.

'I agree,' Canelas said curtly. 'If the debt relationship with the United States is cut, our people will have no cause to accept American orders.'

The others nodded warily. They had come from their home countries – Brazil, Colombia, Ecuador, Mexico and Peru – to call on Canelas in the remote Beni region of Bolivia because they were all in the same game as he was.

Officially Canelas was 'an agro-industrial entrepreneur'. But it was not for the sake of the great herds of Hereford and Santa Gertrudis cattle roaming the 100,000 acres here that the ranch was patrolled by jeeps mounted with machine-guns and anti-tank missiles. The security was for Canelas personally. His was a famous name in Bolivia, largely because of the police's long-sustained failure to arrest him – though they could comfort themselves, as they banked their bribes, with the thought that much of his activity was impeccably law-abiding.

Apart from the ranching, the 'agro' part of Canelas' enterprises centred on the cultivation of a green-leaved shrub which yielded three crops a year on the slopes of the Andes mountains. The selling of those leaves was legal, indeed the infusion made from them and known as 'coca tea' was a favourite Bolivian drink. The President himself was known to enjoy it.

Where the Canelas' operation crossed the borderline of legality was with its 'industrialization': the crude process of turning coca leaves into a dark mush by soaking them in kerosene and water and then having the *campesinos* – the peasants – stamp on that mush to press out coca paste. Various further stages of primitive chemical reaction rendered the paste into cocaine hydrochloride: the lethally toxic cocaine which had to be diluted with sugar, flour or talcum powder before it could be sold on the streets of American and – increasingly – of European cities. The safety was relative. Many of the customers would die of drug addiction in the end.

For many years the US Government had made the acceptance of its Drug Enforcement Agency's activity a condition of economic aid in the Latin American countries where cocaine was produced. Canelas' stroke of genius had been to see that the debt crisis could be used to end this interference.

'If the Yanquis take away the carrot,' Canelas observed, 'why should our governments continue to welcome the stick?'

General laughter greeted this remark, although the others would have expressed themselves with less sophistication. They hadn't made their millions by being polite. But they recognized that Canelas was different. Along with the scars of early brawling, he had acquired a kind of polish.

'This is the moment,' he explained, 'for our central banks to draw courage from an unexpected inflow of dollars.'

'Our goddam government turned down $5 billion from us,' the Colombian cut in aggressively. Overweight and mean-faced, he was feared at home for his brutality, torturing suspected DEA collaborators and openly offering $300,000 for any US narcotics agent, dead or alive. 'Our Yanqui-loving President preferred American aid.'

'Today it's different. We are united.'

'If Rodrigo keeps it that way,' the Mexican said. 'And he'd better.'

'All we need do,' Canelas insisted, 'is bring back some of our profits and make the right ministers aware of our patriotism.' His voice turned contemptuous and hard. 'Holy Mother, are you so frightened of investing in your own countries?' He stared at them all in turn, challenging them to argue. He was not only famous in Bolivia as a drug baron and outlaw: he was also celebrated as a benefactor of hospitals and schools, and a friend of the poor – a kind of Robin Hood.

'It's fine for you,' the Mexican began, then fell silent.

'It will be fine for you all,' Canelas said scornfully, 'if you think with your brains instead of your balls.'

Goaded by him, they eventually reached agreement. They might not be economists but they knew how international trade worked and how savagely the poor of their countries had been hit by austerity programmes. They even greeted his blunt summing up with rowdy applause.

'At first, my friends, our governments thumbing their noses at the Yanquis will be popular. But that won't last if there are no goods in the shops. The crunch will come over short-term trade.'

'So long as they get their money,' Suarez explained, 'the Yanqui trading companies won't care what the hell happens to the banks.'

'In their hearts,' Canelas said, 'all men hate bankers.'

So it was settled. Suarez would assess what inflows of dollar deposits would be needed for each country's central bank to meet its minimum foreign-exchange requirements, and the drug barons would respond by repatriating that amount. Suarez himself would have the delicate task of telling the Latin American ministers in the Columbus Group who their saviours were, and what the price of salvation was. Only the question of solidarity remained.

'The Argentines are the problem,' Suarez admitted. 'But I can keep Lopez-Santini in line.'

However, he had a private word with Canelas before retiring.

'Could you have two girls here for a time?' he asked.

'Girls? What a question!'

'These are schoolchildren.'

'They are?' Canelas considered the implications. 'If they are the ones I think they are, they would be well protected. Send me the co-ordinates of the airstrip. I'll fetch them myself.'

Buenos Aires. 3 pm

'Are we going home, please?'

Teresa asked politely, because she and Gloria had spent all morning locked in a bedroom. But although she still trusted Maria, she sensed something was about to happen. The man, whose name she had never heard, had been out for a long time and when the phone rang Maria had rushed to answer it and sounded pleased and excited at whatever she was told. Almost immediately she had said they were going to eat. So Teresa followed her into the tiny kitchen and asked the question again, in case going home was accidentally forgotten in the rush to do other things.

'You'll be home soon. Now go back into the sitting-room and I'll bring the food.'

Maria herself felt triumphant. The plan was succeeding. She crushed sleeping tablets into the soup, stirred it well, then took the bowls through. The younger girl was already curled up on the couch, her thumb firmly in her mouth. Gloria had been retreating further into herself daily, almost hourly. Now she had to be shaken to make her come to the table and eat. Nothing a shrink couldn't sort out in a few years, Maria thought as she watched, anxious that they shouldn't leave a drop.

'Are you taking us home today?' Teresa asked, putting down the bowl.

'Perhaps.' Maria smiled. Teresa had guts and amazing self-control for her age. She was the sort the world needed, not spoilt brats like her sister. 'In fact, I'd like a photo to remember you by.' She fetched her Polaroid camera and a copy of the morning paper, bought for this purpose. 'Pretend you're a grown-up reading the paper, like Papa.'

'Mummy won't let him read the paper at meals,' Gloria interrupted priggishly. 'She says it's bad manners.'

'Today you can.' Maria choked back a cruder retort. 'Here, hold it up between you.'

She stepped back and took the picture. Seconds later a print curled out. She showed it to them, delighted that the newspaper headline was clearly visible. That would prove the date.

'Can't we have one too?' Teresa asked.

'I suppose so.' Maria thought quickly. All the details of this apartment would be known to the police tomorrow, anyway. Why not? She snapped them again and gave Teresa the print. Then she brought in the leftovers of the *empanadas*, looking at her watch and doing mental arithmetic on the way. The regular Pan Am flight to New York left at six. With only hand-luggage she could probably check in only one hour before rather than the two hours officially demanded for economy-class passengers. But the airport was a long way out. She hoped to God Miguel would be quick. It was bad enough that he'd fouled up his own situation over the visa. If she missed the flight and failed to present the draft in New York first thing tomorrow morning, the whole scheme could still go adrift.

'You're a cop, aren't you, señor. I can tell.'

The wrinkled old woman behind the *kiosko*'s counter peered mistrustfully at Comisario Alfaro, whose charade of gossiping while buying cigarettes had never stood a chance of deceiving her. She was beyond flirting with cops to wheedle her way out of possible trouble, so she took the other course and clawed at them.

Alfaro grunted, weak sunlight picking out the smooth shoulders of his camel-hair coat as he confronted her. He studied the ageing face, wondering what kind of hovel she returned to each night, what stinking worn-out mattress she slept on.

'An hour ago a woman was using that phone. You must have sold her the tokens for the calls.'

'Anyone can buy *costels*. You want them rationed?'

'Who is she? Where's she live?'

'Like I told the other man just now, she must come from those apartments down the street.' The instant concern on his face delighted her. 'What's she done? Won a beauty contest?'

'Other man? Who?'

'The stupid cop who makes threats. I've had enough of you lot for one day, I can tell you . . .' Her words trailed to nothing as she realized she was talking to the air.

Alfaro did not often run at his age. But he ran now, pounding back to his car to summon reinforcements.

Miguel felt he could relax at last. The Lopez-Santini daughters were out for the count: for twenty-four hours minimum he reckoned. Once Maria had phoned from the airport to say she was on the flight he'd taken the precaution she had argued against and injected both girls with a more powerful drug. He was pretty sure that once they'd split the money he and Maria would never meet again, if only for reasons of security. But he had wrapped the two in blankets, as she had wanted. He himself would take the first flight to Rio tomorrow and get an American visa there. There was a risk that Lopez-Santini might dishonour the bank draft, but not much of one in his judgement – not after he'd read the final message in the chain.

The friends who owned the apartment kept a bottle of Mexican tequila in a cupboard. Miguel indulged himself in a small glassful, enjoying the fire in his throat as he swallowed. His burdens were lifted. He deserved a drink. All he had to do was get to the airport himself in the morning. He poured a second shot of the liquor, exultant at success, thinking he would probably never understand Maria. A typical bourgeois intellectual – not the kind he would ever have become acquainted with if Tomas hadn't teamed them up together. She was a mix-up that woman, ruthless one minute, worried silly about the girl Teresa catching cold the next. God damn all intellectuals. He drank some more and was on his third glass when the door-buzzer sounded.

He struggled to his feet. The noise became insistent. Someone must know the apartment was occupied. He limped to the window and pulled back the curtains. Five floors below lay a concrete parking area. Impossible. Take a ground-floor apartment, Tomas had ordered, facing the street so you can see who's there. They had done, originally. The buzzer stopped and he heard a muffled command. He was checking his gun when the first shot shattered the door lock and whined, half-spent, into the plaster of the passage wall.

Westhampton, Long Island. Early Evening

The dry martini and the speed with which Trudy Gianni mixed it were more eloquent than speech. She had caught a glimpse of her husband's face through the kitchen window as he halted the red Mercedes and waited for the automatic garage door to swing up. That one glimpse was enough. By the time he had parked the car and was coming through the elegant white front door she had the martinis shaken and ready on the bar in the living-room. His taut, set expression had signalled unmistakably that the day had been a disaster.

'Been tough, has it?' She kissed him and gave him a quick hug, enough to show she cared and understood without making him feel mothered, then went for the drinks. 'Here, sweetheart. The stuff the doctors don't prescribe. Take slowly and repeat as necessary.'

It was an old joke from the time he'd been in hospital with appendicitis and she'd smuggled in a hip-flask of ready-mixed martini, which the nurse had raised hell about. They were both sure the lift in morale had speeded his recovery. Now she prayed the old joke would work too. He looked badly down.

For what seemed a never-ending minute, Paul Gianni lay back in his easy chair, twirling the glass in his fingers and saying nothing, his chest heaving as if he'd been in a fight. Then he drank the martini in one gulp.

'The Brazilian money didn't come, they don't know when it will and that bastard Roth won't make a loan without collateral. The question is, do we let him have the bonds?'

'We can't.' Grateful that Paul had at least come straight to the point, she perched on the arm of his chair. 'If we ever had to start again, that three hundred thousand is pretty much all we have. It may sound a lot, darling, but it isn't. Not today.'

'Who's talking about starting again?' he stood up abruptly and began pacing the room, his hands in his pockets, shooting remarks at her. 'This is all about keeping going, honey, right? This is about a business I built, about people I employ, about a share-holding worth two million bucks. This isn't my failure. This is some goddam lousy berk in a bank fouling us up. You heard everyone last night? We have a great future. I'm not quitting through a thing like this.'

Trudy sat and listened, sharing his bitterness at the contrast between last night's celebration and today's dilemma, and becoming increasingly afraid that he might have already pledged the bonds.

'I have to do something,' he argued, confirming her fear.

'Paul.' She stood and faced him. 'I want to know. What have you told the bank?'

He stopped his pacing, responding to her directness.

'I said they could have one hundred thousand as security.'

'And how long will that pay the bills? One week, two weeks?' When they were starting up, with four employees in a disused garage, she had known the figures. Now she had lost track. But she did remember one thing vividly from those days of struggle. 'We made an agreement, Paul. Once we had other shareholders we would get out of personal liability. We wouldn't mortgage our souls anymore. If we lose our shares in the company, fine. That's part of the deal. Risking our savings is not.'

'Like I said, I have to do something, Trudy. What kind of guy d'you think I am?' He was getting angry and when they fought, which wasn't often, the violence was liable to become physical. 'You want me to lay off the workforce tomorrow?'

She squared up to him, trying to keep calm, but preferring, if they were going to have a fight, to get it over with.

'Hold a meeting, Paul. Call everyone together and tell them the exact truth.'

'That the bank screwed us?'

'Put it any way you like. Just tell them why there is no cash this week. If they want to keep their jobs, they'll have to wait.'

'Suppose we give them half pay?'

'Paul,' she stood firm, though her voice became higher-pitched. 'If you pledge our savings, you do it without me. Without me and without my consent.'

For a few seconds she thought he was going to hit her. Then his arms dropped limp to his sides and he shook his head to and fro like a vexed bull, frustrated in finding its way out of a pen, and she knew she had won.

'Darling,' she said, moving up and hugging him, 'I love you very much and I'm not letting you ruin our lives, okay? There must be other ways to fix a two-bit bank president like Roth. There have to be.'

After she had shaken him another martini, and one for herself, she began working things out aloud and came to a conclusion.

'Listen, the annual meeting of the Hampton Heritage Society is on Saturday. In Southampton. I have to be there, anyway.'

Paul nodded. Trudy had this thing about conservation and had recently been elected to the Society's committee.

'So?' He didn't see the connection.

'Heritage keeps its account with Bartrum. I'm going to call on Mr Roth and tell him straight. If he gives bad advice to a business he could give bad advice to our committee.'

'He'll just laugh at you. What kind of a threat is that?' The implications began to hit Paul. 'Listen, honey, don't start something rash. That could do us more harm than good.'

'Its on the agenda,' she insisted stubbornly. 'We confirm the accountants, the auditors, the bankers.'

'We don't want to make those kind of waves.'

'Oh yes we do.' If she sounded vindictive it was because, unusually for her, she felt that way. 'You don't know how things work around there, Paul. Southampton people are into every kind of graft, from the parking laws onwards. That's why the local politicians give themselves fancy names like the Probity Party and the Honesty Party. It's because they're all as crooked as corkscrews. I'm going to make waves that'll wash right up to Roth's front porch. Believe me, I am.'

Buenos Aires. Evening

For the first time, Lopez-Santini was actively afraid of the city. When the series of instructions culminated late in the evening at a call-box, he knew instinctively that the trail had now run full circle. If he was walking into a trap himself, this was where it would be sprung.

Going through the pretence of telephoning, while he felt with his fingers behind the box, was a pantomime. He had no token and the nearby *kiosko* was shuttered and padlocked. Then, having located an envelope, he was obliged to move out beneath a streetlamp to be able to read the contents. He felt certain he was being watched, but there was just enough traffic on the street for no single vehicle to be conspicuous. He glanced around nervously as he fumbled with the flap.

Inside was a photograph. He felt a wrench of mental pain as he recognized his children. They were holding a newspaper. Why? What was all this? Then he turned the picture over and saw writing on the back.

'Today they are well. If the draft is cashed we will telephone with the address. If anything goes wrong, they will die.'

Lopez-Santini was the kind who thinks on his feet. As he read the words he realized that the whole chain of messages had been a ruse to keep him busy while the kidnappers fled the country. In terms of finding Teresa and Gloria he was no further forward. He might never be.

He was just deciding he should have foreseen this and asked Alfaro for surveillance when the headlamps of a kerb-crawling car snapped on to main beam, blinding him. He heard running feet and seconds later, as he instinctively turned to escape, a gun was brandished in his face.

'Don't move,' a voice shouted.

He obeyed, raising his hands, expecting at any moment to be pistol-whipped, until he realized that these were not kidnappers. The men around him were uniformed. He was being arrested by the police.

'Keep still.'

Lagos. Morning, Friday June 14th

'I have given your file. If you wait, you will see him.' The cheerful secretary in the Nigerian Finance Ministry, today swathed in another riotously coloured dress, indicated the same bench on which Len Slater had spent so much of the day before.

'I tell you, when I sing, they dance!' The genially rotund lawyer named Ayokolo whispered. 'All it needed was a call from me. Mallam Sule is an old friend.'

During the succeeding twenty minutes Slater noticed that the secretary was unable to make the telephone function, finally slamming down the instrument in disgust. So Ayokolo couldn't have phoned. His suspicions about the degree of the lawyer's influence were further increased when they were shown into a large, air-conditioned office and he found himself shaking hands with an imposing white-gowned African in a small round, embroidered-linen hat. This was Mallam Sule – the 'Mallam' being an honorific meaning 'teacher'.

'There was no need to bring a lawyer,' Sule remarked, in a schoolmasterly reprimand. 'I received your telegram and have the dossier from the Central Bank.'

'Not always easy,' Ayokolo suggested smoothly, seeking to reassert his position.

'What you say is true. The Shagari regime left the bank records in chaos. Those of us who try to remove the corruption face an uphill task.'

'Nothing wrong with our loan, though, eh?' Slater was uneasy at the implications of Sule's bluntness. 'Straightforward two million sterling loan, eh?'

'Two million?' Sule's ebony face creased quizzically as if this visitor was trying to catch him out. 'Not two million. Only one million eight hundred thousand was received by the Central Bank. And not even so much reached the parastatal authority for whom the loan was taken. Although,' he added pedantically, 'that is an internal matter.'

'But that's not right!' Slater felt the sweat rise on his forehead in spite of the chill air-conditioning. 'We loaned you two million. The Bank of Commercial Credit arranged it. Don't tell me you didn't have two because you bloody did. The Minister signed. We made that loan in good faith.' He checked himself, but the damage was done.

'My friend,' a slow anger clouded the Nigerian's dark eyes, 'if less reached our Central Bank then there was not good faith. Not good faith at all. We have been defrauded in London too many times. By banks themselves, by your own bank. Invoices were paid for goods that never existed. Loans ended in Switzerland. What did your British government do?' Sule pounded his desk in a most unscholarly way, his long gown billowing around him. 'Your Bank of England rescued Johnson Matthey. You even arrest the men who were bringing Dikko home for trial. Is this good faith?'

Slater remembered the headlines of the Dikko affair – the corrupt Nigerian ex-Minister who was kidnapped in London and then found drugged in a crate awaiting shipment at Stansted Airport.

'Dikko's nothing to do with this.'

'How do you tell me, when I am the one who knows!'

'We took money out of South Africa. We supported you.'

'This is true?' Sule calmed down instantly and looked enquiringly at the lawyer.

'We have all the papers,' Ayokolo said. 'Please show them.'

Wisely Slater had brought proof of the way Keith Norris had transferred funds for political reasons.

'My friend,' Sule said after studying the documents, 'we like goodwill. I think the government would like to pay this debt. But we must understand something. Ninety-seven per cent of our foreign exchange comes from oil, and the price of oil has crashed. We need the most strict controls on foreign exchange. Who should we pay first? The honest creditors or the ones involved with fraud?'

'But this money belongs to our pensioners.' Again Slater felt he was up against complexities he would never surmount. 'For some it's all they have.'

'We appreciate when an Englishman, one of those who used to be our friends, will help us.' Sule repeated the point. 'Will you help us again, my friend? Can your Union help?'

'How can we?' Shades of the Dikko case flickered in Slater's imagination. AUCAS had members in clerical jobs at airports, docks and freight terminals. 'So long as it's legal,' he muttered.

'Allow me some private words with your lawyer.' Sule waved towards the door. 'Wait outside a little, please.'

Some while later, squashed up alongside Ayokolo in their taxi and sweating profusely, Slater was treated to some obliquely phrased explanations of the arrangement the lawyer had made.

'This is just a question of "one good turn deserves another".' Ayokolo sat twisted round on the seat to face his client, beaming. 'You want funds released from here, our government is trying to obtain release of items purchased in Britain which are held because of what your authorities call "documentation irregularities". The two problems are the same to us. If you can smooth these so-called "irregularities" in London, Mallam Sule will do his best to arrange the documentation here. He is sympathetic because you also are a victim of the corrupt Shagari regime.'

Over lunch in the Federal Palace Hotel, Ayokolo quietly passed across a slip of paper bearing his own Swiss bank account number and a sum in Swiss francs which Slater did not dispute because he had no idea of the exchange rates.

'An advance on my expenses would be in order,' he suggested, adding magnanimously, 'It can wait until you are contacted by our embassy. Then you will know things are moving.'

'This will be legal?'

'My friend, it is nothing more than fair play.'

Slater had no option but to accept this assurance, downing a riotously expensive whisky to seal the bargain. He wasn't sure what attitude Keith would adopt to a blatant trade-off. But then again, why should Keith know?

Much later, with the aid of the hotel cashier, he discovered that Ayokolo's services had already cost £3,000. The businessman on the plane out had been right: this was the white man's grave.

'Herr Seiler.' The manager of the bank's North American branch was on the line from New York and sounding worried. 'You wished me to report if a certain draft was presented here. A woman is downstairs at one of the tellers' windows now, demanding cash. What do you wish me to do?'

'Accept it.'

Seiler hadn't risen to the top of his organization through lack of foresight. He had prepared meticulously for the surfacing of the Lopez-Santini ransom, alerting every branch and representative office worldwide about the existence of this unusual animal: a draft acceptable without identification of the bearer being sought, save through the accompanying letter. He had assumed the kidnappers would not even attempt to cash it at any other bank. He had been right.

'Ask no questions, but say that such a large sum must be brought from the vaults and there will be a slight delay. Keep this line open while that is done.'

'Immediately, Herr Seiler.'

'The video cameras in the banking hall are working?'

'She is being filmed all the time.'

'Good. Then give the orders and hold on.'

Seiler's preparations had included entering Lopez-Santini's various telephone numbers into his personal computerized recall system. Common sense dictated that at this crucial moment in the release negotiation the Minister would be at home, even though it was late morning in the Argentine. He activated the home number. Seconds later Lopez-Santini answered, his tone exhausted and nerve-wracked. He had spent much of the night at the Central Police Station, even after the absurd error of his arrest as a suspect had been resolved.

'Excellency, are your daughters safe?'

'I don't know.'

'Your draft has been presented.' For the sake of security, Seiler did not say where. 'It would now be possible to call the police.'

'No!' The explosive character of the Minister's feelings were evident, despite the faintness of the connection. 'For God's sake, no.' He was terrified that Alfaro's incompetent surveillance could have compromised the deal. 'Give them the money. I will inform you as soon as I have news. Do nothing to alarm the people in question.'

'As you wish, Your Excellency.' Seiler put down that telephone and then gave further orders to New York: 'Make certain every characteristic of this woman is noted, the colour of her clothing, her accent, how she walks, every detail.'

Whilst at this stage he was compelled to respect his client's wishes, the situation would change. The woman, whoever she was, would be walking out with her suitcase of dollar bills into a minefield of problems. For a start she could not deposit over $10,000 in a bank without the Federal authorities being notified: a measure designed precisely to obstruct the laundering of crime syndicates' cash.

Seiler wanted to help his client recover the $250,000 if possible. Yet as he pondered the implications he found himself possessed by an obstinate conviction that there might be more to this kidnapping than a simple ransom. The Argentine Minister must be involved in the current default ultimatum. Although Seiler's own bank had no representative on the rescheduling committee – thankfully his mistrust of Third World politicians had kept his debt exposure to a minimum – he had participated in one loan with Credit Suisse, who were on Osborn's committee and who kept him broadly informed. That had been his reason for attending the Swiss–American Chamber of Commerce lunch: to scent the wind a little further. Now, on a hunch, he rang his colleague at Credit Suisse and asked how far Lopez-Santini had a role in the talks.

'Lopez-Santini? He's acting on behalf of this so-called cartel.'

'*Ach, so!*' A wealth of comprehension illuminated Seiler's surprise. The Argentine had certainly kept that fact quiet. Small wonder he had sounded distraught. He must be under impossible pressure. 'And he takes a hard line?'

'Outwardly. This week he cancelled talks with the IMF. However, from what I learn, he would personally prefer a negotiated solution.'

'Hans, do something for us both. Send a message to New York. Kindly warn either Osborn or Warburton that I shall be telephoning on an urgent matter.'

Seiler sat back in his leather chair and began a debate with himself on the ethics of betraying a client's trust.

Washington DC. 10 am

'I admit this may be more like a blind poker game than a negotiation.' Osborn was keeping his patience. 'We know some of the other side's cards, but we can't see the faces of the men controlling the bids.'

'So do we raise. Or look?'

The man asking was a special adviser to the President named Bud Phillips. He was thirty-eight, sallow, a 1970s whizz-kid economist who through fast political finessing after the last campaign had joined the Office of Management and Budget and gone on from there. He liked to 'crudify' matters. 'Get them in terms the people can understand,' he would say. By 'people' he meant the President. Hence the poker-game comparison. Nor did it faze him that he was 'crudifying' the debt problem to the arbiters of the American financial establishment.

The men round the table in the board-room of the Federal Reserve System's megalithic marble headquarters in Washington included the Chairman of the Federal Reserve's Board of Governors, the Comptroller of the Currency, the Secretary of the Treasury and two members of the National Advisory Council. Although the administration of US financial policy was directed through an interlocking series of formal committees, this meeting was an *ad hoc* one, convened at Bill Osborn's special request. Phillips had not hesitated in letting him know that he was privileged.

'Suppose this default threat's no more than just bluff. How do we raise them? You care to tell us, Mr Osborn?' Phillips didn't mind being rude either. He had the ear of the President and he could pull rank any time he liked.

'Well, sir, I don't believe this is a bluff. Our banking structure being as fragile as it is, I think the ultimatum should be given an immediate political response. There are a number of moves the President could threaten.' Osborn knew they mostly had in-built faults. What he wanted to underline was the seriousness of the situation. 'The President could threaten to suspend aid programmes, cancel arms sales, withdraw military support and block the sale of high-tech equipment. If he wanted to go as far as President Carter did over the Iran hostages, he could freeze assets the defaulting countries hold in the US or in US banks abroad. He could impound ships and aircraft . . .'

'Hey, wait,' Phillips interrupted. 'You want the Russkies moving in to Brazil, Ecuador and Mexico, you want Cuba having a ball at our expense? You cut off aid and arms, who do you think they're going to turn to?'

'Sanctions seldom if ever work,' commented one of the National Advisory Council members, 'and if we sequestrated their assets, they would as sure as hell sequestrate ours.'

'Essentially, Bill, this is a fiscal and monetary problem,' the

Chairman observed. 'As a Governor of the IMF I deplore the threat of default. As Chairman of the Federal Reserve I am as concerned as anyone about exposure of US banks to foreign debt. However, it is not our duty to impose the rule of law on international financial relationships.'

'The administration hustled us into foreign lending originally, and we pretty well kept the world economy afloat after the first oil-price hike.' Osborn was fighting his corner.

'My predecessor encouraged you, Bill, and you weren't unwilling.'

The cautious reaction did not surprise Osborn. Yet the gut problem was political. Whatever the Third World leaders had done with all those hundreds of billions of dollars, the price for servicing their debts now was austerity and poverty at home, and depressing living standards when they'd promised to raise them. That road could lead only to coups and revolutions or default, and what leader would choose revolution? He put the point.

'If you don't raise the threat stakes, then you'll have to raise the aid ones. The Baker plan recognized that aid has to be increased.'

'The President wants to slash aid budgets, not expand them,' Phillips cut in.

'Then you have the other choice . . .'

'You do, not the administration. Speak for yourself.'

'I would rather speak for America.' Osborn's tone went cold enough to have frozen the jug of water on the table. 'I don't believe the mass of Americans want a series of bank failures any more than the banks do. Or lost exports and lost jobs. Bank depositors have votes, Mr Phillips. Many millions of them. I repeat, you have a third choice. If you seriously think this is outside of politics you can plan on bailing out the banks, because if we can't bargain our way out of this, a lot of banks are going to fail.'

'You call that having a sight of their cards?'

'I say that if they show their hand to the world we'll have a banking panic that'll make 1929 look like a minor flurry. May I ask where you keep your own deposits, sir?'

This was naked poker-playing, but Osborn reckoned Phillips liked to get himself into situations where he could slam money down on the table. He was that kind of person. Raising him performed beautifully, yielding an instant dividend.

'Sure, Manufacturers Hanover. Want a better name?'

'May I advise you, sir, that your bank is exposed to 268 per cent of its capital in only six of the twenty-one countries threatening to default. If our negotiation fails it will be immediately insolvent. So will banks in Britain, Europe and Japan. This crisis is worldwide.'

Osborn caught the Chairman's eye, saw the glint of amusement, and allowed himself to play to the gallery for a moment longer.

'Maybe, sir, you ought to go right out and withdraw your savings now. The Moscow Narodny Bank might be a safe place to put them. If it isn't over-exposed in Eastern Europe.'

A ripple of laughter greeted the special adviser's discomfiture – no one liked him – but he recovered fast.

'Okay, so there could be a crisis. Where are the position papers? Where are the threat evaluations?'

'Right here.' Osborn drew a number of folders from his briefcase. 'I thought you might find graphs simpler to understand.'

The irony was lost on Phillips, though it won another appreciative smile from the Chairman.

'As the graphs show, given time, banks can build up reserves against bad debts, and even a low inflation-rate helps. Just like with a mortgage. At the start debt is a high proportion of the house's value. After ten years of inflation at, say, four per cent, the proportion is forty per cent less.'

'So,' Phillips was still out to be unpleasant, 'you reschedule your loans to twenty years, you enlarge your reserves and at the end you write off the debts. What's the problem?'

'The interest. They want it hugely reduced.'

'You could capitalize interest,' the Comptroller of the Currency insisted, 'as you've effectively been doing by loaning new money.'

'We're not taking that road, sir. It worsens the debtors' positons and it doesn't give us either profits or the revenue to pay depositors and shareholders.' Between 1978 and 1983 alone the banks had provided $140 billion of 'new money' and received back $125 billion of it as interest on earlier loans. That road led straight over the cliff.

The Chairman of the Fed had heard enough argument. He was physically a big man and he shifted his bulk upright in a way that clearly indicated he was taking control

'All shareholders take a risk. It's the name of the game. If back in '83 a small bank like Wachovia in North Carolina thought it prudent to create a $22 million special reserve against its Latin American portfolio, why did the big money-center banks scream their heads off when we required them to set capital aside against the worst of their non-performing loans?'

Osborn spread his hands in submission. There was no answer to that and he wished the Fed had been a lot tougher at the time. But the Fed had usually preferred a 'hands off' approach. Not, perhaps, any longer.

'We can require you to cut dividends,' the Chairman continued, 'and make loss provisions and I guess we shall have to do that. You could voluntarily do more. You could restate and reduce your profits for the last several years and you may have to cap the interest rates you charge Argentina, Brazil, Mexico and the rest. Your shareholders will have to bite on the bullet. No one guaranteed their money.'

'Cutting dividends will make it hard to raise new capital and we'll need new capital to build reserves,' Osborn protested.

'The market discounted that risk long ago, Bill.' The Chairman wasn't giving way. 'First National's share price hasn't reflected its book profits for years.' He shifted again in his chair and delivered a verdict. 'We're not talking about a threat to the whole US banking system. We're talking about the top eleven or twelve among 15,000 banks. They may hold twenty per cent of US banking assets, but that's still no reason to be running scared.'

'You mean the government would protect depositors in the interbank market to prevent insolvencies spreading?' Osborn reacted strongly, launching into technical arguments.

'Let's deal with the crisis when we get to it,' the Comptroller suggested. 'Keep negotiating, right.'

'Back in September '84, sir, your predecessor publicly acknowledged he would not allow the top eleven US banks to fail. Will you protect smaller institutions?'

'There are plenty of ways to regulate the financial system,' the Chairman said sharply, 'and we do not intend to be panicked by an ultimatum.'

So that was it, Osborn thought. He had been successful in negotiating the way out of too many rescheduling crises in the past. If he'd failed once or twice they might believe the unthinkable could happen. He began gathering his papers together. He had to get to the National airport to catch the shuttle back to New York before lunch.

'Okay, Mr Osborn,' Bud Phillips wanted the last word, 'what's your strategy?'

'To negotiate with one hand while trying to break the cartel with the other. In which I would have appreciated some help from the President's office.' He rose to his feet. 'Gentlemen, I don't think we have as much time as you imagine.' Then he inclined his head towards Phillips. 'As I said, I can recommend the Moscow Narodny. At least it's protected by its government.'

As he left the room he hoped the manner of his going would have more impact than his arguments.

'Is this for real?' Phillips asked anxiously. 'Osborn had me worried there.'

'It's been around for years. Potentially.' The Chairman smiled reassuringly. 'All the indicators are that with falling interest rates and oil prices down there's enough economic recovery around for default to be unlikely. This so-called option is a typical Third World manoeuvre, and no man's better qualified to handle it than Bill.'

Buenos Aires. 12.30 pm

The Thursday-night dispute with Comisario Alfaro had been protracted, bitter and inconclusive. Back at Police Headquarters, Alfaro had accused the Minister of obstructing the course of justice by negotiating, while Lopez-Santini defended himself by accusing the Comisario of failing to turn up a single clue. Alfaro riposted that the Minister had ruined an operation to catch the criminals.

Overall, it had been a no-win situation for either man. Lopez-Santini had returned at 2 am to his apartment as furious with himself as with the police. He had scarcely slept. Throughout the morning he and Mercedes had waited in their elegant drawing-room overlooking the Park where this whole tragedy began, each becoming more tense and ill-tempered as the minutes passed.

Then Seiler's call from Zurich proved what Lopez-Santini had already imagined. The kidnappers had successfully fled the Argentine. Mercedes exploded into one of her legendary tantrums, beside herself with fear lest the girls had been killed, or left to die in some cruel hiding-place.

'How could you trust such animals!' she kept moaning. 'Holy Mother of God what kind of idiot did I marry? Oh my babies, my poor, poor darlings.'

'You insisted we should pay the ransom.'

'Now you're blaming me! You're as bad as they are.'

Within half an hour of Seiler's call, Mercedes' refusal to acknowledge that her husband had done precisely what she demanded was making the conflict between them unbearable. When she launched into another histrionic outbreak, his forbearance broke. He strode across the room and slapped her face, resoundingly hard, swinging his palm from side to side to shock her out of the hysteria.

'If you can't behave like an adult,' he shouted, 'go to your room.'

She burst into tears and leapt up, clutching her cheeks, and stumbled towards the door, though pausing long enough to spit an insult back at him.

'No Braun-Menendez would treat his wife like this, you peasant.'

After she had gone, Lopez-Santini collapsed into an armchair, as much relieved as agonized. His wife was an over-indulged and pampered bitch. He should have taken to beating her years ago. Not that it helped this situation. The phone rang again. Since the kidnapping its shrill tone seemed to have captured his life. When he answered, feeling his heart pound with apprehension, it was the unmistakable woman's voice, hard-edged yet educated.

'You will find them in Quilmes. Asleep in the bedroom. The doors are locked.' She spelt out the apartment number and the street slowly. He was hastily scribbling on a pad when a click told him the address would not be repeated. He completed writing it down, then rang Alfaro and requested him, formally, to be there in twenty minutes. He wanted the break-in done officially, with witnesses.

When the Comisario cared to exert himself he could make things happen. The unfashionable old apartment block was already surrounded by armed police as Lopez-Santini approached. He was recognized and let through the cordon. Alfaro had arrived seconds ahead of him and after the briefest greeting, led the way up the stairs, flanked by two other officers with drawn revolvers.

'The lift could be booby-trapped,' Alfaro shouted over his shoulder as they ran up.

By the fifth floor both the older men were panting. They looked round at the apartment numbers. Fifty-three was a short way down the dingily carpeted corridor. The door was closed, but the bullet-holes through the lock stared back at them, evidence that someone else had got there first. Gun in hand, Alfaro shouldered his way through, and Lopez-Santini found himself thinking with respect 'at least he leads from the front'. Then what they found drove everything else from his mind. The small sitting-room was empty. The bedroom was not.

On the double bed lay the contorted body of a man, his arms trussed behind his back, his throat slit, his blood congealed and soaked into the bedding. Of Lopez-Santini's daughters there was no sign.

'Dead twelve hours, at least,' Alfaro decided. 'No need for a doctor to tell us that. Have you seen him before?'

'No.' Lopez-Santini felt stunned. This was one outcome he had never envisaged.

'You have not mistaken the address?' Though he concealed it well, Alfaro was horrified not so much by the killing, as by the fact that it had taken place under the noses of his own police, scarcely two hundred metres from the *kiosko*.

'I am sure not.' The surge of hope died as it was born. The coincidence of finding a corpse would be impossible. Theories crowded his brain, until one of the officers called out that he had made a discovery in the sitting-room.

Behind the door there was a cheap imitation-leather grip, unzipped and almost fully packed with clothing. After a cautious inspection for explosives, this yielded a passport, which identified the murdered man. He was Miguel dos Santos, aged twenty-seven, born in Buenos Aires, engineer by profession.

Suddenly Lopez-Santini remembered the snapshot of his daughter, took it from his wallet and began carefully comparing its background details with this room. There was no mistaking the couch the girls had been seated on. Then the newspaper was located in the kitchen. Finally, in the course of a more thorough search, a second Polaroid photograph was found beneath the bed. On the back Teresa had written, presumably for herself, 'Maria took this picture at lunchtime. We are going home soon.'

For the first time since his ordeal had begun, Lopez-Santini openly cried. It was not merely the pathos of the few words, it was the proof that his daughters' release had been imminent. Why else should the woman, in some quirk of decency, have taken a second picture for the girls. Why, unless she was supremely confident of success, should she have let them write her name down? That could only be because they had already overheard it. He blew his nose and turned on the Comisario.

'If nothing else, this reveals the other kidnapper's identity. Now, perhaps, you can find who came here before us, and why.'

Unusually, Alfaro did not defend himself, because he knew the answer and this was no moment to give it. This Miguel and his woman must have been involved in the Flores shoot-out, the caretaker's descriptions fitted. Other *traficantes* must have killed him in revenge. But for what reason did they want the children? When he eventually answered the Minister he was non-committal.

'Unfortunately we have no proof that Maria is her name.'

CHAPTER EIGHT

London. 4.15 pm, Friday June 14th

Knowing what the truth must be, and proving the truth, did not only preoccupy lawyers and policemen – it worried self-respecting journalists almost as much. For the *Trib* it was a point of honour to get things right, no matter how pressing the deadline.

In consequence, when the prints of Maggie's photographs reached Stuart Pendler he had gazed at them with the kind of reverent affection a detective might reserve for a long-sought and blood-stained murder weapon. The roll of film posted hastily in Marsh Harbour a week ago had been delivered in Paris this morning. Although the facsimile transmission to London had blurred the images fractionally, Pendler knew there was no way the Argentine and Polish Finance Ministers could deny having met in the Bahamas last weekend.

Naturally, officials of both countries had issued categoric denials.

However, the Polish Embassy's terse statement had unintentionally clinched his story: 'The Polish government will not participate in such an alleged cartel of debtor nations.' The use of the word 'will' rather than 'would' might have been a grammatical slip by a press attaché possessed of imperfect English. Pendler didn't give a damn. That was what the man had said, and like a skilled attorney he intended to make the most of it.

Writing the story posed familiar difficulties. A reporter's access to secrets is very seldom official, and then it is heavily restricted to 'background use only'. He is forced to work by deduction, confirming details stealthily without revealing his true motives. Today Pendler was in possession of a great deal of circumstantial evidence over and above his personal experience in Great Abaco. The Banco do Brasil was still withholding foreign-exchange payments – that was causing uncertainty in the markets. There had been profit-taking on the stock exchanges, a weakening of the US dollar, a hardening of the Swiss franc, an upturn in gold prices. The smell was of crisis, heavily damped down like a charcoal-burner's fire, but still issuing a tell-tale plume of smoke. The speech Warburton had made in Zurich implicitly confirmed it. Plus the photograph. There are few more effective journalistic devices than printing the denial alongside the proof.

As always, when Pendler began to type into his 'Trash Eighty', the machine which would afterwards transmit his words in a short burst straight down an ordinary telephone line into the *Trib*'s typesetting computers, he began with the climax. If you don't grab the reader with the opening sentence, you'd probably never grab him at all – and you certainly wouldn't grab your editor.

A major international debt default may follow a secret conference of Third World Finance Ministers held last weekend in the Bahamas. They are reliably believed to have formed a debtor-nations' cartel, which could hold the West's bankers to ransom.

From there Pendler went on to recount the evidence, starting with the confirmation provided by the Polish denial and ending with a summary of where the $1,000 billion of Third World debt lay and which banks were most exposed.

Some normally conservative British banks were in almost as bad shape as his own countrymen's – even though the fall of the dollar had improved matters for them, since most loans were denominated in dollars. The Midland had only gone into international banking since 1980 and had already burnt its fingers buying Crocker Bank in California and then having to sell again. Pendler reckoned its receipts in interest and repayments from Latin America probably exceeded its total pre-tax profits – a perilous situation if those payments ceased. The only British high-street bank that could easily ride the storm of default appeared to be the Royal Bank of Scotland, while several of the City's most prestigious merchant banks would be in serious trouble.

There was an expression people used about the Scots. He tried to recall it when he rang Paris to check the editor's reactions. 'Canny', that was the word. The Scots and the Swiss alone had been canny enough to keep their risks well spread in the way bankers used to do, with the Germans a close third. Back in 1981 the West German central bank, the Bundesbank, had seen the writing on the wall and from then through to 1983 German banks had paid no dividends. Their excellent profits had gone into reserve. By 1984 the Deutsche Banke had already put aside forty per cent of the value of its loans to the Third World and Eastern Europe.

Harry Grant was impressed. If there was a European angle, he liked it thoroughly documented. Europe was where most of his readers lived.

'If I don't watch out,' he kidded, 'people are going to be thinking you're the only writer we have! Your Bahamas feature is all over the business page and I'm giving this two columns under the pic on page two.'

'Not the front page?' Pendler pretended unhappiness.

'We have to keep a sense of balance, Stu. Other events have taken place in the world.'

Pendler dropped his objection and expressed thanks. By Sunday, as queries streamed in from the *Washington Post* and the *New York Times*, Harry would be begging for more, which was why he had not mentioned Columbus Cay by name. He'd reveal that after Maggie's visit. It would be crazy to spoil her photographic coup by encouraging hordes of reporters to descend on the place. He was going to keep this exclusive as long as he could. For once his editor was underestimating the impact the *Trib* could have.

New York. 2.30 pm

As Sheldon Harrison ushered her through the door, she heard Osborn saying, in his quietly drawling voice, 'Quite some lady, this. She could knock off a parrot or two . . .'

Suddenly they realized she had entered behind them and rose hastily to their feet – Osborn instinctively straightening his tie, like a college boy caught unawares, Warburton courteously offering her a chair.

'Good of you to join us, Mrs Svenson.' Osborn swiftly recovered his usual urbanity. 'We'd value your advice.'

Mette Svenson took her time settling down, nettled by the remark she had overheard, and suspecting that the reference to parrots involved some obscure witticism. Even after two decades of working in a predominantly masculine environment, she could still be riled by male attitudes. She was honest enough to be pleased by admiration, if it didn't intrude on business. But being divorced, she was too often regarded as a potential lay and her reaction to that was biting. Overall, one of the hardest aspects of her career had been coming to terms with the fact that whereas in fashion or public relations a degree of glamour was an asset to a woman executive, in banking it was suspect.

Not that she thought of herself as a raving beauty. She just had clean, clear-eyed Scandinavian good looks, and because she took care of them they hadn't dulled. Indeed, her early forties had improved her features with a gloss of sophistication, and that again only added to the misleading impression, since at heart she remained as committed a radical as when she was a student.

'How do you find the mood of the meetings?' Osborn asked, when she was evidently ready, earning appreciation for his tact.

'You would like the truth?'

'No point in having anything else.'

In her rise from investment analyst to board member at the Royal Bank of Stockholm, Mette Svenson had not only been forced to prove her abilities constantly – Sweden might be politically liberal, but Swedish men were basically hostile to women in business – she had become adept at reading the minds of those she worked with.

'In their hearts very few believe such a default can happen.' She spoke English with a recognizably Swedish inflection and choice of words. 'They think if we all make small concessions, in the end the debtors will give way, or that the IMF or the World Bank will help.'

'The World Bank could never run to $580 billion.' Annoyance crept into Osborn's voice. 'Would Lopez-Santini cancel IMF talks if he thought the IMF had a role?'

'Intellectually the members of the committee know this. But they cannot think beyond it, except to believe governments will not let them fail.'

'Down in Washington the Fed and the Comptroller don't feel like saving banks this weekend.'

'I don't know about that, Mr Osborn, but you have some very frightened men here. If they lived for a few weeks on beans and maize in a shanty-town they might understand at least why we have this ultimatum.'

'Damned right,' Warburton murmured. 'Military dictators could tell the poor to shut up or else. Now that most Latin American countries are democracies their governments can't.'

'You would like me to tell the committee that? You think it comes more effective from a woman?' She came straight to the point.

'You could add your ten cents' worth.' Osborn doubted if anyone could influence his obstinately worried colleagues. 'In fact, I was hoping you'd help us with something different.'

'Ah,' her inflexion was delicately precise, 'the parrot.'

'The ... oh, my God,' Osborn blushed. 'Don't get us wrong. We call trying to break this cartel "knocking parrots off the perch". It's our other option...' The soft buzz of the intercom interrupted him and he answered with uncharacteristic aggravation. 'We're in a meeting, Sally.'

'There is an urgent call for Mr Warburton from Zurich.'

The secretary's voice was audible to them all. Warburton excused himself and left the room.

'You were telling me about the parrot.' She wanted this curious joke explained in full.

'The debtors could be like a row of parrots,' he grinned disarmingly, 'not too complimentary an image, I admit. If we could persuade a few of them that default would do more harm than good, then the ultimatum might collapse. Jim has already talked the Poles off the perch. Unfortunately, Poland isn't a key country. The Argentine, Brazil, Mexico, they are ... well, you know all this. I'm planning on spending the weekend in Brazil and I'll take in Colombia on the way back. We have to break Latin American solidarity on this.'

'And which bird have your selected for me?' She could guess easily enough. Only one of the nations had a woman president. 'The Philippines?'

'Correct.' Thanks to the incredible greed of the Marcos family, and equally appalling mismanagement, the Philippines were over $26 billion in debt, sixty per cent of it to commercial banks. But they were recovering. 'The currency's strong. Logically they should have no temptation to default.'

'And Mrs Aquino might like a Swedish negotiator more than an American?'

'Your country always has appreciated the Third World's point of view better than most.'

'Thank you.' She smiled. She had not met Osborn before this week and she liked him. 'I will go to Manila if you like, after I have delivered my ten cents' worth.'

'Herr Seiler, I am afraid you are speaking in riddles.' Warburton had endured some five minutes of ultra-discretion during which all the Swiss banker had managed to convey was that he had an unnameable client with an unnameable problem. The committee was due to reassemble shortly. 'If this is sufficiently important, could you come to New York?'

'It is too late. Here we have now eight-thirty in the evening. All flights have departed.'

'You will have to be more explicit, clearer.' They certainly went to bed early, the good Swiss.

'I do not wish to break the trust of my client. But this information is important for us all.' Seiler was evidently struggling with his conscience. 'There is a man from South America with whom you have dealings at this time.'

'A man with a rich wife?'

'*Richtig!* This man has today paid a large sum for his children.'

'Go on.' Warburton felt his stomach tighten.

'But he does not find them. Now he is afraid they are with other people. I tell you because you should know of this pressures on him.

'I'm extremely grateful.' No wonder Seiler was being cautious on an open line. 'I assure you this will be kept completely confidential.'

However, just as he was expecting the conversation to end, the Swiss unleashed a final burst of frankness.

'I tell you also because I have known this man some years. He has a good brain and what he does with you is not in his character. I think perhaps there is a connection.'

Merciful heaven, Warburton thought as he rang off, poor José-Maria. Of all crimes, kidnapping was one he loathed most. It was calculated, callous and inhuman. If the Swiss was correct, it added an extremely ugly dimension to this whole business. He sat for a few minutes trying to reason out why organized crime should be connected with the cartel's ultimatum. He failed. But as he went to join the committee it occurred to him that the jetting around South American capitals which had always been an essential part of Bill Osborn's rescheduling diplomacy might no longer be safe, or prudent.

Buenos Aires. 5.30 pm

Four men had now been murdered in connection with the kidnapping. Lopez-Santini had paid and lost $250,000. Men would kill for a lot less than that, Comisario Alfaro reflected. In the shanty-towns they would kill for pesos. But not *traficantes*: they killed to protect the most lucrative trade in the world. So why did they so badly want the Minister's daughters? There was no major drug-enforcement programme in the Argentine to disrupt.

The police files had revealed that Miguel dos Santos' brother had belonged to the Junta de Coordinacion Revolucionaria and he himself was a suspected revolutionary, though holding a respectable job from which he had taken two weeks' holiday. Why should a JCR member be pursued by *traficantes*? What deal over the children had dos Santos defaulted on?

There were aspects of these crimes Alfaro could not yet fathom and remarks made by the old *kiosko*-owner suggested that his own men were involved. The only sure way to protect himself was to inform the Minister before some nosey reporter made that connection too. He phoned the apartment and caught Lopez-Santini in an unusually aggressive mood.

'A miracle. For once you get in touch when you're needed.' He had inevitable suspicions that the police tap on his phone was linked to the second abduction of Teresa and Gloria and the irony that he had authorized that tap only angered him more.

'How can I be of service, Excellency?' The Comisario was unexpectedly obsequious, which only served to heighten the suspicion.

'I want an extradition request to the United States authorized for the woman Maria. She drew the cash in New York. You must contact the American authorities. I am going there myself tomorrow.' This was not in fact true. He was going to meet the reptilian Suarez in Bogotá, then to New York. But he wished to pressurize Alfaro.

'I must warn, you may achieve nothing, Excellency. Even if they arrest this woman, even if that is her name, she will not know who the *traficantes* are.'

'You are certain they have my daughters?' Anxiety eroded Lopez-Santini's confidence. He sounded totally jet-lagged again, as he had been the previous day. 'This is not another rumour?'

'I regret, Minister, that there is no other explanation. You will be wasting your time in New York.'

The attempt to give him directions rekindled Lopez-Santini's anger.

'My Ministerial arrangements are my affair,' he snapped, 'and if you wish to find a lead to the *traficantes* I suggest you start with every official in your headquarters who knows of the tap on this telephone. Kindly do that, Comisario. And as for the woman, Maria, it is my opinion that she may still be waiting in New York for her dead accomplice.'

Alfaro was on the verge of replying, equally tersely, that his responsibilities were to the Ministry of Justice, when he thought better of it. The two Ministers were known to be friends.

New York. 3.45 pm

Making notes for the record, Sheldon Harrison realized that the committee was way off finding a solution to the crisis. The great majority of its thirty-one members would accept another rescheduling, would even agree a small proportion of new lending, full well knowing it would be simply used by the debtors to pay outstanding interest. But they would not accept receiving significantly less interest than they were paying to depositors. He didn't blame them either. In conventional terms that was the straight road to ruin. As the Monopoly game rules say: 'Go directly to jail. Do not pass Go, do not collect $200.'

None the less, Bill Osborn was making a final plea for 'flexibility' and its urgency was compounded by knowing about the hidden pressures on the Argentine negotiator.

'Mrs Svenson, gentlemen. Although Poland has now quit the cartel, we still have to deal with twenty countries through a single negotiator, and Señor Lopez-Santini has been given little or no latitude for compromise.'

'That's absurd,' a British voice interrupted.

'On the contrary,' Osborn observed mildly, 'it's what our German colleagues call *realpolitik*. They know damn well that if all the Arabs and pension funds and small investors we've accepted deposits from hear about a default they'll want their money back and we won't have it. Outright default is not an option we can live with. We have to achieve a conciliatory default to keep those loans technically performing.' He looked around the long table apologetically. 'You may not have appreciated how painful this is going to be.'

'Just how painful?' demanded the banker seated next to Harrison, who had lent more recklessly than most to Mexico.

'I would like to offer a fifteen- to twenty-year rescheduling, as against the thirty years that they want, and an interest-forgiveness of three per cent.' He glanced at Harrison. 'Pass around our calculations, will you, Sheldon.'

Murmurs of protest began even before Harrison had handed out the figures.

'Bill's crazy,' Harrison's neighbour exclaimed. 'Rescheduling ought to give us higher margins. This would cost half our profits! Our stock would hit the floor.'

'I hear you, gentlemen,' Osborn raised his hand for silence, 'and I'm sorry. The big money-center banks are going to need fifteen years to establish adequate reserves and their smaller correspondent banks will just have to live with that. Our own Federal Reserve advocates capping interest rates and is going to insist that we cut dividends. It's going to hurt. But it's preferable to a default.'

'Please.' Mette Svenson had decided to add her ten cents' worth. 'There is reckless borrowing and there has also been reckless lending. We have all been guilty of that. Let me tell you a story. In Sweden in summer we like to wear simple leather sandals with wooden soles. So my own bank – I tell this against ourselves – offered loans to manufacture these in Africa. Of course the money is accepted because it gives work building the factory. But in that part of Africa there is not the right wood, not enough leather and the people never wore wooden shoes in their lives. So the project has closed and we do not get the money back. I think that is our responsibility, not the Africans.'

An insulted silence greeted her comments, but she persisted.

'We should accept that of the $580 billion we have lent, very little will ever be repaid. This debt structure is a house of cards and Third World countries will not feel guilty at all if Western institutions collapse with it.'

'My dear lady,' an elegant, rather patronizing Briton interrupted, 'a collapse simply cannot happen. Our governments and central banks will not allow it. They'll create a lifeboat for us.'

Christ, Harrison thought, if there's one sure way to encourage a default it's by telling everyone out loud that governments are standing by with a financial raft.

'Sir,' Osborn's patience was wearing thin, 'I guess in Britain the Socialists might be happy to have banks under government control. In the United States no one would.'

'Such dependence on the State is dangerous,' the German agreed.

The wrangling continued for a further hour, by which time people were looking at their watches. All except the New Yorkers had flights to catch. Osborn called the meeting to order.

'I have no authority to call a vote. You can go home right now if you prefer. But I need a collective decision.'

A few minutes later, after several shows of hands, he had a reluctant mandate to offer a fifteen-year rescheduling and a one per cent forgiveness of interest. Even that would cost millions of dollars annually and it still required ratification from the two thousand or so smaller participating banks.

'I'd like telexed confirmations by Sunday night,' Osborn said as he wound up the conference, 'though I can't pretend that I think this will bring home the goods. Brazil, Mexico and the rest are going to want fresh loans in addition, whether they deserve them or not.'

Afterwards, in the privacy of his office, Bill Osborn made light of Mrs Svenson's contribution.

'Well,' he told her, 'I guess that what wasn't sauce for the ganders still could be the right stuff for the goose. You and Mrs Aquino should hit things off pretty well. How soon could you leave?'

'Tomorrow morning? I must make a report to Stockholm first.'

'Tell your people we have to talk the more responsible leaders out of this cartel. It's the only way of cutting a default down to manageable size.'

'I think they will agree.' She smiled wryly.

'You talk those Filippinos around, and I'll join your club. They're a key country in this. And be careful with the generals. No one can govern without them and they might just be on our side. They won't want to lose our military aid.'

'But I cannot speak for the American administration!'

'Nor can we, that's the hell of it. Those guys can take a hint, though.' He grinned. 'And I'm sure you know how to drop one.'

When she had gone, Osborn began preparing himself for his swing round Brazil and Colombia.

'You think I should take in Mexico City too?' he asked Warburton.

'A waste of time. Their problems are close to insoluble, and from what I hear they're in a violently anti-American mood.' Warburton paused and cleared his throat unnecessarily. Osborn looked up from the papers he was sorting out on his desk. 'Violence down there may not be confined to words. Are you sure you should go, Bill?'

'Hell, Jim. I take the normal precautions any executive takes these days. Travel economy, never have a chauffeured limo waiting around. I've been to Rio dozens of times and the Governor of the Banco do Brasil's expecting me, goddamit.'

He began the process of lighting a cigar, methodically slicing off the tip and then warming the end with a match.

'We agreed a strategy. We have a weekend when nothing's happening on the markets and the banks are closed. I'll tackle Brazil. You deal with your friend Lopez-Santini. If his children are being held he might appreciate some help. Either way, if we can knock those two off the perch we've half-way cracked the problem.'

The cigar glowed as he took the first deep draw.

'And we have to crack it before some lousy clerk or secretary leaks the story to the press. This weekend could be the last breathing space we have.' He blew out smoke. 'No, Jim. I can take care of myself. I'm heading south tonight.'

London. 11 am, Saturday June 15th

'Wake up, Len. There's a man to see you.'

Len Slater, sleeping off the jet-lag, lifted his head dozily from the pillow, and rubbed his eyes with his knuckles.

'I'm fair buggered, love. Why can't you leave me be?' He'd hardly been in bed two hours since his overnight journey.

'You must get up, Len. He's in the hall.' She stood by the bed ready to help him, his leg was always that stiff in the mornings. 'He's a black,' she added, *sotto voce*. 'From the Nigeria High something or other and it's urgent.'

Painfully, Slater got up and walked to the window, adjusting the trousers of his striped winceyette pyjamas before twitching back the curtains to peep out. He didn't want neighbours getting the wrong idea.

Out in the road, double-parked with outrageous disdain for the local Fords and Vauxhalls, stood a long black Mercedes saloon, with a uniformed chauffeur standing beside it. Already kids were gathering to stare. Slater recognized the model – the 600, the biggest Merc of them all – because he'd seen so many in Lagos: a lot more than was healthy in a place that couldn't pay its bloody debts, he'd thought at first. When he discovered the system of bribes and kickbacks that provided limousines his thoughts had become unprintable.

'He'll just have to wait, love,' he ordered grumpily. 'Sit him down in the front room.' He'd been looking forward to a day off.

As he shaved and dressed he could hear Gladys calling from the kitchen, offering tea. 'Two sugars or one, Mr . . .?' But the reply was muffled by the parlour walls. He supposed the man *was* from the High Commission – the equivalent, in Commonwealth countries, of an embassy. It was astonishing that either the pedantic Mallam Sule or the lawyer Ayokolo could have sparked such immediate action. Nigeria had not noticeably been a place for getting things done.

The front room in this semi-detached house was reserved for big occasions like Christmas or birthdays and had an unlived-in air, with china ornaments and carefully framed photographs on highly polished pieces of furniture. When Slater entered, the Nigerian was sitting uncomfortably on the edge of the blue-moquette-covered sofa, a half-consumed cup of tea on a gleaming table beside him. He rose immediately to his feet, revealing himself to be tall and well-built, wearing a grey pinstripe suit that would have done credit to Savile Row and a club tie. He spoke with a near-perfect Oxford accent. Later, looking back, Slater would find it hard to think of him as having been an African at all, so English were both his voice and his manner.

'How do you do.' The Nigerian shook hands with military firmness. 'My name is Ironsi. Lieutenant-Colonel James Ironsi, Commercial Counsellor at the High Commission. For me it's a great pleasure to be here again,' he smiled down at his tie which Slater noticed had an owl embroidered on it. 'Staff College. And Sandhurst.'

'Glad to meet you. Please sit down.' Slater was now as much taken aback by the visitor's impeccable credentials as by his unexpected arrival. If the man had introduced himself as a duke he could hardly have created a greater impact. It was difficult to believe that he, the ascetic Muslim, Mallam Sule, and the effervescent, self-serving lawyer, Ayokolo, all belonged to the same nation. 'Well, er, what can I do for you, Colonel?'

'I was hoping if you were free we might have lunch. Lagos asked me to discuss your little problem, which I am sure we can do something about.'

Slater hesitated. He'd promised Gladys a run in the car sometime over the weekend. On the other hand, if he could report on Monday that the two million was on its way . . .

'There's quite a decent place near Windsor,' Ironsi prompted, 'Pity to stay in the city on a day like this.'

'I'll just have a word with the wife, if you don't mind.' He caught an appeal in the Colonel's quick glance. 'She won't be coming. Gladys understands about business.'

A few minutes later, with his wife's disgruntlement clear in the way she said goodbye, Len Slater was stepping into the luxurious interior of the Mercedes while the chauffeur held open the door.

During the three-quarter-hour drive through London's outer suburbs and past Heathrow to Windsor the Colonel kept the conversation flowing with polite questions about the Amalgamated Union of Clerical and Accounting Staffs. Since Len Slater knew more about his union than anything else, not excluding snooker which was his sole recreation, the two men got on famously.

'Have any trouble with the Airports Authority?' the Colonel enquired as they drove near the new Terminal Four on the south side.

'Nothing serious. The bosses would like to cut overtime, but they've not a chance – not with the workload.'

'So your members are hard at it, are they?' The Colonel laughed genially. 'Partly our fault, I'm afraid. We're freighting stuff from here as well as Stansted now. The absurd Dikko affair still causes mistrust there, even though it was years ago.'

Relieved to hear the kidnapping disapproved of, Slater began talking about AUCAS members again and the subject of freight did not recur until they were half-way through their lunch at an Elizabethan manor house converted into a hotel, all linenfold panelling, old oak and sporting prints.

'Frankly, Mr Slater,' Ironsi remarked, 'clearing some of our freight is being very troublesome. Export documentation, signatures. I suspect we don't know the right people at Heathrow yet.'

Slater's forkful of steak turned dry in his mouth despite the sauce. Mallam Sule had mentioned document problems. What exactly was he being asked to do?

'We have the same trouble as you had in Lagos until you found Daniel Ayokolo. Everything's simple with someone who knows the ropes, eh? Now this shop steward you mentioned, the one who's a supervisor in the freight area, he must know how to speed things up.'

'All depends . . .' Slater struggled to swallow the meat. He was a long way from happy at Ironsi turning out to be a friend of Ayokolo. So much for first impressions. 'This is legal, isn't it?' he asked cautiously.

'My dear fellow. I can tell you frankly, there is nothing underhand. We have been waiting many months for a delivery of computer software. Last week it reached Heathrow at last and there was some alleged irregularity in the export documents. The consignment was delayed. Last night we obtained new documentation. All signed. All correct. There is a Nigeria Airways flight tomorrow night. We must have it on that flight and, let me tell you, the weekend is one hell of a time for clearing anything through Heathrow. Not because of the Customs. They're always on duty. But because of the ground staff.'

'Tomorrow?' The request sounded reasonable, but the shop-steward's address was at the office. 'That could be a bit tight. Wouldn't Monday do?'

'Monday will be a bad day.' Ironsi summoned the waiter. 'What would you like next? A sweet? Cheese?' They ordered and he took up the thread again. 'As a friend, Mr Slater, I can warn you that by Monday night it may be impossible to transfer back your £2 million.' He allowed the mention of the full sum to have its effect.

'Let me be quite frank. For reasons I cannot reveal, a lot may happen on Monday in relations between our countries. I would like us both to be free of that stress.'

Tactfully, he then spoke of other things until they were securely in the Mercedes again and starting back.

'I have the documents with me,' he said, taking a folder from his briefcase. 'We have to drive past the airport. We could stop and see this friend of yours.'

'Now?' Slater almost fainted. The man must be out of his mind, wanting to turn up in a bloody great gin palace with CD plates and a black chauffeur. The lads would take it for granted that there was something fishy going on.

'I can wait for you.' Ironsi guessed the difficulty.

'They work shifts. He may not even be on duty.' In fact, Slater couldn't remember his name, only that he'd been admitted to the pension scheme through a fiddle, since shop stewards, though Union officials, were paid by their employers, not by the Union. And then it came to him: Kevin Gates.

'I tell you what,' Ironsi was determined and he knew the quirks of the British character, 'we'll go to another freight shed. You walk round and see if he's there. Say you dropped by on the off-chance. If he's willing, come back to me for the folder.'

Very reluctantly, Slater agreed. They turned off at the Heathrow perimeter road and reached the freight area. Feeling acutely conspicuous, he walked to the nearest shed, was directed to another, and eventually obtained two pieces of information: Kevin was off until tomorrow midday, and the airlines they handled included Nigeria Airways. He returned to the limousine greatly relieved. At least he could think about this arrangement now – sleep on it, as it were.

'Too bad,' Ironsi settled back in his seat, affecting to make light of the disappointment. 'Shall I send a driver for you?'

Flattered in spite of himself, Slater declined. He'd take Gladys to Windsor Castle, thereby dressing the occasion up a bit for Kevin's benefit, and phone beforehand too. A thought struck him.

'Don't quite know how to put this,' he muttered, 'but if an exporter's agent were doing this, well, the lads at the airport get used to a bit of bunce.'

'Ah, no problem.' Ironsi's bulging wallet appeared in his palm as fast as a gun might have done in earlier days, and he stripped out a quantity of £10 notes. ' "Bunce",' he said reflectively, 'a new word for my vocabulary. As you probably know, we call it "dash".' With the money he passed across a visiting-card and the folder. 'Tomorrow you will act as my courier, and first thing

Monday I will act as yours. The transfer will be made at once. On that you can have my word.'

During the rest of the short journey the conversation flagged.

'A pity our relations with Britain aren't better,' Ironsi remarked at one point. 'Your government never understood the Dikko business.'

'I'm relieved you didn't approve of that.' Slater unintentionally revealed his silent train of thought about illegal exports.

'Absolutely.' Ironsi shook his head at the incompetence of previous regimes. 'To kidnap Dikko for a show trial was absurd. We should have shot him in the street and had done with it.'

Beni region, Bolivia. Morning

Teresa woke slowly, aware first of daylight and crisp linen sheets around her and drowsily supposing she was back at home. Then she realized there was something wrong with the room. The ceiling was a rough white, not like her own bedroom. She opened her eyes fully. The walls weren't pink like hers, either. They were whitewashed too. Where was she? In hospital? She had been in hospital once and she remembered the white walls.

'Feeling better, *mi chiquita*?' The woman's voice sounded rough but kindly, speaking Spanish with an unfamiliar accent.

She tried to hoist herself upright and was rewarded with an agonizing stab of headache.

'Not so good, eh, my little one? Lie down again if you want. Nobody's in a hurry today.'

Teresa obeyed, staying quite still, frightened to move.

'My head hurts,' she said to the ceiling.

'Never mind. It will get better, *chiquita*. I would give you medicine but El Señor says I must not.'

Slowly the terrible throbbing pain ebbed away and Teresa began to sit up, this time with great caution. The room was large, with simple furniture. Bright sun streamed through the windows. Sitting in a wicker chair was a woman wearing a long voluminous skirt and with a brightly coloured poncho around her shoulders. She had a wrinkled dark-brown face and black hair drawn tightly back into a plait. Teresa recognized her instantly as a *campesino* of Inca descent. It was unusual to come across someone so dark-skinned, and the air felt warm, too warm for winter. She was mystified.

'Am I in hospital?'

'No, no,' the woman drew out the words soothingly, 'this El Señor's hacienda, my *chiquita*. Would you like food? He has told me you can have anything you want. Toast and jam, milk, orange juice, bananas . . .'

'I would like some milk, please. I expect Gloria would too . . .' Panic seized her. She had fallen asleep after Maria left. What had happened. 'Where is Gloria?' she cried out, and instantly a warning surge of headache returned.

'The *gordita chiquita*? Don't worry. She is in another room.'

'Is she all right?'

'Of course she is all right, little one.' The woman heaved herself out of the chair and came across to the bedside, gazing at Teresa in admiration. 'So pale, so pretty. Don't be afraid. I shall look after you.' She darted her fingers forward to stroke Teresa's cheek as though the skin were irresistible. 'I wish I had a little white daughter like you! Now, you would like to eat?'

'May I get up first, please?'

'Of course, my little dear. I will fetch your clothes. They were all washed yesterday, washed and ironed.'

'Yesterday?' Confusion reclaimed Teresa's mind. 'What is today?'

'Today? Saturday, of course. You were fast asleep when you came last night.'

'Saturday?' She struggled with her memory. Something terribly important was happening on Saturday. The hockey match! 'What time is it, please?'

'So many questions! Curiosity killed the cat. It's the middle of the morning, *chiquita*.'

'We'll miss the hockey match,' Teresa slipped out of bed, realizing with surprise that she was in someone else's nightie. 'The match against Michael Ham. Please, I must get dressed.'

'Hockey?' The old woman couldn't pronounce the word. 'Some kind of game, is it? I don't know about that, but El Señor said you could ride the ponies in the afternoon.'

Teresa stared at her, then tiptoed carefully across the polished wooden floor to the window. The hacienda seemed to be on a slight hill. Outside was a clump of trees and beyond that, so far as she could see, right to the blue grey horizon, stretched grasslands dotted with trees and grazing cattle. She felt the pleasant warmth of the sun on her face, then turned back into the room.

'Please, where are we?'

'Oh *mi querida chiquita*, where do you think? On El Señor's ranch! You came with him yesterday, do you not remember?'

'No.' She remained confused. 'Who is El Señor?'

'The boss, of course, the owner, and he has gone away again.

Now stop this fretting in your mind and I will bring your clothes.'

The woman left. She had strict instructions not to reveal Señor Canelas' name, otherwise the two girls were to have what they wished.

In American eyes he might be a vicious criminal; in the eyes of his colleagues a feared king among drug barons. In his own eyes he was also motivated by honour, and no harm would come to Lopez-Santini's daughters on his property.

'They are the children of a bereaved friend,' he had told the housekeeper. 'They have gone through a difficult period. Look after them well.' He had seen no reason to explain that they had effectively lost a whole day of their young lives while, kept under drugs, they were driven in a van 700 kilometres north into the Santiago del Estero, from where he had fetched them, piloting the plane himself in careless defiance of the Argentine's border controls.

Southampton, Long Island. Midday

Controversies engendered at Annual General Meetings of the Southampton Heritage Society most often centred directly or indirectly on its rivalry with the older-established Southampton Colonial Society. This occasion was no exception. The ladies dominant at the meeting – in a room loaned them on the 1644 thoroughfare called Job's Lane – were in self-recriminatory mood. The Heritage Society had overspent its budget in the fiscal year now ending and might be forced to abandon founding a small museum of colonial farm implements in the next.

'I don't have to tell you how close this project is to all our hearts,' Mrs Ruffels, the socially ambitious matron who was the chairperson remarked, gaining loud applause, since the scheme would give the neatest possible slap in the face to the Colonial Society, which inexplicably hadn't thought of it first. 'We're just going to have to make the very most of the money we have and maybe launch a special appeal.'

Trudy Gianni, at the committee table, clapped loudly. She didn't give a damn about colonial farm implements, but she now had the perfect opening to attack the Bartrum Bank. She'd spent all yesterday researching its commitments, and they were genuinely horrific. By the time she was through, that louse Ray Roth would feel he'd been dug, ploughed and harrowed. No question he would, because she'd noticed him come in late and take a seat at the back. As its banker he liked to think of himself as an unofficial patron of the Society.

Her moment came with the auditor's report on the accounts.

'May I make an observation?' she asked.

'Go right ahead, Mrs Gianni. That's what this meeting's for.'

'We have this statement which includes $53,000.40 on deposit at the Bartrum Bank. Well, I am sorry to say this, but there are things happening to investments in the outside world that you may not all be aware of.'

'Is this relevant, Trudy?' Jane Ruffels was a friend of Rosalind Roth and she could see Ray stirring anxiously in his chair at the back.

'I'm afraid so.' Once she was on her feet, Trudy Gianni was hard to stop. 'The money we deposit has to be loaned out again. That's a bank's normal business.' She kept her voice very calm, very clear. 'What worries me is that our bankers have made very large loans to the Argentine, Brazil and Mexico – $47 million altogether – and a week ago Brazil stopped making interest payments.' A ripple of whispering swept the hall and she saw that Roth wanted to stand up in protest. She raised her voice to be heard above the chatter. 'In fact, Brazil has stopped making any payments at all, for anything.'

'Mrs Gianni, please!'

Unfortunately, Mrs Ruffels' intervention had the opposite effect to her intention. Silence fell, but Trudy was still on her feet.

'The Society can't afford to lose $53,000. I'm sorry to say this about a neighbourhood bank where many of us have accounts, but I think we should transfer to an institution that is not involved in risky foreign lending.'

Uproar followed and Trudy Gianni sat down again. She noticed people were already leaving, presumably to call their husbands, though as it was a quarter century since American banks had opened on a Saturday there would be nothing their husbands could do.

'Ladies and gentlemen, please.' Jane Ruffels, darting furious glances at Trudy, tried to restore quiet. 'Order, order, please.' Slowly she succeeded. 'Ladies and gentlemen, our trusted banking adviser, Ray Roth is with us. Can we please let him speak. Ray, please come forward.'

With lumbering, uncertain steps Roth made his way through the audience towards the committee, his face the mirror of the agony he felt.

'Now,' she was set to castigate that jumped-up bitch in public, 'I have no doubt that Mr Roth can give us complete reassurance.'

'Sure, Mrs Ruffels.' He was so perturbed that he forgot to address his listeners, 'Bartrum Bank is perfectly sound. No one need worry. Your savings are safe.'

'Do you deny what I said?' Trudy spat it out before anyone could stop her. Roth gave an audible sigh of despair and shook his head slowly from side to side.

'It is true we have loans in Latin America. Yes, we have problems with Brazil. But we're expecting those payments to come through any day.' He summoned enough anger to turn towards Trudy, 'As this lady knows.'

'What I know is that they never do come. Your twenty million was loaned for six months – five years ago!' She stood up. Any future she might have had socially in Southampton was finished.

'Mrs Ruffels, I resign.'

As she marched out, several people booed. But far more appeared stunned. She had sworn to put the knife into Ray Roth and she'd done so. What she only began to appreciate when women hurried after her to ask uncomprehending and frantic questions on the tree-shaded sidewalk of Job's Lane, was that she had also sparked a local panic.

New York. Midday

From long experience, James Warburton accepted that in a crisis Saturday and Sunday were no different to other days – except that you had no staff. He was clearing some of the immense paperwork associated with the co-ordination of rescheduling when the telex came. In fact, he wasn't entirely without staff. Sheldon Harrison and Bill Osborn's secretary, Sally, were on duty in the First National building this morning.

'I just can't think why this wasn't sent up before,' Sally said apologetically, handing across four copies of the telex on different shades of flimsy paper. 'I guess the security men don't know who you are.'

The telex originated in London at 10 am British Summer Time – eight hours ago. It was from a press officer at the Banking Information Service in Lombard Street, and it began tersely:

INTERNATIONAL HERALD TRIBUNE NEWSPAPER CARRIED FOLLOWING ARTICLE THIS MORNING, QUOTING YOU. URGENTLY REQUEST ADVICE ON REACTION WE SHOULD GIVE.

Normally, Warburton's well-scrubbed complexion, looking fresh out of a Turkish bath, revealed remarkably little. Now, as he read the text, watched by Sally and Sheldon Harrison, his expression showed distinct signs of alarm and his jaw-muscles tightened.

'Take a look at this, Sheldon.' He detached the pink copy. 'In my view, the shit has now hit the fan.'

Harrison read the copy, finding what Stuart Pendler had written uncomfortably accurate, and not in the least liking the sentence tacked on at the end.

NEWSPAPER ALSO PRINTS APPARENTLY GENUINE PICTURE OF ARGENTINE AND POLISH FINANCE MINISTERS AT RESTAURANT IN THE BAHAMAS.

'How in hell does this reporter know where the cartel met when we don't? He must have heard your speech in Zurich, too.'

'He did. The question is, how can we contain the damage? Sally.' She approached, shorthand pad ready. 'Telex all the committee members, drawing their attention to this newspaper report. Nothing dramatic. Simply that. And we have to warn Bill in Rio.' He addressed Harrison again. 'We must also locate both Lopez-Santini and the Pole. They must issue denials.'

'They already have done.'

'I must have missed that.' Warburton found the passage in the telex. 'Clever stuff. That man Pendler's no fool. Where is Lopez-Santini?'

'His family say he's on the way here.'

'Track him down. I must speak to him. Phone the Argentine Consul at home. Make him earn his allowances for a change.'

'At least we have the whole weekend.'

'The whole weekend? My dear boy, you've spent too long in the white heat of Long Island's technological revolution. Your brain must have been cauterized. In Tokyo at this moment it is Sunday morning, in the Gulf sheikhs are finishing their sheep's eyes or whatever they consume for dinner, in London the Connaught is serving cocktails. The *Herald Tribune* sells in all those places and the Japanese will have been brooding over this report and preparing to react the moment the markets open on Monday, if not earlier. They're great ones for off-the-floor trading. I've known them track a stockbroker down to his favourite pub in Kensington on a Sunday and do a ten-million deal then and there on the telephone.'

'Twenty-four hours is better than nothing.'

'We haven't got twenty-four hours. At weekends American

banker may play golf or watch baseball. While their British colleagues entertain at their country houses or watch cricket. They're all switched off. But the brokers and dealers aren't. Those twenty-eight-year-olds in the City who earn three times as much as I ever have and live on the phone will be dumping their girl-friends, revving up their Porsches and heading for the office. They're paid to be ahead of the competition. They'll find a way to trade, with settlement on Monday.'

'Can't we issue a denial?'

'Not one that would be believed. On Monday, when responsible leaders are back at work here and in London, perhaps. But by then the panic will be under way. What brokers call a "flight into quality" – out of dollars and into gold, out of ordinary shares and into government bonds – will start rolling back westwards through the time-zones from Tokyo tomorrow, getting more unstoppable all the way. When it hits here it'll be a tidal wave.' Warburton grunted angrily. 'That damn reporter may have started something no one can control.'

CHAPTER NINE

New York. Saturday June 15th

In one important detail, Warburton's predictions were over-optimistic, impossible as that would have seemed to Sheldon Harrison as he watched his chances of getting home to Water Mill steadily whittled away.

Warburton was right that the full flow of computerized dealings which wash billions of dollars, pounds, yen and deutschmarks around the world from Monday to Friday could not gather into a tidal wave until full trading resumed in Hong Kong and Tokyo on Monday morning. Because the banks were closed, the whizz-kid brokers' bargains could not be settled until then, so they simply accumulated like water building up behind a dam.

The forgotten detail was that every Saturday night sees an influential flood of information released worldwide as Sunday newspapers roll off their printing presses in every democratic country, and there are, anyway, no significant financial centres in the Communist Bloc.

On this Saturday, the first editor to wrestle with the problems posed by Pendler's story was at the *Asahi Shimbun* in Tokyo. The *Asahi Shimbun* boasted the largest daily circulation in the world – over nine million copies – and served a nation that was uniquely newspaper-conscious. On average, every Japanese family bought more than one paper a day. However, the editor was under pressure. The *Shimbun* was essentially a newspaper of fact, not opinion. He ordered a résumé of Pendler's piece to be carried as a news story, prefaced by 'Reports are circulating in Western capitals that . . .' and left full coverage to the Monday edition.

The reactions of Sunday newspaper editors with more breathing space in India, Africa and Europe – to all of whom the story was potentially of immense importance – were similar. They let rip with their editorial comments, while their news pages carried a rehash of Pendler's story, spiced with whatever their own financial writers had been able to dig up from the files.

In London, the dilemma for the 'serious' Sunday newspapers was acute. They all carried extensive business sections, serving the élite of their readership who were executives and professional people. That same élite also controlled their major source of revenue: advertising. If the paper missed out on a murder or a train crash, no one would complain too much. If their much-vaunted in-depth coverage of the City remained silent on an international financial débâcle like this, those business readers would feel savagely let down.

In New York, editors had more time at their disposal than almost anywhere else. Furthermore, the most authoritative journal of them all had fewer qualms or hassles than the rest over reporting what had by now been christened the 'world debt crisis'. The New York Times was part-owner of the International Herald Tribune, its editors knew Stuart Pendler and trusted Harry Grant's judgement. They could legitimately request an expanded and updated version of the original report, exclusive to them.

Well before the final front page of the New York Times' Sunday edition was 'put to bed', the paper's Tokyo correspondents had begun filing new copy about agitated Japanese brokers and currency-dealers establishing an extensive 'off-the-floor' market, with frantic buying of gold, even though the computer 'books' of the London and New York dealers were closed. To compensate for the risk, huge margins were being quoted. Whatever errors of guesswork Stuart Pendler might have made, this was hard, genuine, front-page news. The story had begun to feed upon itself.

London. Morning, Sunday June 16th

On Sunday mornings Gladys Slater deliberately let her husband oversleep. When he did come down, the papers were waiting in the kitchen so that he could enjoy them with his breakfast. The tabloid they took had decided to splash the news, being short of more trivial sensations this weekend. When Slater discovered it was in the 'heavyweight' paper as well, he had to push away his bacon and eggs, unable to eat more. Now he knew why Colonel Ironsi wanted the shipment out today and why repayment of the two million might be impossible after tomorrow. He took his cup of tea to the back room, where the telephone was, and began hunting down the shop steward at Heathrow.

Len Slater was not the only executive to leap for the telephone in Britain. Bank directors, fund managers, import–export traders, anyone with money tied up internationally, all began contacting the responsible officials of their organizations and warning them, if they did not already realize it, that the opening of business on Monday would be a potentially disastrous moment of truth. Many drove straight to work and began assembling the data for instant decision-making in the morning while, as Warburton had forecast, the dealers and brokers began trading informally. So, as Sunday wore on, a tidal wave of financial panic did gather momentum, rolling back westwards from Tokyo and Hong Kong to engulf Europe and sound alarm bells in North America.

Southampton, Long Island. Morning

The Roth family home stood four-square on Meeting House Lane, looking for all the world like a dolls' house come to life. A white-columned porch along the front contrasted picturesquely with dark-stained shingle walls, in which three symmetrical rectangular windows lit the rooms above, while above them the roof was steeply pitched in the shape of a white-framed pediment enclosing a wide window for the attics. Rosalind Roth had fallen in love with it at first sight and had brushed aside Ray's wish to be nearer Dune Road. 'This is off South Main Street,' she had said firmly, 'and that suits me fine. Besides, the garden's pretty too.'

It was. High trees framed the house, shading the lawn, and a small circular driveway curled round in front of the porch. If this wasn't one of the fashionable mansions along the sea-front, at least it was a miniature of one.

Not that the newsboy delivering papers appreciated any of these attributes. His practised concern each Sunday morning as he cycled through the entrance pillars was to toss the 400-page bulk of the *Times'* numerous Sunday sections on to the porch without slackening speed, let alone dismounting. Today, as he sent it flying through the air, he might just as well have been throwing a bomb.

The resounding thump of the newspaper landing on the planks brought out Ray Roth in person, in his dressing-gown, scooping up the bundle and immediately retreating inside again.

Early this morning, he had woken in a sweat that had nothing to do with the warm June night. In his dream, Meeting House Lane had been beseiged by reporters and photographers with flashbulbs popping, while behind them crowds of depositors surged forward and the village police made no attempt to hold them back when he appeared. Hands were grabbing to lynch him when his own screaming brought him to.

Even knowing these were mere imaginings and seeing the driveway deserted, he still shrank inside again as fast as if it had all been real. Now he was relying on the *Times* to prove that the nightmare of financial collapse was only fantasy. He took the paper to the kitchen and spread it out on the pine table, so anxious to reach the business section that he almost missed the secondary front-page headline:

FINANCIAL PANIC IN TOKYO

Even this did not instantly connect until he noticed the subsidiary line.

Debt Default Threatens US Banks

He read on with horror, compulsively hoping for some kind of let-out. There was none. Plaza was listed among the most-exposed US money-centre banks and there were ominous references to 'many hundreds of smaller institutions being at risk through their participation in syndicated loans, particularly to the notorious MBA countries: Mexico, Brazil and Argentina'. For the first time, Roth learnt in black and white how those three debtors had caused a hushed-up crisis right back in 1982 – and Plaza had led him into lending to all three within months of it. In fact, he realized with shock, Bartrum's money had very probably gone to pay Plaza's overdue interest – and not so indirectly, either.

Unable to stop himself shaking at the storm which must break the moment any corporate depositor read this and added two and two together, he rang Schuster's home number. Yesterday, the bank's Treasurer had been out of town. Today, thank God, he was back.

'You gotta come over. I know it's Sunday. This is an emergency, Dale. Have you read the *Times*? You haven't? Well, do that thing and come straight on here.'

He went upstairs to dress. Rosalind was still asleep and he tried to avoid disturbing her. With his tossing and screaming she must have had a lousy night. But all the while he was washing and shaving he felt like screaming again, because his last conversation with Paul Gianni kept coming back into his mind, and its implications had begun to scare the hell out of him.

Yesterday, he had called Gianni at home, after the Heritage Society meeting, demanding an apology.

'You realize your wife has slandered my bank,' he had raged.

'And you've screwed my company, Roth. If I don't have the Brazilian money Monday morning, I'll be bussing every one of my workforce who banks with you to Southampton. Could be three hundred or more. You know what they'll do when they get there? They'll take out their savings. Expect a long line, Roth – a long line and an angry one.'

Even yesterday, challenging Gianni had been a mistake. This morning it looked like a disaster. There was now no way he could advance more of the $700,000 to ACE Techtronics, and when that kind of a line formed others joined. Gianni would be certain to alert the local papers, reporters would arrive . . . The scenario didn't bear thinking about. Not because a single depositor would lose a single cent in the end, but because of the adverse publicity.

Too late, Roth had appreciated that there were two sides to Gianni and his blonde, all-American wife. There was the acumen and energy which had built their business, and there was this vicious Latin reaction to being, as they saw it, betrayed. He desperately needed counsel.

Half an hour later, a shaken Dale Schuster arrived, joined him in the kitchen for coffee and began trying to make a plan.

'Okay, Ray.' He knew the dangers of panic and realized the first necessity was to calm his superior down. 'What Gianni's doing is strictly symbolic. He's just promoting images out of the Great Depression that don't apply. He knows the FDIC guarantees deposits up to $100,000. And suppose his workforce does arrive, we have plenty cash in the vaults, like we're required to. They don't all have their money in demand deposits, either. Must be some still have seven- or twenty-eight-day accounts.'

'Not many.' Roth switched his mind off the appalling long-term cost of a bank being rescued by the Federal Deposit Insurance Corporation and on to a more immediate worry. Two worries in fact. He raised the easier first. 'A lot of customers have deposit accounts with checking privileges, Dale. How are we going to monitor those tomorrow?'

Dale winced. Recent innovations had made it increasingly difficult to monitor the flow of funds through a bank – any bank. Deposit accounts at high interest with no withdrawal notice required and deposits which could have cheques drawn against them were only two. Not that Bartrum could have resisted these ideas any more than they could have resisted issuing cash-cards. There was a financial-services revolution sweeping both America and Europe which was turning banking from its safe, traditional form into a business where the Treasurer lived on a permanent tightrope.

In traditional banking you knew exactly when your depositors' money became due for repayment, and this principle was still the bedrock of money-market lending, from overnight funds onwards. But Schuster had no means of knowing when the small-saver holders of Bartrum's deposit accounts would start withdrawing money. Worse, they didn't even have to come to one of the bank's branches. They could use their cheques to transfer everything they held to other banks or thrift institutions; they could use them to obtain cash from friendly storekeepers; or they could use them for straight purchasing.

'Tomorrow,' Roth said, 'we'll have no way to tell if we're being hit by ordinary customers or not. We'll have to wait until the checks come through.'

Whereas customers' deposit accounts used to be a source of stability, now they were as volatile as current ones. Usually the flow out would be balanced by flows in. A vital aspect of Schuster's job was to monitor those flows, so that if the bank's liquidity ratio declined, he could 'go out' to raise funds and restore the bank's liquidity. Such very short-term borrowing was the daily routine of a bank treasurer's life the world over.

However, if there were any kind of panic, that outflow could escalate hideously during the day and Schuster would have to 'go out' a second time, phoning around the money markets and those large corporations which regularly lent their surplus cash short-term for the benefit of slightly higher rates of interest. Corporate borrowings were the source of Roth's second, far worse, fear. Bartrum Bank held around $230 million of them, mainly 'at sight', which meant the owners could withdraw at any time. Usually they did not. They happily left their money to go on earning its fractionally better rate.

'What if the markets close on us? What if corporate lending officers start switching funds after reading the papers? We could be millions down in hours and no way to get funds.'

Being unable to raise short-term and overnight money was a banker's worst nightmare. Then the only solution was to pay higher rates and then, inevitably, word would get round that you were in trouble of some kind.

'Then we go to the Fed,' Schuster said. 'That's what the discount window's for.'

The Federal Reserve was the 'lender of last resort', through a borrowing technique called 'discounting'.

'One of us may have to go to New York, Dale. You're the Treasurer.'

'Jesus Christ!' Schuster exploded. 'I have to be where the action is. Right here.' Ray never seemed to learn. He should have stayed in real estate. He got frightened because he knew enough to get scared but not enough to be a professional. Being President was about the worst position from which to learn how a bank really worked. If Ray had accepted he was only a figurehead, things might have been okay. He might have listened to advice about those goddam MBA loans.

'Listen, Ray, we have a vice-president holed up in New York, right? If the corporations start pulling money out and Plaza refuses us funds, then Sheldon Harrison can earn his pay a little. Sheldon can go to the Fed. Hell, he knows more about what the real problem is than any of us.

Bogotá. Morning

'Forget it. They had your picture. You can't make denials. Anyway, who the hell wants to?'

Rodrigo Suarez lounging in the sun on the terrace of the villa he had been lent for the weekend, challenged Lopez-Santini with apparent confidence. Further off, a couple of girls lay in bikinis by the pool, occasionally turning over languidly and smoothing more lotion on their lithe tanned bodies. Suarez liked them in pairs.

'Listen,' Suarez continued, 'we were due back at Columbus Cay tonight. You postponed the meeting to Wednesday. Why in hell do we need a meeting at all?'

Suarez's eyes strayed to the girls by the pool. Without them around, yesterday's technical discussions would have been unbearable. Yesterday had been bad. The Colombian Minister had declined to commit himself, even though narcodollars had begun to filter back into the country and the Central Bank knew the country's foreign-exchange position was improving. On top of that, Lopez-Santini had been insistent on achieving a conciliatory default.

Then, like a miracle, just as he was organizing threats to be delivered in Buenos Aires, the newspaper stories had broken.

'Be a realist,' he went on, reaching for a rum and Coke, 'in Bolivia we don't give a damn. The Mexicans hate the *gringo* banks. Here they don't want to be slaves to Yanqui aid conditions. Peru by-passed the IMF long ago and has interest arrears going back to 1984. 1984, I tell you. No nation in the entire Group wants another rescheduling. So why pretend we're not going to default when in two days we are?'

'We gave an option, not an ultimatum.'

Lopez-Santini did not intend yielding. His contempt for Suarez grew by the minute. Last night he had been cold-bloodedly offered a woman and he'd been hard put to decline politely. If the Bolivian had displayed minimal tact, if at dinner he'd found himself next to someone attractive and she'd proved to be un-attached, well . . . But Suarez's whole approach had been insult-ingly crude, and typical of the man.

'I am in honour bound,' Lopez-Santini persisted. 'I gave an option. On Friday night, Osborn asked for an extension of time. I must allow that time. It is in no one's interest to promote a crisis ahead of then.'

'Why the hell should we play to their rules?' Suarez began to get angry. 'This time we make the rules, José-Maria, and no one compels us to honour options.'

Lopez-Santini bridled. He loathed this drug mafioso calling him by his Christian name. Worse, he was sure their absent host had been connected with a ruthless financial scandal a few years back, centring on a $70 million syndicated loan put together by Chase Manhattan, of which $13½ million had gone missing. The junior official in the Finance Ministry who noticed it first had been killed in a car crash, the head of a commission appointed to investigate had been shot, a government lawyer had also been shot and computerized records had been erased. The whole story was symptomatic of the known fact that around ten per cent of Colombian foreign borrowing was never entered in the National Budget – it was siphoned off by racketeers like Suarez's friends.

'I tell you,' he repeated, 'we shall still have to trade with foreign countries. I am deeply embarrassed by these press stories.'

'Past history,' Suarez commented brutally, and for once he was justified. 'Since you can't change the past, forget it. If the world thinks we're defaulting, it saves us argument.'

'A meeting is essential, if only to confirm a collective decision. I still intend to work for a conciliatory default. That is why I am going to New York tonight.'

Suarez winked at the girls, not that they were aware of it. He winked as he would at an accomplice, because this was where he was going to put one over this lousy, lily-livered academic, who had no business to be fouling up the real world.

'So you leave as the famous Osborn arrives?'

'Osborn?' Lopez-Santini was thrown off balance.

'You didn't know?' Suarez was swift to exploit an advantage. 'Just proves he's acting behind our backs, the bastard. Not that he stood a chance of keeping it quiet. His visit to the Central Bank tomorrow's about as secret as a whore's profession. Personally, I reckon he's taking a risk. Colombians don't like being double-crossed.' He let this idea sink home. 'You could have legitimized things. However, if you have to be in New York . . .'

'Unfortunately, I have urgent personal matters . . .' Lopez-Santini hesitated, fully comprehending the implied threat, torn because he was required to swear an affidavit regarding the ransom payment. 'I have to be there.'

'Your daughters?' Suarez swung his legs off the reclining chair and sat with his backside distending the blue canvas, though his eyes hardly left Lopez-Santini's face. 'Your daughters are in New York?'

'No.' Lopez-Santini stared back, suspicions crowding his mind. He himself had not mentioned Teresa and Gloria. 'In point of fact,' he said, adjusting the truth to test Suarez's reactions, 'I am going to see some lawyers. My daughters have been kidnapped.'

'Holy Mother of God!' The whistle of faked surprise caught the attention of the girls by the pool, who both sat up and then, relieved that this was not a call for their services, slumped back on to the sunbeds. They'd had an exhausting night.

'Is there anything I can do?' Suarez asked, altogether too concernedly.

'You?' The suspicions swelled to a surmise in Lopez-Santini's mind, an absurd surmise. Absurd until he remembered how drug-trafficking knows no frontiers. He looked back at his colleague, calculating how close to the bone he could cut. 'Our police believe the girls are in the hands of *traficantes*. The theory makes no sense, since the ransom demands have come from the ERP. Either way, I would do anything for their return.'

'Sure. Any decent father would.' Suarez made a show of thinking this through. 'I still have a few connections from the past.' He laughed, less pleasantly than he had intended. 'Even though all that is behind me.' The Argentine was on the hook, he saw precisely how to play him. 'You'd like me to put out feelers?'

'Discreetly. The men have shown they're killers.'

'They have?' Suarez again affected sympathy. 'Those guys are not the easiest to handle. Ever. What are your kids' names?'

London. 4 pm

The call from Warsaw made Stuart Pendler's day. He could have danced. Since morning he had been labouring for tomorrow's paper, splicing agency material with his own observations of activity in the City, normally dormant on Sundays. His usual contacts among brokers had refused to comment, fearful of spoiling their own trading positions in advance. Inevitably, his theme was speculative: how the markets would be hit on Monday. A single new fact to hang a story on is worth a page of speculation. Until the call came he lacked one.

'Mr Pendler?' the query in a recognizably central European accent followed a rigmarole with the operator and others. 'My name is Kryst. I am speaking on behalf of the Finance Minister. Your article has caused Dr Kaminski considerable distress. We wish to clarify certain things.'

'Why is he distressed?'

'You turn our Embassy's denial into a confirmation. This is incorrect. The Minister is not participating in discussions.'

'See here, Mr Kryst,' Pendler was prepared to defend himself, having no inkling where this complaint would lead. 'I was in that restaurant. He was with Lopez-Santini.'

As Kryst began to reply, another voice cut in, harsher, more authoritative. Pendler guessed Kaminski had been listening.

'You have misunderstood.' The Minister's English was laboured and guttural, but clear. 'There was a meeting, yes. After consideration, the Polish government has decided it is not in the national interest to take a further part.'

'May I quote you, sir?' Pendler was scribbling shorthand, his attitude changed.

'Yes. Poland will honour its international obligations. You may say that.'

Either the picture or the story must have caused one hell of a ruckus for Kaminski to be putting this on the record. Probably because default would make the economy more dependent on the Soviet Union. He posed the obvious next question.

'So you will not be attending the next meeting?'

'On Wednesday, no. But this is not for you to quote. You may say we wish to expand our trading relations with our neighbours in the Common Market.'

Kaminski made several more anodyne observations, concluding by warning again about quotations out of context. Reluctantly, Pendler promised to respect what could and could not be attributed directly to the Minister. Then he whooped with joy. He had an exclusive interview which deserved to lead the paper, plus the crucial date of the next conference.

'Debt-crisis cartel will meet Wednesday.'

The headline rose before his eyes, even though it was the one part of the story he did not write – that was done by the sub-editors. He had an absolute beat on everyone else. As for the location, Columbus Cay, he would try holding it over for Wednesday.

He was typing the story when he realized the date must have changed. Wednesday was the day for which the Club had accepted Maggie's booking. He rang to warn her.

'Don't worry, love.' She took it calmly. 'We'll still be there. If anything, more so. To coin a phrase, every picture makes a story.' How she proposed arriving she did not explain, nor that she was getting there a day earlier.

Len Slater had done the job as early as Gladys would let him, telling her they just had to pop into Heathrow on the way to Windsor and maybe on the way back again for a minute or two.

'All to do with yesterday, is it?' she had not been deceived. 'Well, it'll be nice to have Sunday lunch out for a change. We don't often, do we, dear? Count my blessings, I suppose.'

The shop steward, Kevin Gates, had accepted the two envelopes without fuss, the one with the documents, the other containing £80 in tens.

'Administrative instructions,' Slater had explained, as he handed the second one over the counter. Kevin had nodded.

'Okay, Len. No problem. Mind waiting for the waybill?'

'Waybill?'

'The airline's receipt. Gives the flight number, the weight, the number of packages, all that. Your friend who's sending this lot'll need it for sure. Won't take long.'

'Don't want to keep the wife hanging around. I'll come later.' The truth was he hadn't wanted to be hanging around himself, especially if anyone questioned the documentation. The waybill thing puzzled him – Ironsi had said nothing about bringing papers back. Obviously he'd have to, though.

So he had spent the other £20 on lunch and petrol and was now calling in again to collect the waybill. He left Gladys in the car and walked up the steps of the loading bay, then along into the small office in the end of the freight shed, where you rang a bell and waited for someone to come. Eventually Kevin was summoned.

'Lucky you weren't any longer,' he said. 'Need your signature on the T2L.'

'What's that?' Traces of alarm showed immediately in Slater's lined, rather gaunt face.

Gates eyed him, curious. Len had bent the rules for him,

fiddling an AUCAS pension when he was already on the British Airports Authority one, so he'd retire on two. One favour deserved another. He'd been happy to expedite the shipment. There'd been no need for the eighty quid either. Len must be losing his grip. Anyway there was no way he'd sign someone else's T2L for eighty quid or eight hundred. Messengers occasionally did and Len was only acting as a messenger. Still, he wondered if the old man knew what the consignment was. If not, he ought to.

'T2L's the Customs form,' he explained. 'Thought your friends might have done one in advance. Since you're here, we'd better just check the other docs.'

He removed the sheaf of papers from the folder one by one: the insurance certificate, half a dozen copies of invoices, an export licence from the Department of Trade. Slater took his spectacles from the pocket of his tweed jacket and put them on. From being a blur the description of the consignment resolved into legible typing: '30 Laser rangefinders. 30 Mk 3 Laser gunsights. 20 Laser bombsights. 200 image-intensifiers . . .' Christ alive, this wasn't computer software! The list of items continued, all of them military-sounding, '60 intruder-detection devices . . . Total value £1,830,000. F.o.b. London.'

'Interesting stuff,' Gates remarked. 'Not that the Customs people are objecting. They've had the export licence all the time.'

'My friends said there'd been a hold-up.' Slater was intensely relieved to hear the export licence hadn't been the trouble. The Customs and everyone else would instantly smell a rat if he'd brought a new one and then asked for it back, which he had been on the verge of doing.

'The exporters told us to hold everything a week ago. Said they couldn't release the shipment yet. If it hadn't gone by tomorrow we'd have told them to come and fetch it. Looks big this shed, but there's never enough space. Cost them a bomb in daily charges.' He laughed. 'Right word, eh? Bomb. Well, this set has the signatures. Only needs the T2L.' He pulled out the Customs form.

For a moment Slater still baulked at signing, covering up with a pretence of reading the paperwork. He noticed the invoices had been stamped by a bank and countersigned with the usual scrawl. The exporting company had signed too. The airline had stamped them. At least he was in good company. He added his own signature to the T2L.

'Okay then,' Gates said, cheerfully. 'Here's the waybill. Your mates at the company'll want that. Won't get their money from the bank without it when the consignment's f.o.b.' He produced the second envelope and handed it across. 'No need to give me "administrative instructions", Len. You should've known that.'

Slater mumbled an apology, taking both the waybill and the rejected kick-back. Kevin refusing cash was more ominous than any other aspect of this mission. Nor could he ask why, with other staff in earshot.

'So the shipment will leave tonight?' he confirmed.

'Be loaded in about an hour. Here today, Lagos tomorrow.' He grinned. 'Bad luck for the buggers on the receiving end. Laser sights are what the Yanks used on that Tripoli raid.'

'Thanks, Kevin.' Slater did not expect him to reply 'Anytime', and he didn't.

This might be all legal, but it smelt wrong and they both knew it did. So what had been wrong with the documents? The Customs had accepted them, the airline had accepted them. He just didn't know.

As soon as Gladys and he were home he rang the Colonel, who sounded surprised about the waybill.

'Send it to me, I suppose. You can put it in the post.'

'And . . .' Slater didn't want to mention the two million on the telephone.

'My dear chap, as soon as that consignment's unloaded, yours will be on its way.'

New York. Afternoon

The hotel was a cheap establishment on West 25th Street, where comings and goings attracted little attention and there were many local Hispanics. Maria had chosen it partly because Miguel might feel less conspicuous in a racially cosmopolitan area, partly because she had stayed there once before and it had been essential for the rendezvous to be fixed before either of them left Buenos Aires.

She was starting to worry seriously. Miguel should have checked in Friday night. Or, if he'd been forced to spend a whole day in Rio obtaining a visa, yesterday. He had the phone number. He had not called. She had sat in the room for hour after hour, waiting.

The room was at the back, looking into an internal well, a deep tunnel of gloom which direct light never reached. There was a so-called shower-room, little more than a cubicle with a spray fitment, a faucet and crevices into which the cockroaches scuttled as she entered. The suitcase of dollar bills stood in the closet. The suitcase was the other worry.

The choice of the first bank she visited on Friday had been a lucky break: a very lucky one. She'd spun a tale about having just sold her car for cash. The teller had said that that was okay, the authorities were only concerned about the movement of sums over $10,000. 'I guess its the laundering of drug money they want to stop,' he explained. Hiding her tote bag from his sight, she had extracted $9,500 and passed it across.

'You have some identification, Miss. Driver's licence? Social security card?'

Stifling an instinct to gather up the bills and walk straight out, she had been obliged to open an account in her own name. After some delay, she was issued with a passbook and left, realizing with a touch of despair that the banks closed at three and she could never dispose of $250,000 in the time. It was impossible to carry the suitcase around. She would have to use her tote bag, returning frequently to 25th Street to refill it. Quite apart from the risk of being mugged, she would end up holding a minimum of twenty-six passbooks. That would be crazy. So she had opened only four accounts – what normal citizen could plausibly want more in a single city – and had to lock the remaining $212,000 in the suitcase inside the closet.

Initially the situation had merely infuriated her. At home in Buenos Aires she could have disposed of the cash. Here she had no friends, no revolutionary connections – another illogical item added to the score she would settle with Tomas. Nor was she so imprudent as to look for criminal outlets. That would be an invitation to a knife in the back.

By Saturday night her normal self-contained calm was rippled by cat's-paws of fear. Miguel hadn't shown. Could Lopez-Santini have double-crossed them and brought in the cops? Suppose they informed New York? Not so many Argentine citizens travelled to and fro. Even though her name was not Maria, she began to feel unsafe. She ought to get out of the States again.

By Sunday morning she'd made up her mind. If Miguel hadn't come by noon tomorrow, she would take a chance and fly out to somewhere like the Bahamas where they didn't ask so many questions.

Finally, around 5 pm, the combination of fear and worry prompted her to take an almost equal risk. She went down to the young desk clerk and asked for a call to Argentina. He regarded her with suspicion.

'Guess you have to pay in advance,' he said. 'You have the money?'

She gave him a $20 bill and the number.

'In the booth,' he pointed to a grimy cupboard housing a telephone extension. 'You want person-to-person?'

'I'll speak to whoever's there.' She could think of no other way to trace Miguel except through Ramos – Ramos who had saved them in the car-park shoot-out and who expected to share in Miguel's pay-out. Except, again, that Ramos had disappeared thereafter. The only chance was a bar where, on account of his dark complexion, they knew him as 'El Negro'. The nickname had advantages, with the desk clerk eavesdropping.

'*Hola!*' She made it sound as if she was just round the corner. 'Is El Negro there?'

'I will ask.'

A long pause, 'Who wants him?'

'A friend of Miguel.'

'Miguel?' A longer pause. She could imagine the asides. Then Ramos himself came on the line and recognized her voice.

'Hey, where are you?'

'Not so far away. I'm trying to find Miguel.'

'I'm looking for that son of a bitch myself. He still owes me.'

She rang off as quickly as she could.

The acne-marked desk clerk regarded her with unblinking dishonesty. 'Four minutes, that'll be thirty-six.'

She fumed, paid and told him she was checking out tomorrow. She would fly to Nassau. The Bahamas had no restriction on the import of currency – they welcomed it for the casinos. All she had to do was get through the Customs and Emigration at JFK. Compared to fighting off the *traficantes*, that was nothing.

Bogotá. Afternoon

The gunman had never before been offered so much. A *mestizo* born of mixed Indian and Spanish blood, he was young enough to try anything, old enough in experience to succeed. The drug barons wanted a Yanqui killed and had nailed $100,000 to the contract. It wasn't the gunman's business to ask why. He was concentrating all his craft on the objective: a middle-aged Yank who would leave the Tequendama Hotel shortly before 9 am tomorrow morning and take a taxi to the Bank of the Republic on Carrera 7, not far from the Plaza Simon Bolivar.

The gunman called himself by a single name, Pedro, as if he were a famous bullfighter. He spent the early evening reconnoitring, calculating concealment, angles of approach, ways to escape. The hotel presented obstacles. If the taxi was ordered – as surely it would be – the American would walk straight out from the lobby and into the vehicle, leaving himself minimally exposed. On arrival he would be a simple target. The police guarding the bank would be unlikely to assist the occupant of a taxi. The American would pause to pay the driver. The disadvantage would be having so little cover on a main street. The gunman consulted his paymaster. Could the police confine their attention to the victim for the first thirty seconds? The paymaster thought they might.

Water Mill, Long Island. 5 pm

Reclining in the afternoon sun on the lawn at his home, where the mown grass stretched down to the sedge by the pond – the 'pond' was a small lake in size – Sheldon Harrison found it hard to believe that there was a panic starting anywhere, least of all here. He was in slacks and a polo shirt. The neighbour's boy was contentedly paddling his yellow canoe out on the water. He would have dismissed the crisis entirely, or at least until tomorrow, if he hadn't been back from New York at Ray Roth's insistence and if Roth and Schuster hadn't been beside him on the lawn.

As always when he was agitated, Roth was pounding the air with his fist, reiterating the briefing Schuster had already given.

'If the Fed wants our book of mortgage notes, you pledge them. They're good collateral. They're good, aren't they, Dale?'

'We have a good-quality book,' Schuster confirmed, anxious to calm Roth down. 'We have good customer notes from all over: auto agents, department stores, industries.' Like ACE, he thought bitterly, whose notes would soon be backed by little more than partially owned plant and a mortgaged factory. He hurried on with the list, in case Roth suffered the same realization. 'We have state securities, certificates of deposit . . .' If Roth wanted reassurance, he'd mention everything the Fed might accept all over again.

'You want me to take the notes themselves?' Harrison asked. 'Or do I just need authority in writing?' He had never performed the duty of borrowing at the 'discount window'.

'They should let us earmark our own collateral.' Schuster spoke with conviction. 'We're in good enough standing at this moment in time.'

The discount window was no longer the principal instrument of central bank operations. The Fed expected banks to go to the open market first. Schuster would be obliged to try corporate lending-officers and money-brokers before he sent Sheldon into action, and those people might require the actual documents.

'I guess we can keep the notes here. We're in good standing.' Schuster repeated.

'Are we?' Roth's agitation compelled him into physical movement. He heaved himself out of the canvas chair and began pacing the grass. 'You think we are? We have seventy-one million in capital and reserves and the loans to those goddam MBA bastards are forty-seven.'

'No problem,' Schuster insisted.

But Roth was walking away, figures stinging his consciousness like a swarm of bees, and he did not hear. He went towards the pond and the swarm followed, circling his head, buzzing and darting at him. Monies deposited with the bank totalled way over $840 million. Only a thirtieth of that had to be withdrawn tomorrow and his uncommitted reserves would be consumed. Only a thirtieth and he would have to begin calling in commercial loans, telling auto-dealers he could no longer underwrite their Fall floor-planning, cancelling stand-by letters of credit. If that wasn't enough, individual overdrafts would have to be called in, ultimately mortgages foreclosed on. The Fed's 'last resort' lending was essentially short-term.

The figures stung unbearably. Forgetting the others, he wandered down towards the reeds bordering the pond. The boy in the canoe waved and he raised a hand mechanically, envying him the placid water. The reeds seemed to grow higher as he approached, ready to envelop him. He noticed a track. There were tiny pebbles on the track as it led to the water, and the buzzing around his head diminished as he trod it. He wished he were in a boat like the boy, able to paddle away under the road-bridge and out into the wide expanse of Mecox Bay where the swarm could not follow.

'Ray!' A shout disturbed this dream of sanctuary. He turned, realizing his shoes were wet. Harrison was coming down the lawn. 'Ray! I guess if I'm going back tonight we should fix that paperwork.'

Roth nodded. As he trudged slowly back, the figures began to buzz round his head again.

New York. 8 pm

As the Avianca flight from Bogotá touched down, Lopez-Santini reflected how ridiculous it was that you could fly direct from any capital in South America to New York, yet communications within the continent remained complicated and poor. Few things illustrated the neo-colonial relationship more clearly. Not that this occupied his mind for long. His lawyer and the Consul should be meeting him here at Kennedy, ready to drive him straight to call on the police captain in the precinct where the kidnappers had cashed the draft.

The Minister was both annoyed and concerned at having crossed paths with Osborn in Colombia. He would make the point forcibly with Warburton tomorrow that *he* was the negotiator representing the Group. If Osborn met an uncompromising reception down there, he had only himself to blame. Meanwhile, the kidnapping came first.

When he emerged from Immigration, a process only somewhat facilitated by his diplomatic passport, the lawyer and the Consul were waiting. In the limousine he asked various questions.

'The bank has given its video to the police?'

'This afternoon, Excellency.'

That was progress. They now had pictures to help them hunt for the woman, about whom he possessed only one useful fact: she was an Argentine trying to unload a lot of money in a hurry. Plenty of his fellow citizens had infinitely larger sums deposited in this city, but he could not believe that there would have been many with $250,000 in cash here over the weekend. Lopez-Santini had abandoned trying to conceal his predicament from the Consul. He was determined on action at all costs.

James Warburton dined by himself at the Carlyle Hotel, unable to be seduced by any of the more exotic dishes on the king-sized menu – more like the programme for a gala performance at Covent Garden Opera than a *carte du jour* – and settled for a grilled steak. The *maître d'hôtel* understood perfectly, ordered the other place-settings at the table to be removed by a *commis* waiter, suggested a 1978 burgundy to accompany the meat, and tactfully left the Englishman to contemplate whatever was on his mind in peace.

He had a lot to think about. Bill Osborn's message from Rio this morning had been unsettling. The Governor of the Banco do Brasil had begged for patience and indicated that foreign exchange would very shortly be released to meet trade credits. In Warburton's view, this simply confirmed the theme he had pursued at the Swiss–American Chamber of Commerce: that the debtor nations would square off their trade debts to the outside world before a default, since the totals involved were relatively small and would be vital for them to keep their import–export businesses going.

Meanwhile, Harrison's attempts to track down Lopez–Santini had failed. Warburton could only suppose that the Argentine would surface shortly. Then Harrison had left for the rest of the day to attend to what sounded like a nervous breakdown on the part of the Bartrum Bank's President.

To cap it all, responses from the rescheduling committee members were falling far short of what he and Osborn considered the minimum the debtors would accept. Yet they all reported disquieting indications of that man Pendler having sparked a major panic.

When the wine waiter brought the burgundy, his spirits recovered briefly. Sardonically challenging the future, he raised his glass and privately toasted 'Black Monday'. God knows where the expression derived from, but whoever coined it had possessed remarkable prescience.

Tokyo. 9 am, Monday June 17th

If you were a stock and securities trader and hoped for a six-figure salary, plus bonuses, before you were thirty, you needed several qualities. You had to be an innovator, dreaming up new financial formulas to attract your clients; you had to be able to make instant buying and selling decisions on the telephone whilst watching prices flicker and change on a VDU screen. Overall you had to possess a brain that could outstrip a computer, because the computer could only forecast the way a trend might continue and you could do better: you could sense when the trend would reverse.

At twenty-nine Jock Anderson had all these abilities finely honed, which was why he headed the Tokyo office of a London stockbroking firm owned by an American financial conglomerate. The Americans wanted results all the time. Anderson was a Scot, a mathematics graduate whose speed with figures had led into this unexpected career. He was not an innovator on the scale of whoever invented the Eurodollar, the offshore dollar in which investments were free of US withholding tax – or any other government's tax – and from which had developed a multi-billion Eurobond market. But Anderson had devised a method of attracting the ultra-conservative and American-oriented Japanese into British government bonds. This job was his reward.

Anderson had decided on Sunday that there would be a stock-market panic and that British government bonds, which gave fixed interest with guaranteed security, were going to boom at the expense of industrial shares. The Japanese were notorious for 'off-the-floor' trading and for doing it any time of the day or night. When the phone calls started flowing into his home on Sunday he was ready. At their close of business on Friday evening, the traders in his London office had passed a statement of their 'inventory' of stocks with indications on which to quote. This was his starting point.

'Here is our position,' the traders had said in effect. 'We're holding a bull of £300 million and a bear of £120 million.'

The 'bull' was a list of stocks the firm owned and expected to sell at a profit. The 'bears' were stocks they had contracted to provide later and expected to be able to buy more cheaply before delivery was due.

Anderson was based in Tokyo in order to deal. But he had to balance both sides of this 'position' as he traded. The greatest danger would be contracting to sell more of the bear stocks and finding that the price in London rose sharply tomorrow morning, leaving his firm with a loss. In the broking business, prices changed all the time, if only by fractions of one per cent – but fractions could spell millions. One half of one per cent of the inventory available today represented £1,500,000.

On a Sunday he had one advantage. He could demand that the Japanese dealers telephoning him at home committed themselves irrevocably before 8.30 on Monday morning, half an hour before the Tokyo Stock Exchange opened.

However, by teatime on Sunday he had become concerned at the volume. If the representatives of other American-owned rivals like Salomon and Goldman Sachs were doing the same, which he could bet a haggis to a rusty horseshoe they were, the pressure tomorrow would be intense and the prices they'd been making could prove too low. A dealer has to deal but he isn't compelled to do so at weekends. From four o'clock onwards he had his wife Isobel answering the phone, regretting that he was 'unavailable'.

By 8.30 on Monday morning every single bargain Anderson had entered into had been confirmed and he began to smell huge profits. There was a definite flight developing out of corporate stocks and into the safety of guaranteed government bonds.

Quick telephoning around dealers in bullion, commodities and currency revealed a comparable rush to buy. The VDUs in his office, charting off-the-floor deals in equities, showed falling prices.

Tokyo had one of the largest equity markets anywhere. Its stock exchange was the second busiest in the world – next after New York – and the Japanese were inveterate small investors, putting as much as twenty per cent of their disposable incomes into savings. Those small investors were unlikely to be selling yet, but his Japanese opposite numbers must be expecting them to. He decided to ring London to confirm his intentions. His plan was to force the market up every point he could.

'I agree, Jock,' his boss decided, when the call woke him at his Belgravia apartment shortly before 1 am London time. 'If this turns into the bull market you expect, make the highest prices you can and limit the quantities. If they bid enough, they'll get the bonds: if they don't, they won't. Keep in touch.'

The boss, named Philip Lindsay, apologized to his wife, though she was inured to these midnight disturbances, switched off the bedside light again and lay on his back thinking for a while. He had read the Sunday papers. He had expected a flight into quality. If Tokyo was like this, then when the pressure hit London and New York there was likely to be chaos. He reached out and fumbled to set his electronic alarm for an hour earlier than usual. He would need to be at work ahead of the rush.

In Tokyo, when the Exchange opened, Anderson began explaining to vociferous if invariably polite clients that there was a lot of demand for British government 'gilt-edged' stocks. With virtually every bargain struck, he jacked up the price. Within half an hour, he had marked £11 million of sales. Within an hour, the prices London had been quoting on Friday night were as out of date as Roman coins, and he was restricting individual deals in size.

By midday he was in a potentially perilous 'bear' position on short-dated British bonds, and was offering only those with a longer five- to fifteen-year coupon, while his assistant hastily bought financial futures on the Singapore Stock Exchange as a hedge against the price rises. The VDUs in his office – as a foreigner he was not permitted on the floor of the Tokyo Stock Exchange – showed tumultuous falls in local Japanese equities. History was being made, and when that happened, above all times, a trader could not sit back and wish it wasn't. A dealer had to deal. Fortified by frequent cups of green tea – a local custom he had adopted – Anderson rejoiced and dealt.

Disturbance and fear are the shrewd dealer's natural allies. When Tokyo closed and he transferred his computer 'book' back to London he had sold over £300 million of bonds, many long-dated. In the fullness of the next week, his firm would make a £20 million profit on his day's work.

'It's a flight into fixed-interest with a vengeance,' he commented as he telephoned through his analysis of events to Philip Lindsay. 'If the central banks don't intervene, I think the equity market will collapse tomorrow, and ordinary punters will cut and run to anything they think will hold its value.'

He knew there were certain things the conservative Japanese were unlikely to invest in – art and diamonds among them. He was predicting Western reactions.

CHAPTER TEN

London. Morning, Monday June 17th

Philip Lindsay had left his Eaton Square flat at 7.10 am and been at his desk half an hour when Anderson's closing call came through. Unlike his subordinate, he found himself wondering if the electronic age of dealing would cope any better with this evident emergency than the old system, or whether the speed and sensitivity of its reactions, coupled with the billions of pounds, dollars, yen and other currencies involved, would merely intensify a panic.

Back in the days when stockbroking was a profession for gentlemen, and only individuals could be members of the London Stock Exchange, Philip Lindsay's great aunts and uncles used to write – or sometimes daringly telephone – to their brokers and ask advice on whether this or that share should be bought or sold. The brokers themselves acted on clients' instructions, while men called 'jobbers' held a pool of stock and traded with the brokers. This gentlemanly system had not prevented his grandfather from being wiped out in the 1929 crash.

Those clients and brokers would both have been stupefied by the way Lindsay's firm operated today – as much by the capital involved as by the computerization. In their day, a stockbroker who bought for his firm, rather than against clients' orders, took notorious risks. Yet Lindsay's company owned its £300 million inventory of 'bull' positions. It was their equivalent to a shopkeeper's stock.

Six decades after the 1929 crash, sterling was no longer the world's dominant currency and Britain's financial citadel, the City of London, had been stormed by the megabuck. Most stockbroking firms and discount houses had been forced to sell out either to American financial conglomerates or to British merchant and commercial banks. There was no other way they could compete after the so-called 'Big Bang' had opened the Stock Exchange to outsiders.

On the memorable date of October 27th 1986, everything had changed. The gilt-edged jobbers became 'market-makers' and the trading with which Lindsay's firm had been concerned turned into a telephone market. Although in the mind of the public the Stock Exchange's trading floor, with its distinctive hexagonal pitches, remained symbolic, a substantial proportion of its £2 billion daily turnover had transferred to a less tangible nexus of phone links and computer databases, with deals and prices displayed on terminals available throughout Britain.

Lindsay was the partner who had adapted best to this ruthless transition. He had survived and prospered at the cost of an horrific working day and threats from his wife that if he did not pay more attention to his family they were heading for the divorce courts. When he had left the regular army prematurely she had never imagined he would have such a flair for dealing. His success was partly due to its being underlaid by dispassionate self-discipline.

After Anderson's call he briefed his trading staff with his customary succinctness.

'What we're going to be faced with is a massive flight into fixed-interest stocks, and the greater their liquidity, the better. A lot of the demand will wash straight through to US Treasuries, and I imagine the discount houses here will run out of Treasury bills very fast. The key for us will be gilts.'

In financial terms 'liquidity' meant holding either cash or assets which could be converted rapidly into cash. With the solvency of the banks in question no one would put money on deposit in the ordinary way. The best haven was in so-called 'government debt': fixed-interest bonds and bills issued by governments to raise money. Anyone holding those had guaranteed interest and guaranteed repayment; provided the governments themselves were sound. The best governments were the American, Japanese, Swiss, German, Swedish and British. The best bills were very short-term ones, due ideally for repayment within three months, like British Treasury ones.

Short-term bills were easily resold, because their repayment date was so close, and hence they had high liquidity. This Monday the principal aim of brokers and investors was to take positions in funds which could be shifted fast as the international situation changed.

'Only short-term paper, Philip?' one of the traders asked.

'We'll mop up as much as we can, but don't be afraid to go long. This pressure must bring rates down and when it does we can make a killing in longer-dated paper.'

The point about the stocks was simple. Government bonds carried fixed interest rates. If you paid £100 for a 10 per cent bond, then it paid exactly 10 per cent. If demand forced the price up to £110 then that bond's interest yield fell in proportion to 9.1 per cent. Eventually, as the clamour for short-dated bonds brought the interest rates down, the stocks that were longer-dated would respond, and their value would rise. A trading firm like Lindsay's had to replenish its inventory constantly. The obvious way was to get into longer-dated bonds ahead of demand for them.

The traders asked a few more questions, already imbued with restrained excitement, and returned to the rows of VDU screens, telephones and time-zone clocks in their trading-room. By the time New York opened, the atmosphere would be at fever pitch.

It was around lunchtime that Stuart Pendler realized that the story he had originated was now beyond his capacity to report. The huge surge of selling which had begun in Tokyo took shape as it rolled back around the world, but in London all he could do was observe the crest of this wave as it roared through Europe, gathering a greater weight behind it every hour, eventually to crash on the American markets, when they opened.

He had started by writing comment on the London Stock Exchange, quickly replacing conventional phrases like 'stocks post losses', in his draft article, with 'British industrials show fifty-point fall'. Then, as he read the Reuter tape and spoke to the few dealers who were prepared to spare a second, he appreciated that what he had taken for a 'flight into quality' had become something a lot simpler: a rush for liquidity at all costs.

From Japan, news agencies reported entrepreneurs buying up car-tyres and batteries, while housewives rushed to the stores to stock their deep-freezes. Ordinary Japanese investors, who mistrusted foreign stocks, had sought refuge in their own government's yen bonds, creating a huge bull market. Otherwise they relied on the great household gods of their national economy for protection, like the Mitsubishi Corporation. Bank shares were hard hit and at lunchtime panicky citizens began queueing in the streets to withdraw their savings.

The Sydney markets had reacted similarly, though with no panic. In Singapore, which depended entirely on supplying other industrial countries with commercial goods and services, the *Straits Times* Industrial Index dropped sharply in instant reaction to the dangers of recession. In Hong Kong the Gold and Silver Exchange was experiencing intense speculative buying, while the Hang Seng Stock Index dropped like a stone. Fortunes would be made and lost in the Crown Colony before the sun set.

But the underlying story was the same worldwide. A vast flow of funds was looking for safe havens and hoping to find them in Europe or the United States.

The snag, Pendler knew well, was that Europe had no havens large enough: the Bank of England issued only £5 million in Treasury bills each week; the supply of West German guaranteed *Schuldschein* bonds was small; and Swiss securities were hard to get. No one would part with holdings of high-quality Eurobonds, like those issued by the World Bank and the Kingdom of Sweden, except at a grotesque mark-up. By contrast, the US Treasury made available $150 billion of short-term bills a year.

That was it. The only financial market capable of accepting the vast flow of money was New York, and the world's most acceptable debt instruments, as they were called, were US Treasuries. Since those could only be bought with dollars, there was a wild trade into the dollar, which was rising fast against the yen. So was the Swiss franc and the Deutschmark. Sterling was steady. That puzzled him, until he appreciated that the British banks were not seen as being in such peril as American ones, although their shares had sunk.

By three in the afternoon, Pendler had a clear enough picture to start writing a report. There were three legs to the world's financial stool. Government bonds were going up; major currencies were firm because bonds had to be bought with them; ordinary shares – equities – were crashing, with the banks suffering worst of all. A panic had begun. When small investors learnt from the radio, TV and newspapers what was happening, their precious portfolios would already have depreciated twenty per cent, unless they were in government bonds. That panic could only become more intense. He was putting this on paper when his phone rang with news he ought to have anticipated.

'Mr Pendler? You don't know who I am and it is better that you don't.' The voice was British, slightly effete, with a breathlessness appropriate to a gossip column. 'You may like to know that certain Arabs are withdrawing funds from London.'

'Who?' Pendler was alert at once.

'Some Gulf sheikhs. No names. My firm has had instructions to withdraw more than three billion pounds today. We have also concluded a hotel sale at a long way below the intended figure.'

'Who are you? How can I believe this?'

'It'll show up in the money markets.' The phone went dead.

'Christ,' Pendler thought, 'if the Arabs pull out there will be trouble.' Their money was at the root of the debt problem. They'd lent short, often only overnight and at the most for a few months, on and on for years. But the banks had lent that money out again long, relying on the Arabs constantly rolling over the bulk of the loans. The Arabs had begun withdrawing funds after the oil-price falls hit their revenues. If this anonymous caller was right, they were getting out of property too. This was news in its own right – it was the Arabs who had started the London property boom.

Pendler finished his story with the sentence: 'Meanwhile, in London Bank of England officials were understood to be conferring with other central banks on moves to prevent commercial bank insolvencies if the Third World debt default is confirmed.'

When he reckoned the copy had filtered through the computers in Paris he rang the editor and found himself under unexpected attack.

'You've gotten us a great story, Stu,' Grant said sarcastically. 'How many billions of dollars d'you reckon its going to cost the West?'

'There's $580 billion of bank money . . .'

'And how many bank failures?' Grant cut in. 'How many millions unemployed?'

'Hey,' Pendler came alive in protest. 'I didn't invent this thing. I found out it was happening.'

Two hundred miles away, Harry Grant wiped his forehead with the back of his hand. He was exhausted.

'I've had my lines jammed with calls from angry bank officers half the day. They have a point. There is a flip side to this story. There are the banks' defences.'

'I mentioned that the central banks are getting together.'

'Sure.' Grant had to admit the reporter's job was to report the news and the news was of growing panic. 'Just the same, Stu, you can't cover this out of London. No one could. We'll be leading with Wall Street reports. I want you back on the original thing: this debt cartel and Western defences against it. You still have a beat on that.' Ruefully, Pendler agreed.

'Here,' Grant continued. 'Let me read you something that came in earlier from Manila. On second thoughts, I'll summarize. It's about the Philippine government giving an undertaking to some Swedish woman banker that it will not, repeat not, participate in a default.'

'Confirms my story.' He left unsaid that it would probably only worsen the panic by its implication that other nations were defaulting.

'I'd like you to speak with this woman and find out what it means. Our Stockholm stringer can profile her. You get the financial deal.'

'Must be a run-up to the cartel's next meeting. Like the Poles quitting.'

'Precisely. You get back on that. We have an avalanche of copy on the panic. I want to know what's going to stop it. How the commercial banks are acting, what support structure the Bank of England and the Fed are rigging up.'

Pendler accepted the order. He didn't trouble to point out that if any single item of news would make a default certain, that item would be that the Western governments were ready to bail out their banks. If they were, why should a Nigerian, a Brazilian or a Mexican bother to negotiate? They'd know they were going to get away with it.

Bogotá. 9 am

In keeping with his low-profile policy, Bill Osborn had not re-quested an official car to ferry him from the Tequendama Hotel to his meeting with the Governor of the Central Bank. He had breakfasted in his room, pondering the limited and biased account of the debt crisis in the local newspapers, and wishing Colombia was less remote from the mainstream of events. In Brazil they had more than pretensions to leadership; theirs was a powerful nation, a major force in Latin American development. He was moderately confident that the Brazilian authorities would live up to their promises. By contrast, Colombia was backward, its ordinary people accustomed to endemic violence, its presidential system inherently weak because even the most admired leader was pro-hibited from a second term. What effect would publicity for the default have on his discussions here? He was thinking this through and finishing his coffee when the reception rang to say his car had arrived.

'You're sure?'

'It is for you, señor.'

'Have the driver wait in the lobby.'

Osborn was immediately suspicious. He had not needed Jim Warburton's counsel to keep his wits about him here. The locals would snatch the spectacles off a tourist in the street, let alone watches or wallets, and knife him if he resisted. Kidnappers everywhere played the three-card trick with cabs, deluding the victim into picking their vehicle from the line.

However, the uniformed driver standing near the reception desk in the lobby carried identification and a letter confirming the appointment at the Central Bank. He shepherded Osborn out to a limousine with a practised mix of deference and speed, while a porter trailed behind with the luggage.

'I shall take you to the airport after, señor,' the driver explained as he set off.

During the short drive Osborn noticed that the traffic fumes were as bad as ever. Reputedly, the combination of smog and the rarefied air at the city's 8,000-foot altitude could make it hard to light a fire in Bogotá. Well, he thought, that's appropriate, since I'm here to damp a conflagration down. He turned his mind to the next step. Publication of the cartel's existence threw his whole negotiation with Lopez-Santini into a dangerous new perspective. The US regulators would be intervening to protect the dollar today. As for that braggart of a presidential aide, Bud Phillips, he almost hoped Manny Hanny would go down. Not that it would. The banks to fail would be small outfits like Sheldon Harrison's in Long Island. Osborn wished now that he had cut out this side trip. Colombia's debt was not so vast. He had taken a risk in not returning to New York until tonight, relying on the extra time Lopez-Santini had reluctantly agreed. Warburton could cope internationally, but it would be less easy for a Briton to talk turkey with the US authorities.

'We are almost there, señor.'

The driver spoke over his shoulder, and Osborn came out of his reverie, recognizing the old and dignified bank building ahead. Children were playing tag on the sidewalk – there seemed to be children everywhere in this city – and as the driver slowed he noticed a mid-1950s Studebaker parked near the bank entrance. His son would go crazy for that, bad as its condition looked. A young man in jeans was leaning against it, his elbow resting on the door. He turned his head in curiosity as the limousine glided past, then was hidden from Osborn's view by the bulk of his own veteran car.

As the limousine stopped, one of the policemen guarding the bank entrance stepped forward, while the driver darted out to run round and open the door. Briefcase clutched in his left hand, Osborn ducked his head to emerge, unable to avoid the moment of awkwardness inherent in alighting from the back seat. He straightened up while the driver held the door. Then, as he made for the entrance, a colossal blow hit him in the shoulder, spinning him round, and the next instant a tearing pain wrenched his chest. He fell, his spectacles clattering into the gutter, only distantly hearing a fusillade of shots hit the Studebaker as his consciousness faded.

*

'My younger colleagues in London think they work long hours,' Warburton confided to Sheldon Harrison. 'They're fooling themselves. This is a twenty-four-hour-a-day game,' he laughed gently, 'and it could get worse.'

Senior executives in the big investment banks, like those in all the thirty-nine primary dealing firms who underwrote all issues of US government bonds, routinely reached their offices before 7 am and spent twelve hours there, snatching a sandwich for lunch. They earned their high pay. When they arrived they were briefed by staff who had been on night shifts monitoring positions taken by their branches or subsidiaries in Europe and the Far East. Firms like Salomon Brothers and Goldman Sachs traded around the clock and earned $400 million a year off inventories worth as much as $8 billion. Today their turnover would be colossal.

Effectively, the momentum of the selling wave had hit New York long before the stock markets opened, and by 10 am Warburton and Harrison themselves had already devoted two and a half hours to wrestling with the implications for the rescheduling committee. Bank shares had sagged like a hot-air balloon with the burner off.

'If we fail to reach agreement with Lopez-Santini by Wednesday,' Warburton remarked bluntly, 'this fall in share values is going to expose a great many more banks than it's threatening now.'

Harrison didn't argue. He knew. Bartrum Bank's capitalization – the market value of its equity – had stood at $51 million on Friday and it had reserves of $20 million: total $71 million, as against its $47 million of Latin American debt. If Bartrum's shares fell to half last week's price the figures would be appallingly different. Capitalization under $26 million, reserves still $20 million: total less than $46 million against the $47 million debt. Bartrum Bank would be insolvent even without a single other loan or advance going bad. The same could happen to hundreds of others. And if the $230 million of short-term corporate deposits were withdrawn . . . he didn't like to think about that situation.

'What was the London price fall?' he asked.

'One hundred and forty-one points on the FT Index. I'm not surprised we're getting all these telexes. Everyone's worried stupid, and it won't help the banks one iota that the equivalent of the whole Third World debt will be traded today and a few financiers will end up multi-millionaires while the poor continue to starve.'

That was the rub. All the financial activity of a normal day – the $100 billion of currency exchanges, the 125 million separate deals struck on the New York Stock Exchange, the commodity-trading in items from gold to soybeans, the sales of US Treasuries through those thirty-nine primary dealers – would combine like a giant magnet to draw money out of deposits with the banks and into whatever was perceived as safer. As figures, the trillions of dollars that washed around the markets were incomprehensible. The figures would only become real in terms of bankruptcies, mortgages foreclosed and private loans called in.

'Do we know where Lopez-Santini is yet?' Warburton asked, almost rhetorically, since Sally would have brought in any message. She shook her head. 'We'll have to go on chasing that Argentine Consul.'

The only cheering news was when Mette Svenson arrived, unannounced, having completed her Philippines' mission.

'They accepted Mr Osborn's outline terms,' she told them, delight showing through the fatigue of travel. 'I thought after, maybe I could do better. I am not sure.'

'You've done marvellously,' Warburton assured her. 'If you're not too tired, perhaps you could help us work out a consensus of agreement for the other banks.' He indicated the telexes Harrison was working on.

'Is Mr Osborn not here yet?' she enquired a few minutes later. 'I had expected to see him.'

'God willing,' Warburton consulted his watch, 'he'll be through with the Governor of the Colombian Central Bank about now, and back with us tonight.'

London. 4.45 pm

Richard Stephens was delighted. He sat in his shirt-sleeves at his ornate desk, perspiring gently from the early summer heat-wave which had hit southern England at the weekend, and playing with figures on his calculator and watching the VDU.

Through shrewd appreciation of what Sunday's news meant, he had achieved a month's turnover before lunch. His bank might be among the smallest investment-banking concerns operating amid the fabulous wealth of the Middle East, but he had still made a fortune today. He had done it quite simply by starting to telephone his Arab clients in Saudi Arabia and the Gulf at four in the morning – his time, not theirs – and suggesting that if they wished to save their financial skins they should move everything they had out of London banks and London property.

Enough of the sheikhs had already been nervous about investments as a result of oil-price falls cutting their revenues. They had responded.

Stephens was now so busy that he had to hand a hotel deal to an assistant, who accepted a price of £5 million, which was a long way below last week's valuation. No matter – their cut was two and a half per cent. But the real profit came from what he had been doing flat out all day: shifting funds. By the afternoon, he had either taken back, or arranged to recover, £3 billion of short-term paper. The American and British banks concerned had protested that panic was unnecessary. They had completely missed the point: it was vitally necessary in terms of Richard Stephen's commission. He showed further profit when he reinvested on behalf of his sheikhs in US Treasuries and Swiss deposit accounts. As he had pointed out to them, the Swiss might pay extremely low rates of interest compared to American or British banks, but they were the only banks in the world where deposits would be safe in a crisis.

The process of making these switches would take up to three days, and while it lasted it was a bonanza. It was to help keep the bonanza running that he had briefly made his anonymous phone call to Stuart Pendler. The *Trib* was air-freighted to the Gulf, and it would do no harm for his more reluctant clients to read about what their rival sheikhs were doing. All being well, he would scoop in a further yield of selling orders early tomorrow.

The only call he did not want, but felt obliged to take, was from Len Slater. The old fool was blathering on about his Nigerian two million. Had the money come in yet?

'Let's face it, Len,' he had let fly, 'this is not a tremendously probable day for anything to arrive from Nigeria, least of all funds.'

By the late afternoon, Philip Lindsay's forecast had proved correct. While equities and bank shares had slumped, turnover in gilts had been enormous.

'The market's bigger than us,' he reported to New York. 'I think we should now start selling short and buy again when it cracks. In the meantime, we'll borrow bonds from insurance companies and fund managers.'

'You reckon this bull will collapse?' The American recognized the danger. Lindsay was proposing to switch from buying as prices rose to selling what he did not yet possess, in the belief that they would fall. To do so when the market was up and running required strong nerves.

'There's rumour about the Bank of England supporting the commercial banks. If they don't, there'll be a loss of confidence in sterling. That and huge profit-taking could turn this bull into a bear.'

'You're in the game to deal, Philip,' the American decided. 'You deal.'

When Lindsay rang off he knew this would be the most nail-biting week of his broking career. He sat debating his suppositions again. People seemed to have forgotten that the British banks had made some provision against a Third World default. Furthermore, the situation was crucially different to that in the United States, with its many thousands of banks. When only five dominated the British domestic scene it was unthinkable for the Bank of England not to bail them out. There would be repercussions later, certainly. Shareholders would find their dividends were savaged. Inflation would increase. But today's scramble into ultra-safe government paper was unjustified. It was in the United States that they faced real trouble. He would stick by his views. If he was correct, his strategy would earn a colossal profit. If he was wrong, he'd be out of a job.

Hauppage, Long Island. 10.20 am

Paul Gianni's temper had not been improved by the way the bank officer at Plaza had spoken to him.

'I appreciate that, sir,' the man had said. 'We have your details on file. No Brazilian payments have been received. When they are, you'll be notified.' He had then cut the next question short. 'We're busy here right now, sir. Like I said, you'll be notified.'

Gianni could not know that Plaza was struggling to answer queries from precisely 102 correspondent banks which its senior executives had lured into MBA syndicated loans. Nor that the President of Plaza was in Washington, personally seeking assurance from the Comptroller of the Currency. If the default took place, Plaza would be insolvent more than twice over, and it was the duty of the Comptroller to order closure of any insolvent banking institution. Plaza's President was asking him to look the other way for a while, so that a merger could be arranged or some other safety net put in place.

Not that Gianni's reaction would have been any different had he known. He'd probably have snarled 'Tough luck, baby!' and done exactly what he now did: run down to where the workforce was assembled on the factory's floor.

'Okay, fellers,' he announced, standing atop a crate so that they could all see him, 'let's go. Maybe when we hit Southampton the goddam Bartrum Bank will decide to find some payroll money hidden in its goddam vault.'

New York. *11.10 am*

The Immigration Officer checking outgoing passengers at J. F. Kennedy airport was watching for any woman in her late twenties travelling on an Argentine passport. He asked Maria where she was going and let her through, at the same time pressing the buzzer for assistance. She never noticed the hold-up caused by a plain-clothes officer coming to the desk as she passed relievedly on to the departure lounge.

'Could be the one. Description fits,' the Immigration man explained. 'She's on a Nassau flight . . .'

The plain-clothes officer had photographs printed from the bank camera's vidoetape. He went through to the departure lounge, accompanied by two police officers, whom he told to stand outside. Then he unobtrusively surveyed the waiting passengers, made comparisons with the pictures and ordered the airline staff to announce a ten-minute departure delay when they saw the police come in. He wanted everyone distracted. He did not want a gunfight in this crowded area.

When she noticed the cops Maria tensed, staying rigidly seated. She had no weapon except bluff. The announcement began. Instinctively she turned towards the sound.

'Miss Maria,' the plain-clothes man was standing in front of her. He was young and spoke softly, 'I guess you may have to miss your flight.'

She looked around. The two cops were a short distance on either side, fingers resting on their holsters. They did a poor job of looking unconcerned.

'Why?' She tried to sound surprised. 'What's the trouble?'

'We'd like to talk with you.'

The plain-clothes man was extraordinarily cool. None the less, she hefted the tote bag carefully in case they got the wrong idea. The cops followed close behind as she left, ignoring the stares and whispering as the other passengers realized things had been happening besides the announcement.

Once outside the lounge they snapped handcuffs on her and hustled her away through a staff exit. She thought of struggling then, furious at giving up when they hadn't even found the money.

'Forget it, lady.' One of the cops read her attitude.

Twenty minutes later, her checked bag had been retrieved. If she had not been so self-disciplined she would have cried. The whole business had been an abortion. She cursed Miguel for his failure to arrive.

London. 7 pm

At first Gladys Slater mistook him for a salesman. After the chimes sounded in the hall she had cautiously opened the front door to find this man in a blue blazer, carrying a briefcase, on the doorstep. He had a patient, weary look in his eyes, and she assumed he was selling insurance.

'Not today, thank you,' she said firmly.

He didn't move or smile, just held out a card in a protective plastic cover.

'Metropolitan Police, Mrs Slater. I'd like to speak to your husband, please.'

She gawped at the warrant card, let him in and hurried upstairs. Len was changing. She closed the bedroom door behind her.

'What shall I say?'

'Tell him I'll be down.' Slater tried to calm himself by dressing meticulously. The day had been catastrophic already. The two million had not come through, via Stephens' bank or any other. The Nigerian High Commission had insisted Colonel Ironsi was out of town.

When Slater entered the parlour, the policeman was sitting precisely where Ironsi had sat only two days ago. He was in no doubt about the connection.

'Good evening, sir. My name's Paulson. Detective-Inspector. Fraud Squad.' The weariness had vanished, as it always did when Paulson knew he had come to the right place. 'I'd like to ask a few questions, if you don't mind. I understand you signed a Customs declaration at Heathrow Airport yesterday.'

'Yes?' Slater sat down. This was going to take time.

As the questioning proceeded, he found his mood swinging violently from hope to fear. Hope when he realized no Customs or export offence had been committed, confused apprehension as Paulson reached the crux.

'The exporter's signatures on those documents were not genuine, Mr Slater. The Export Manager had withheld his signature until his bank received confirmation from Nigeria that there was foreign exchange available for the consignment. It was f.o.b., Mr Slater. You know what that means?'

He did not. He stayed anxiously silent.

'"Free on board" means that the exporter's bank pays him on receipt of copies of the shipping documents. In this case it could not because, in spite of promises, Nigeria never released the funds. The Export Manager only found out that the consignment had left when he sent a truck to bring it back. He'd like to know who signed those documents, and so would we.'

Slater tried to explain his role, while the detective took notes. He explained about Keith wanting to fight apartheid and about Richard Stephens, whom he was sure was crooked; about the businessman on the plane; the lawyer Ayokolo; the ascetic Mallam Sule; the Colonel who was anxious to help; his own fears about the pension funds, and a lot more. Long before he was through, Slater sensed that he didn't believe a word, that no one would believe what he'd been through to recover his union's money, would assume that he must have conspired with Ironsi in return for a personal kickback. Eventually he went and brought down the remaining £80.

'Here,' he handed the four banknotes over, 'I spent twenty on lunch for me and Glad, and that's the rest.'

Paulson took a long white envelope from his briefcase, slipped the notes inside and sealed it. He wrote out a receipt.

'Now, sir,' he said in a not unkindly voice, 'might be best if you accompany me to Scotland Yard and make a formal statement. You don't have to. I just advise it.'

He'd come across some unholy muddles in his time with the Fraud Squad, but for stupidity and incompetence this took a lot of beating. The Nigerian would claim diplomatic immunity. The gunsight-manufacturer was £1,800,000 in the hole. Slater himself, the old fool, had walked straight into a charge of fraudulent misrepresentation. Big money mesmerized some people. Paulson felt genuinely sorry for him. In court he might escape with a suspended sentence. As for Stephens, the Fraud Squad had been watching that one for months. It was an ill wind that blew nobody any good.

The headquarters of the Bartrum Bank was an elegant three-storey red-brick edifice of classical proportions on Hampton Road, with a stone-columned portico entrance and white-painted colonial-style windows. No one here liked high-rises, and even Roth's detractors admitted the building graced the area. Roth himself was in his spacious office overlooking the street when the first of the eight buses comprising Paul Gianni's invasion fleet halted outside and began disgorging passengers.

However, he was unaware of the tragi-comedy about to engulf him until an assistant entered to warn breathlessly that long lines were forming at all the tellers' windows in the banking hall. He squinted down at the road. A tailback of men and women, from their workday clothing demonstrably straight out of a factory, was forming on the sidewalk below. As he watched, the fifth bus unloaded. By the time he had summoned the village police all eight had come and gone, and a line beginning at the stone portico stretched the whole length of the block.

'Listen, fellers.' The cop who'd been sent was in his shirt-sleeves. He tried to sound relaxed as he addressed the men at the head of the line outside, while his colleague watched from their patrol car, coloured lights flashing on its roof. 'You're obstructing the sidewalk. Why don't you come back later, huh?'

'This is a free country, ain't it? We're just standing in line for our money.' One of the supervisors, clad in a white coat, showed his bank passbook with his name in it: Donovan.

The cop hesitated. As a rookie, he was uncertain whether these strangers were breaking any law. On the other hand, the way Southampton Village regulations were framed, they just had to be. This was a tight little town, and the local politicians made sure it stayed that way. Like in the Marines, there was an offence for every situation. He returned to the patrol car for advice.

In those few seconds Gianni himself appeared, a reporter and a photographer trailing him. He faced the head of the line, raised his fist in the air and started a chant.

'We want Roth. We want Roth. We want Roth. We want Roth.'

The whole length of the line took it up and, like a jack-in-the-box jumping up when the button's pressed, Roth struggled through the crowd to appear on the top step under the portico.

The flashbulbs popped, as in his nightmare. He held up his hands, warding them off, trying to speak.

'It's okay,' he shouted. 'I tell you, it's okay. Your money's safe. You can draw it anytime.'

The chant stopped as Donovan called for people to listen. They were reasonable men and women. Gianni had briefed them on what this was all about. 'Don't act up,' he had instructed. 'Play it cool. Just stand in line and I'll do the rest.' Now he stepped forward, the reporter scribbling madly, the two cops temporarily leaving well alone.

'I'm glad to hear that, Roth,' he said with biting clarity, 'because I'm coming right in to collect these people's payroll cash.'

Roth faltered, raising his hands again, as if for silence; in reality for self-protection.

'Seven hundred thousand dollars my firm is due. We'll take it back with us.'

'We . . .' Roth began to stutter, tried to get a grip on himself. 'I can't do that. The money hasn't come . . .'

He could scarcely have phrased the truth worse. Those who could hear him assumed he meant that there was no cash in the vaults. Those at the back interpreted his despairing expression the same way. A great shout rose up, followed by a verbal fusillade of insults.

'We want our money, you bastard.'

'Trickster.'

'Let us in.'

The line broke up, fanning out in a surge for the portico. The cops leapt into action, flailing riot sticks, aiming primarily to head off this assault on the bank. They clubbed their way to the entrance, pushed Roth inside and ordered him to lock the doors, then stood four-square in the portico, guns drawn, until the wail of sirens indicated that reinforcements were on the way.

Gianni and eighteen others were arrested. On police advice the bank stayed closed. As the reporter wrote, with slight exaggeration, Southampton had seen nothing to touch this since the Red Indian raid when Thomas Halsey's unfortunate wife, Phoebe, had been scalped in the 1660s.

The irony was that Roth maintained a prudent six per cent of the bank's $840 million's worth of liabilities in deposits at his various branches. Far from being short at Southampton today, he had earlier organized security vans to deliver an additional $3 million in varying denominations in case Gianni carried through his threat.

Up until minutes before the riot, he had been totally pre-occupied with his real problem. This centred on the less prudent $230 million of 'sight' money which the bank had on its books from a variety of corporate sources, which boosted lending capacity and helped counterbalance the lack of flexibility in the Latin American loans.

Now, he literally trembled at his desk while conferring with Schuster. They had both begun to realize that publicity following the police's over-reaction to a situation that had been containable could spark corporate withdrawals which the bank could not sustain. Roth's nightmare was becoming reality.

New York. 2.10 pm

The first brief message that Bill Osborn had been gunned down in Bogotá reached First National by telex at lunchtime. Just after two, a phone call from the US Embassy there brought Sally, taut and in shock as if she had witnessed the shooting herself, searching for Warburton.

'Bill's been shot.' She could not believe what she was repeating. 'They say he's "seriously ill" with a bullet in one lung and another in the shoulder. Someone called a *marimbero* shot him outside the Central Bank – I have the US Consul on the line.'

Warburton hurried to Osborn's office, explained who he was and went straight to the vital matter.

'Can he be moved? He should be in hospital here. Can you arrange a plane?'

The Consul sounded dubious. 'Might be better to send one down yourself, sir.'

There was no point blaming the diplomat. Embassies were seldom empowered to incur that kind of expense. He asked for Osborn to be ready for transfer first thing in the morning and then had Sally connect him straight to the ultimate source of authority. But Bud Phillips at the White House was evasive – so much so that, uncharacteristically, Warburton lost his temper.

'Mr Phillips,' he said angrily, 'the reason they tried to assassinate Bill Osborn is that he was applying the diplomatic pressure you refused to apply. You owe Osborn a lot. I'd like one of your Air Force planes with a medical team sent down to fetch him back.'

'Who the hell d'you think you are?' Phillips didn't like this kind of talk from anyone, least of all from a foreigner.

'I'm Bill's deputy in this negotiation. I have no political allegiance here; I don't even hold a green card. If you want the *Washington Post* to print the full story of how you personally refused to help the banks and you now refuse to help Osborn, fine. If you haven't organized something within two hours, I'll send a plane myself.'

When he rang off, Sally, to his amazement, gave him a quick kiss.

'That's the right stuff,' she said warmly. 'They do owe Bill a hell of a lot.'

'We have to look after him,' Warburton said, 'and we're going to get significantly tougher. As you might say, this is now a completely different ball game.'

New York. 4 pm

'I am happy to talk with you, Mr Harrison. But I'm not so sure I can help.'

It was as an indirect favour to Bill Osborn, whose shooting horrified him when he heard of it an hour ago, that Edward Channon was receiving Harrison at the New York Fed. Indirect because, although the debt crisis was the reason, Harrison was in New York on behalf of Bartrum Bank.

'What Ray Roth needs is $100 million for a week.'

'You've tried other sources?'

'Our Treasurer has. Corporate money is hard to come by today.'

'The understatement of the year.' Channon was basically sympathetic. He had been monitoring the markets closely, and things were looking worse than they had done in December 1982. The wave of panic had hit New York every way as hard as anyone could have predicted. Traders in the giant primary-dealing firms like Goldman Sachs and Salomon had been handling tens of billions of dollars. The dollar itself had risen against virtually every other currency as foreign demand for US Treasuries surged in and the Fed was conducting urgent open-market operations to stabilize both interest rates and the currency. On the Stock Exchange bank shares had plunged close to thirty per cent, and industrials had dropped through fear of a cancelled contracts and job-losses.

'You've tried the interbank market?' Channon asked.

'We couldn't get what we need.'

Channon knew billions of dollars were being withdrawn from banks and that every one of the money-centre giants had been borrowing heavily on the international market. But he also knew what Harrison really meant: that the rates being quoted to

Bartrum had been punitively high, because it had no great reputation.

'We are the lender of last resort,' he agreed, 'but not in all circumstances. What is your exact position?'

All he wanted to learn could be read in a balance sheet. Harrison had prepared one. The essence, done in his neat handwriting as Roth had dictated the figures to him, was simple:

Liabilities	$ million	Assets	$ million
Deposits	840	Cash	52
Capital	51	Federal Reserve Deposit	101
Reserves	20	Loans	758
	——		——
	911		911

'Our problem,' Harrison admitted, 'is that, of those deposits, nearly $230 are at sight. Corporations are starting to call them in.'

'You mean, there's a run on your bank?'

'Not yet.' Harrison saw no reason to mention the riot that had made Roth all but hysterical on the telephone. 'However, in this kind of a crisis there could be a run on a lot of institutions.'

'True.' Channon weighed the figures again. 'Doesn't alter the fact that if that $230 million goes, you'll be worse than out of cash. And remember our reserve requirement has to be met this Wednesday.'

'It's there.' That was the $101 million, the twelve per cent of deposits required by law to be lodged with the Fed.

'Could your shareholders put up more cash?'

It was all Harrison could do not to reply with a caustic joke. If Roth's description of events was correct, no shareholder would even look at such a proposition. What was more, he hadn't broached the worst aspect.

'Mr Channon,' he said carefully, 'it would be dishonest of me not to tell you that, of our loans, $47 million are with the Argentine, Brazil and Mexico.'

'You're in a perilous situation.'

'We are hoping . . .' Harrison corrected himself. 'Mr Osborn's committee is hoping that the default will be averted. We expect an answer to our proposals on Wednesday.'

Channon considered this. 'What collateral is your Mr Roth offering for a $100 million advance through the discount window?'

'We have a good-quality mortgage book, in excess of $150 million. Could that be earmarked?'

'I'd prefer to have the paper here. How about the morning?'

'The Treasurer will bring it.'

'Right.' Channon made a note. 'We will advance $100 million until Wednesday afternoon. Now listen, Mr Harrison, I want us to understand each other. Your bank is close to insolvency. If either panicky corporate lending officers run out on you or the MBA loans go non-performing, you will not be able to meet your Fed requirement in two days' time.' He glanced at the basic balance sheet again. 'Your share price must be falling with the rest. I cannot guarantee the Fed giving further substantial support. Your Treasurer will just have to talk those corporate officers into staying with you until this crisis passes.'

After Harrison had left, Channon made further notes. He judged Bartrum Bank's chances of survival at rather less than evens. What worried him more was that it wasn't the only small bank being hit by the panic. He had thirty-two others in the New York Federal Reserve's District besieging the discount window for emergency funds and wondered how many more there were in trouble nationwide. The last survey had shown that 209 major US banks had fifty per cent or more of their capital and reserves locked up in Third World loans. Those were major banks. How many smaller Bartrum equivalents were there in addition?

CHAPTER ELEVEN

New York. 6 pm, Monday June 17th

'Where the devil is Lopez-Santini?' James Warburton's anger was only just under control. Two hours ago Sally had received an unspecific message about the Argentine Minister being delayed by 'matters of the highest importance', and they were still waiting in First National's conference room.

'What kind of a guy is he?' Harrison asked, mainly to let Warburton release his irritation.

'Sophisticated and shrewd. He'll know exactly what chaos he's causing. The only explanation is the one the Swiss banker hinted at: he's paid a ransom, and for some reason his children haven't been returned.' Warburton helped himself to a whisky from the liquor cupboard. 'There are very nasty undercurrents in all this, Sheldon. I hope to God he isn't being deliberately prevented from coming. We badly need a public statement to damp things down.'

Harrison needed no telling – not after his earlier interview at the Fed. The brilliant vengeance inflicted by Paul Gianni might make Bartrum a special case, but not so special. The crisis, which First National's President and Warburton had agreed would take a full working week to heat up, was reaching boiling point a lot faster. This Wednesday, the alternate Wednesday which was the statutory day for banks to meet their reserve obligations to the Federal Reserve, now looked like being melt-down day unless Lopez-Santini accepted the carefully typed offer that lay in front of them.

The counter-proposal that Warburton had cobbled together, despite communications with other banks being grotesquely impeded by the very crisis they were trying to defuse, went a great deal further towards the cartel's demands than anyone would have agreed last Friday.

'Nothing like the shadow of the gallows for concentrating the mind,' Warburton had remarked cheerfully as he had passed the final, much annotated, draft to Sally.

That had been three hours ago, and three hours was a long time. In five hours the Tokyo Stock Exchange would be opening: it was Tuesday morning in Japan. Although traders around the world, from Amsterdam to Melbourne, would be working in shifts and bedding down as best they could in their offices, the general public would not. The general public would still live to a normal rhythm, waking, breakfasting, reading the papers and listening to the radio, then being seized by a new day's fears. This afternoon the San Francisco Stock Exchange had reported sharper falls than New York; Tokyo would take it up from there. The velocity was increasing relentlessly.

The only good news – and it could not be publicized – was that the central banks had at last taken notice and formed an emergency committee at deputy-governor level. But it would not assemble in Washington until tomorrow and Warburton was placing no reliance on its coming up with more than short-term support. The cartel had possessed the initiative from the start. Only the cartel could defuse the crisis by accepting long-term measures. So where the devil was its spokesman?

Furthermore, did Lopez-Santini know that Osborn had been shot?

Lopez-Santini was compelling himself to remain calm and objective – not easy for a Latin coming face to face with the kidnapper of his daughters.

The Police Captain was doubtful of this confrontation's value.

'Refuses to talk. Not a goddam word except when she wants the washroom.'

Maria was being held at his precinct headquarters while the District Attorney decided whether cashing the draft constituted an indictable offence in the circumstances, or whether she should only appear in court to contest extradition proceedings. As yet she had no legal representative. That could explain her silence. Lopez-Santini believed he possessed a weapon with which to break it.

The Police Captain led the way through to a small interview room, bare save for a plain table and hard chairs. Maria was seated, two armed officers standing behind her. The extradition details included the charge of murdering a chauffeur. The Captain was taking no chances.

Lopez-Santini sat down on the other side of the table, studying her features. She stared back with the ferocity of a cornered lynx, her grey-brown eyes fixed on his. He found such fury in a well-formed, clear-skinned, intelligent face both disturbing and frightening. He ought to be the dominantly angry one; she should be cowering. Yet it convinced him that he was correct. Teresa had trusted her. He was sure he knew the reason.

'Can we be alone?' he asked.

The guards did not move. They stood with their feet apart, shoulders square, hands itchingly loose. The Captain hesitated.

'You sure?' Lopez-Santini nodded. 'Okay. We'll be right outside the door.'

He watched her closely as the police left. Then he slipped the Polaroid photo out of his wallet and placed it in front of her.

'Read what is written on the back.'

With obvious reluctance she obeyed. A little tremor crossed her face.

'You double-crossed us, you bastard,' she said.

'We were both double-crossed.' He kept his tone even, unemotional. 'Teresa and Gloria were not in the apartment in Quilmes. The photograph was. So was Miguel dos Santos. His throat had been cut.'

The tremor returned. Her lip quivered. Some of the hate left her eyes. Lopez-Santini had guessed right. She had no idea of what had happened after she left Buenos Aires.

'We suspect it was the *traficantes*. Do you know who?'

She said nothing.

'You saved the girls from them once. Why? What is the connection? I must know the connection.' He went on, recounting the search, playing on how he knew Teresa must have liked and trusted her. He was close to giving up when she uttered a name.

'Tomas Catala.'

Then, still silently, her head bent, she began to cry.

Miami. Evening

There were only two kinds of girl who could take a jet-set vacation at the drop of a hint – that was, unless a boyfriend paid. They were the very rich, and airline staff. Maggie Fitzgerald knew no one in the former category who was flexible-minded enough for her Columbus Cay mission. Anneke Los, on the other hand . . .

'Sure, and I'm offering you the most fantastic skin-diving in the Western world,' she had baited her suggestion with Irish hyperbole, 'in a place neither of us is likely to be affording again.'

'So what is the catch?'

Anneke was a scuba-diving fanatic, a trim and powerful swimmer who kept a map on the wall of her Amsterdam apartment marked with all the places she had been skin-diving. The red pins mainly dotted the Mediterranean and the Indian Ocean: Malta, Crete, Eilat, the Comores, the Seychelles. As a KLM air hostess she travelled on her own airline at only five per cent of the fare; on any other at ten per cent. She had a gap on her roster. The temptation had been overwhelming.

However, she had guessed when Maggie Fitzgerald telephoned that the suggestion might not be entirely altruistic.

'So what do I have to do?' she had insisted.

'Pretend we're both on holiday. As you will be.'

So this Monday evening they were at the start of the trip, and also in luck. They had checked in to one of the less expensive hotels along Miami's beachfront – discount by courtesy of Anneke's job – and been joined by a flying friend of hers for drinks. His name was Jake and he was an instructor at a local air-training school.

'Where d'you say this place is?' he enquired, after Maggie had enthused appropriately over the water-sports paradise they were bound for. 'Columbus Cay? Isn't there some kind of a private landing-strip?'

'Most unfortunately,' Maggie smiled impishly, 'we've lent out both our yacht and our plane. We were going to take a scheduled flight to Marsh Harbour tomorrow.'

In fact, from her brief experience of being frog-marched across the island, she had no memory of an airfield.

'Too bad.' Jake winked at Anneke, whose arrival was the kind of surprise he liked. She might not be so tall, but she had one helluva figure. 'Maybe I could stand in for the absent crew. Can't be more than an hour or so in the Cessna. You like me to check the strip?'

Maggie hesitated. The last thing she wanted was an amorous American hanging around Anneke. The essence of her disguise, apart from having dyed her hair, was that they were two single girls adventuring together.

'Be a pleasure,' Jake insisted. 'Don't come back 'til the afternoon.'

He went and phoned his airfield, returning jubilant.

'Thought there was. Columbus Cay has a grass strip suitable for light planes only, and they do the Customs routine. We'll leave at eight, if that's okay with you ladies.'

'You're a lovely man,' Maggie accepted graciously. 'We'll consider that a date.' She was delighted too; this would bypass the normal Immigration, unless McLellan, the Columbus Cay Manager, created difficulties.

New York. Evening

In the end, Lopez-Santini came for dinner at the Carlyle, and Warburton's intended recriminations were largely put aside when he saw the change in the Argentine's appearance. A single week had left the skin beneath his eyes grey and his fleshy cheeks sunken. It was as though a portrait artist had crudely imposed the decay of ten years on his features. He apologized, mentioning events beyond his control, asked for a whisky on the rocks, and drained half the glass at a gulp.

'We heard about your daughters,' Warburton said quietly. 'You have our deepest sympathy.'

'You heard?' His surprise faded as he remembered the Buenos Aires press reports.

'Are they back with you?'

Lopez-Santini shook his head. The reason for his being so late was that after interviewing Maria he had spent three-quarters of an hour tracking down Comisario Alfaro on the telephone to insist that the man Tomas be arrested. Alfaro had not been optimistic, albeit agreeing that Tomas probably knew the whereabouts of the girls.

'I am truly sorry.' Warburton was determined to keep this discussion statesmanlike. He now presented his own bad news with deliberate restraint. 'We have also had a shock. Bill Osborn was shot in Bogotá this morning.'

'Holy Mother of God!' Lopez-Santini's sharp intake of breath told its own story. 'Dead? Who shot him?'

'Mercifully Bill wasn't killed, but he's badly wounded. They say the would-be assassin was a *marimbero*. Is that some kind of revolutionary group?'

'It means that he was a marijuana-trafficker.' Recollections of Suarez's threats ran through his mind. 'In the Argentine we call them *traficantes*; in Mexico the cocaine-runners are *coqueros*. There are many names.'

'Are they connected with your daughters' kidnap?'

'I think so.' Lopez-Santini was becoming convinced that the real intention was to keep him under pressure even though he had broken off the IMF talks which would have begun today. Why the kidnapper Maria had quarrelled with the *traficantes* remained mysterious. And was Rodrigo Suarez involved?

'José-Maria,' Warburton leaned forward confidentially, 'when kidnap and murder become part of a negotiation then you and I must both change our tactics. Would you bear that in mind while we discuss our proposals?'

'Perhaps.' If his admission was grudging it was because at the best of times a man cannot see far into the future, and this evening Lopez-Santini was exhausted.

During dinner the three men argued over the proposals that Harrison and Warburton had hammered out.

'There are no great technical innovations,' Warburton said. 'We've gone further than the fourteen-year rescheduling offered to Mexico. We're suggesting twenty years and we're prepared to reduce all loans from interest at the US Prime Rate to LIBOR, which cuts them a percentage point. And on top of that we'll allow a two per cent forgiveness.'

'Our own committee will not accept that.'

'Believe me, José-Maria, it's a great deal further than anyone would go before today's panic on the markets. Are you forgetting how many executives and treasurers we have to persuade? Mexico alone has debts to 550 different banks.'

'I regret your proposal is not enough.'

'What do you want, then? A payments pause? Repayments in local currency instead of dollars?' Warburton was being forced back on his last-ditch suggestion, the only one that did more than tinker with the problem. 'If we let this crisis fester two or three days more you'll have reduced the Western banks to a condition where they couldn't lend the Third World more if they wanted to. Their stockholders would vote out the boards. They'll institute a freeze that will hurt you as badly as you've hurt them. It's not in your interest to break off relations with the Western system.'

'With that I agree.' Lopez-Santini was picking at his food, totally lacking appetite. He was unable to forget the danger his daughters were in. 'However, such a breaking-off may be inevitable

'You and I know each other well enough to be honest.' Warburton vividly recalled a merchant-banking friend remarking that maintaining historical prejudices against certain countries had saved his firm a great deal of money. 'Men may have been created equal, theoretically. Countries emphatically were not. There are always going to be nations like yours with the abilities and natural resources to be leaders; and there are always going to be ones which, in my friend Sheldon's phrase, will be basket-cases.'

This was Harrison's cue, and he took it.

'Realistically, sir, Haiti's been an independent state since 1804 and Liberia since 1847. But they never have gotten themselves organized and maybe they never will. Uncle Sam just goes on propping them up. That's fine for government. It's not so great for the banks.'

'I must object to that statement.' Lopez-Santini felt obliged to make some protest.

'We can go on producing technical solutions to stave off default, but those are precisely what got us into the present predicament,' Warburton said. 'The Third World can only prosper by its own efforts, and those won't succeed unless the natural leaders – your own country, Brazil, Kenya, India, the Philippines – show the way. If your cartel forces us to a crunch, José-Maria, the banks are going to write off their investment in the basket-cases and concentrate on helping the responsible ones – who, incidentally, will be the ones that encourage private initiative and private capital.'

Warburton paused. It was no accident that he had named certain countries. Kenya and India had never joined the cartel. Brazil and the Philippines were defecting from it.

'It is impossible for me to tell my colleagues that.'

'I do not expect you to. I merely hope that your country will follow Brazil, the Philippines and Poland in abandoning the cartel.'

'You are inventing this?' Lopez-Santini became wary despite his tiredness.

'No.' At last Warburton allowed his anger to surface. 'We don't do business with gunmen. We had hoped that you would dissociate yourself from the cartel as several others have. Publicly. We need a public statement to calm this situation down.'

'I am sorry. I cannot make any statement until your proposal has been considered on Wednesday evening.'

'Wednesday evening!' Warburton was shocked. 'By Thursday this crisis could be out of control. Where are you meeting?'

'I regret I cannot reveal the location.'

'José, let me tell you. Our proposal may not remain open that long. You told us Rodrigo Suarez is your co-negotiator. What is his view?'

'He is in favour of default.'

Effectively the discussion ended there, although Warburton had a final card to play. He gripped the Argentine's hand warmly as they said goodbye.

'If there is any help we can give over your daughters, let us know. The Drug Enforcement Agency might have some information.'

'Thank you, no. Our own police are following leads.'

None the less Warburton reckoned he had left their guest with a thought to sleep on. Back in the bar for a nightcap, he took the idea a stage further. Harrison had miraculously found time to research Suarez's background.

Warburton read the material with amazement. 'If the kidnap isn't connected with this, Sheldon, I'll eat my hat. You're going down to Washington to meet Bill Osborn's plane. Why not talk to the DEA while you're there? They have agents all over Latin America, or so I've heard.'

Harrison agreed. A scheme had come into his head that might be hare-brained. Or it might not. Either way, if the other side fought rough he saw no reason why they should not do the same.

Tokyo. Midday, Tuesday June 18th

Jock Anderson was in his element. He sat, telephone in hand, bog-eyed from watching the VDU screens displaying prices in all the Far Eastern markets, riding this roller-coaster for all its worth. This was a bull market for the history books, and he was talking every client into buying long-term bonds, knowing that when the bubble burst Philip Lindsay's 'bear' strategy would pay off beyond belief.

'Yes, sir.' He was always polite with the Japanese, ultra-polite. 'The market is going up fast. The stock you want did trade at $106\frac{1}{4}$ earlier.' He glanced at one of the VDUs, saw it was touching $106\frac{5}{8}$ and gave himself a wide margin. 'I can give you twenty-five thousand at $107\frac{1}{8}$. No, sir, I can't make that price. Well, for an old client, 107. Twenty-five thousand. Yes, sir. That's a deal.' Last week its price had been 88.

The day was a constant spiel, a constant calculation of spreads. He only came to his senses when his wife stormed into the office, a most unusual occurrence. She was distraught.

'I've been trying to phone you all morning,' she almost shouted in desperation. 'What am I going to do? I can hardly afford to buy rice. The queues are enormous and the prices have gone mad. If you want to eat this week, you'll have to give me more cash.'

What was that verse of Rudyard Kipling's?

Philip Lindsay, glad to be briefly out of the hubbub of the trading-room, drew on a cigarette and tried to relax in his office. 'Enforced rest,' the army used to call it, and no bad idea when you were overtired and liable to make wrong decisions. He compelled himself to watch the lazy curl of smoke and let his thoughts drift similarly for a few minutes, but the verse he had learnt by heart at school kept nagging his memory. Unable to recall the words, he tried to dismiss it.

The financial crisis was tightening all the time. This morning's newspapers had carried prominent advertisements by all the major banks assuring clients and shareholders that there was no cause for panic. However, they had been neatly upstaged by the largest savings bank, whose announcement was confined to assuring depositors that it had no Third World investments, let alone loans. This all made a nice contrast, Lindsay reflected, as his cigarette-smoke dispersed, to the days of the great tombstone advertisements when banks proudly proclaimed their new commitments in South America and Africa.

Meanwhile, a further £1,000 million Treasury tapstock was anticipated this afternoon as the Bank of England sought to calm the markets. It would not succeed. Trading in the long room downstairs, with its screens and time-zone clocks and streamers of telex hung on the walls, was more frenetic than yesterday. The same was happening on the floor of the Stock Exchange itself, where the *Financial Times* 100-share index had dipped below 1080 from a level around 1570 last week. By any precedent this was a catastrophic slide. At the same time, gilt-edged had risen thirty per cent. This bull market could not last.

Lindsay remembered the day after the American raid on Tripoli in the spring of 1986. That tiny convulsion in world affairs had caused a sufficient flight out of equities for the Treasury-bill interest-rate to fall half a point in response to rapidly hardening prices. This week the Bank of England's minimum lending rate, displayed on a screen at the Stock Exchange and monitored in his office, had fallen two and three-quarter points already.

Such a situation would not be allowed to continue. The Bank of England would have to guarantee sufficient liquidity for the commercial banks to meet the outflow of Arab and other funds which was the subject of this morning's headlines and which within months could cripple the economy. They would have to announce a 'lifeboat'. The question was, how soon? More specifically, would the fund managers from whom he was borrowing bonds in order to deliver the millions he was selling under his 'bear' strategy remain happy? He was giving them the normal one half of one per cent extra interest, and borrowing bonds was a familiar procedure. But what if the fund managers decided themselves to sell and take the profit? He reckoned that the end of the week would bring the crunch. If the market hadn't turned by then, he was in trouble.

As he jerked himself out of the largely ineffective 'enforced rest', the verse of Kipling sounded in his mind.

> 'If you can keep your head while all about you
> Are losing theirs and blaming it on you . . .'

A few hundred yards from where Lindsay was forcing himself to keep his nerve, a champagne cork plopped out of a bottle of Moët et Chandon guided by the practised fingers of Richard Stephens.

'Here's to another billion,' he toasted his partner, bowing in mock solemnity. 'We are rich men, Gervase. As our Muslim friends would say, "Allah Akbar".'

Stephens had cause to consider God was Great. Even though that reporter Pendler had cautiously not made a separate story out of his leak, the mention of it had yielded a plentiful harvest for this morning's early phone-calls to the Gulf. The Bank of Commercial Credit was pulling funds out of London at a rate which would have caused Stephens' Socialist friends, had they been in power, to institute immediate exchange control. The joke was that grapevine rumours suggested that the Gulf States' central banks might shortly join the Bank of England in a support operation. That meant Arabs were now running scared in both directions: frightened for their cash deposits and, conversely, worried for their completely illiquid investments in British industry and property.

A knock on the door disturbed Stephens' celebration. His secretary came in.

'Excuse me, sir. There's a gentleman insists on seeing you . . .'

The words were barely spoken before a burly man in a blue blazer entered the room and held out his warrant-card.

'Detective-Inspector Paulson. You are Mr Richard Stephens? I should like to ask you a few questions about a certain Nigerian transaction.'

'But . . .' Stephens put down his glass on the great carved desk.

In the next hour, New York would become fully active. He had a hectic afternoon ahead of him. 'We are extremely busy, officer.'

'So I see, sir.' Paulson eyed the champagne bottle sardonically. 'None the less, we should appreciate an immediate interview with you at the Fraud Squad.'

Buenos Aires. 10.20 am

Comisario Alfaro's luck had turned. Having derived little save humiliation from the kidnap case, he had at last been blessed with a break. His men had picked up Tomas Catala at five this morning at his room on the university campus where he was a lecturer. They had brought away a bagful of subversive literature. Catala was without question in the Junta de Coordinacion Revolucionaria. The problem was making him talk.

Back in the days of the dirty war, the army would have beaten and tortured him until they had a confession, then thrown him alive from a helicopter into a swamp or the sea. Democracy and intellectual influences on an elected government made this option impracticable.

At the same time, Alfaro needed results. He had compromised by hosing down Catala with cold water, leaving him without clothes and shivering in a furniture-less cell for three hours, then interviewing him, still naked, under arc lights. If there was one thing calculated to distress the middle class, it was being naked. Catala tried to hide his private parts with his hands.

'Your accomplice, Maria, has confessed.' Alfaro had thrust the original of the Polaroid snapshot in front of the lecturer's face. 'She fell for those kids. Never trust a woman, Tomas. We know how you organized the kidnap. We have sworn statements linking you to five killings.' This was fabrication, but there was no way the man could know. 'Tell us where the kids are and we'll drop the murder charges.'

Catala had looked up, spat in his face, and received a lip-splitting punch in the mouth as reward, which left him sprawled on the floor.

Two hours later, still bleeding, he changed his tune, fractionally. He was not going to reveal that the *traficantes* funded the JCR and had demanded a *quid pro quo*, but he did want to get himself off the murder rap. From the protective intellectual sanctuary of the university, where left-wing conspiracy was a way of life, it had seemed easy to tell Maria that the chauffeur must be silenced. He had not even used the word 'kill'. Now, shivering and increasingly demoralized in this cell, things looked painfully different.

'The girls are in a neighbouring country,' he admitted. 'I don't know where. They'll be released when Lopez-Santini releases our country from debt.' He reverted to momentary defiance. 'You can tell him that from me.'

Alfaro left the man to freeze, the arrogant son of a bitch. He knew the country must be Bolivia. The dead *traficantes*' vehicle had been registered up near the border. He telephoned New York and was able to give the Minister that information before he left for the Bahamas. He himself would contact the Bolivian police, but without hope of real collaboration. He had done all that he could be expected to do for the moment. Effectively, the girls' safety lay in their father's hands.

Southampton, Long Island. 9 am

The day, three short of the summer solstice, had dawned bright and surprisingly crisp for this often humid maritime climate. The sun shone benifently on the white stone portico of the Bartrum Bank, and a spirit of hope imbued Ray Roth's feelings, despite the terrible pictures in the paper of the riot around this same spot yesterday. When the double doors of the bank swung open at nine o'clock precisely, it was Roth himself in lightweight grey suit who performed the duty, and then stepped forward into the sunlight.

There was a small crowd outside and, inevitably, a photographer.

'Come on in, folks,' Roth said, 'everything's okay. It's business as usual.'

'Is the depositors' money safe?' a reporter called out.

'Sir, we have plenty of cash in the vaults. There is no problem.'

'You won't be calling on the FDIC?'

'We will not. Right now we have no need of their $16 billion.' He mentioned the figure of the Federal Deposit Insurance Corporation's available reserve deliberately, to impress. 'Not one solitary cent of it.'

If the bank ever did, that would be the end of his own career and of Schuster's. When the FDIC stepped in to protect depositors, one of its rules was that the failed management went – and without compensation of any kind.

For several minutes Roth made a show of welcoming customers, in order to give picture opportunities. He was determined to repair the public-relations damage Gianni had caused.

As he returned to his office, the confident image sagged. On the doorstep there were no problems. Inside there were. Soon the out-of-town cheques drawn yesterday would arrive to be honoured. Neither he nor Schuster had obtained fresh corporate or interbank money and he was kicking himself for giving Harrison the delicate task of approaching the Fed. He had barely re-entered the building when he was brought a telex from Plaza in New York. The telex began:

REGRET INFORM YOU MEXICO LAST NIGHT SUSPENDED FOREIGN-EXCHANGE PAYMENTS WITH IMMEDIATE EFFECT . . .

New York. 10 am

The President of the First National Bank had been in conference with his board since breakfast. He now asked Warburton to join them, and after reiterating thanks for his prompt action in bringing Osborn back from Bogotá, posed the question which mattered.

'What are the chances of ending this default threat, Mr Warburton? We need to know. Our stock lost over a quarter of its value yesterday; Mexico's playing rough; the Banco do Brasil hasn't come up with the short-term trade payments it promised; interbank money's showing distinct signs of drying up. We're running out of liquidity.'

'At this moment, I should say that the crisis is turning the default into reality faster than anyone can stop it. There must be a real temptation for members of this cartel to decide that they've no longer any need to bargain.'

'As bad as that?'

'We do not even know where the cartel meets, or which nations originated it. As for the attack on Bill Osborn . . .,' Warburton became coldly furious whenever he thought about that crude and cowardly way of seeking to frighten the banks, 'I hope your Federal Reserve is as shocked as we are.'

'I should say so. Bill has gotten more done by being shot than he could have any other way.' The President checked himself. 'Don't misunderstand me. Than he could have done any other way within the time.'

'Time is crucial,' Warburton agreed. 'We've barely a day and a half in hand.'

The Mexican action last night could only be construed as a further deliberately delivered challenge, and he wondered who had orchestrated it. Various financial packages had been strapped together for Mexico after the earthquake, followed by the 1986 oil-price fall, made it impossible for her to service her $97 billion debt, except at the price of extreme popular discontent. If one package failed, another was always put in place. The Chairman of the Fed had narrowly averted more than one repayment crisis by personally flying down secretly to see the Mexican president. Washington officials might despise Mexican corruption and incompetence, but when it came to the crunch they never dared contemplate political chaos on the United States' southern border.

Columbus Cay, Great Abaco. 10.20 am

What with one delay and another, Jake's six-seater, twin-engined, Cessna was an hour late circling the Club before landing. Maggie and Anneke enjoyed a brief panoramic view of the translucent azure sea, beaches, white boats moored at jetties and thatched buildings among palm trees. Then with a gentle bump they touched down on a grass strip at the further end of the island and rumbled to a stop.

They hardly had the baggage out before a jeep roared up, the instantly recognizable, neatly bearded figure of McLellan driving. He swung himself out and came across.

'This is a private club. We do not accept casual . . .,' he began.

'These ladies have reservations.' Jake was about to prove his worth. 'They didn't hire me to fly them from Miami for the hell of it.'

Maggie snapped open her bag, extracted the French travel-agent's folder containing their vouchers, and held it out. McLellan's gaze flicked over her face, but he was more concerned with the documents. His attitude changed to one of embarrassment.

'You're the French guests?'

'We are indeed. Except that I'm Irish and my friend is Dutch.'

'I am extremely sorry. We telexed the day before yesterday . . .'

'We left the day before yesterday.'

'Hey, mister,' Jake exploded, 'they came all the way from Paris, France, okay? Don't tell us you have no accommodations. We flew in, remember? There's hardly a goddam soul around.'

'We have arrived,' Anneke put in firmly, 'and we are staying.'

'Please get in the jeep.' McLellan made a gesture of exasperated surrender. 'We have an unexpected conference. I cannot guarantee rooms after tomorrow.'

'Then we shall be sueing.'

Maggie remained determinedly uncompromising, even when they had been shown to a comfortable small villa with its own lounge, and McLellan, wary of the storm he had unleashed on himself, had sent them complimentary flowers and fruit. Soon after, they transferred themselves to the pool for a swim before Jake flew back, and were comfortable in deck-chairs when a steward came across and spoke to Anneke.

'De gentleman over dere is axeing you like a drink.'

They all gazed in the direction the Bahamian indicated. On the far side of the pool a lean, moustachioed man reclining in a long chair raised his hand and waved.

'Jesus, he has some nerve,' Jake muttered.

'Nothing ventured, nothing gained.' Maggie waved back, gesturing the man to join them.

Unhurriedly, he rose to his feet and strolled over. Of medium height, he was handsome in a coarse-featured way. A gold cross suspended from a chain nestled in the curling black hair on his chest. Jake, who was no ladykiller, looked him up and down disgustedly. Taking no notice, the man stood in front of them and spoke to Anneke with a strong Spanish accent.

'Nice to see other people here. I have been the only one. My name is Rodrigo – Rodrigo Suarez.'

'I told you that manager guy was lying,' Jake said to the girls, disregarding Suarez.

'You are also staying?' Suarez smiled thinly at him, more like a knife-thrust than a smile.

'Me? I'm the pilot.'

'Ah, the Cessna. Myself, I prefer a jet. My Lear is at Marsh Harbour.'

Maggie sat up and stretched out a hand to Suarez. Another ten seconds and the men would be fighting.

'I am Maggie. This is Anneke. Why don't you sit down.'

In the course of the stilted conversation which followed, Suarez revealed that he was waiting for a business associate and would be making a short trip in the afternoon before returning tomorrow. The 'short trip', he boasted, was to Mexico.

'You like to see the plane? A beauty.' He touched his fingers to his lips. 'Come this afternoon. A boat can bring you back from Marsh Harbour.'

'Guess I ought to be getting along.' Jake was thoroughly discomforted.

'We'll see you off, Jake,' Maggie insisted. She had no desire to go to at Marsh Harbour. 'Come on, Anneke.'

'I have drinks waiting when you come back,' Suarez called out as they walked away to find McLellan and the jeep.

After Jake had taken off, swinging round to roar low over the pool and then pull up defiantly into the sky, thumbing his nose at all concerned, McLellan asked them to complete their arrival formalities.

'Who's the Latin lover?' Maggie asked when they reached the reception.

McLellan glanced up from examining her virginally new passport.

'A guest.' He looked at her more closely. Something about this woman stirred memories. Disregarding the hairstyle, he concentrated on her eyes and mouth. Then he slammed her passport down on the counter. 'Miss Fitzgerald, we warned you off Columbus Cay ten days ago.'

'To be sure and so you did.' Maggie overplayed her Irishness deliberately, mocking him. 'I was completely forgetting. And are you not the very same Pat McLellan was sacked from the Crillon for embezzling travellers cheques? Are you not the very man? And did you not run the kitchens in the Sante prison for a while after that?

'You little bitch,' he murmured.

'Wouldn't the authorities here just love to know such a thing, Mr McLellan. And the travel agents.'

He stared at her, discountenanced. He had never ceased regretting the stupidity which had ruined his career in Europe. Once the Bahamians got to hear of it, the demands for kickbacks would never cease. He handed Maggie back her passport.

'You'll have to leave when the conference starts tomorrow.'

'Tomorrow is another day.'

'We'll see.'

McLellan felt he could afford to temporize. Tomorrow that humourless spook from Nassau named Garrard was sure to turn up. Garrard would deal with these two in very short order and without listening to a word they said. He watched them wander back to the pool, where Suarez was waiting. He had already refused to provide the Bolivian with women. 'And the best of luck to the pair of you,' he murmured. Suarez had made no secret of his tastes.

Andrews Air Force Base, Maryland. Midday

Two medics lifted Osborn's stretcher out of the US Air Force Boeing with infinite care, carrying it through the aircraft's door on to a hydraulically operated platform. A third medic held aloft the snake-like tube of a drip attached to Osborn's arm. He had not only suffered loss of blood but had also become dehydrated in Bogotá's rarefied air.

As the platform lowered them to the tarmac, Phillips, Harrison and an Air Force colonel stepped forward, the colonel saluting stiffly.

Osborn raised his head a fraction and essayed a grin.

'Hi. How's business?'

'The Chairman of the Fed's in Mexico City right now,' Phillips answered. 'A central bankers' committee is in session. We have our ambassadors throughout Latin America . . .'

He was interrupted by a white-coated doctor.

'If you don't mind, sir. Maybe later, at Bethesda.'

Osborn lifted a hand weakly as they placed him in the waiting ambulance. 'Thanks, fellers.' He lay back, thinking that if he had achieved nothing else, at least he had made the President's office take note.

From Andrews AFB Harrison drove himself to the Drug Enforcement Agency's headquarters, where he had a lengthy discussion with the Director. He learnt that Suarez was a known drug mafioso in Bolivia and there were rumours of his having attended a meeting of drug barons on Canelas' ranch there recently. However, there was no mention of children.

'These are vicious men,' the Director remarked. 'We'd like to nail them, but I doubt we ever will. It's a $100 billion-a-year business and they have hundreds of traffickers for every agent of ours. We'll give you any help we can, of course. You should go down to Miami; that's the nerve centre for Latin American operations. I'll warn our people to expect you. As the admen used to say, "Let's run this idea up the flagpole and see if anyone salutes it".'

Harrison was left to speculate on whether either Warburton, as a representative of the banks, or Phillips, at the President's office, would.

*

London. Early evening

The kangaroo court was being convened after working hours at the AUCAS headquarters. Its verdict, Len Slater knew, would be more hasty and more vengeful than any he might later face in a genuine court of justice. Keith Norris had convened it and while he fought publicly for members' rights against the bosses, he was as contemptuous of the Union's own employees as any nineteenth-century mill-owner.

The court assembled in the conference room, with its windows open because of the heat and letting in the grinding noise of traffic in the Camden Road outside. The black-and-white photos of the Union's past General Secretaries gazed down, grim-faced, from the walls.

Keith Norris presided, flanked on his left by the other pension-fund Trustee and on his right by the Union's Treasurer. The three men were both judges and jury. They looked stonily at Slater, seated alone at the far end of the table. Keith opened the proceedings.

'Brother Len, no need to waste time explaining what we're here for. You stand accused of losing £2 million of our funds, failing to maintain proper control of other investments, accepting bribes in cash and kind and overall betraying the interests of your fellow members. What's your defence? If there is one.'

The snideness of Norris' tone made it evident that the verdict had already been decided. None the less, Slater made an attempt to justify himself.

'You ordered me to invest in black Africa, brother,' he said in as strong a voice as he could muster. 'If I had lunches with the banker who you . . .'

'At the Ritz, wasn't it? You had sausages and beans I suppose? Who d'you think paid in the end?'

'Let 'im finish, Keith,' the other Trustee intervened.

Slater sought salvation from this potential ally. At least the other Trustee was familiar with pension-fund procedures.

'Bill knows we had to balance our investments. Of the five million, two were in government fixed-interest, two in equities, and one in property. We chose blue-chip equities, Keith.'

'And what are they worth today? Two-thirds?'

'The crisis isn't my fault.'

'I put it to you, brother,' Norris assumed a quasi-legal tone, 'that if you had not betrayed the principles of the Labour movement, if you'd invested with co-operatives and not with capitalist companies, that the other two million would be worth more today, not less. Now, what about this cash the Fraud Squad say you had from the Nigerian? And why was Kevin down at Heathrow in our pension scheme when he had no right?'

As Slater tried to answer, his voice grew husky. None of the three would accept that he was more sinned against than sinning. It wasn't long before Keith switched from being prosecutor to delivering the verdict.

'I'd hoped that there would be some kind of extenuating circumstances.' He sought quick confirmation from the other two. 'We don't find any. Goes without saying you can have your cards and clear out tonight. For betraying the interests of the Union I reckon a fine of £10,000 and expulsion from membership.'

The Treasurer touched his elbow and a brief confabulation ensued.

'All right,' Norris agreed, then looked back at Slater.

'You're a lucky man today, believe you me. We'll dock that ten thousand from your pension. A thousand a year for ten years and you can have a week to hand over the house and car. To make it easier, you can be on pension from tomorrow. Reduced, of course, seeing as you're two years short of retirement.'

Slater stared at them, dazed by the savagery of the fine. But Keith had not finished with him yet.

'I'll leave a thought with you, Len. Having the pension now's a concession. You've no automatic right to it yet. If you should think of taking us to the High Court or any of that Tory nonsense, we could change our minds. About that and paying the fine by instalments. You play tricks with us, brother, and we'll play tricks with you.'

When Slater had gathered together his personal papers he left without saying goodbye to anyone. He dreaded telling his wife that in seven days the house wouldn't be theirs anymore. On the train-ride back to Hendon, clutching his stick, his briefcase and several plastic bags full of correspondence, he began to realize that there was one compensation. Gladys would give him a terrible time, but she would understand. She'd always said she wouldn't trust Keith to open a packet of crisps for her because he'd steal the salt. Not that they put those little blue-paper screws of salt in anymore.

*

Edward Channon was becoming acutely concerned at the volume of funds being sought through the discount window by banks whose liquidity appeared to be threatened by the crisis. When major New York money-centre banks like First National and Plaza asked for hundreds of millions it was indicative of serious pressure on them. Last night's Mexican suspension of foreign-exchange payments, coming on top of Brazil's, had thrown the money markets into turmoil. There had been a virtual repeat of the nail-biting evening of December 9th 1982, when the same two countries had left the New York electronic interbank clearance system - known by the acronym of CHIPS - $360 million short.

In 1982 the shortfall had been due to small American banks instructing the Fed Funds brokers not to lend their money to Latin American banks. This time the prohibition was tougher. Wary treasurers had forbidden lending to any bank involved with Latin American loans, from the big money-centres downwards. So, if the Fed itself did not provide money, many hundreds of banks could be unable to meet their obligations.

Technically, Channon faced no difficulty. He could provide cash against assets within hours or even minutes. His problem was that he could not provide liquidity to banks that were no longer viable, as he had been forced to tell the Treasurer of Bartrum Bank this afternoon.

'Mr Schuster,' he had said, 'don't blame young Harrison. Blame your loans being seriously mismatched. You've not only lent out a very high proportion of assets – around eighty-seven per cent it seems – but a third of those assets are deposits on call and you've lent them out again long-term, not least in Latin America. I'm sorry, but with Mexico suspending payments as well as Brazil it is not within my remit to authorize any further advance.'

'What the hell's a lender of last resort for?' Schuster had stormed. 'Don't tell me you'll have First National or Plaza close their doors. You're hitting us small guys who can't fight back.'

'We closed down Penn Square on account of its non-performing loans,' Channon had replied tightly, keeping his temper, 'and Continental Illinois was only saved by Morgan. There's nothing sacred about being a bank.'

But when Schuster had departed in a rage, Channon had to admit to himself that there was. His chairman had flown to Mexico City today to help save the sacred names of Chase, Citibank, Plaza and the rest. If the chairman failed and Osborn's committee failed, then the near-inevitable collapse of Bartrum would not be an isolated incident which the system could survive. It would be the start of a devastating chain reaction and the Federal Reserve System would have to mount the fastest and largest rescue operation since its creation in 1913.

When Sally buzzed through to say she had a Mr Stuart Pendler on the line, Warburton's instinctive inclination was to refuse the call. Moments later he was extremely glad he had not done so.

'Hullo.' The journalist's voice had that fractional echo sometimes imparted by the transatlantic phone. 'I just heard about Bill Osborn. I'm sorry. In connection with your negotiating there's something I think you ought to know. Maybe relevant. Maybe not.'

'Yes.'

'You know a man named Suarez?'

'Not personally.' Warburton wondered where this was leading.

'He's in the Bahamas with Lopez-Santini and now he's flown to Mexico.'

'Has he, by God! What else? You have any details?'

Pendler related a proportion of what he had just been told by Maggie.

'How do you know this?' Warburton demanded. Without question Suarez must be endeavouring to undermine the Chairman of the Fed's visit.

'Never reveal sources, I'm afraid. But Suarez is flying back tomorrow in his own jet. I'm telling you because I can't publish this yet. My story is that the debtor-nations' meeting is imminent.'

'Where?' Warburton was impatient now. 'I urgently need to talk to Lopez-Santini.'

'Take me with you, and I'll tell you.'

Warburton thought quickly. He could use Pendler. He agreed.

'It's called Columbus Cay. You fly to Marsh Harbour. I'll be with you in New York tomorrow.'

'Thank you, very much. Tell me, why are you revealing all this?'

'I don't like my countrymen being gunned down. Also, I would like to be in at the kill.'

It was not an argument Warburton could fault.

CHAPTER TWELVE

Mexico City. 10 am, Wednesday June 19th

The Learjet, sleek as a dream, handled more like a fighter than an executive plane. Suarez occupied the co-pilot's seat during the take-off, revelling in the power that punched them in the back as the jet began to roll. His fingers light on the controls, he followed through the captain's movements as the nose lifted sharply, the wheels juddered and parted company with the tarmac, and they streaked up into the hazy sky.

The Lear's exhilarating performance matched Suarez's mood. Down there, at the centre of the sprawling dusty gridiron, which in a few more years would be a city of thirty million people, almost all impoverished and under-nourished, he had left food for thought with the Finance Minister. Alvarez's predecessor had achieved such political unpopularity by toeing the American and IMF line that he had lost his job.

'Why dig you own grave, *amigo*?' Suarez had asked, as they pulled on cigars at the Minister's residence. 'The Columbus Group was your creation. For all practical purposes the default has taken place. Have the Western banks collapsed? The hell they have!'

The argument was superficial. So far there had only been rising public panic, violent decline on the stock markets and withdrawals of bank deposits. The full effects of a default had not yet been felt; Suarez had skirted round that.

'All the Fed wants is not to have to bail out the *gringo* banks. Holy Mother, whose side are you on? The President of the United States or ours?' Here Suarez had edged his chair closer and assured Alvarez that if, inexplicably, defending Latin American interests did cost him his office, he would not go short of money himself.

However, the clinching argument had been Mexico's own

national economic predicament. When Alvarez revealed details of the Chairman of the Fed's proposals, Suarez had been able to ridicule them with devastating effect.

'Agricultural credits? Trade-promotion assistance from Japan? Since when have the Japs drunk tequila? Do you believe the banks would put up four billions of new money right now? Their stockholders would go berserk. Anyhow, since when can the Fed give orders to Lloyds or the Deutsche Bank?' Speaking colloquially in Spanish, as opposed to the stilted English of international meetings, Suarez could be caustic. 'You say this pie in the sky adds up to $7 billion?'

'Eight, they hope. Our President is favourably influenced.'

'Eight? When you have nine billions arrears of interest? What does Mexico gain from that? Minus one billion dollars! We agreed to face the banks with an ultimatum. Will the President receive me?'

That had been a billion-dollar question in itself. Suarez knew his own reputation was low. He had been forced to utilize his status as Lopez-Santini's deputy negotiator, a role that tasted as bitter as gall. However, the devil was behind him, in the shape of Canelas and the other drug barons.

When he had been admitted to the Presidential Palace this morning, he had adopted an appropriately flattering approach, deftly quoting the President's own words back at him, and almost surprising himself with his eloquence.

'Your Excellency,' he had said, seated on an absurd gilt chair in a vast reception room. 'Your message to our meeting ten days ago was a stirring one: "We will not pay our foreign debts with recession, nor unemployment, nor hunger." Señor Lopez-Santini took that message to New York. Tonight we shall have the answer. We have no doubt that the banks will respond with terms far more favourable than the Federal Reserve has proposed. All we have to do is keep our nerve and maintain our solidarity.'

When he left, the President had shaken his hand with unexpected warmth.

'If I have misjudged you in the past, forgive me. Your heart is in the same place as ours: with the workers and the *campesinos*.'

Now, settling into one of the Learjet's armchairs, as it reached its 40,000-foot cruise altitude, Suarez reviewed his tactics and felt sure that Alvarez would arrive at Columbus Cay with Presidential approval. All that remained was the manipulation of Lopez-Santini.

Yesterday, Suarez had conducted a carefully oblique conversation with the Argentine at Columbus Cay. He had said that acquaintances of his had tracked down Teresa and Gloria. They were in his own country, Bolivia. Those holding them were keenly interested in the negotiation and would release them unharmed the moment it was successfully concluded. Suarez regretted he could arrange no other outcome.

'I have already paid and lost one ransom,' Lopez-Santini had remarked angrily. 'Why should I believe this?'

The obvious answer was that it was too goddam bad if he didn't. What Suarez had actually said was that if the Group reached agreement on Wednesday evening, he would personally telephone a contact number in La Paz and Lopez-Santini's daughters would be released to the Argentine Embassy. He suggested that Mercedes Lopez-Santini should be waiting there. From what he had heard of the Minister's wife, she would exert irresistible pressure once she was within hours of recovering her daughters.

As the jet passed over the Mexican coast, on track across the Gulf towards Great Abaco, Suarez was unable to fault the scheme. The contact in La Paz was Amado Canelas himself, utilizing a villa near the Bolivian capital. Indeed, this Learjet belonged to Canelas, under a legitimate meat-trading company's name. He would be pleased at today's success in Mexico. The drug-barons' manipulation of the Columbus Group was within sight of victory. Suarez used the plane's telephone to call Canelas and tell him.

'Our footballers defeated the West,' he joked. 'Now we shall.'

Canelas laughed. That was another business with which they all had connections. But ultimately he responded with a warning.

'Remember, Rodrigo,' every syllable was distinct, 'what we want is a default. No compromises. Not a conciliatory default. An absolute one. You fix that, and everything will be fine.'

London. Late afternoon

The bond market was becoming hesitant, its upward momentum slipping. All day Lindsay had watched the flickering figures on the VDU screens, and as the uncertainty developed, his pulse quickened. Professionals only bought what they could trade at a profit. He was still determinedly selling short, borrowing bonds literally by the million from pension-fund managers and insurance companies to fulfil his contracts, convinced prices must eventually fall. But first they had to peak.

A trader was like a mountaineer in cloud, knowing by instinct the high point of his climb must be close, yet unable to confirm his position. On the other side lay a potentially precipitous descent. If he were caught wrong-footed at the crossover, he was in trouble.

'I don't think they'll go much higher,' Lindsay told one of his younger traders, who looked anxiously up, telephone in hand, about to do a deal. When Lindsay advised, dealers in the trading-room reacted. His instinct was legendary. The trader hastily switched his phone to another line, cutting off his own call. Better that than make a wrong decision or prevaricate.

'You think so, Philip?' he asked. 'You could be right. Prices are so high the effective interest rate on Treasury 1992–96 is down to six and seven-eighths. It's the lowest ever.'

Lindsay smiled to himself. On that particular stock, carrying a nine per cent interest coupon, it probably was. Before the rat-race of inflation took hold, when he had joined the army, three per cent was the norm. No matter. When effective interest rates fell as low as this, things would happen internationally. They must do. The pound would fall, too, on account of investment in Britain becoming less attractive, and the Bank of England would not only step in to support the currency, it would probably go further. Even if its 'bill mountain' had been eroded by demand already, it would issue more bills to flood the market, bring prices down and hoist British interest rates back to levels that were internationally competitive. In other words, the Bank would manipulate an end to the bull market, and bonds would decline.

'I'm damn sure the market's peaked. Go hell for leather selling short,' he ordered, 'and say your prayers, because this will be a ride to remember.'

Once the market gathered momentum down the far side of the peak, the big investors who had rushed into government bonds since the weekend would rush to get out again, and speed the collapse. It would prove no different from any other kind of panic-buying followed by any other kind of panic-selling: except in scale. Money was a commodity, and shortages of any commodity raised the price; surpluses then resulted in an over-correction. The price of oil, the commodity at the root of the whole Third World debt problem, ought to have been enough of an example to anyone. From $3 a barrel in the late 1960s it had raced to $30 ten years later, and then sunk right down to $9 in 1986. The difference with the stock market would be that it wasn't the sheikhs who would lose: it would be the ordinary investors.

He had hardly returned to his office, preparing to check his instincts with banking contacts, when a personal call from Scotland reminded him of exactly how hard those ordinary investors could be hit. His sixty-eight-year-old aunt was on the line, worried sick by what she had been reading in the papers.

'Philip, dear. I must have some advice. My ICI shares are down terribly, so are Courtaulds. I daren't look at Midland Bank any more. My stockbroker up here thinks I should sell them all and buy gilts. What would you do?' A plaintive note crept into her usually placid voice. 'Philip, those industrial shares of mine are hardly half the value they were last week. And I'd done so well in the last few years.' She sounded close to crying. 'The broker said I'd still show a profit if I sell.'

'Do nothing of the sort, Aunt Laura.' Lindsay wished he could wring the bloody broker's neck, for exploiting her fears instead of calming them. His aunt was no speculator. She had bought blue-chip shares. Advising her to 'take a profit' during a crisis was like telling her to throw half her future income in the Firth of Forth. 'Gilts are about to collapse and once this is all over equities will recover. Don't sell, Aunt Laura. Hold on.' He would have added 'tough it out' if he had thought the phrase would mean anything to her.

The brief conversation reminded him forcibly that although he expected his own firm to end up with an £80–£90 million profit from this panic, if ordinary investors lost their nerve they could see their savings destroyed. The process was terrifyingly simple. If Aunt Laura sold out today she would lose half the value of her equities. If she then bought gilts and they sank back to a sensible level next week, she would lose another third. Her portfolio had been worth around £70,000. A fortnight of fear-inspired changes could see it reduced to £23,000. She would suffer for the rest of her life if she panicked now. Only the broker would profit and, of course, the more shrewd investors she sold to and bought from.

Unless he was wrong, and this became a full-scale 1929-style crash. Then everyone would scramble into cash and cash alone.

He began ringing around to find out what was happening at the banks and discount houses. The answers were not as comforting as he had hoped.

'Between ourselves, Philip,' a director of one of the largest told him, 'there have been very substantial outflows of Arab funds. We've always been careful not to become hooked on the sheikhs. Even so, we're having to exercise very tight controls. Cutting back our interbank lines of credit to the USA and Canada, for example. That's where the crunch is going to come, and the news from Mexico is not encouraging.'

'There will be a default?'

'My dear fellow, if I knew the answer to that I'd be on the phone to Ladbrokes now.' Ladbrokes the bookmakers were renowned for accepting bets on almost anything. 'We certainly can't rule out a default. The Bank of England's keeping a lifeboat alongside, so to speak. Apparently several smaller American banks are in serious trouble already. In my view, the American banking structure is extremely fragile. Thank God we're not so badly exposed ourselves.'

Afterwards Lindsay tried to evaluate the advice. A Bank of England 'lifeboat' meant 'printing money', as the papers called it, by giving loans to the banks. That, in the long term, spelt inflation, and inflation inevitably eroded the attractiveness of bonds as compared to equities. Basically, he decided that if he could survive a further and worse panic he would be proved right. He steeled himself to continue selling short.

Finally, prompted by the banker, he rang Ladbrokes himself. The odds they were offering against a default were not encouraging. Seven to four on. Lindsay believed in backing his own judgement. He laid out £1,000.

When he finally transmitted his book to New York that night he remembered an old Oriental proverb about 'the hospice whose signboard reads *Decision* – in whose beds the few who find it can be sure of sleeping well'.

If he enjoyed no other comfort tonight, at least he had found that place.

Hauppage, Long Island Midday

The factory doors were open – which was about all Gianni could claim. He was down, sure, but he wasn't out yet. A skeleton staff, working voluntarily for half pay, was handling deliveries of finished electronic products held in stock. That was in the warehouse section. The main assembly hall was deserted; the lines of partially completed radar components and aircraft radios motionless and silent, starting to be flecked with dust. Everything was exactly as it had been when it had stopped at ten on Monday morning, down to the trash in the cans and the occasional cigarette-butts. ACE Techtronics' production was closed down in every practical way except legally. Gianni stood by one of the benches and traced a sad finger-line in the dust.

The closure had come about faster than he could have imagined. The backlash of his publicity operation against Bartrum had hit ACE only fractionally less fast than it had hit Roth. When the pictures appeared yesterday, Gianni's financial backers had lost confidence as swiftly as Bartrum Bank's corporate depositors had. His wife, Trudy, subdued, miserable and blaming herself, was upstairs now with his secretary sorting out paperwork.

From somewhere close there came a hammering noise, staccato blows like a nail being driven into wood, shattering the silence. Gianni spun round, momentarily foxed, then realized someone was attacking the assembly-hall doors from outside. He raced round through the warehouse. Standing by the locked entrance were two men, one holding a notice while another attached it with hammer-blows to the door.

'What the hell . . .' Gianni shouted, running to confront them, and astonished to see that the men were in suits.

'Bailiffs,' one said gruffly, pointing to the paper protected by a transparent plastic covering. 'Notification of a claim on this property.'

'You can't do that.' Gianni was moving to tear it down when the other wrenched his arm away.

'You just leave that, mister. You have a mortgage on this building, right? They're foreclosing.'

Stupified, Gianni read the text. When he had penetrated the legal jargon it told him that if the finance company did not receive overdue payments within seven days, they intended to take possession. The document asserted their rights of ownership. He left the notice where it was and went back up to the office.

'Sweetheart,' Trudy was holding out a file, 'do we cancel this microchip order or postpone?' She saw his expression. 'What's happened?'

He was telling her when the phone rang. He picked it up himself. This was no time for the usual secretarial barrier between the boss and callers. The man on the line sounded typically East Coast, laid-back, self-confident. In a second Gianna recognized it was the goddam officer at Plaza he had spoken to about the Brazilian money a week ago.

'Yeah. What is it?' All his antagonism surfaced.

'Glad to say we've received a transfer from Brazil, sir.'

'You what?' The miracle had come about.

'One hundred thousand dollars.'

Gianni's exultation faded as fast as it had surged. One-seventh part of the first payment. What the hell were the bastards playing at, he demanded.

'We wouldn't mind knowing that ourselves, sir. The Banco do Brasil say they're giving total priority to trade debts. Yours is one of over four hundred partial payments we received this morning. They need your electronics. I guess you'll get the rest within a few weeks. Where do you want the hundred thousand sent? Not to Bartrum Bank, I imagine.'

'You're damn right, I don't.' For a moment Gianni contemplated managing without a bank at all, then thought of the Bank of the Hamptons. So far as he knew it had never been on this foreign-lending kick. 'You make out a draft,' he ordered. 'I'll drive right down to Manhattan and collect it.'

'Whatever you prefer, sir. Next time, may I suggest you have a letter of credit drawn on us in New York. Bills of exchange are . . .'

'Sure,' Gianni wasn't listening. 'Trudy,' he shouted for his wife. 'Don't cancel those microchips. Postpone.' He restored his attention to the Plaza officer. 'Tell me something, what is this all about? Why are they paying some guys and not others?'

'We reckon,' the officer sounded more laid-back than ever, 'that these trade-debt settlements are the preliminary to a Latin American default.'

'I thought that just happened?' Gianni had been too preoccupied to read about the crisis – he had been living it.

'No, sir. It could happen any day. You've been lucky.'

'Lucky!' Gianni just about blew up. 'You call me lucky!'

'We have over a billion dollars in loans out to Brazil. Maybe that puts things in perspective.'

Gianni wouldn't have cared ten cents if Plaza was a hundred billion down the tube. He said he'd be in Wall Street before two, and rang off.

It was only later, humming down the Long Island Expressway in his red Mercedes, that the corollary of the banker's casual comparison hit him. If Plaza was up to its eyeballs in Latin American debt and a default made it insolvent, how would he receive the rest of the Brazilian money? When he reached the bank, after a major hassle parking, he demanded to know if later payments could be routed some other way.

The young bank officer scrutinized him with amusement. This was Bartrum's client, and an excessively rude one at that, and Bartrum was a walking corpse, anyway.

'Could be pretty difficult, sir. We negotiated that bill of yours through our representative out there. I guess you'll have to stick with the way it's all set up.' He blinked at Gianni. There hadn't been many humorous moments in the past week, and here was a practical joke just sitting up and begging to be played. 'Our Board Chairman's hosting a prayer session tonight. You care to join us?'

For a second Gianni thought he was serious. Then he seized the draft and walked out. To hell with Plaza. If he could show this evidence to his backers, maybe that attachment notice on the factory could be withdrawn.

*

'How you doin', ladies? You Mister Suarez's frien's?'

Maggie rolled over on her sunbed by the pool. Staring down at her was a Bahamian in the loudest, multi-coloured beach-shirt she had yet seen. She recognized the man: Garrard.

Tilting her straw hat over her eyes, so that it partially hid her face, she squinted up at him.

'I suppose you could be saying that,' she conceded. 'Mr Suarez invited us for dinner this evening, to be sure.'

Had Garrard failed to recognize her? It seemed unlikely, although she was not festooned with cameras as before. She was relying on a pair of small Minoxes, the sort a tourist might have, and was being careful only to use one at a time. While Anneke was scuba-diving yesterday she had achieved all the coverage she needed of the Club and, of course, had snapped Suarez by the pool. More riskily, she had sneaked telephoto shots of him conferring with Lopez-Santini. She had been keeping her ears open, too. Her call to Stu after Suarez left for Mexico yesterday had been loaded with information – not least that Lopez-Santini appeared tired and on edge, and the two men had quarrelled. Lying in the sun, she had been contriving how to photograph the arriving delegates unobserved.

'Miss Fitzgerald, Miss Los?' Garrard whipped a notebook from his riotous shirt-pocket.

'Have we some problem?' Anneke came to life, speaking with a distinctively Dutch articulation of the words.

'No problem so long as you keepin' away from dis conference.' Garrard paused and stared down at Maggie. 'You givin' trouble and I'm tellin' you, Mister Suarez frien' or not, you goin' to be sleepin' de night in jail.'

'I don't know what you're talking about.' The protest was for Anneke's benefit.

'All right,' Garrard flipped the notebook shut, 'you have a good day and don' think you'se foolin' me. Be seein' you terreckly.' He walked away.

'Not a very nice man.' Anneke commented. 'What was he talking about . . .' She stopped in mid-sentence. Maggie was off, hips swinging in the one-piece swim-suit, sandals clacking angrily on the stone-laid surround of the pool.

At the reception, McLellan was busy with security men, checking in delegates. He spotted Maggie coming, but could not escape as she threaded her way through the group of chatting politicians to the desk.

'Mister McLellan,' she leant against the counter, speaking quietly, 'the luck of the Irish may not be enough. You keep that man Garrard off our backs, will you?' She smiled with the kind of sweetness that poisons drinks, and mimicked the drawn-out Bahamian accent, 'All right?'

'Felipe, when does Señor Alvarez arrive from Mexico?'

'He has promised to be here for the meeting at 4 pm, Excellency.'

Lopez-Santini checked his watch for at the least the twentieth time this morning. He and his aide were taking lunch in the shade of the verandah outside his villa at the Club, and the tension which had made it hard for him to enjoy food yesterday was becoming worse. His stomach felt completely knotted up inside him, and his back and neck ached. When he recalled Suarez's blatant threat he found it impossible to swallow. His mouth simply dried up.

'Felipe.' He could no longer conceal what was going on. 'My wife will soon be arriving in La Paz. You know the reason?'

'Your daughters?' It had not been hard to guess why the Minister was so distraught.

'They may be released tonight.' He could not openly admit the linkage with this negotiation, but he intended Felipe to reach his own conclusions by continuing straight on to that subject. 'What is your view of the rescheduling-committee's proposal?'

'Mine?' Felipe was taken aback. His normal job was writing drafts to his superior's orders, and he appreciated just how loaded this question was in every way: economically, politically, personally.

'From our Argentine point of view, a conciliatory default must be preferable. The last few days have demonstrated better than any computer model how disastrous outright default could be. For the Western creditor nations, I mean.' He plunged deeper into these controversial waters. 'Whoever tried to assassinate Señor Osborn damaged our position.'

'I agree. It was despicable.'

'It is not only the Poles and the Filippinos who have dropped out.' Felipe consulted his notes. 'This morning, telex cancellations have come from Chile, Egypt, Malaysia, the Sudan and Thailand.' He passed across an annotated list.

Lopez-Santini scanned the figures, confirming what he already knew. None were major debtors. Egypt owed $22 billion, Chile $20 billion: between them all they barely owed as much as Brazil or Mexico. They were all allies of the United States and recipients of US aid. But that was not the essential point.

'The international credibility of our Group has suffered,' Felipe remarked.

'Much worse.' His aide must be afraid to frame the real crux in words. 'Apart from the token presence of Indonesia and a few Africans we now represent our own region alone. A majority for a conciliatory default may no longer be obtainable.' If Suarez's campaigning had been fruitful, it definitely would not.

'Unless we propose one, Excellency.'

'Felipe.' He refused to discuss the impossible. 'Arrange a call to the Embassy in La Paz. I must speak to my wife.'

While his aide did this from indoors, a mood of unrelievable gloom enveloped Lopez-Santini. He had been left no options by Suarez. Whether the attack on Osborn was a total blunder or a master-stroke of tactics hardly mattered now. He would be forced to defeat himself in the very hour he might have succeeded. As soon as he returned to Buenos Aires he would resign, even though by then the damage would have be done. Once the default was announced, the Argentine people, whose economic future the President had trusted to his care, would be sentenced to years of avoidable and unnecessary hardship.

Had Lopez-Santini been a professional politician he might have shrugged the failure off. Survival is the name of the political game and he would live to fight another day. Because he was not a politician, but an idealist, he buried his head in his hands as if the action could blot out the humiliation he was destined for at the meeting later.

Straits of Florida. 1.40 pm

The Learjet's route purposely veered south of the direct and shortest distance to Great Abaco, passing clear of the Marquesas to run over the centre of the straits between Cuba and Miami. Once past longitude 80° W the computerized inertial navigation system would bank the plane gently left and take it the remaining 270 miles to Marsh Harbour. The captain had punched in all the data before the take-off. He was some fifty miles south of Key West and still fourteen minutes from the turn when things went wrong.

'Excellency.' The captain had hurried aft to inform Suarez, his head brushing the low ceiling of the cabin. The Lear was a fast jet but not large. 'Señor.' He had to rouse the Deputy Minister from sleep.

Suarez brought himself out of what had been half dream and half wishful thinking about the coming evening with Anneke and that other girl, who was too tall for his liking.

'What are you saying,' he demanded irritatedly. The captain was pointing at the round window beside his armchair. He glanced out and was transfixed.

Riding perilously close to their own wingtip was a warplane, missiles hanging beneath its wings, the angular nose and sharply outlined fin as threatening as a patrolling shark. Alarmed, he peered across the aisle at the other side. Framed in the perspex was the first plane's twin which like it bore the words, in black paint on the silver fuselage, 'US Air Force'.

'We have been ordered to land at Miami,' the captain said, and Suarez noticed that he was sweating in spite of being in his shirt-sleeves.

'They can't do this. We're in international airspace.' Suarez roughly yanked his seat-belt open and moved forward to occupy the captain's seat, putting on the headset as he did so. He searched for the transmit button, found it and spoke, garbling the radio procedures he had once fleetingly learnt.

'We do not wish landing at Miami, repeat we do not want any landing.'

'Sierra Golf Juliet,' the crisp voice of one of the Americans alongside gave their callsign, 'you will commence descent to Miami now. Four thousand feet per minute. Heading zero one zero.'

'I protest. This is piracy.'

'Listen, bud. Someone down there wants to talk with you, right. Now start losing height.'

Suarez had his fingers on the control column, anyway. Suddenly he tried to take over, pulling back so hard that the autopilot disconnected. The nose tilted violently. The captain leapt to pinion his arms while the second pilot struggled to regain level flight.

'Down you bastards, not up. You wanna go down the fast way with a missile in your backside?' the fighter pilot's voice crackled on the radio.

'Señor,' the captain did not relax his hold. 'I am in command. Kindly leave the flight-deck.'

'They can't do this,' Suarez hoisted himself out of the seat. 'It's a hijack.'

'They did it to an Egyptian airliner over the Mediterranean. We have no choice. Please return to the cabin and sit down.'

Compelled to be quiet for a moment, Suarez realized that the Yanquis must think Canelas himself was on board. He began to swear richly and methodically. He knew he had long been on the DEA's wanted list himself. His only protection would be the diplomatic passport he carried as a Deputy Minister.

Then a worse thought hit him. He picked up the intercom telephone by his seat and shouted a question.

'Have you carried coke on this plane?'

The second pilot's head appeared in the narrow doorway.

'Not for two weeks. The floor has been cleaned.' The man's face was as pale as Suarez felt. If the Customs found any trace of drugs the crew's arrest was a foregone conclusion. 'Do you wish us to inform Señor Canelas?'

Should they? On reflection, no. The Yanquis would be listening in to their transmissions. He would only incriminate himself.

'Tell Nassau we are being compelled to land,' he ordered. 'Lodge complaints.' That way the Bolivian authorities would protest and Canelas, eventually, would be told. He did not expect protests to help him much.

New York. 2.30 pm

'This place is where?' Warburton had been unable to find it on the map spread across his desk. Outside, the weather was stoking up towards the midsummer heat and humidity which made New York unbearable. Planning how to reach a holiday island promised relief from that, though whether they would be welcome at Columbus Cay seemed questionable.

'Maps don't mark it,' Pendler explained, pointing with his finger, 'it's near Marsh Harbour.'

'You were deported from there as well as Nassau?' Warburton's eye twinkled. Reporters were fair game. 'You know, Mr Pendler, I'm not sure if you're an asset or a liability. If you come it's on one condition. You file nothing until I say.'

'Hey, that's pretty tough.' However, he did not complain. This would be a world exclusive, though he wished he knew what the banker's scheme of action was.

'Furthermore,' the urbane geniality had a hard underlay, 'once we're there you're on your own. I'll take you in to this airstrip. I can't prevent you being thrown out again.'

Pendler thought of the spook Garrard and reckoned Maggie must have found a way round that problem. Her disguise wouldn't have fooled a child. Not that he wanted to be dependent on her. This was his story.

'I think,' Warburton said carefully, 'we might follow your friends' example and nightstop in Miami. Can you be ready by 3.30?' He supposed another hour would give Harrison long enough.

'Hell!' Pendler exclaimed. 'I haven't filed today. Harry Grant will fire me.' The morning had been occupied with the flight from Europe. 'Is there anything new on the crisis?'

'On *your* crisis?' Warburton lifted a greying eyebrow. 'Would you like me to write a book about the last twenty-four hours?'

'A paragraph would be fine.' Pendler was rapidly tuning into this sardonic approach.

'Well, the Dow Jones Index is at its lowest for eleven years. Any moment now the Japs who rushed into US Treasuries will decide to opt for cash.' Warburton sought to encapsulate the position. 'The fact is, the banks' liquidity ratios are being shot to pieces. Some are already calling in overdrafts and loans.' He showed Pendler a telex. 'That is one of literally hundreds. Our rescheduling committee is under siege. If we can't avert this default, fifty or more of the 209 most exposed American banks could be insolvent by the end of the week. I know of one which may not last as long as that.'

'And the Fed?'

'The Chairman made a trip to Mexico which apparently failed. Whereas the Bank of England has let it be known that there's a lifeboat available for British banks, the Fed won't commit itself for fear of encouraging the default. All it's doing is giving the big money-centres limited support through the discount window. And it's letting the small fry squirm. I've no doubt the aim is to convince the debtor nations that they could lose in the long term. Personally, and don't quote me, I consider it is a very dangerous form of brinkmanship indeed.'

Pendler stopped scribbling notes and asked for the use of a desk. Whilst they were waiting for the next move, he could at least get something across to Paris. He was unaware that the Fed was not the only organization involved in brinkmanship this afternoon.

Southampton, Long Island. 3 pm

The Bartrum Bank was closing to customers for the day and Roth was in mortal fear that those finely panelled white doors giving on to the columned portico where he had been so humiliated might never reopen: at least not under his presidency or direction.

Roth was upstairs in the Treasurer's room, not as sumptuous as his own, but impressive enough. He might as well have been in a padded cell, beating his fists against the walls of figures which were imprisoning the bank and him.

'Dale,' he beseeched, 'what happened to our controls?'

Schuster used to boast that he ran the tightest establishment this side of Fort Knox.

'Ray,' he said tiredly, 'our liquidity controls couldn't cope with all these corporate withdrawals. We have eighty-four per cent of our assets loaned out and maybe that wasn't prudent. Don't bug me about it. You agreed. The fact is the Fed will not accept all those loans to auto-dealers and other guys as collateral. Not when we also have $47 million of non-performing assets in Brazil and Mexico.'

'But you always controlled the leverage?'

'Sure. We kept a twelve- to fifteen-times ratio between capital and deposits. Never worse. That ratio just flew out of the window today and no one could have stopped it. On Monday we had issued capital and reserves of $71 million, right? And we had $840 million deposits. Less than twelve to one, right? Safe. Acceptable to the regulators. What happened today? Brazil and Mexico went non-performing. Our capital goes down to $24 million. That goddam ratio is now thirty-five.'

'It's just a ratio, Dale. Don't mean anything. We still have cash in the vaults. $21,538,213 of cash.' Roth had the precise figure on a slip of paper. He'd had all the branches count every bill they possessed. Schuster looked at him in despair. Unless he was so mind-blown that he'd flipped back into a kid's perceptions, Roth knew damn well that money wasn't just cash. Money was electronic transfers constantly moving in and out of banks' accounts with each other and with the Fed. In the last two days virtually all the Bartrum Bank's transfers had been outwards.

'Ray,' he said, 'we could survive if no one wanted their deposits back. Before Gianni shot his mouth off and the papers printed all that junk they mostly didn't. We had $230 million of deposits at sight and we'd lent them out again in loans. Yesterday and today $220 of that $230 million drained away. We covered it with the Federal Reserve deposit of $101 million, $20 million of the cash and the $100 million Sheldon borrowed at the discount window.'

'So?' Roth computed simple arithmetic in his head. The figures spun less confusingly, the walls began to retreat. 'So?' he argued, 'we made it. We also repaid $10 million to small depositors and we're holding twenty-one in cash.' He mopped his forehead with a silk handkerchief. 'Christ, you had me worried there.'

'Ray,' Schuster spoke softly, in the sympathetic tone he used to reserve for wheedling widows' savings into his thrift association back in the old days. 'Ray, we're all loaned up and we still have other obligations. To private depositors like Gianni's guys. To the Fed. Remember?'

Roth looked confused. Shit, Schuster thought, he should be in hospital, or back home under sedation – any place except heading a bank.

'Twelve per cent of our deposits has to be lodged with the Fed this afternoon, Ray.' His tone was becoming tougher. 'Even after all those withdrawals that's still $72 million. We just don't have seventy-two million bucks.'

'You always said you could massage the figures.'

'Jesus Christ!' The total unreality of this conversation finally got under Schuster's skin. 'We're insolvent, Ray. I can massage repayment dates. I can't massage seventy-two million out of nowhere. Bartrum Bank is insolvent. Insolvent.'

Roth stood up, swaying like a punch-drunk boxer as he fought to push the walls away and the figures buzzed around his head.

'I have to find Sheldon,' he shouted. 'Sheldon knows those MBA loans aren't going bad. We have to make him tell the Fed.'

Before Schuster could stop him, he was out of the room and pounding down the stairs towards the side-entrance of the building.

Miami. 3.20 pm

Suarez was still sweating, and not only from the climate. Since the Learjet had touched down an hour ago far too much had happened.

The aircraft itself was on a concrete hard-standing in the hot sun, guarded by armed customs agents in blue uniforms, while others removed the seats. A sniffer dog had detected traces of drugs in the cabin, and yapped excitedly around the floor. In a moment the floor itself would come up, and agents would be peering with torches into every accessible part of the airframe.

The officer who had arrested Suarez after the landing had let him watch this, and also made a point of driving him past the enclosure where over three hundred aircraft of all types and sizes stood impounded as the result of drug offences.

'Guess that's where your friend Canelas' plane's a'headed for,' he had commented.

Suarez's protests that he was on a diplomatic mission had earned him no Brownie points.

'You're not accredited to the USA or the United Nations. Sure, we'll check with the State Department. Ain't going to make no difference, though. Far as we're concerned you're just an ordinary citizen. Well, ordinary as a *coquero* can be.'

After that they had left Suarez half an hour by himself to meditate and sweat some more until a young officer in slacks and a blue shirt unlocked the door and entered the room. Although the shirt had neither badges on the arm nor the words 'US CUSTOMS' emblazoned in yellow capitals on the back, he had the right clean, determined look. Suarez did not question his credentials.

Harrison pulled out a chair and sat himself down by the table.

'Okay,' he said bluntly. 'You have an option. Either you can be charged and go before a Federal Grand Jury in Miami . . .'

'Or?' Suarez spat the question out. He might be scared of how Canelas' would react, but he was not a coward.

'Or you can release Lopez-Santini's children and someone may decide you do have diplomatic status.'

Suarez stared in surprise and disbelief.

'I am not holding those girls. What are they to do with this?'

'You play it your way.' The officer stood up. 'The Grand Jury sits next week. Be our guest.' He walked out. The lock clicked.

Ten minutes later Suarez was hammering with his fists on the door. After a short pause the officer re-entered.

'You have a telephone? I must speak to my own country and the Bahamas.'

'Sure. If you're calling Columbus Cay I should tell them you'll be late.'

As he escorted Suarez to a customs agent's office, where the calls could be monitored and recorded, Harrison reflected that this had worked even faster than the DEA reckoned it would. Not that Suarez would be reaching Columbus Cay tonight. They wouldn't let him go until the two girls were definitely free. Furthermore, what with the Learjet being impounded, the Bolivian would be dependent on a charter and he was going to find that impossible to arrange before the morning. But what seemed to amuse his collaborators in the DEA more than anything was how Suarez was going to explain the loss of the jet to its owner.

'You must try scuba-diving once, you have to.' Anneke urged. 'It's so fantastic.'

They had lazed by the pool all afternoon while Maggie kept a weather eye on the goings-on. There was a definite tension. Suarez had not reappeared. Lopez-Santini's assistant scurried to and from the telex machine in the offices of the conference centre: she knew because lengths of telex message trailed from his hands like streamers. Small groups of delegates would wander past, deep in conversation, glancing more apprehensively than admiringly at her and Anneke. Perhaps it would be a good thing to clear off for a time.

'All right,' she agreed. 'You've talked me into it. Where do we go this fine and lovely day?'

'Charlie's reef. It's a coral garden. Only twenty-five feet of water. Angel fish, parrot fish, vase sponges. It's another world. I promise, you'll be hooked.'

'Not literally, I hope.'

'Oh, no one uses lines.' Anneke's sense of humour wasn't the greatest. 'We don't fish. We use the speargun.'

When they collected the gear she demonstrated the weapon. Made of aluminium anodized black and weighing only a few pounds, the speargun fired a two-and-a-half-foot-long shaft fitted with a steel tip. A ten-foot length of braided nylon cord was attached.

'What a very nasty device,' Maggie commented. 'Is it powerful?'

'Oh,' Anneke laughed, anxious to prove she was jokey at heart. 'This will go straight through a shark. Or a man. It will go through a man, easy.'

The digital clock in the conference centre was showing 15.58 – 3.58 pm – and the delegates had been seated some minutes before Alvarez arrived from Mexico City.

Lopez-Santini conferred hurriedly with him, discovering that Suarez should have been back an hour and a half ago. Was there a snag over the children? Fear gripped him.

'Rodrigo Suarez has a report to present as well as I,' he argued quickly. 'We should delay the start.'

Though astonished at the Argentine deferring to Suarez in any way, the Mexican willingly agreed. His final session with his own president had been tricky. He needed time to consult with the Brazilian co-sponsor of the meeting; and he would also want Suarez's support in lobbying votes at the end. He and Lopez-Santini went together to the podium and expressed regret that the absence of certain delegates compelled a postponement of two hours. The meeting would reassemble at 6 pm.

Water Mill, Long Island. 4 pm

The gate in the long, white picket fence was open when Roth drove up, giving him a surge of hope that Harrison was at home.

On the way out from Southampton, along Route 27 and past the ornate sign announcing that this was the oldest village in New York State, his thoughts had grown more and more disordered. By the time his Buick was scrunching the driveway gravel at the old clapboard house they were linked to reality in only one, all-consuming idea. Harrison knew what was going on. Harrison had the answers.

Harrison was not there.

The matronly housekeeper who answered the bell did her best, suggesting numbers to contact. Seeing Roth's distraught state she let him phone from the long, low-ceilinged hallway room. But no one knew where Harrison was. Even the British banker affected ignorance.

'Sheldon's been out of town a lot since Osborn was shot. I'm sorry I can't be more helpful. Can I take a message?'

Roth declined the offer. The buzzing around his head was becoming insistent, deafening. The housekeeper, finding him standing, irresolute, offered coffee. He refused that, too. Eventually he wandered out through another door to the terrace. The sun was shining on the old trees and down there was the pond, placid and welcoming.

The swarm around him seemed to guess he had a refuge where it couldn't follow. As he trod the grass it attacked, driving him faster towards the safety of the pond and, as before, when he neared the water the intensity diminished.

He found the path through the reeds, with its tiny pebbles, and he walked on out. His feet churned the muddy bottom and his suit became soaked. He didn't notice. His gaze was fixed on the peaceful centre of the pond, where he would be safe.

242

Columbus Cay, Great Abaco. 5 pm

Garrard accepted the unexpected with phlegmatic calm. When he was summoned to speak to Suarez on the telephone, he went to the office at his own pace and understood the two messages perfectly. First, the Bolivian had been delayed and Lopez-Santini was to be told by the manager. Second, he was to have a talk with those two women, on his behalf. The Bolivian said they needed talking to. Garrard didn't ask why. The Bahamas were a major trafficking centre and he had been on the mafiosi's payroll for a long time. He assured Suarez he would fix those two and went down to the jetty.

In Miami, Suarez put the phone down with some satisfaction. This sting could only have been set up by agents of the DEA, and by methodical thinking he had identified them. Garrard would do the rest.

The customs officer monitoring the call made a note that the Bolivian had woman trouble. He did not worry further because the hijack had been organized on information received.

La Paz. 5 pm

Teresa was nervous, though she tried hard not to let it show. The man who had dropped them off on the street had said they must walk five hundred metres and they would find a big house with a sign saying 'Embajada de la Repubblica Argentina'. She took Gloria's hand firmly in hers, and began to walk.

The city was dirty and busy. Car horns honked. People on the sidewalk jostled them. They had to cross an intersection where the lights didn't work properly and policemen in white helmets, carrying guns, directed the traffic. Then they reached the Embassy with its emblazoned sign.

Minutes later, both girls were being overwhelmed with hugs and kisses in an anteroom.

'Oh, my babies, my little ones.' Mercedes was in tears of joy, embracing them again and again, holding their faces tenderly to gaze at them. 'Oh, but you're half-starved, you poor darlings. What did those cruel people do to you?'

After a while, when they had settled on a sofa, Mercedes noticed that although Gloria huddled against her, clinging like a baby,

243

Teresa had shifted to sit upright and apart. 'What's the matter, my darling?' she demanded. 'Aren't you glad to see me? Aren't you happy?'

Teresa stayed quite silent for several moments before she spoke in a calm, considered voice.

'The hacienda was lovely. We had such nice meals and rode ponies in the afternoon. At least I did. But I think Maria was the nicest person, though I was frightened of her at first.'

Mercedes stared at her elder daughter, shocked, bewildered, unbelieving.

'Oh my God,' she whispered.

'Please, Mama.' Teresa appeared not to hear. 'When are we going to see Papa? I want to tell him all about it.'

Columbus Cay, Great Abaco. 5.45 pm

Maggie spotted the approaching powerboat while Anneke was still in the water. Their boat was large and slow with a fibre-glass awning and plenty of space. As the powerboat curvetted around in a half-circle, throwing up spray, Maggie recognized the man at the controls and knew this wasn't a social call. She looked around. Anneke's head and shoulders were visible over the stern. She handed the speargun up to Maggie. Their own boatman was seated in the bow by the anchor-rope and starting to take lazy notice.

Garrard throttled back, his boat instantly settling in the water, its momentum carrying it onward. He hefted his gun into his right hand. These two were going to Marsh Harbour and into custody. Directly. No questions. They'd stay there until Suarez arrived. No questions and no arguments. His powerboat coasted closer. Ten feet. Eight. He stood up, hefting his automatic into his right hand to reinforce his authority, and shouted.

'You two bin givin' trouble. You comin' wid me.'

It took Maggie several seconds to realize what the short, stubby shape in Garrard's hand was, and in the same instant that her temper surged at being nakedly threatened, she realized she was clutching a form of weapon herself. Instinctively raising the speargun, she yelled at him.

'Leave us alone. Go away.'

'Put dat down!' Garrard was taking no chances. He prepared to fire in the air as a warning. Once. More for the benefit of the boatman's evidence than anything else. If Suarez wanted this pair killed he'd have said so. Any shooting had to be strictly defensive. He raised his gun.

Anneke, hearing the shouts but hidden from the action, dropped back in the water and swam round the diving-boat's stern in time to see Garrard pointing his gun, apparently at Maggie's head. She kicked out hard towards the powerboat, reaching up to haul violently on its side as the explosion of the shot stunned her hearing. The boat rocked. Garrard groped for support, unintentionally firing again.

The second bullet thudded into the diving-boat's hull and Maggie didn't hesitate any more. Garrard was hardly six feet away and was already recovering himself. His next shot wouldn't miss. She levelled the speargun, fumbled a moment with the unfamiliar trigger, and pulled. Line snaked out behind the shaft as it struck him square in the chest. He screamed and fell heavily back into his own boat.

Anneke hoisted herself up on the short ladder hooked to the diving-boat's stern, as the old boatman, a faded baseball cap pulled down on his grizzled hair, came aft under the awning.

'He tried to kill me.' Maggie found herself shaking all over. A few feet away, Garrard's body was lying in the boat, one arm protruding incongruously above the coaming, its hand limp, and near it lay the speargun's line. She averted her eyes, unable to look. Even though he was a big man, Garrard could not have survived the impact of the spear.

'Don' you worry, miss.' A great grin illuminated the boatman's face. 'I seen all dat. What you done, dat de best ting anyone done aroun' here in years.'

'How was this starting?' Anneke, having missed the beginning was still mystified. 'Why did that man have a gun?'

'He's de shootin' kind, miss.'

The boatman took a wooden-poled boathook from its stowage place. Leaning out, he caught the bow of the powerboat, and pulled it close. Maggie turned away. He took the speargun and placed it by Garrard's body, then secured the line to the powerboat and pushed it clear again.

'Fraid you'se goin' to lose dat spear. We better take de boat and de body someplace won't be divin' and send dem both to de bottom.' He was still smiling delightedly. 'Miss, I'm tellin' you. Dat man bin givin' us trouble for years.'

From the brief uninformative message, Lopez-Santini had assumed that Suarez would be delayed only an hour or two. Then came a barely audible phone-call, distorted by interference, from La Paz. The children were safe. Mercedes, as far as he could distinguish her words, sounded too emotionally drained to speak coherently. No matter. Teresa said hello. He threw his hands in the air and embraced Felipe.

'A thousand congratulations, Excellency. How did it come about?'

'I do not know.' He was so overjoyed he did not care. 'But we need no longer wait for that mobster Suarez. We can distribute the conciliatory default proposals and recommend acceptance.'

'I am afraid Mexico will not support us.' Felipe was saddened to place so immediate a dampener on his Minister's relief. 'Señor Alvarez's aide has warned me. They are canvassing votes.'

'I was afraid that might happen.' Lopez-Santini shook his head, angry because defeat seemed always an inescapable part of victory; angry at his joy turning sour.

'I shall insist that they consider the proposals overnight. There can be a vote in the morning. If we lose, we lose.'

EPILOGUE

*Columbus Cay, Great Abaco. 11 am, Thursday
June 20th*

The hexagonal conference centre with its pagoda-like roof, set
among palm trees and casuarinas, intrigued Warburton. Somehow
this kind of tropical luxury had eluded him during his banking
career.

'Quite a place for a conference,' he murmured to Harrison. 'You
Americans think of everything. What "decision-making aids" are
you going to invent next?'

He had time to ruminate because they were waiting outside for
the Columbus Group's decision. Waiting in comfort on a terrace,
with a steward attending them, it was true, but still waiting. Last
night Lopez-Santini had invited them to fly across from Miami
after breakfast, though with no guarantees. Warburton had expressed the hope that, whichever way the vote went, he would be
allowed a chance to address the delegates. It might be a last-ditch
chance, even with Suarez still detained by 'formalities'. But it
would be better than no chance.

The click of Maggie's camera interrupted his thoughts. She had
been dancing around them like a dervish ever since their plane
had landed. Maggie and Anneke were in absurdly high spirits,
perhaps on the rebound from yesterday's shock. A mammoth
thunderstorm had blown up last night and the general assumption
was that Garrard's boat had sunk in it. McLellan was displaying
gratifyingly little enthusiasm for a search – that was good news.
So was something else. When Maggie realized that the third
person in the light aircraft was Pendler she had felt the most unexpected emotional relief. So much so that she had run forward
on the grass and hugged him.

'Hey, that's nice,' he had said, kissing her in return, though
hardly appearing as bowled over as a man who only a week and a

half ago had had his attention more sharply focused on communicating bedroom doors than on financial crises might have been. 'How are things?'

'Eventful. I'll tell you later.'

'This story,' he had said, 'is about the best I've ever had. I could write a book.'

That was the snag about Stu, she thought, as she darted around taking quick shots of him talking to Warburton. He had a one-track mind. Looking at the bright side, perhaps it could have advantages, though.

'You reckon I can come into the conference with you?' he was asking Warburton.

'I will use my best offices on your behalf.' Already the banker was slipping into the kind of formal phrase he would be employing on the delegates.

'By the way, did Lopez-Santini get his kids back okay? Wasn't there some kidnap deal?'

'I believe so.' Warburton deliberately let slip an indiscretion. 'I understand a ransom was paid.' Eventually someone might piece together the relationship between events. But he hoped not. The less Pendler and this girl knew about how their information had been utilized, the better. Meanwhile, it was enough that their interests and his own coincided.

The Argentine's aide, Felipe, came out of the conference centre.

'Señor Warburton.' He handed across a slip of paper. 'This was the vote. Very close indeed.'

Warburton scrutinized the figures. 'Do they want me to speak?' he asked warily.

'They are prepared to listen,' Felipe said and led the way inside, with Pendler and Maggie trailing behind.

Pendler spotted several observers' chairs at the back of the hall and quickly settled himself down to start recording his impressions. He was thankful that no one had challenged his and Maggie's right to be there. A second later, Harrison joined them, wondering whether Jim or Bill Osborn could organize a rescue operation for Bartrum Bank. He had heard late last night of Roth's suicide. Only a take-over could save the bank from closure. He reckoned this operation should have earned some goodwill.

There was no applause as Lopez-Santini led his guest to the podium. Glancing around the audience while arranging his papers, Warburton noted both significantly vacant seats at the horseshoe-shaped table and distinct hostility on several faces. When Latin Americans were vexed, they showed it. By contrast, the Africans' faces were as expressionless as they were unlined by age. You could

248

really only tell Africans were old if they had greying hair. He wondered which way the 'basket-cases' had voted. Probably in favour, since their need for funds was unending. It was the strong who could afford to default and, matching the country name-cards on the desks to the faces, is was evidently the strong whom Lopez-Santini had been up against.

'Excellencies.' The Argentine raised a hand for silence. 'I would like to introduce the distinguished banker and Deputy Chairman of the rescheduling committee, Mr James Warburton.'

Pendler listened, noting every detail of the hall and of the delegates, aware of the Latin Americans' antagonism.

'Your Excellencies.' When he addressed an assembly Warburton's voice acquired a deep resonance. 'I have the honour of speaking to you in circumstances of greater promise than most of my friends in the financial community appreciate. Interest rates have fallen and are unlikely to recover. Oil prices are at a level which must stimulate economic activity generally. None of these improvements can be exploited unless we restore stability to the financial markets with the greatest possible speed.'

You can say that again, Pendler thought, surprised that murmurs of assent greeted the remark. He flipped over the page.

'Your Excellencies, only a negotiated and conciliatory solution to our dispute can restore that stability. The past week has demonstrated how extremely fragile the world's financial system is.'

Pendler suddenly remembered Harry Grant's remark, in the century ago of last week, to the effect that experts did not consider a default probable. Presumably high-wire walkers took the same view of the dangers inherent in their profession. The experts had been looking pretty damn stupid these last few days. The system had just about fallen off the wire. As the Briton paused he gave a comparable impression that he was balancing his words with the greatest care.

'Your Excellencies,' Warburton said, 'I am relieved that you have voted in favour of our proposals . . .'

Top Fiction from Methuen Paperbacks

While every effort is made to keep prices low, it is sometimes necessary to increase prices at short notice. Methuen Paperbacks reserves the right to show new retail prices on covers which may differ from those previously advertised in the text or elsewhere.

The prices shown below were correct at the time of going to press.

All these books are available at your bookshop or newsagent, or can be ordered direct from the publisher. Just tick the titles you want and fill in the form below.

Methuen Paperbacks, Cash Sales Department,
PO Box 11, Falmouth,
Cornwall TR10 109EN.

Please send cheque or postal order, no currency, for purchase price quoted and allow the following for postage and packing:

UK	60p for the first book, 25p for the second book and 15p for each additional book ordered to a maximum charge of £1.90.
BFPO and Eire	60p for the first book, 25p for the second book and 15p for each next seven books, thereafter 9p per book.
Overseas Customers	£1.25 for the first book, 75p for the second book and 28p for each. subsequent title ordered.

NAME (Block Letters) ....

ADDRESS..

....